Robert H. deCoy's riveting biography of Jack Johnson rips the veil of invisibility from the life and career of one of the world's greatest fighters. The "Great White Hopes" were little match for Jack Johnson's "Black Power."

JACK JOHNSON
THE BIG BLACK FIRE

By Robert H. deCoy

An Original Holloway House Edition
HOLLOWAY HOUSE PUBLISHING COMPANY
LOS ANGELES, CALIFORNIA

Published by
HOLLOWAY HOUSE PUBLISHING COMPANY
8060 Melrose Avenue, Los Angeles, CA 90046

International Standard Book Number 0-87067-581-1
Printed in the United States of America
Cover design by Bill Skurski

Dedicated
to
Those who were with me during the year that was,
with faith, fire and concern.
The married couple
Odell & Pearl Pierce
my nephew
Emile Wilson
The Parents who bore me
Robert, Sr. & Cleo L. deCoy
The offspring of my marriage
Sheri-laine & Teri Laine
Then, Two Friends who Prophecied it
Quinin "Q" Williams
and my editor
Milt Van Sickle
with
Roselle Kahn
who believed me
along with
Sharon and her father Jerry Bloom

JACK JOHNSON

AUTHOR'S PREFACE

I knew Jack Johnson well and lived with him for a brief span of time, before his death.

My father knew and introduced me to him. My mother adored him as did all of the children she bore my father.

When I became of age, I spent more time with him, for as a child I had heard my father say, many times, to me:

"Son, the only black man who was able to become a champion and a hero to his people was Jack Johnson.

"He struck a double blow, inside or outside the ring, with everything that he did.

"A black man who becomes a hero must be able to strike 'the double blow.' One for himself, and the other for the people that he was born of.

"Mention any black man in American history," my daddy would challenge me, while I was yet but a child, "and you'll find that none of them could hold the shoes of Jack Johnson.

"But his people wouldn't recognize him, 'cause they were too damn scared and jealous of him. Jealous, because he looked upon himself as a kind of Black King. Jealous, on the other hand, because they were too scared to like him—for fear of white folks."

I used to talk with Mr. Johnson everytime that I met him, while I was a child and then when I went into the army, 1942-1943, each time that I met him, listened, and I found that when people would listen to him, he had the wisdom of all of the ages. Especially, the modern age.

I knew long ago, as I asked him questions, that one day I wanted to write his true story as he told it to me —piece by piece.

But, how else would I be able to tell his complete story, unless I listened to him tell it in parts, so that one day I might be able to put all of the pieces down in writing.

This much I have tried to do. For Jack Johnson had become a God, my only hero, and, as a Black Boy, I needed a real black hero to keep going. Somebody who showed me that: "You could beat the game, only if you challenged the odds."

Robert H. deCoy

INTRODUCTION

THE FIRE SIDE SUBJECT

Jack Johnson was not just "A Black Fire," blazing with the speed of a demon. He was a Fire Side Subject as well. He was the rage of humanity, blowing across the landscape of three or more continents. He was "The Black Emperor Come," demanding tribute of his subjects.

He was the King of the Commoner, who slept with white queens, showing only the black of his ass to white kings. He was the raging fire of black vengeance, a burning bush speeding across the highly combustible plains and prairies of social customs. He singed them in bloody-hot defiance.

He was not only the talk of the town, but also of whorehouses, outhouses, courthouses, White Houses and black houses, of palaces in kingdoms and empires. Everybody knew Jack's name, from presidents to paupers.

The Invincible, the Genius, the Cocksman, the Crook, the Creditor, the Collector, the Creature of Christ, the Black Clown. They called him all of these.

He raced his cars at incredible speeds, while his incredible conduct caused riots among the races. He seized the opportunity to defy death as a daily diet. Daring, destructive, dangerous, devious, deceiving was Jack as he lived. So, he died, going out fast, not even bothering to slow down in 68 years. He went out speed-ing fast, the same damn way he came in, as he had told a Chicago motorcycle cop who had stopped him one day.

This is one of the many tales told about Jack, which has been told, retold, documented and attested, vowed, vouchsafed and sworn to on a stack of Bibles. So, there's no reason to doubt that it did happen.

This incident took place in Chicago, the mythical Nigger Heaven where Jack lived and spent much of his time.

That particular day, Jack Johnson was out driving along Michigan Avenue, in his white Stutz Bearcat with the gold-plated dashboard, with a pretty white, pink-toed, blonde bitch alongside him, the wind blowing her pretty, long silk hair as they sped along the avenue. How fast he was going, he couldn't even tell, for Jack Johnson was never one to look at his speedometer.

He was in his usual hurry, "to-get-some-place-that-he-had-to-be," when a cracker cop, siren screaming, came up on his motorcycle and waved Jack over to a stop.

So, anyhow, "out of jealousy and envy, along with the sight of this pretty white broad," the cop began writing him out a ticket for speeding.

Jack eyed the ticket, and looked at the cop, grinning.

"About how much is this gonna' cost me, boy?" Jack asked.

"About fifty of them hard-earned dollars you been making," replied the cracker.

Now, we must remember that skilled labor in those times paid less than two dollars a day. But Jack was still grinning as he reached down into his pocket and came up with a wad of money, a bankroll big enough to choke a horse. He peeled off a gold-sided hundred dollar bill, and extended it across to the cop.

"Here, boy. You pay it. And hold on to th' change."

He put his car into drive, pecked a kiss on the blonde's white forehead, and laughed.

" 'Cause I'm comin' back th' same gawd damn way!" said Jack, as his car jumped away from the curb like a bullet, putting smoke and rubber in the white man's face.

*   *   *

". . . . Speakin' of Jack, now . . . as anybody could tell you, back there in his time, there wasn't a man nor bull alive, who could whip the likes of Jack Johnson . . . insides the ring, neither outsides of it . . ."

". . . Black as a tar-baby with a mouth fulla' gold,
         Smooth as black satin,
         A champ, from his soul . . ."

". . . That's what we used to say 'bout him, awright . . ."

". . . They use' to say other things, lots worse than that 'bout him, too. . . . Them white folks, I mean . . ."

". . . It wasn't just white folks. Let's stick with th' facts. Many a black preacher, along with most educated Niggers hated Jack much more'n th' white folks did . . ."

". . . That's because he screwed up their minds so bad. He could twist up th' minds of a white man an' a college-trained Nigger, just as fast as he could twist up a white woman's tail . . ."

". . . They say, that's what kept him into trouble all of th' time . . ."

". . . You mean that's what gave *them* troubles, all th' time, seeing 'Old Black Jack' climbing in an outa' white women's beds . . ."

". . . Yeah, they even named it *'White Slavery.'* But,

Jack didn't give a damn much for Black Slavery. He sure was against that, awright . . ."

". . . They could go see him, standin' there on two legs to fight white men. But his layin' betwixt th' legs of white women's was something else. There wasn't no law against it. So, damn it, Congress went and passed one, called th' MANN ACT . . ."

". . . An' made it retroactive to git him too! You ever hear th' likes? . . . That Congress an' them courts is a bitch when it comes to Niggers like Jack . . ."

". . . It sure in th' hell is. They even went further, an' made it a fed'ral offense to transport prizefight moving pictures 'cross state lines. Just to keep folks from seein' how badly Johnson was whippin' up on white boys . . ."

". . . Shucks, them was just two federal laws. Man! It would be too hard and too many to count 'mongst all of th' state, county and city laws that were passed on accounta' Jack an' his shenanigans . . ."

". . . Did you know that they went an' named that big One-O-One, Howitzer Cannon after him, during World War I . . . Able to shoot more than thirty some-odd miles . . . Sometimes they called it 'Big Bertha,' but sometimes they called it 'l'il Arthur,' for Jack."

". . . Hell, th' American Infantry and Artillery soldiers used to paint his name on th' bullets and shells 'fore they fired 'em into th' German lines . . ."

". . . No wonder 'bout that. Did you know that Jack could jump ten feet backwards, from a standin' position? An' I ain't never heard tell of another man who could perform that feat—even jumpin' forward—without a runnin' start . . ."

". . . Hell, th' first time that he did it was just after his broken thighbone had healed, where a mean racehorse had gone an' kicked him a coupla' months before. He did it on a bet, with some white men and Niggers who didn't believe he was well 'nough to fight again . . ."

". . . Shucks, that ain't nothing. He once hit a Texas steer, head on with his fist, and knocked him plumb out with one punch. An' it's a matter of record that he once did th' same to a bull he was fighting, after he had decided to take up bullfighting an' become a *matador,* over in Spain . . ."

". . . Man, Jack could do anything that he set his mind to. Did you know, that with just a fifth-grade education, he learned enough to teach himself to read French, Italian, Spanish . . . and that he could speak seven languages . . . German, Russian, Portuguese, as well as English . . . ?"

". . . And they tell me that mostly always he was reading and quoting from Spencer and Chaucer. He even rewrote Shakespeare's *Othello,* so he could play it on the stage. Only, Jack refused to play Othello as a tragedy. He said that it wasn't . . . for a fact . . ."

". . . An' there was also a spiritual side to Jack Johnson, too. Don't forget that. Course most folks won't admit that much in his favor. He used to preach in church, right good sermons, after he come to give up on prizefighting . . ."

". . . Hell, he did that even 'fore he got through prizefighting. He even went out in Danville, Illinois one night, all by hisself, and preached a sermon to th' Ku Klux Klan, right in front of their burnin' cross . . ."

". . . Yeah, them crackers just sat there, scared shitless, an' listening for thirty minutes or more. They figured that Jack musta' come out with an army of Niggers hidin' behind them in th' darkness . . ."

". . . They say when they saw him drivin' away in his white Thompson Flyer, all alone, they was fit to be tied. So they compensated by runnin' around all night, beating up on any an' every Nigger who come into sight . . ."

". . . Yeah, he was always doing something like that, causing other people misery . . ."

". . . But, he give 'em some joy an' some hope, too. Jack did more to change this country than any black man who ever lived. . . an' along with that you can include most of the white folks they call heroes . . ."

". . . Changed boxing . . . he changed th' laws, he changed people, he damn near changed everything, when you come right down to it . . ."

"He was a fighter, that's for sure, as well as many other things . . ."

". . . He was all that an' a damn sight more. Did you know that when he opened up his nightclub in Chicago back in 1912, one New York white writer named 'Wurra Wurra' McCloughlin wrote, '. . . Jack Johnson is unquestionably the biggest thing in Chicago . . . and I include the stock-yards . . .' "

". . . An' that ain't all that he wrote. They tell that Jack had a room up in his club, covered with leopard skins and mirrors everywhere. He called it his *'joie de fille* salon' for his entertainment with white girls. It had them white reporters shook up about what went on up there. So, McCloughlin asked one of 'em, after she had taken her turn, and come on downstairs, 'What goes on 'mongst them mirrors and leopard skins . . . ?' Th' bitch said, 'I really couldn't tell you, chum. But you ain't lived until you've seen yourself in bed with that black monster, in seventeen different angles and directions . . .' "

". . . See? Now, you know a white woman givin' an answer like that to a white man, 'bout a Nigger in bed, is 'nough to blow his mind, even nowadays . . ."

". . . Niggers, too . . . Now, don't be prejudiced. Even Booker T. Washington was so shook up that he told th' white Y.M.C.A. in Detroit, when he addressed them, '. . . Jack Johnson has harmed rather than helped the race. I wish to say emphatically that his actions do not meet my approval, and I'm sure they do not meet with the approval of the colored race . . .' "

". . . See there? An' just think. Booker T. got caught in that New Yorker Hotel coming from a white woman's room, by a cracker who beat him so bad, he never got over it. Just jealous of Jack Johnson who did it right out in th' open . . ."

". . . But, Jack Johnson did everything right out in th' open. He was The Flash of Light and The Burning Flame!"

". . . The Black Fire! The Big Smoke! They called him both."

". . . He was The Avenger, Destroyer, God an' th' Devil, all rolled into One . . ."

". . . He rolled awright . . . 'cross five different Continents, burning up everything as he went along . . ."

". . . Some say he rolled in on that 'Galveston Tidal Wave' . . . They say his being there when the tidal wave hit was a signal to th' world of his presence on earth . . . Cthers say that th' tidal wave rolled in to quench The Big Black Fire of Jack Johnson before it got to burning out of hand. But it failed to make it. 'Cause Jack was able to survive the Flood, preparing for th' things that was to come . . ."

". . . If you ever saw a Black Fire burning, then that was Jack. For a Black Fire burning is nothing but Spirit and Force. It can't be put out like white fire. A Black Fire has to burn its own self out, by itself . . ."

CHAPTER ONE

"WELL, TO TELL THE TRUTH . . .!"

Well, now, to tell the truth, there's so much fact mixed with fiction concerning the fighting and loving in the life of Jack "L'il Arthur" Johnson, that you can hardly separate the two. But, one thing surely can be relied upon, whatever you hear. And the one thing is, "Whatever you hear that sounds like fiction, is sure for certain, to be the truthful fact."

"Still and all, you've just got to use your mind and imagination and take yourself back and remember what it was like to be an *American Black Boy* with a dream of becoming great in *The Great White Way* they call *Life in America*."

And to transport yourself back to that time isn't always too easy, unless you are fully aware of what Jack Johnson himself once said: "The Great White Way, called Good Life in America, ain't nothing but a bare black-ass lie!!" Of course, it took Jack more than half his lifetime before he came to recognize this fact. Though he had been suspecting it all along.

And to keep on telling the truth, as to how he came to learn that his suspicions were altogether right, then we've just got to go back to live with him and learn, learning as he learned how to make a black ace, highest card of the deck, while drawing for a royal flush in spades during a poker game.

Or to throw the dice from your fist, in speedy combinations, so that "Two, Three or Twelve" won't come to crap-out on the first roll. And that the only real winners are the ones who make it "natural," throw seven or come eleven—the only two ways to keep ahead of the game.

Catching points is a hassle, especially six and eights made the hard way or easy. Or to make ten and four, "jump-straight-in-the-door," is the only way to keep beating the house from on-insides. But the White House will make sure that you never do it. So, they leave you but five and nine, because the "bar-bet" is for the Nigger. Going out "six-ace"—seven—is the only way a Nigger can look like that he's keeping even. Playing the field will get you nothing for your nickels in the long run of life.

Now, some say that he rolled in on the Galveston Flood. Others say it was his Black Spirit that summoned it. But whatever the truth, this much we know, that Jack Johnson and the tidal wave are synonymous in that they were the two most prominent events to hit Galveston, Texas. And that they both were destroyers. The tidal wave was merely water. John Arthur Johnson was fire. Black fire! Both rose and rolled across the landscape of life, taking their tolls, changing the courses of living, leaving in their wakes, many changes and alterations, thus illuminating the glaring futility of man and his manufactured inventions in opposition to the creations and manipulations of God.

At first, nobody ever sees, or recognizes the manipulations and creations, or the reincarnation of Gods on earth. It is only in retrospect, or in reflection that a person ever admits, or even senses, "I saw God or the Works of God." The presence of God makes a people uncomfortable. Jack Johnson, "The Big Black Fire," made people uncomfortable—unaccustomed to the presence of God, as we are. Then, the presence of God makes us resentful, awed, fearful, vengeful, hostile. Was it not the same, with the presence of Jesus of Nazareth?

Some folks started calling Jack, "The Black Sinning Son of Satan." Which could be true. For he was born on Devil's Island—a name the natives gave to the island of Galveston, Texas. That hot speck of land in the Gulf of Mexico, twenty miles long and two miles wide in some places, connected to the United States by a bridge.

Other folks claimed that Jack just blew in on the tropical bay breezes to be born on the last day of March, 1878. And the sea waves had already, from that very day, "started boiling up and churning," finally building and boiling up higher to become a tidal wave, and to spill all over the Island some 22 years later, on September 8, 1900, scraping the people from the land. It became known as "Jack Johnson's coming-out party." For thereafter, he would burn across the hearts and souls of men, as the water had washed them from the face of the earth at Galveston.

He was to say of this Galveston Disaster later, when his enemies and persecutors had joined to discredit him: ". . . I saved many lives when the great Tidal Wave engulfed Galveston . . . the greatest of modern times. Thousands of persons lost their lives . . . Avaricious men appeared on the tragic scenes with boats and wagons, charging a fee of several dollars to convey these unfortunates to safety. When I had encountered these men, I compelled them to go to the rescue of the victims . . . or I took possession of the rescue conveyances myself, and piloted the threatened ones to safety. I spent many days in relief work after the catastrophe, feeding the hungry, caring for the sick and injured, and burying the dead, but industrious newspaper writers, in 'seeking topics concerning me,' never chronicled these events. The records of the Galveston authorities, and those of the Relief Committees, will substantiate what I have related in this connection . . ." (from *Jack Johnson, In the Ring and Out*)

Jack was 22 years old when it happened. Between the time of his birth and the rising of that flood, he had become a man. Many things happened there, between the time he was born and the tidal wave.

Well, to go back to the start, with his growing. There was little that he did which was spectacular.

As a kid he was a coward, or so he was called. The boy just loved people and hated to fight them, although he grew up fast to be a pretty good size of a boy, before he made twelve. That's when he ran away from home. At the age of twelve.

The boy was a dreamer. His mother made a note of that. Just shortly after he was born, a colored lady spiritualist named Miss Dinah came to see him, looked at his baby-palm hands, and prophesied to his mother:

"This child is gonna eat his bread in many a country. . . ."

When his mother and Miss Dinah used to repeat this prophesy to Li'l Arthur as he grew up toward twelve, he admitted that he couldn't help but feel that he was marked out for a "special destiny." He used to dream of what it would be.

He finished the fifth grade when he was going on thirteen. And nothing in particular had happened. While working with his crippled father, who was a school janitor, cleaning up the school every day, he kept the prophesy close to his heart. Hoping.

He would watch the sea-ships, sailing out of the bay, wondering if he were meant to go with them. He felt the same way as he watched the night freights and passenger trains pulling out for New Orleans, or to New York City.

Hs father was too stern and eager to give whippings. His mother was severe with her scoldings. His sisters and brothers insulted and jeered him because of his unwillingness to fight back. And when he had to fight, he could seemingly never win any of his fights.

So, with two dollars in his pocket, he climbed from the attic-bedroom window and slid down the rain-pipe to the ground. Then he headed on out to the railroad yards, running away from home. The first big try for adventure.

He traveled all night and fell asleep on the rods of his first freight train. Only to wake up in the morning, to learn, to his frustration, that the box car that he was riding had rolled around all night, but had never left the freight yards. His directions were better on the second try.

It has been said that Jack Johnson was a pure-blood African, of Coromante stock. Those were the African tribes of New York, led by Quaco, their chief, who back in 1741 had nearly succeeded in burning up all of New York City. Some have suggested that Jack went to see what damage was still visible.

Others say that he went up to meet with Steve Brodie, his hero, who had jumped, and survived his jump, from the top of the Brooklyn Bridge.

Whichever is true, it is known for certain, that he only got as far as Atlanta, Georgia, where he nearly starved to death before he got a job in a racehorse stable. Then he began to act as if he were Isaac Murphy, the black Kentucky Derby three-time winner. He began exercising the horses too hard in the mornings, so he got fired, without enough money for his fare back home.

Later, many times in his life, he was asked to recall, and to explain why he was afraid to return home by the same means he had left, "riding the rails," the rods of the box cars. His answer was always:

"Fear, man, fear. Of what I saw happen more than a few times while trying to make my way on up here. I saw white men, called 'yard-dicks,' taking the black bums and hoboes they could catch and throwing them underneath the rolling wheels of the trains, to kill or dismember them, whichever it went. This was the price a Nigger could pay when and if they caught him. That was enough to scare any young boy in his teens like me."

For the next two years or so, Jack Johnson traveled in between Boston and New York, working as a dishwasher, stable cleaner, or at any odd jobs he could find. But mostly he went begging and starving, unemployed. He visited the libraries, the museums and art galleries wherever he could find them. Mostly in the winters, for these places were always kept warm. He learned to feed his mind and fill his spirit in the warmth of these places, compensating for the empty stomach and freezing chills which ravaged his young body.

He read and studied the speeches of Frederick Douglass, the brilliant Negro antislavery leader. He visited the Metropolitan Museum to stare at the picture of Quaco, his forbear, being burned at the stake for leading a slave rebellion. He studied the history of the Coromante Tribe, that fierce African nation which had spawned him, and which, for the sake of freedom, went wild. He knew that the British had paid indemnity to the Colonial slave owners, rather than return them to slavery, after America had gained her independence. He knew that the remainder of his people had been settled off Nova Scotia and down in the Barbados Islands as "free and independent subjects of The Commonwealth." He learned of the heritage his forbears had left him.

Then, after two years away, Jack started out again, slowly making his way back home to Galveston. The longing for his mother, her cooking and frying, and the taste of watermelons, and the summer sun and bay breezes had taken its toll on the lonely young black boy of fourteen.

The trip back home took more than four months, going the round about ways, ranging almost from the Atlantic to the Pacific coasts, interrupted by many days in jails which seem to have no end, even though his sentences never amounted to more than a week or so.

He was nimble enough to avoid most of the brakemen, the "shacks," or "yard dicks" or hostile hoboes eager to throw a body underneath a rolling train. He was not so lucky, when it came to begging handouts. For this is what he was generally picked up for and, arrested as a vagrant, was locked up in jail.

Along the way back down home, he listened and learned the songs of the road, with the "I-don't-give-a-damn air," from the Caucasian vagrants in his jail cells. But, he liked best of all to sing, along with the black boys of his race, the hymns of lament called "them low-down blues." Sometimes he just stretched out on his cot, staring at the ceiling, as he listened to the songs.

He learned the art of shooting craps, the mark of crooked craps, the use of a knife, which was standard equipment on the road. He learned to "rassle and tussle," to box bare-knuckled, and to choke, to throttle a man lifeless in self-defense.

He learned the brutality of white men, because of his color. How to be "kicked in the ass" and bear with it. He learned to respect the emphasis of their authority, and their re-emphasis with clubs, fists and guns.

The boy was never so fearfully impressed with a white man's intentions until he was kicked from his cell by the Town Marshal of Idaho City, who unlocked the jailhouse door to release him:

"Nigger, if I ever see you again, I'm going to shoot

you in the head, and then put the pistol in your hand . . ."

Eventually, the runaway boy arrived back home.

His mother worriedly began scolding him again, now that his father had grown too weak from paralysis to rise from his sick bed with any regularity. Besides, "Li'l Arthur" had grown up so in the two years away from home, he could not be beaten and treated like a child any longer.

As a result of his mother's prayers and constant pleadings, young Jack took a job on a milk wagon at a salary of a dollar and a quarter a week. He departed this job for a better one at Gregory's Stables, exercising horses in the mornings. This afforded him to go double-or-nothing with his wages, utilizing the crap-skills he had learned along the road. His hero at the time was still the great Isaac Murphy, Negro jockey, whom he imitated every morning with the horses. He ran the horses so hard, that when he turned them over to the clients, the animals were no good for the rest of the day. So, the manager fired him, warning him to stay away from the stables, and to quit offering his services to clients or he would call the sheriff.

To the relief of his parents, "Li'l Arthur" found another job, serving as apprentice in a bakery, a profession he loved. There, in a short time, Jack became an expert at baking pies and cookies and making cakes. He became known for his ability to make bread. But, wanderlust overtook him again. Once more he elected to leave home. This time he went by water, and he stowed away on a steam-freighter headed north.

A short distance out, he was discovered and put to work, to pay for his crime of stealing passage. He was kept a virtual prisoner aboard, forbidden to go ashore as the ship docked at New Orleans, Mobile, Key West, Savannah, Norfolk, and other points. He was frequently beaten severely by the ship's cook, a white man, and when the passengers discovered the mistreatment, out of sympathy, they took up a collection to pay his expenses the remainder of the trip to Boston.

This treatment so burned into the soul of Jack Johnson, he never forgot it. Thereafter, whenever he was aboard a ship or frequenting the harbors across the world, he always scanned the faces of the crews, looking for that chief cook whom he had sworn to kill if he ever found him.

Jack admitted that his humiliation and suffering aboard ship was the thing that had changed him from a happy-go-lucky, adventuresome boy into a hardened man, knowing his first hatred, preferring to die rather than be subjected to such cruelty at the hands of any white man again.

The ship docked at Boston, and young Jack began roaming, "searching around Th' Cradle of American Independence" . . . the home of Crispus Attucks, the Headquarters of Frederick Douglass, Hubert Harrison and other 'Stand up and Fight' Negroes of the past. He met William Monroe Trotter, who had won four scholarships to Harvard, and who was so brilliant in his studies that upon completing his undergraduate work, Harvard had given him his MA without further study.

But Jack had no formal education. And he learned that he was unable to meet and talk with the Black Back-Bay Elite of Boston, whose snobbery as to color and college was "much hautier than that of all Boston Back-Bay white folks."

He decided to stick it out anyway. He began supporting himself as best he could. He went out and began to work as a drifter in the racehorse stables. He was still light enough to work as an exercise boy. And he learned that "if you have a way with horses, any trainer would take you on, without questions." He did this for nearly three years, passing on from stable to stable. But his square meals per day, or per week, were less than the horses which he was hired to exercise. He yearned to return home, but never earned the fare to take him back. He was afraid to return again by "hopping a rattler" and riding the rails as he had once done. His explanation later in life was: "I was showing signs and symptoms of that famous Nigger disease called 'white folks fear' . . . I was mad enough fighting myself not to admit it. I was willing to fight anybody else to prove it wasn't so. I had never learned to fight, that is, standing up and fighting. So, I decided to learn. I would have to learn, before I could risk riding the rods to go home again . . . that was the year 1895."

He was but seventeen years old when he learned of a forthcoming prizefight between Joe Walcott, "The Barbados Demon," of Coromante stock, (not to be confused with "Jersey Joe" Walcott of the mid-twentieth century) and his opponent, "Scaldy Bill Quinn," a white man. They needed sparring mates in their training camps at Woburn. Jack decided to try the white man first, feeling that "Scaldy Bill" would prefer to have a colored sparring mate, since his opponent was also of that race.

"Get out of this camp, nigger!" Scaldy Bill told the black boy, after he had applied and begged for the job, or a try at it. "If I ever catch your black ass back around here, I'll kick you out on your face."

The boy left, suppressing his rage as the tears rolled down his cheeks, frustrated with his humiliation, hunger and misery. He then headed to the Walcott camp.

Jack first met the wife of the man who was to become champion of the Welterweights. Mrs. Walcott invited him to eat, inquired his age, which was seventeen. She noted his height was six feet even. He revealed that he weighed one-hundred-fifty pounds.

When Walcott saw him, he looked around and laughed. "Son, you're gonna need some more pork chops. So, you come to help me out? Awright, you're here. You ever had any kind of experience at this sort of thing?"

When Jack replied, "None," Walcott laughed again.

"Okay, son. It don't matter. You'll get it. There's got to be a first time for everything. Come on, put on th' gloves. Let's start with your training. It's a great game, if you just remember, don't forget. Pull in your chin."

As they sparred, Walcott saw no reason to pull his punches after the first round. His fists ripped to Jack's ribs like bullets. But the kid stood and took it. For this treatment was no comparison with what he had received from the railroad "shacks," the sheriffs, the cook and his crew, which had brutalized his body during his travels. Besides, now his stomach was full. This inspired him with confidence. So he took the punches smiling and came back time and time again to receive more of what the Barbados Demon, the mighty Joe Walcott, could dish out.

What Jack took and gave back in exchange impressed Walcott so, that in a few weeks, as the match approached, Joe told Howie Hodgins, his manager, that when he fought Quinn, he wanted the young Johnson in his corner as a Second.

The boy had a major purpose in helping to get Walcott ready. Vengeance. He had a strong and vicious pride, and when hurt deeply, he would seek out his enemy for vengeance. This canny observation, on the part of Joe Walcott, was to be substantiated over and over in the years that followed as Jack Johnson approached manhood, and emerged the greatest champion of them all. Many a white man, facing him as an opponent, was to learn about this vengeance. Along with Frankie Childs, a black man who once refused to allow

Jack to sleep on the floor in the warmth of his room on a freezing Chicago night. Tommy Burns, who had cried, "All black cats are yellow on the inside. That nigger ain't nothing but a black cat!" Or Jim Jeffries, who announced, ". . . I've got no use for *any* living nigger. I've got less use for a nigger named Johnson."

During the match, it was obvious that on points, Joe Walcott was leading "Scaldy Bill" Quinn, beyond a shadow of a doubt. But Johnson the kid was not satisfied; when Walcott asked him, "How am I doing?"

"You're not doing too good. But you ain't doing too bad. To yourself and the others, you might seem to be breaking even, maybe. You better take the fight to him, to make sure. 'Cause if it comes to a vote, looking anything like even, you'll never get the verdict over a white man."

Walcott followed the instructions of his young protégé, so that in the seventeenth round "Scaldy Bill" dropped to the canvas, a senseless, bleeding hulk of a man. Jack Johnson left the corner and went over to stand above him and to gaze down at the bloody mess of Quinn, huddled in a helpless heap. Smiling in satisfaction, his pride was temporarily satiated with the sight. His job was done, he had saved for his fare home. Once again he headed out, going South.

As any straggler would say, "Johnson strayed 'long the way . . . ." He stopped off along the route to purchase a big bass viol', which he taught himself to play. He gambled to pick up a few more pieces of money—and lost the rest of his bank roll in crap games. Joe Walcott had now departed, so there were no more sparring partner jobs in the offing.

He returned to the stables and to racing horses, which was easy. Although now too heavy to ride any but the top weights, he was more than skillful in controlling the tempers of "the mean ones." But, soon, he met his match, and was kicked in the thigh by a brute, which snapped his femur like a matchstick. Miraculously, he was dragged from the stall before the horse had succeeded in kicking him to death. He lay there and cried, pleading with his boss.

"If I could just get home, sir. To see my mother, my sisters, and my poor father before he dies."

The boss responded—as Johnson later told it, "The night before, somebody had told him, 'It's good luck assured to kill a Chinaman. But it will double your luck for certain to help a broken-down Nigger.' "

His superstitious white boss, amenable to any suggestion that would change the present course of his luck at the tracks, dug down into his pockets and gave the crippled young Negro the price of his fare back home.

He was shipped back by boat, to keep the strain off his leg, allowing time to give his broken bones a chance to heal. But upon arriving in Galveston, the boat was quarantined. He learned that smallpox had broken out aboard. But, throwing his bass viol' overboard, allowing it to float attached to a string, "Li'l Arthur" went below and found himself still skinny enough to squeeze through a porthole under the cover of darkness, and he waded ashore, despite the leg that had been broken.

He hobbled home, soaking wet, appearing at the door, and presenting his mother with a huge, dripping bass viol' as a present. She had watched him come, hobbling up the road in the darkness toward the house. She looked at his gift, and ". . . uttered not a mumbling word . . . just turned back into the kitchen to put on a pot of hot coffee for me."

As he sat drinking coffee and eating, she began to upbraid him for the worry and misery he had caused them. "She never even touched the gift I had brought her for more than a week . . . till one night she came up as I was sittin' there on the porch, playing it and singing her favorite hymn, 'Swing Low, Sweet Chariot' . . . I saw that had got her. I saw th' tears in her eyes. Then, she looked at me and tried to smile before she went inside th' house. That's when I knew she had forgiven me."

CHAPTER TWO

NOW, THE WAY I HEAR IT TOLD . . .

Now, the way I hear it told—and some folks substantiate th' fact, that "Tiny," Jack's mother, made him stay 'round th' house helping with house chores and th' cooking, till his thigh-bone had connected back and healed up completely. Just how long it took, folks don't say. But one thing is certain, that it didn't take too long, and soon Jack was out on the streets of Galveston showing off. He astonished some white folks, and a few Niggers who hung out over on Avenue K. On a bet, he blew those cats' minds by making a backwards jump of ten feet, from a standing-straight position.

They say that he went back to the bakery to work, baking bread, pies and cakes. But that wasn't paying him enough money. So, he went down to the docks and got hired.

Now, there was a man on the docks called "The Big

Bully," who passed every day among the workers demanding a token tribute in cash from those he met as he patrolled. Jack was warned of the man, even though he had met him just a few nights before in a crap-game. The Bully had lost a quarter bet to Johnson, but had snatched up the quarter coin, after losing the bet, and walked away. Jack did nothing at the time, but shortly after, the two of them met and fought it out—one of the bloodiest fights ever witnessed on the docks of Galveston. They used everything to fight with, anything either one could lay his hands on. It ended with The Bully being carried off with a steel-hook in his arm muscle.

Those who had witnessed it marveled at "Li'l Arthur's" quickness with fist and foot. They ran by to tell "Tiny," his mother, about it, while she sat on the porch shelling peas. She said not a word, pretending to watch the scrawny chickens pecking in the dirt in front of the porch steps. She just sat there waiting until "Li'l Arthur" came home.

Then she scolded him for his conduct and for acting so tough; he answered back: "Mama, tough times just go to make tough people."

He quit the docks and went to work downtown in "Professor Herman Bernau's Sporting Gymnasium," where he was hired on the record of his fighting abilities. However, his job was not to give fighting instructions, but rather to keep the place neat and clean. Still, the position afforded young Johnson "a chance to use the punching-bags, after regular hours." And to exercise with the weights and with the pulleys. The owner also gave him the special privilege of buying two pair of boxing gloves at a wholesale price.

Upon getting off from work, he would frequently carry his boxing gloves and stroll up to the corner of Avenue K and Eleventh Street, where "all of the boozers, bettors, thieves and hustlers hung out, just three or four blocks from my house."

He would walk up to a man, anybody who looked rough, throw him one pair of the gloves and start to pulling on the other pair himself. This was a dare, the challenge for an informal bout "just for fun," to the awe and delight of the spectators. He always won.

They say he could predict every blow he was going to make. If Jack said that he was going to hit you next in the eye or in the mouth, you better believe it. 'Cause that's just what he'd proceed to do, next lick he got in. He had started to making a science out of using boxing gloves.

But his mother wasn't for it; nor was his father who himself had been a bare-knuckled fighter in his younger days.

He couldn't ride racehorses any more because of his size, and because of the way he would race them. The bakery ovens? No, too hot and too many hours for the mealy-mouth wages they paid. The docks were out because of so many fights and killings. And his crapplaying and boxing made his family ashamed of him. So, it was agreed, that he would go over to the mainland to find work as a waiter in the hotels there.

It wasn't bad. He liked it. Because there he could hear them playing the newest tunes from Europe. And he could watch th' big-time white acts sing and perform. But, he'd get caught each time, watching the parties from New Orleans and seeing the white people of Paris perform. The manager would jump him, coming up from behind, catching Jack as he watched from behind a ballroom pillar. Then he would fine him 25c for loafing on the job.

So, Jack split-the-scene and made his way to Dallas, "up north in Texas." After hanging around for a while, he found a better job for himself in a paint-shop.

But, when the foreman was out of sight, he had fun sparring around with another young Negro named Wally Lewis, who also worked there. All those who watched him in Dallas would agree that, "He's a comer." And that he would go far in boxing, if he stuck with it.

"Li'l Arthur" did well in Dallas and went back down home to see his family and celebrate. A family holiday, his making nineteen!

At the same time he arrived, the traveling circus came to town, featuring Bob Tomlinson as the sideshow attraction. Inside his tent, Tomlinson challenged "all comers," promising five dollars to anyone able to stand up against him for four rounds!

"Five dollars, for stayin' just four rounds?" Jack joked to the colored men around him. "Why, that's better, or as good, as a week's salary for some poor colored man 'round here. For five dollars, man, I can beat that cracker, much less than get five for stayin' four."

In a few minutes Jack stood up and volunteered to try. One colored helper rushed up along his side and whispered:

"Don't let him push you back into that canvas wall of th' tent. There's a cracker hiding there with a baseball bat to help him out, if you're too tough."

Johnson smiled in gratitude, but the Negro had disappeared into the crowd.

Tomlinson took him lightly, confident that it would be over within a few seconds. A few minutes later he recognized that this was a serious mistake. The action was all his, he had called all of the shots. But the young Nigger wasn't down after three rounds. It wasn't as easy as the local white boys had promised him.

He attempted to spin Johnson around, faking a clinch to push, but the young Nigger was proving that he knew how to clinch professionally—something he'd learned from the Great Joe Walcott.

The fourth round came. Five dollars at stake. Now the black boy came to life. Driving punches! Jabbing! Hooking and feinting like a pro! They never even got near the tent-wall where Tomlinson's helper was waiting with the bat. The white man reeled and sagged, ready to go down. Two minutes later, the bell rang. One minute short. It saved the white man from a knockout. Another lesson learned and never forgotten. "Three-minute rounds would be cut down to two minutes, if it looked like a white man was going to be knocked out by a black one."

He related this lesson at the dinner table, one to be learned and remembered, as the Johnson family ate fried chicken that night, prepared especially in celebration of his victory.

After that, "Li'l Arthur" became a local celebrity, especially with white folks who gave "stag-parties" which featured six Niggers pitch-forked into a ring, where the last man left standing received five dollars. It was called "The Battle Royal" and was generally staged at the Royal Sporting Club of Galveston.

Johnson won so many of these events that it became a habit for all of the five other black contestants to immediately gang up on him from the start, trying to eliminate him at the beginning. But he always found a way to divert their efforts, turning them against each other with his remarks, his biting comments, his taunts, which were later to become the trademark of his ring career.

By now "Li'l Arthur" had come to the crossroads of his career. After so many "Battle Royals," white folks sat up and began to take particular notice, looking around for some really professional fighters to book him with.

The records are contradictory. Some say his first fight

was against Jim McCormick, "The Galveston Giant," on February 11, 1899. Others state that his first one was with Sid Smith, in the same year.

Jack himself is quoted in one of his biographies, saying that his first recorded fight was with "Klondike," May 6, 1899, in Chicago. But it is known that he fought professionally before leaving the South and going up to fight in Chicago.

And it is a fact that he did go traveling around the country looking up men willing to fight him. And he did make it up as far as Chicago between 1899 and 1901, as his autobiography says.

However, there is no record of earlier fights in his own book, ghost-written in 1927. It starts with his loss to "Klondike Jim Jefford" and his fight with John Lee in 1901.

Then he decided to give up fighting and come back home to his mother. And he got married somewhere around that time, too. It is certain he was home when the Galveston Tidal Wave struck Texas and the Devil's Island. He was 22 years old when the flood hit Galveston.

CHAPTER THREE

WHEN THE FLOOD ROLLED IN

The big flood rolled in on a tidal wave the eighth day of September in the year 1900. The total of lives lost and property destroyed has yet to be determined. But, as it rolled in from the sea, covering the sky with darkness, one thing is certain. John Arthur Johnson was standing there, confused by the coming of the wave, but daring to brave and to defy it.

He told about it later: "The sky became queer. Because of the dark gray shadow of the sky, you couldn't see the wave. And at the time, there wasn't even a flutter of the winds at the crossroads.

"It came in silence, like a thin curtain of gauze was being spread out, covering the sky from the sight of the earth, with a million specks of dust clouded over it, blowing across the sky so as to cover the sun from sight.

"For a while, the dirty gray gauze curtain hung over the city. Then, I went into the house uneasily and took out my bicycle, while my mother sat sewing, humming a sad hymn there in the lamplight.

"Coming out of the house, I challenged my friend Ambrose, who was sitting near the front porch astride his bike-seat.

" 'Come on, bastard! I'll race you down to the beach.'

He followed me without comment, until we were headed downhill.

" 'Hell, Nigger, you couldn't race a turtle.'

"We sped past many people who were headed uphill from the town, others in confusion were headed the other way, downhill toward the sea, like us. I didn't notice until later that their faces were haunted, looking terrible, like they were fleeing from some nameless demon.

"Me and Ambrose, my friend, never made it down to the shore. Some man got in front of my bike, and tried to pull it from under me. I kicked out at his face, to make him let go of my bike. He fell back into the street, as a mad rush of people followed him, trampling him under, and almost running over me, too.

"Then, I heard a scream. The scream of a woman, crying out.

" 'Oh, Lawdy, don't hurt my child!'

"The groaning crowd passed, swayed and looked back. Then everybody began to wail and moan. In a moment everybody was screaming, running in all directions like a thundering herd of wild cattle.

"The wind from the sky came out like Heaven had burst open and all the dead souls and spirits of Hell had been turned loose. The sky exploded, the winds sounded like a thousand sirens had been let loose across the face of the earth. Seems like it hit the far corners of the earth, making a curve in space, then bouncing back like a boomerang, roaring and screaming, going around the roof of the world, then belching out in fury.

"I stood and looked at it coming back in, like a black bolt of lightning exploding against the top of the hills, uprooting the trees, lifting houses, machines and the bodies of the people, so that they flew through the air like matchsticks. And that's when I went down to my knees, my bike was blown clear from under my legs like a rubberband. As I fell, I saw the bike crash and bend like wire around a tree.

"Then, all of the legs of the world were running over

me, seems like. Boot legs, bare legs. Legs of women, children, men and animals. From my knees I lashed out against them with my fists, butting with my head. I tore at them, trying desperately to rise up to my feet. When I arose, I saw the winds sweep down a crowd of men, women, and children as if they were cornstalks in a field cut down by one sweep of the scythe. The body of a young child flew past my head, as if it had been shot from the mouth of a cannon. I watched her little body crash into the stones and brick of a wall.

"I began screaming myself, from the bottom of my lungs calling out for Ambrose, who had disappeared.

"I turned back toward home, thinking of my family. My mother, and my father who was unable to run or protect himself. At the top of the hill, I turned back to look down, for I dared not look up into the sky. I watched the people rushing up toward my position. Then I saw the sea, rising up. Rising higher in one single black, black wave. Rearing higher than the heavens, reaching out toward me, clutching out to claim me in one pounce. Then, it came down, like a single hand of God, with many fingers clutching to claim all of us who stood within its grasp.

"The sky split with a roar that shook the earth. A mountain of water smashed down. Now, no longer did I see faces of people, animals or buildings. I only heard the roar of the sea, like a mighty wall of iron which had crushed out everything before it.

"I flung out to grab a woman, who was being swept away by the tide. Her children were hanging onto her skirts. I held the children for a while, until the floods sucked them from my grasp. I watched them disappear beneath the swirling flood of murky waters.

"An old man rose to the surface of the waters, crying out. 'Thank you, Jesus. Save me.' Then he vanished underneath a wave that rose up to claim him.

"Then, I found myself kicking. Swimming and clawing, struggling with all my strength to keep myself afloat. I treaded water to reach high ground, when something caught my hand, as I was making my way up a standing tree. I paused ready to lash out. But, nobody was there. Only the face of Ambrose, who screamed.

" 'Jack! Your mother and family. Don't forget them.'

"I knew that my mother and my family were trapped helpless in our little house. I slid down, fighting, lashing, swimming and wading through the water, treading the streets eddying with water—now, as deep as a lake—to find my way home.

"At last I found it. On the flat roof of our house there were people, all bunched together waiting for the end. As I made my way toward them, the second wave hit, roaring down the streets, from behind me. The dead and the dying were all around me, littering the sides of the narrow street to my house.

"As I drew closer, I saw and heard 'Harry the Carter,' and other white men, calling from their skiffs and their wagons, calling up to the people on the roof.

" 'Here you-all go. Only a dollar a head up to safety. Anybody with a dollar, we'll take you up there. Dollar a head . . . dollar a head . . . dollar a head, all it takes . . .'

" 'Harry the Carter' was the first one I could get to. I reached up and pulled him down from his wagon. The lights of the city flickered and blinked out, just about that time. The area was covered over with darkness, but I had him in my grasp. In the last light, blinking, I struck out at his face.

"I reached up for the reins of his horses. He came at me again. I turned, calling out to the people to climb aboard. The other white men in boats rowed away to seek a more peaceful place for their saving business.

"I took another swing at Harry and we went down together, fighting to the death under the hoofs of fright-

ened horses. No holds barred, we fought in the darkness
and the water, among dead cats and dogs, fowl and
dead swine, punching wrestling, kicking, until I sent
him reeling beneath his horses. He came up floundering. Then I could see his bloody white teeth between his
bloody, watery lips, pleading, 'Give you half, Jack, I'll
give you half, please. We split, fifty-fifty, I promise.'
That was the last time that I hit him. He either drowned
or swam away. I encouraged the people and my family
to get aboard the wagon and clucked the mad horses to
haul us to higher ground and to safety.

"I yelled to everyone else crowded together on the
roof-top.

" 'Climb on! Free for everybody!'

"This I did all night long. Although there were many
others that I caught along the way, both black men and
white men, with carriages, boats and wagons, charging
destitute and desperate people a cash fee to carry them
to high ground.

"As I came across them, I made them change their
tunes—with a horsewhip and with my fists. I must have
fought with at least a half-dozen or more of such men.
Those who wouldn't comply, I took their wagons or
boats and placed somebody else in charge from among
those who were willing to aid me.

"It was the same sad story for days. More than five-
thousand souls had been claimed by the flood.

"The weather cleared up, and the blazing sun came
down on Devil's Island. I climbed to the top of a hill to
look down on the damage. I could hear the hymn-songs
of my people coming up to me from all around, the
wails of widow and mother prayers crying out for their
dead loved ones, children calling out for fathers and
mothers, whom they would never see again, departed
ones who would never answer their calls again. Not in
this world.

"Funeral pyres were burning all over the town. The air was filled with the smell of smoke and burning flesh. The corpses were piled in heaps, pushed into deep trenches, or packed into the holds of small boats, moving out to the sea to surrender the dead that the wave had claimed.

"I knew that those sights and sounds would never leave me. I would never be free of those memories, not ever.

"I decided to leave Galveston soon after the disaster was over, to make my way to the North, or elsewhere, with the only skill I knew, which was fighting. At least it was the fastest way to make it, so I could come back and get mama and the family.

"I vowed that I would deliver them from this scene. Even if it was to kill me, I decided it would be better to die trying to do so."

CHAPTER FOUR

ON THE WAY UP

Now, after the flood had settled, Jack tried to settle down. He fell in love and got married to a pretty light-skinned girl of the town named Mary Austin. Cultured and refined, she was; she disapproved of his fighting for a living. When he wouldn't give it up, she deserted him. His first knock-out blow at the hands of a woman.

The next came at the hands of a man. "The Graduate Professor" of boxing, Joe Choynski, came to town. A man known for inexhaustible endurance and the concentrated force with which he could strike an opponent down in the ring. They also called him "The Polish Jew."

The fight was advertised as, "A fight to the finish," which of course was illegal, even then.

Choynski lowered the boom on Johnson in the third round.

It might not have been the hardest punch ever aimed at Johnson. But, for sure it was the hardest one that ever landed on him. It came like a rocket and caught Jack in the temple.

They say that he dropped as if he had been shot. They had to pour cold water on him to bring him around. Then, when he opened his eyes, he was staring dead into the face of Cap'n Luke Travis of the Texas Rangers.

"Now, you two boys are going over to be guests, for a spell, in our 'Cross-Barred-Hotel'." So he took them on to jail.

Aside from that knockout, there was another good lesson, which Jack had come to learn the hard way.

"Place no faith in the words of a white man, even if he represents the Law."

Captain Travis had assured them, even though a fight to the finish was illegal, nothing would be done about it. The Rangers had come to see it, not wanting to spoil the sport, delaying the arrests of the principals until it was all over. Choynski had cut their pleasure too short. Young Jack had been their disappointment, going down too quick.

But, this jail term paid off dividends for "Li'l Arthur." For the fight was continued daily in the courtyard of the jail. The warden demanded it for his own entertainment, the amusement of the guards and other prisoners, as physical exercises for the Jew and the nigger.

As fighters go, Choynski had a good heart, and was generous enough to give Jack a few lessons during these daily sessions, for more than three weeks.

"A man who can move like you should never have to take a punch. Don't try to block, man, you're fast enough to move clear out of the way. Forget blocking!"

So, it was there in the jailyard that "the cat style of boxing," the Jack Johnson style, received the polishing touches, under the scrutiny and instructions of Joe Choynski, "The Professor."

Very shortly, a tobacco-chewing judge came to the prison and watched them fight. When they were finished, the official told the guards.

" 'Bout time you can turn 'em loose now, boys,"

Free and relieved from the experience, but obviously shaken, Johnson struck out to cross the desert to California, "Riding the rails," to points West, to begin a serious career in professional boxing, which seven years later would enthrone him, Champion of the World.

"Li'l Arthur" would lose but two fights after this, and one of these by a fluke. To Marvin Hart in 1905, in San Francisco. And to the great Joe Jeanette later that same year. He fought the latter numerous times, "whenever they were short of change."

Jack improved so fast, and became so good, that he could hardly earn money as a fighter. Even offering his services as a sparring mate.

His opponents, both black and white, along with their managers and promoters, would insist on "arrangement before his fights." The outcomes were precluded. Johnson must not win. The decisions were to be "draws," or "no decisions."

"Frequently," he related, "I was not to knock them out and was forced to let them go the distance.

Such conditions filled him with such rage that his only release during his bouts was to taunt, clown and laugh as he went about cutting and slashing his oppo nents to ribbons. Sometimes, he would break the agree ment and knock his opponent out. Only to find that there were to be no more engagements in the near fu ture.

But, he came to the attention of Tad Dorgan, a lead ing sports reporter, the boxing authority of the Wes Coast, to whom all prize-fighters, managers, and pro moters paid homage.

It was Dorgan who pulled Jack aside one day, to say: "Kid, I think that you've got it. You are going to beat them all. Mark my words."

The Big Fire not only marked the words of Tad Dor gan as a prophecy, which awed him no end. He later vis ited a fortune teller that he had heard about, disguising himself as a day laborer.

In his autobiography, *Jack Johnson—In the Ring— and Out,* "Li'l Arthur" describes his visit:

"I was careful, or thought I was, to conceal from her the real nature of my occupation. But I did not fool her. She at once told me that I was a boxer, and recounted some of my past life with such accuracy that I was as tounded. She proceeded to tell me many things con cerning my future, some of them so fantastic and so im probable . . . that I departed from her presence feeling that she had drawn a highly imaginative picture of my life. She predicted that I would be the heavyweight boxing champion; she told me of my forthcoming mar riages and of various affairs that I was destined to have with women . . . of the adventures and travels that were to mark my later life; of my conflicts with the law; of the accident which nearly cost my life in Spain, when an automobile turned over with me; of my sickness, which nearly ended in my death; of my return to America and the events of the following years. . . .

"In the years since, events and circumstances have come to pass with little deviation from the manner in which she foretold them. I still do not make an admission of being superstitious, but . . . the record stands . . ."

Upon his return to San Francisco, broke, hungry, despondent, Jack found things no different. In order to eat, he was forced to become chief cook and bottle washer for a traveling troop of roving professional prize fighters organized by Sailor Tom Sharkey. But as part of his education, he learned more-tricks-of-the-trade.

He was shown that by saturating the bandages in a solution of gun cotton and whiskey, he would make a concrete-casing around the fists, inside the boxing gloves. He learned to watch closely as they applied the practice of "slipping the peter" to an opponent. That was to lace the food and drink of an opponent with hashish. He learned the latter the hard way. As it was done to him, by his own manager, aided by Jack's new wife, Clara Kerr, a Negro beauty, whom everybody knew as Sadie. However, this fact was never substantiated. Jack himself had never wanted to believe it, even after Sadie had run away with one of his best friends, robbing him of every bit of clothing, every piece of jewelry, and every dollar and cent he had to his name.

His white manager was Frank Corella, a bail bondsman, known as "The Furnisher," who was then working Jack up into "good money matches." He had made and saved some money, bringing it home to Sadie. He had showered her with gifts, clothes, jewelry and money, which they both were more than amply supplied with. Much of this Sadie gleefully turned over to Johnson's best friend, her lover, Willie Bryant, a discredited trainer of race-horses.

The time grew near when the two had planned "to pick the crow clean." Corella signed Johnson to fight George Gardner, from County Clare, Ireland, generally accepted as the Light Heavyweight Champion of the world. The fight was to take place in March, 1902.

Between the three—Clara, his wife, her lover Willie, and Corella, his manager, "the peter was being slipped" to Johnson. One thing was certain. His manager was in on the deal, sending out his agents to bet large bundles of money on the Irish champion, while he strutted around a pitched tent making but token bets on his own fighter.

Sadie and her lover were also making plans.

Nine days before the fight, Johnson was leaving Harry Corbett's Saloon on Ellis Street, after having been allowed to sip a beer there, becoming the "first of his race" ever to do so. Upon departing, he staggered and became dizzy, falling in a heap on the sidewalk, moaning to Corella that he was sick.

After a spell of vomiting, he was carried home to his wife. He ran a temperature of 102 for the next week. Under Corella's orders, Sadie fed him water biscuits, milk and soda until he bloated. Before ring time, he had another attack of violent vomiting. The job had been done. He walked down the aisle to the ring, his arms across the shoulders of his two seconds, barely making it under his own power.

The white folks came in howling for "some black nigger blood." Corella took further precautions to make certain they would have it. The ring was spattered with it. Johnson's blood, as Gardner knocked him from pillar to post. Between rounds, Corella dosed his weak fighter with straight shots of strong rye whiskey.

By the twelfth round he was reeling from belly-

cramps, dizzy spells, and one of the worst beatings that
Gardner could administer. The champion closed in for
the k ', missed the haymaker that brought him to a
. .... with Johnson. A desperate man, a wounded animal, a cornered tiger.

The champion said later, "It looked like the eyes of
death and murder were starin' into mine. It was the evil
eye of doom, I swear it . . ."

Johnson chopped him murderously, three merciless
digs to the body. Gardner backed away thereafter, and
ran for six more rounds. Finally, in the 19th and 20th
rounds, "Li'l Arthur" caught up and beat Gardner into
a senseless hulk. "Slippin' him the peter" hadn't worked
as planned.

But the plans of Clara and Willie Bryant to pick the
crow clean went off as scheduled. For when he arrived
at his apartment, they had gone, with his money, his
clothes, and his jewelry.

"I just laid down and cried like a baby," Jack later
said. "I learned that Frank Corella had vanished, too,
with my part of the gate receipts which he had collected.

"I wished for my mother, just as I prayed down
God's curses on white men, and all other Nigger
women. All, except the one who bore me.

"I swore before God nevermore to trust anybody. In
my rage, I punched holes into the walls with my fists. I
wanted to shatter them, to make certain that I would
never fight in the ring again.

"Then I went out into the city, roamed the streets for
days, drinking, starving, with one single purpose in
mind. To find Clara, if I could, and to make her come
back. Then to take Willie by the neck and throttle him
to death.

"I refused all offers to fight any more. I became a
derelict, caring about nothing.

"Everybody was saying, 'Johnson is through. Finished. Washed up.'

"I roamed everywhere I could in efforts to find Clara. I took on fighters, all of whom I had beaten, in order to keep eating. Finally the urge to find Clara was satisfied. I caught her and Willie coming out of a hotel in St. Louis one night. But, strangely enough, I didn't want to kill him. I took Clara with me to Chicago. In a couple of months, she left again. And I knew well that after that time, she would never come back.

"I 'went to the dogs' completely. One night, while standing slouched against a corner saloon, I heard a man pass and say, 'That's him, Jack Johnson. Washed up, man. He couldn't even hold the hat of a good man, now.'

"When I heard that, I started to run somewhere to hide. I didn't know where to hide, so I just hopped the next rattler out of town. It carried me to Pittsburgh, to New York and back. Working as a sparring partner for anyone who would hire me. Very few did, and none were eager to."

CHAPTER FIVE

ON THE RUN FROM HIMSELF

"Did you ever see a man on the run, from himself?" I heard Jack Johnson ask one day in Chicago.

Although, he was talking to some other folks who were standing there at the bar with him, he turned around and looked me dead in the eye and asked.

"Did you ever see, or hear of anything like that, friend? You ever hear of a man running away from himself, and trying to catch up with the same thing that he was running away from, all at the same time?"

He didn't wait for me to give him an answer. He just kept on. Already knowing what my answer would be.

"It's natural bitch, my friend. A natural born, pure bitch."

"Imagine," Jack said. "Running from yourself. 'Cause you're scared that th' very same self that you're running from is gonna catch up with th' very same thing that you're scared of catching, while you're running away from the thing that's gonna catch up with you?"

Wow! He had scared me, along with everybody else in listening distance at the bar. Then, he went on to tell some of the stories and experiences while running from himself, to catch up with himself.

Seemingly, he went everywhere. Fighting in tanktowns. Fighting any and all comers, to keep a piece of bread in his stomach. But starving and drunk most of the time.

He even went back to fighting those "Battle Royals" again, which was way below his status—as white men would put up a pot of money, he remembered. Pitchforking—six Niggers in a boxing ring together. Pitting them all against each other, to see which "One Nigger" could survive.

Jack took this, while on his way. And he kept on running, all over the country. He ended back in Chicago—starving, without a place to lay his head.

Back in Chicago, he came across Frankie Childs, a fighter he used to barnstorm with who Jack thought had become his friend.

The Hawk, meaning the cold wind, was pitching in "Chi Town" that winter. Frankie felt sorry for Johnson —down on his luck—and invited him to come up and sleep on the floor of his one-room pad.

Jack was so happy that he cried like a baby. Grateful to sleep on the floor near the pot-belly stove, glowing red-hot with welcome.

But a few nights later, Frankie came home, woke Jack up and put him back out into the cold-freeze. Seemingly, Frankie had brought his cousin, from back down in Arkansas, with him. His cousin had just blown into town. Frankie claimed, that he "had to have the floor where Johnson had been sleeping, for his cousin's comfort."

Li'l Arthur offered to take over in the corner and sleep without cover and pallet, if he would be allowed to stay for the night, at least.

But, Frankie still said no. Jack would have to go back out into the night and the freezing, sub-zero

So, he went; but he never forgot. Later, he was to beat Childs almost to death in the ring. Then, long years afterwards, when Jack was on his uppers, Childs came weather.

in to beg for a handout. And Jack told him, "You better get the hell away from me. And now!"

That goes to show you how deeply Jack felt. How unforgiving he could be to an enemy.

Naturally, Johnson survived that freezing cold night, after Frankie Childs had turned him out into the cold. He prayed as he walked, and found a nickel in the torn lining of his coat, which must have slipped down from the pocket, long ago. With this nickel, he bought a cup of coffee and stayed at the counter until the place closed up.

So, daylight came, and he was able to sleep in the slot of a corner building without freezing to death. Jack left Chicago and struck out for fights on the West Coast again. At Los Angeles, he managed to get a match with Jack Jeffries, called "The Other Jeffries." His brother, Jim Jeffries, was Heavyweight Champion of the World —and specialized in "nigger hating and nigger baiting." Although a three-to-one underdog, "The Big Black Fire" polished off the "Other Jeff" with a knockout in five rounds.

Johnson learned that this was the only way to do it. For, whenever he was in the lead, bringing his white opponent close to a knockout, then the regular three-minute rounds were cut short by a minute or more to allow his white opponents to be saved by the bell. And by this time he had become newspaper copy, having beaten the best of black boys, such as Frankie Childs, Denver Ed Martin, Joe Butler and the like. White boys had set up "the color line" against him—and he seldom managed to dent it. But Jack Jeffries was white, and brother of the champion. Now, San Francisco and the West Coast wanted to see more of The Big Black Fire.

Word spread east, and Johnson got himself a fight in Boston, Massachusetts, in the spring of 1903. He was to take on the protégé of John L. Sullivan—a white boy named Sandy Ferguson. Sullivan claimed he was the coming champion.

Ferguson's friends took precautions to make sure that the Cap'n Sullivan would be right in his opinions. They called on Johnson a half dozen times carrying guns, showing them to Jack, making certain that he got the point.

"John L's got big plans for this Ferguson boy. You understand what we mean, nigger?"

Jack rolled them a round of his "Uncle Tom Eyes" with the whites showing. But they didn't get it. He nodded meekly.

"Yassuhs. I understands. I sure do. I 'spect that you'all and th' Cap'n wants me to be nice and let your boy go. And then, you'all is gonna be nice to me."

They stood to go, satisfied. "That's th' point, boy. And there's a hundred smackers in it for you to be nice. But, a very short life, if you don't."

Now that's the night that Jack Johnson caught up and found himself. That night.

Jack Johnson admitted to me, "I came that night to realize. No matter what I had been guilty of doing, I had never been guilty of giving up and laying down because somebody else told me that I had to do it or die. I also found out, that what people had thought I would do, and what I knew I would do, were two different things. What I thought of me, and what other people thought of me, were as different as a pig and a sow. I decided to die. One way or another. But, I would try to beat the living hell out of that white boy, that night. And I did."

And the records show it.

Johnson beat Sandy Ferguson so badly, in front of the men and their guns, that Ferguson took his foot and kicked Johnson in the groin, dropping him to his knees.

But rather than let the fight continue the white referee awarded Johnson the fight "on a foul."

The first, of many race riots in Johnson's life, ensued. The crowd tore the ring-posts, destroyed the ring, while Jack fought himself free . . . out of town and back on the run again. But this time and thereafter, to fight again. And to keep on fighting. No longer against himself, but from now on, against those who were fighting him.

CHAPTER SIX

THE BIG BLACK FIRE IS BACK

Johnson headed west and picked himself up another white manager, which seemed to be what every Nigger needed if he was going up some place in the white world.

He hired Sam Fitzpatrick—or as they say, Sam thought he had hired Jack Johnson.

Jack went to work on his projects. But Johnson's fights in the ring were much less frequent than most fighters. Nearly always, he would agree to let the fights go the limit—fifteen, maybe twenty rounds. He would go the duration, seldom knocking them out—especially white boys.

But, it would be torture. And not only for Johnson. He had gotten into the habit of taunting his opponent. Telling him where he was going to hit him next. Then he would admonish him, scolding him for making mistakes—like a teacher in a classroom. Naturally, the opponent would try harder to kill him. Then, he would warn him. But, there was never a question as to when he could take him out and end it.

In the year 1905, he was scheduled to meet Sam McVey again, whom Jack had already beaten three or more times, but who had got lucky enough to hit and stun Jack in one of their fights. Sam was what the white folks called: "A good nigger," loved by all, because he knew his place with white people and conducted himself in the "proper manner."

Then too, Sam McVey had beaten the great Harry Wills, the man whom, later, Jack Dempsey paid off rather than meet in the ring. Around that time they were saying, too, that Johnson was scared to meet Harry Wills. Seemingly, people had forgotten that Jack had beaten him, too.

So they met again, McVey and Johnson, at Mechanics Pavilion San Francisco. All over the town were signs and sketches of Jack Johnson, being held down by some white men while they castrated him.

At the ringside that night more than five or six hundred people came in carrying signs, playing dirty songs, spitting and jeering at The Big Black Fire.

They went to getting their kicks, flipping burning cigarettes and butts up against the naked flesh of his back while he stood or sat in his corner of the ring.

Jack Johnson took it all in silence—his flesh burning and saying nothing, as he concentrated on Sam McVey. By the time he knocked Sam through the ropes and out, Jack's black back was blistered with angry cigarette burns.

After "creaming" Sam, Jack moved back to his corner and kicked his wash bucket, filled with snot, spit and blood, into the faces of the ringsiders near his corner. Shouting:

"Allow me to serve these refreshments!"

Another riot resulted. But, he was again over the ropes and down the aisle to the trap door.

The Vigilantes patroled the streets of San Francisco throughout the night in search of him. But to no avail. For later, "The Big Smoke" was sitting, laughing and loving, across the bay in Oakland, in the parlors of "Madam Sweetmeat," the most prominent "Lady of the Night" in Northern California. She had once declared:

"Jack Johnson is the best man to ever drop his boots alongside my bed. And the only man who could make me drop my drawers at a moment's notice without having one cent in his pocket."

By the time 1906 had rolled around Johnson had fifty-six fights registered to his credit, not counting the innumerable exhibitions, Battle Royals and other "arranged" bouts, never officially recorded. And he had lost but three of these. One to Klondike, one to Choynski and "the fluke" to Marvin Hart. It was agreed, even among many of his enemies, that he deserved consideration as a title contender.

By then it came and narrowed down to a matter of his color and race prejudices. Some boxing authorities and biased sports writers, having to justify their prejudices, made many proclamations:

"His record is not impressive enough to be a challenger," ignoring the fact that among his fifty-four victories he had defeated Jack Munroe, the only man who held the distinction of knocking down Jim Jeffries, the retired champion, for a count. Or that he had beaten another top challenger, Joe Grim, knocking him down eighteen times in a "no decision" bout.

Most of them kept insisting that he meet the very same fighters that he had beaten before, over and over. They kept insisting, too, that Joe Jeanette, another colored boy, could take him. Forgetting that once Johnson had beaten Joe Jeanette and another good fighter-puncher, Walter Johnson, both on the same night.

So, that year Johnson was obliged to meet Joe Jeanette in no less than four bouts to convince the fans, despite claims of the Caucasian "fight experts" and sports writers. On January 16, he beat Joe in a "no decision" contest of three rounds at New York. He won again in a fifteen round contest at Baltimore in March. Then again in September, six rounds, "no decision," at Philadelphia. And once again on November 26, ten rounds, "draw," at Portland, Maine.

Jeanette's managers, along with Johnson's manager, Sam Fitzpatrick, had agreed that the judges would render "no decision" or "draw," regardless of the outcome—unless Johnson was the loser.

In early 1905, Jim Jeffries, the Heavyweight Champion, had retired undefeated. He designated Jack Root and Marvin Hart as the two contenders for the championship, and he agreed to referee their title match in July, 1905. Hart won, but shortly thereafter, he was defeated by a fighter called "Tough Tommy Burns." His real name was Noah Brusso, but no one objected when he used a different name. (Unlike Cassius Clay, who is no longer "acceptable" now that his name is Muhammed Ali.) Soon after gaining the crown, Tommy Burns took off for Europe—possibly, it has been said, in order to avoid a match with Johnson.

Up until this time, Jack Johnson had battled more than six hundred rounds of fighting. He fought everywhere: in backyards, butchershops, slaughterhouses, circus tents, garages, jailyards, regular gymnasia—and even on shipboard. Yet, the champions consistently refused to meet him, even though he had waded through more than sixty-three fights, losing only four. And one of these losses was by a fluke. Johnson fought Marvin Hart in March, 1905 (before he became champion), and the referee got so excited (at least, that's the way he told it) that he raised Hart's hand as victor, when really he had meant to raise Johnson's. So, they let it stand that way.

By that time, too, Jack had beat all of the best. Sam McVey, three times; Sam Langford and Joe Butler, once each; Sandy Ferguson, three times (he fought him four times, but there was a verdict of "no decision" in one of the fights); and Joe Jeanette, whom he fought seven times (and was beaten by him once). But except for four times, no one could claim to have defeated him. Besides Marvin Hart and Joe Jeanette, he had lost to Joe Choynski—as mentioned previously—and also to Klondike in their first match. (He later defeated Klondike twice.)

In 1907, the largest purse that Johnson had earned was $1,200—his largest to date—in a bout with a white fighter, Bob Fitzsimmons.

They said Johnson couldn't punch, but he punched Fitzsimmons into a soggy heap. Then, they put him up against "Fireman Jimmy Flynn," who was carried from the ring with a broken jaw, after an eleventh round knockout.

Jack had beaten all of the black "White Hopes," and all of the white "White Hopes" were falling apart at the seams. Jack even begged the retired Jim Jeffries to come on out of retirement and fight, now that his protégé Tommy Burns had "flown the coop."

Even some white folks weren't satisfied with Burns as a World Champion. So, the Los Angeles newspaper reporters went to talk with Mr. Jeffries.

"Mr. Jeffries, would you fight Tommy Burns?"

"Nothing doing, I'm out of the game," he answered.

"But suppose the public insists that you come back and defend the title."

"The public can go to hell," said Jeff.

"Well, suppose that they say that you are afraid," asked another reporter.

"Then, I say that they can still go to hell."

But, with nobody around to give him a fight, Jack was finding ways of staying in the papers. He seemingly didn't need money, " 'cause them white broads had begun to lay it on him."

He was stopping the traffic on Fifth Avenue, New York. Riding around in a chauffeured white Stutz, he was wonderful to see, wearing a twenty-pound bearskin coat and two of his pretty white women sitting alongside of him. Jack called them his "personal secretaries."

He was blowing their minds, for sure—the "white-minded" folks, that is.

One thing about Jack was his wit and his humor. If you asked him a silly question, he would cap right back with an answer that would floor you. Like the time one white reporter asked him.

"Mr. Johnson, why is it you seem to prefer the company of white women to those of your own race?"

Jack Johnson just swelled up and answered him right back.

"Because, they enhance me more than my women do. And in return, I allow them to bask in the limelight, temporarily."

And to prove that he let them enhance him and "bask in the limelight temporarily," he came back to Chicago and picked up on the prettiest white whore, they say, in the Windy City, named Belle Shreiber. She offered to live and hustle for him, if he would let her. Which he did. She was to confess and admit that she did, some five or six years later, in order to get Jack sent to jail. Even though she was working in a whore-house when he found her, he was later accused of dis-honoring her, transporting her for carnal purposes.

It is a known fact, seldom admitted, that white women chased Jack around offering their favors, much more than he was chasing them.

Like the time he left this same Belle Schreiber to come out to train for his fight with Jimmy Flynn, "The Fireman," in San Francisco. This same Belle Shreiber caught a train to follow and join him, without his knowing. Johnson was at his training camp, an inn that he had rented between San Francisco and Sacramento. He was intent and concentrating on the fight. Even the innkeeper's daughter had been warned by his handlers to stay away.

But, as the story goes. Down at the train station, Belle Shreiber met up with another white girl from New York, Hattie McLay, a jeweler's daughter, whom Jack later claimed to have married. She had come from New York with the same idea in mind. A surprise visit.

The two white girls met in mortal combat, right there in the station. Each one, almost tearing the other's clothes off. The police came and stopped them, but one of the colored attendants had called Jack on the phone. Jack came up before the police took them off. He made them promise that if they would behave themselves, he would divide his time between them, alternating the nights, during his training. They both agreed. But now you know that this agreement didn't set too well with the reporters and the police officials who stood there and heard it.

Anyhow, as Jack tells it later, after he had put each one to sleep with his loving, he would climb down a rope and head back to his private quarters to get some much needed rest.

This went on, until one night Jack got caught. Or

thought he did. As he was sliding down the rope from Hattie's window, one of those nights, he heard a hard breathing below him. He just knew that it had to be Belle, with her hot temper. But, it wasn't.

When Jack dropped to the ground, he was pounced upon by the innkeeper's daughter grasping, clamoring for the "sight and feel of my private."

"I'll scream if you don't." But she was already at it, as Jack related later. "Like she thought I was built of leather down there. I've never seen a girl get so frantic. And I'd known a lot of frantic women, up to that time."

It was only a few days later that he regretted the incident. When he wouldn't comply for an encore, or promise to "divide myself by three nights," including her, she told her father that she had been raped and thought she was pregnant. "After that, it almost came to the point that that damn rope was going to have two uses for me. One for climbing and the other for hanging."

The innkeeper shouted and screamed about Jack "ruining his poor little baby, with his gigantic, oversized 'thing.'" Fitzpatrick and the others tried to calm him with a pay off for his "baby's lost virtue." The fight being but a few days away.

The reporters got the story. It was whispered around in all circles. Photographers cashed in on the gossip. "Dirty book comics" appeared all over. *Jack Johnson and his Girls, Black Ape Splitting the White Princess,* and other titles. They featured cartoons of Jack, with an oversized, out of proportion penis, in grotesque positions with little white virgins, "ruining them for a respectable life."

Fans flocked to the camp for a sight of his oversized member—which shortly became *The Talk of the Town,* the county, the state and the country.

In mockery, Johnson accommodated "their perverted

curiosities." One accommodation he would live the rest
of his life to regret. He began to appear for his sparring
sessions with his penis wrapped in gauze bandages, en-
hancing the size for the benefit of his "admirerers,"
strolling around the ring, arms raised, effecting the awe
and fascination of all, both men and women, who believed the stories they had heard and the plots of the little pornographic cartoon books.

In defiance, for many bouts thereafter in America
and in Europe, whither the legend had followed him, he
would enter the ring so wrapped and bulging at his
groin. Thus, the legend was accepted as a truism.

Even the white men who knew better grew more
enraged, daring not discuss the "subject of Johnson's
size," in the presence of their ladies, many of whose
curiosities would not be satisfied by just the talk or the
sight of it.

Back in the East, it was discussed as if it were a re-
cent discovery, up till then ignored.

John L. Sullivan, the great bare-knuckle champion
and barroom brawler, took a moral stand against "that
nigger's public conduct." Publicly, he criticized Johnson's "savage performances with white women," his
drinking and public conceit. Carefully avoiding the main
subject: "The size of a nigger's penis is not to be discussed in public."

By that time Johnson had been introduced to a new
drink, by a former British soldier who claimed to have
seen service in Her Majesty's Indian Forces, where he
himself had discovered "The Rajah's Peg." Jack adopted the drink as incomparable after the Britisher had revealed "The Rajah's Peg" was the same as an ordinary
cocktail, except that brandy was used instead of Scotch,
and champagne was substituted for water or soda. It
was to be sipped through a straw. Jack had a special
straw made of gold to sip his Rajah's Peg.

The Northern California Vigilantes were active again, recalling Johnson's last visit to their area, and were busy making death threats. Placards again appeared with hooded white men holding down the body of Johnson and castrating him.

Discussions were held to find means of demanding that the nigger would have to appear in the ring "properly covered" and be forced to wear something other than the tight-fitting regulation boxing trunks of the time. Especially if films of the fights were to be taken.

The retired Jim Jeffries, upon hearing of ". . . the horrible and irreparable ruin this nigger had performed upon helpless white women . . . ," left his retirement, and trekked to Northern California to personally seek vengeance. And not in the ring.

He caught Johnson in a saloon with Belle and Hattie and challenged The Big Smoke to step into the back room with him and we'll lock the door. "Nigger, I dare you to."

But, Jack just rose and answered. "What good is that gonna' do for me?"

And with dignity, he departed the place, Belle and Hattie holding onto each of his arms. Both laughing.

The word got back to New York. One New York reporter analyzed in printing:

". . . Johnson at work has the grace of a dancing master . . . he knows that he could dance away from Jeffries, in a dance that would end up, with Jeffries on the floor. But a locked room is no place for dancing. Johnson knew, that if he killed Jeffries with a boot or a knife, he would hang . . . ."

John L. Sullivan spoke up again. "Why was he afraid to take Jeff on in a private fight? When I was champion I took anybody on, anywhere! He's a yellow dog. That's what he is. My boy Kid Cutler would kill that dinge."

When Johnson read the statements, he simply replied by directing his manager, Fitzpatrick.

"Sam, get me Cutler."

Fitzpatrick tried to persuade Jack against it. His arguments failed.

"But, you'll only be fighting for peanuts," Sam protested.

"I've done that before. And I might have to do it again. But that won't be the case here. You do the arranging, I'll do the fighting.

"Just do what I tell you. There'll be a crowd, 'cause Sullivan is gonna be in Cutler's corner. That'll draw a crowd, and all of them better get in there early."

Five weeks later, at Reading, Pennsylvania, Fitzpatrick and others woulld learn what Jack had meant with his parting comment, as Johnson and Kid Cutler met for a scheduled twelve rounds.

The house was good, even better than The Big Fire had predicted. "Captain" John L. Sullivan came down the aisle, leading Kid Cutler to his corner. The Kid's manager had already collected their share of the gate receipts, which was stowed away in a leather satchel and placed in the hands of an off-duty detective from Philadelphia.

Sullivan was introduced, took his bow and pointed to his protégé. "I now give you a champion of the people. The next champion of the world."

The cheering died down as the bell rang. Cutler stepped from his corner towards Johnson, who was then sliding, his usual "flat-foot shuffle," and smiling.

Cutler feinted at Jack's head. Johson stepped in, made a movement with his left arm, "as if catching a fly" . . . a swift movement. The fight was over as Kid Cutler crumpled to the canvas.

Later, others would be credited with "the shortest prize fight in history."

Fans sitting in the back rows thought it was a heart attack. Those at ringside thought they saw the blow land. The referee was counting ten as Jack was about to climb through the ropes, not caring to wait for his hand to be raised in victory.

But, he paused and grinned again, turning back to Sullivan as the count was completed and the handlers were carrying the unconscious Culter to the corner, and called out above the bewildered murmers of the crowd.

"How did you like that one, Cap'n John?"

CHAPTER SEVEN

IN CHASE OF A CROWN

Johnson returned to New York and remained in the headlines, strutting and driving through Harlem with his 690 Thompson Flyer, displaying his white women—many others beside Hattie and Belle Schreiber—while issuing public challenges for Jim Jeffries to come out of retirement and fight in the ring

Tommy Burns the champion had sent word from abroad, "I'll take care of the nigger when I return to America."

It looked as though Tommy would never return. Sam Fitzpatrick, Johnson's manager, had remarked:

"I don't think Burns will ever return until Jack Johnson either retires or dies."

Then, Jack became intent on winning another kind of crown, by electing to become King of the Speedways, as a race driver. He challenged the king, Barney Oldfield, who had been clocked recently with an automobile speed record of more than one-hundred-thirty miles an hour. Jim Jeffries, the retired champion, had acted as Oldfield's mechanic.

"Since Jeffries is scared to come out and meet me in the ring," said Johnson, "then, I'll just have to go out an' beat him and his partner on the speedway track with my 690 Thompson."

Of course Jack was no slouch at speed with cars. He was known to have driven at over a hundred on the highways and streets.

Oldfield accepted the challenge and in October of that year they met in a duel at Sheepshead Bay, Long Island.

A capacity crowd turned out that day to see Johnson end in a black smear in a pool of black oil and blood.

Jack cut his car across in front of Oldfield at the start and almost took them both over the rails. Then, he swung back and Barney was fit to be tied, his car bouncing sideways. He hit his throttle and took off after Jack, caught up with him, and you could see nothing but smoke and smell the fresh burned paint. He came close to brushing Jack off the track.

It was a battle for two laps, with Oldfield ahead all the way. Then, Johnson's 690 began to show the pace, sputtering, he was forced to pull over to the side and quit with motor trouble. But it was more than "motor trouble" for Barney.

The AAA (American Automobile Association) barred Barney Oldfield from the tracks and racing for

*Born on March 31, 1878, in Galveston, Texas, John Arthur
Johnson quit school after the fifth grade and went to work
in a local gym and discovered the sport that would make
him a legend. Inspired, he began working out and bought
himself a pair of boxing gloves. Photo: Schomburg Center
For Research In Black Culture.*

By the time Jack Johnson was born, Jim Crow laws and such organizations as the Klu Klux Klan were established throughout most of the nation and especially in the Midwest and the South. Churches, schools, and even prisons were segregated. Photo: Library of Congress.

Jack Johnson's flamboyant lifestyle did not make him popular among whites, and caused consternation among many blacks. He hung out in nightclubs, drove fast cars and dated fast women—mostly white women. Photo: Schomburg Center For Research In Black Culture.

Of his four wives, Lucille Cameron, a former Chicago University student, seems to have been the one steady factor. Their marriage lasted fourteen years and it was primarily on Lucille that Jane Alexander's character was based in The Great White Hope. *Photo: Library of Congress.*

Jack Johnson finally caught up with reigning heavyweight Tommy Burns—who'd dodged fighting him for two years—in Sidney, Australia, at Christmas, 1908. Burns had referred to him as "a nigger, a coon and a coward." Johnson vowed to pay him back and he did that in full and more. Photo: Library of Congress.

Johnson beat Tommy Burns so badly the day after Christmas, 1908, that the fight was stopped by the police. Jack London (above), famed author and sports writer fled the arena crying in rage. In an editorial he wrote for the New York Herald he pleaded for Jeffries to come out of retirement. Photo: Library of Congress.

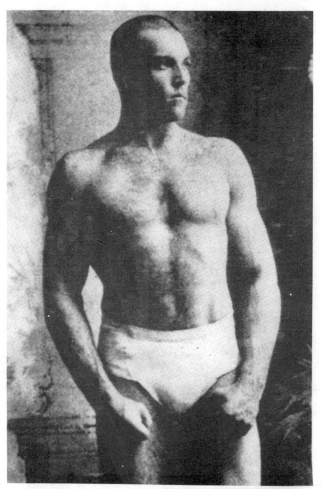

Jack London's choice for "a great white hope" was retired heavyweight champion James J. Jeffries. His fighting size at six foot, two inches, was 220 pounds. However, in retirement he'd gained a hundred pounds by the time of London's call for his return as a "great white hope." Photo: Library of Congress.

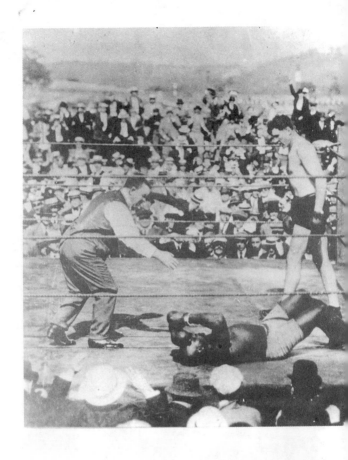

World Champion Jack Johnson fought challenger Jess Willard in Havana, Cuba, on April 5, 1915, in what was billed as another "Battle of the Century." For his match with the last of "the great white hopes," the blazing after-noon sun pushed the thermometer to over the one hundred mark and Willard, "the cowboy from Kansas" wore the

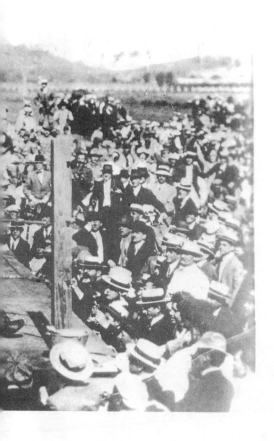

much put upon Johnson (in actuality, he was fighting for a prison pardon), down. By the 26th round what the newspapers called "a tired old Negro" was feeling the effects of the heat and was knocked out. Photo: UPI/Bettmann.

Before his death, Jack Johnson's life followed a multiple of careers, which ranged from boxing exhibtions, to owning a Los Angeles nightclub (The Showboat), and from religious evangelism to the vaudeville stage and extended to a walk-on as an Ethiopian General in the opera Aida. *Photo: UPI/Bettmann.*

He could beat any white man
in the world.
He just couldn't beat all of them.

From the play and performances that won The Pulitzer Prize, The New York Critics Award and The Tony Aw

20th Century-Fox Presents A Lawrence Turman-Martin Ritt Producti

The Great White Hope

Starring James Earl Jones, Jane Alexander.

Produced by Lawrence Turman. Directed by Martin Ritt.
Screenplay by Howard Sackler based on his play.
Produced on the New York Stage by Herman Levin. PANAVISION Color by DE LUXE.

*Howard Sackler's 1960s Broadway play based on the life of
Jack Johnson,* The Great White Hope *starred James Earl
Jones and Jane Alexander. The play created a sensation
and eventually won the Pulitzer Prize, The New York Critics
Award and The Tony Award. Photo: Eddie Brandt's Satur-
day Matinee.*

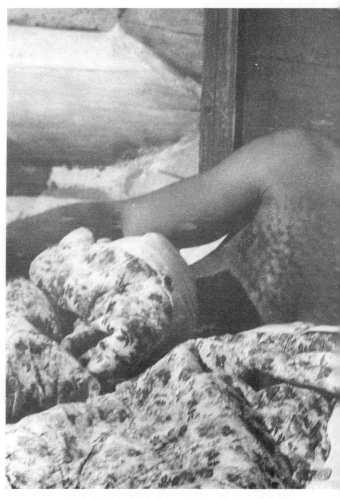

A scene from the 1970 film of The Great White Hope *in which James Earl Jones and Jane Alexander reprised their Broadway roles. The film was acclaimed by critics and, to the surprise of many who thought the husband-wife relationship between Jones and Alexander would offend a segment*

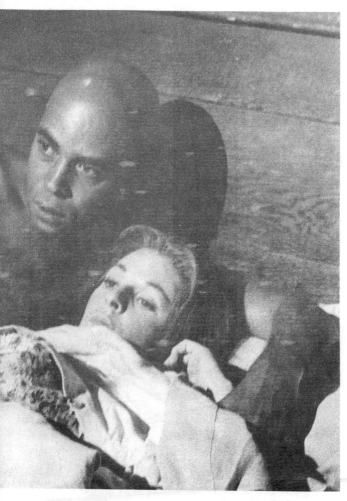

of white filmgoers, was widely popular with audiences. Both Jones and Alexander were nominated by the Academy of Motion Picture Arts and Sciences for Best Actor and Best Actress for their roles in the film: Photo: Eddie Brandt's Saturday Matinee.

Caught in Europe, broke and without many prospects at the onset of World War I, Johnson was pressured by both the French Foreign Service and British Intelligence for "patriotic services." Johnson chose the British over the French and traveled to London with Lucille where they

were given protection by Parliament. He was sent to Russia as a confidential agent to Tsar Nicholas II. This still from The Great White Hope *recreates that time in London. Jones and Alexander are shown standing in the automobile at center. Photo: Eddie Brandt's Saturday Matinee.*

June 11, 1931. Jack Johnson, at the age of fifty-three, was forced to take part in a series of boxing matches in a "barnstorming trip around the United States." Still in good shape, he met Dynamite Johnson in Los Angeles to kick off the tour. Photo: UPI/Bettmann.

two years for competing in an automobile race with a Negro.

Then Johnson decided that he still wasn't going fast enough in his race for the heavyweight crown. He was being detoured by troubles. Women troubles. Aside from the others, Hattie McLay and Belle Schreiber were acting as his "personal secretaries." Both, without pay. Jack began to talk and make plans to go to Europe and catch Burns, to make him fight for the title.

In 1908, Sam Fitzpatrick went to England and made a deal with the British matchmakers. He posted a two thousand five hundred guarantee purse, of which Johnson would only get five hundred pounds, for a bout with Ben Taylor, the "Olrich Terror." The fight was set for July of that year.

Fitzpatrick agreed that Jack Johnson was to fight in Taylor's own backyard, in Plymouth, England. A friend of Taylor's, named Eugene Corri, an Englishman, would be the referee. The rounds would be cut down from the regular three minutes, to two minutes. They were not to use the standard "skin-tight gloves," but were to use six ounce gloves instead. And, further, Jack Johnson would have to win the fight by a knockout, in order to win the bout. It was to go only ten rounds; twenty minutes instead of thirty minutes.

Ben Taylor was built like a mother lode of granite and hadn't ever been knocked off his feet. After going eight rounds, two minutes each, it looked hopeless for Johnson. So, Jack grabbed and clinched him, then jumped back, screaming to the referee:

"He bit me! That bastard bit me on my ear."

Taylor stepped in, protesting his innocence, dropping his guard and Johnson's "Big Berthas" went home. Right! Left! Taylor was down and out.

But, The Black Fire didn't wait for the count. He didn't have to. He was off and running. Down the aisle to a trap-door escape hatch, and through it before the British sports, who had witnessed the fight, started to riot in confusion, protest and fury.

After that fight, Johnson sent forth his challenge to the champion, Jim Jeffries, again. But, the white man answered in his usual manner. "No dinge is any good. All coons look alike to me."

His saying this resulted in a popular song of that time, which was to be played by a band whenever Johnson appeared to fight—including his fight with Jeffries, years later.

"All Coons Look Alike to Me."

The prospects of a Johnson-Burns fight had gained international attention. Many were coming to believe that, "Burns is running away from fighting a black-ass nigger."

Edward VII, ruler of Great Britain, got into the act by making a comment on Johnson's behalf by calling Tommy Burns, the champion, a "Yankee Bluffer . . . in my opinion."

When Johnson heard of the King's statement, he commented.

"I want to thank His Majesty for his sentiments. But he has committed a typical British Blunder. Tommy Burns is no Yankee, he is a Canadian. Nevertheless, His Majesty is a sportsman, specializing in 'rats,' so he oughta' know about Tommy."

The king *was* an expert and keen sportsman. He was one of the world's best judges of rat terriers. They say that nothing pleased him more than to see his dogs turned loose against a barn full of rodents.

He also started a fad which benefitted the taxidermist trade when he had a bear stuffed to serve as a hat rack.

When Johnson had prepared to go to England for the fight with Ben Taylor—and hopefully, also with Burns

—Belle Schreiber pleaded and cried to go along. As did Hattie McLay, who promised further:

"If you get rid of Belle, send her away and marry me, I'll make my father lend us the money for passage and financing the trip."

But, Jack wouldn't marry her, and never did— though it has often been reported that he did. But, he did take her along as his secretary, introducing her as Mrs. Johnson. In return, her father loaned them six hundred dollars and they sailed for London.

Belle was left behind. But, as Jack and Sam planned on their quest for the championship, Hattie planned on her quest for marriage.

Hattie began to drink. In London, they were noticeable. A Paddington, London, landlady evicted them after Hattie threw bottles at Jack's head during the night. The landlady claimed that all of her crockery was broken.

While Hattie was left home, brooding and drinking, Johnson and his manager Fitzpatrick went about seeking to arrange fights—and to eventually get Burns into the ring for a title bout. But, by this time, Tommy had left for the continent.

They were broke when Jack wired back to America to Hattie's father for another five hundred dollar loan. The father sent it, but upon one condition: "That you send my daughter back home."

Johnson wired back, "Good deal."

But it was nine months later that she did go home. She insisted upon remaining with Jack. She was with him when he did finally fight Burns for the title in Australia.

In the meantime, while down on their luck, it was then that Sam Fitzpatrick made arrangements committing Jack Johnson to that "Set-up Suicidal Fight" with Ben Taylor, which was held in Taylor's back yard.

And when he did it, he did it in secrecy in the London Sporting Club, while Jack was standing outside on the front steps of the club.

The incident occurred at Covent Gardens, London, the exclusive National Sporting Club, whose members attended wine suppers in formal evening dress in the dining room, then retired after dinner to the great hall where they would witness a bout or two.

"Privately staged to aid the digestion, with a wager or two in the offering."

Here, the best fighters of the Empire performed before some of England's most prominent VVIP (Veddy, Veddy, Important Men), according to Johnson. Including the Earl of Lonsdale, Sir William Eden (Anthony Eden's father) who had once distressed the members by appearing in a black jumper jacket, a diamond stud, black tie and a white waistcoat.

"Peggy" Bettinson, the National Sporting Club director called Fitzpatrick aside, upon greeting them at the door.

"Have him remain out here on the mat while you come in and we discuss the matter," said the director.

Fitzpatrick moved over to Johnson and said. "Now, you just stand here on this mat while I go in and talk with them. And don't you move one peg, you hear?"

"You know that I won't even move a muscle, Sam," Johnson answered, biting his lip.

"Just be sure you don't now," Fitzpatrick warned further.

Johnson closed his eyes, fighting back the tears. The door closed behind Fitzpatrick and Bettinson.

He stood there for three hours, immobile as a statue, while delivery boys in passing jeered, whistled and spat in his direction.

Finally, Fitzpatrick appeared at the door.

"Come on in, Jack. Everything is all set. They want you to come in so they can see you."

Johnson followed him into the halls, into the big room; the Britishers turned and cheered in his direction.

"Take off your clothes Jack," Fitzpatrick instructed him, while taking a drink offered on a tray by a waiter.

"They want to see what physical shape you're in. And what chances you'll have against their boy, Taylor."

Jack obliged him. Fitzpatrick had not even asked him if he cared to have a drink of water. His clothes dropped to the floor til finally he stood in his underwear before the assembly of Englishmen.

"There he is, gentlemen," the manager boasted as if selling his product from the slave block. "This is my nigger," Sam continued, obviously flushed from the British whiskey he had been consuming over the past three hours. "Look at him! Feel those muscles if you will. Then tell me if you don't think that he can take your man Taylor out in ten."

Johnson closed his eyes that they wouldn't see his resentment as he swallowed down the heavy lump of rage that had risen to his throat, as the British, tinkling the ice in their drinks, sipping from their glasses, walked about feeling his muscles, pinching, probing, stroking parts of his naked anatomy, commenting in admiration on "this most ex'trawd'nary' specimen."

With closed eyelids, Jack listened to the comments and the fantastic arrangements that Sam Fitzpatrick had made, already described earlier, with these British sportsmen. Especially the voices of Lord Hugh Lonsdale, Sir Hiram Maxim and N.S.C. director Bettinson.

"Why, he'll surely demolish Burns, no question. . . ."

"But, you promise that he'll knock out our man Taylor in ten, or your guarantee is forfeited, correct?"

Fitzpatrick assented.

"But, with six ouncers, not the regulation skin tights that this bloke customarily wears."

Jack kept his eyes closed, his face impassive as he heard the humiliating conditions his manager had committed him to.

"Then, should he carry off Sam Taylor and go on to win the title, you will have him return afterwards to fight some suitable opponent under our auspices, correct?"

After half an hour more of such discussion, Johnson was allowed to dress, while Sam and the others went into another room to formalize the agreement.

He was not offered a drink, nor a chair to sit down on. But, he would remember his treatment at the hands of these Britishmen, and that of his white American manager. His indignation against all white men was practically complete. But, he did not tell Fitzpatrick until seven months later, after he had wrested the crown from Tommy Burns.

As he went into training for his forthcoming fight with Sam Taylor, Jack tried to drown his contempt for Fitzpatrick with drink, remembering another manager who had represented him, Frank Corella, who had "slipped him the peter" and bet against him. He began to see little distinction between Fitzpatrick and Corella. He was sullen, drinking and fighting with Hattie concerning her overconsumption of English beer and the inflaming Irish whiskey.

His hatred for the British snobbery could not be concealed. Fitzpatrick had scheduled him for a warm-up bout against an Irishman, Al McNamara, in June about three weeks before his main contest would come off, so that the English bettors could observe him in action.

From the very first bell, The Big Black Fire discarded his usual style and tore across the ring with a murderous attack of raining blows that sent the Irish fighter reeling before he could swing a single blow, sending him down for a count. Three times in three minutes, McNamara went down from the onslaught. The third time he was saved by the bell. As they dragged McNamara back to his corner to revive him, Jack reached down into his waist belt and came up with a tiny American flag, skipping back to his corner gaily singing the words of our unofficial national athem:

"My country, 'tis of thee . . . sweet land of liberty . . . of thee, I sing . . ."

The Britishers rose to a man at the intended insult (the tune being the same as the British national anthem), while Johnson laughed.

The devastation was continued in the second, third and into the fourth round, until McNamara dropped "like a slaughtered pig," unconscious. As he fought Johnson had exchanged insults throughout—with the angry ringsiders, taunting McNamara, warning Sam Taylor who sat there as to what was in store for him. Sam Fitzpatrick cringed and admonished him to no avail. As the referee's count was completed over the unconscious Irishman, Johnson bowed from the waist with courtly formality and threw kisses to all those around, as "bobbies" collected in the ring ready to escort him down the aisle and prevent the angered crowd from performing mayhem upon his person.

But, news of the "Black bloke's performance" against McNamara had paid off. For in the pubs that he frequented the British underworld fringe championed him wherever he went. The crowd flocked to see him pitted against Sam Taylor, that giant of a man who had never been knocked off his feet. The betting was overwhelming when fans learned of the conditions under which the "Black bloke" had been committed by his manager to fight Sam. He must knock him out to win. Two minute rounds. Six ounce gloves. If Taylor remained on his feet at the end, then the nigger would lose.

Again Jack showed his contempt for English sporting conditions, with his own brand of unsportsmanlike conduct, in the eighth round, "employing a dastardly trick, catching Sam unfairly . . . to knock him out. It was the trick of a yellow dog . . ."

Then, as they carried Taylor out and into his dressing room, Johnson sat puffing, fighting a hangover, demanding an "egg beaten up in a bucket of stout and champagne" as a restorative.

Although he was the rage of London's pubs, the "proper" English sports promoters had their enthusiasm soured and were opposed to giving the "tricky blighter a fighting chance to come to even odds with Tommy, because of his unorthodox behavior in the ring and out. Improper, really, in the eyes of any sporting Englishman."

The Canadian title holder smelled money and decided the sum was about right, as well as the time, for his meeting with Johnson. He took up the cry:

"I've been saying that a dinge is no good and yellow. He could never fool me with the yellow trick he pulled on Taylor and get away with it.

"I'll not only fight him, but whip him, as sure as my name is Tommy Burns."

Forgetting that his real name was Noah Brusso.

Fitzpatrick began to prevail upon Johnson to allow him to do the speaking and answer the questions. As he attempted to put "dignified answers into Johnson's mouth."

"Mr. Johnson's answer to Mr. Burns is, 'The question of yellow streaks should be answered in the ring, not out of it.' "

"I am ready to engage Mr. Burns on any terms—and may the best man win."

"It is in the good name of my people that I stand ready to fight with Mr. Burns. And will be the first to acknowledge him if I am defeated."

Still, such obliging statements did not help seal the breach, nor heal the wounds which Johnson's conduct had inflicted upon English and Irish pride.

Then, finally the Angel appeared in the person of Hugh D. McIntosh, former bicycle racer and member of Parliament, founder of the British milkbar industry, the man who had speculated in New Zealand to buy up all of the flags and buntings in New Zealand just prior to a visit there by the U.S. Naval fleet, so that all of the official welcomers were forced to pay his price before they could have suitable decorations and flags . . .

Johnson and Fitzpatrick were impressed with McIntosh and his ideas for the fight, as were Billy Neal, Burns' representative, as he laid out his plans with bombastic English enthusiasm.

The fight would be held in Australia, where lived the most enthusiastic and dedicated fight fans on the face of the glove. He also knew the place, unfolding a map he pointed, where the stadium would be built to accommodate the crowds. He jabbed at the spot:

"Right here, gentlemen. Rushcutter's Bay, on the outskirts of dear old Sydney. We'll bill it: 'The Fight of the Century.' "

The papers were signed. All parties agreeing to fight under the promotion of Hugh D. McIntosh, who went right to work convincing an Australian lumberman to "lend him the lumber" to build it with, with a promise to return it after the fight was over.

"He was a wheeler and a dealer. A 'weak spot' feeler," and McIntosh proved it further in his bargaining with Fitzpatrick, during Johnson's absence, when the manager revealed to Jack that he had signed him for a meager five thousand dollar guarantee and expenses, while Burns had been given a thirty thousand dollar guarantee plus expenses. Then, recalling Fitzpatrick's "dealings" as in the Taylor fight at Plymouth, Jack was sure that his manager had signed him, with an extra bribe for himself on the side.

He left for Australia dejected within, but did not reveal as much to his manager nor his "wife," Hattie McLay.

Arriving in Australia, he went directly to McIntosh and attempted to secure a larger guarantee, "or not fight."

But, McIntosh had taken insurance on the fight, as well as Johnson's life. He reached down into his drawer and pulled a pistol, which he pointed at Johnson, explaining:

"Nigger, you'll fight or die. It's of little consequence to me, except for the enormous amount of trouble I've taken to make this fight. And remember, not a darn thing will happen to me for letting this gun go off, accidentally. If you bring off a good fight, I give you my word, there'll be something else in the kitty for you. I'm laying a heavy bet that you win. You do that and I've got a couple thousand more that I am winning for you. You'll get that, with no split with your manager."

Johnson returned to his training, hopeful that the white man would keep his word, if he won.

"He could give two peck to a jaybird and beat him to a tick," Johnson said of McIntosh later. So, Jack comforted himself with the idea of winning after Fitzpatrick revealed the news that Burns was showing little or nothing in training to cause them to doubt winning.

The two parties and the promoter could not come together in deciding on a referee. All were brought together for the first time to settle it. Burns brought a revolver to the meeting, walked over to Johnson, spinning it around on his finger under his nose.

"Hello, you stinking nigger scum, so we meet, huh?"

Johnson never flinched.

"That's right, you yellow-assed Canuck bastard. I'm finally getting your tail in the ring."

Handlers rushed forward, pulling them apart, relieving the struggling Burns of the revolver and holding him.

Burns shouted:

"Why, you black son of a whore. You wait, I'll kill you in that ring."

"With what, Tommy?" Jack laughed. "I laid one of your bitches back in London one night. She said that you didn't last but for one round. And that was after using your mouth. One round, Tommy, with your mouth."

Burns tore free and snatched an inkwell from the desk, hurling it at the laughing Johnson's head. They were finally able to force Burns into a chair across the room as they discussed, rejecting every possible suitable referee that was mentioned.

Finally, Johnson stood up and spoke, addressing McIntosh.

"Listen Mr. Mac', it's like this. I know that for every point scored for me, I'll have to earn two, because I'm black. I just want to make sure that I get one point anyway. There's only one man that I think I trust enough to give it to me . . . and that man is you, yourself."

It was a rough spot for McIntosh, who made no claim to knowing the finer points of a boxing referee. But, seemingly neither camp had any objections. So, it was decided. The promoter would referee the match. He promised to study and make himself familiar with the Queensberry Rules, from the book.

Johnson was remembering, that McIntosh had promised to bet on him. So, at least he had to give Johnson his due, if he still thought that he would win. He only hoped that the man hadn't changed his mind, since their talk.

CHAPTER EIGHT

THE BATTLE OF THE CENTURY

It was Christmas day, at Rushcutter's Bay on the outskirts of Sydney, Australia. The fight that the whole world had been waiting for finally took place.

The year was 1908. More than thirty thousand white souls, two white women and but a handful of blacks were sitting there in the open air stands as the two fighters came down the aisles to their corners. The rest of the world sat by, waiting for reports to come in by wireless telegraph.

Any and everybody was there who could raise the price of passage to Sydney. In all the little towns, the houses and the cottonfields: Texas, Louisiana, Georgia, Tennessee, Alabama and Mis'sippi, colored folks were praying, weeping and dancing, having visions of Jack Johnson winning.

The race was come awake, after many years of trial; Jack Johnson was the Black Jesus, our deliverer, after so long a wait in hopelessness. The black man was on the march at last, serving notice to the world. We were ready to take on all colors, beat them and win, for the title of the world.

The few black men at the ringside backed Johnson to the hilt, taking all they could get and afford from the white folks who backed Burns to the last shilling, at odds of 7 to 4, for the white boy.

When Jack heard about the odds in his dressing room, he quit smiling and cried:

"Here I am," he said to his manager. "The best chance in the world I'll every have of cleaning up. And I don't have nary single pound to bet on myself. Can't even pay the hotel bill that we owe."

But, then they thought of something else. They thought of it only after the police had begun to gather at the ringside, prepared to stop things if the nigger was getting killed. If they stopped it, then it wouldn't solve anything. It would be declared "no contest." Could the referee give points on a decision, as he saw it then, based on what had gone on before? They asked Burns to decide, since he was champ. He promptly said yes. The referee could decide on points. That is just how sure he felt about winning.

The stuffed Christmas turkeys were left cold on the dinner tables in Sydney that day, while all the men and boys, fathers and sons, went out to the fight, climbing on top of the rooftops, fences and hills to be first hand witnesses to the fracas.

With the sun blazing down at 11:10, in the ring, Jack threw off his fancy robe, giving folks a sight of black splendor that made them take in their breaths.

He was smiling all along.

The first bell rang at 11:15. They spring at each other, tooth and nail. Burns and Johnson.

But The Big Black Fire is blazing, proving that he has come to humble the flesh and soul of a white man.

Even if the white man thought that his name was Burns.

Jack steps back from a flurry of blows and uses his right uppercut, which no man then or now has ever mastered at delivering without telegraphing it ahead of time with his feet. Flat on his two feet, he delivers the right uppercut, ripping into the stomach of Burns, continuing on up to connect with his jaw, landing with bonecrushing force.

The champion of the world is lifted from his feet, and his head hits against the floor as he lands. The punch is "heard around the world," in a flash, serving notice that the age of white supremacy in the fight ring is over.

The people roar. But the roar is cut short, listening to the toll of the referee . . . five . . . six . . . seven . . . eight . . . Burns climbs to his feet again. Johnson moves in, clubs with a right hook, that had once felled a full grown Texas steer into unconsciousness. Burns reels and rolls, as Jack follows with the next punch, then the champion throws a punch of his own, his hardest, which causes Johnson to laugh as he taunts:

"Poor li'l Tommy. Did someone kid you into thinking you were a fighter, huh?"

Burns covers himself into a bundle to protect his head and body as Johnson rains a succession of blows against his biceps. All of them whistling through the air to land and further bruise the muscles of his arms. Red spots appear where each punch lands. The bell rings.

Everyone knows that the round has been cut short.

Johnson dances back to his corner, prancing, high stepping, singing the national anthem.

Johnson dances out in the second round, taunting Burns to come in and fight.

"Show me something, man. This thing is scheduled for twenty rounds. Them people out there are betting on you."

Then, he wings in a right that drops Burns to his butt.

He bounces up like a rubber ball and clinches Johnson, who looks at McIntosh in protest.

"He's holding, ref."

The crowd laughs at the bluff. Then Burns turns to Johnson still holding, screaming.

"Break, nigger! Fight like a white man!"

Johnson laughs and takes measure, rattling a tattoo of punches to the white man's stomach. The champion reels away back, peddling, maneuvering, running backwards around the ring, Johnson in pursuit.

"What you scared of, white man? Where you tryin' to run? Ain't nothing to run from . . . except this damn good whippin' that I'm gonna give you. Stand up and take it . . . ain't you got no guts?"

The champion's backers try to give him encouragement, shouting.

"Go, Tommy boy! The bigger they come, the harder they fall." They chanted in unison. "Bigger they come the harder they fall . . ."

Johnson is laughing when the bell rings.

The brave bettors, the backers of Burns, shout directions and instructions during the one minute rest period.

"Wait him out, Tommy . . . Go to his stomach . . . Make that nigger come to you . . . You're the champ . . . Make him bring it to you, Tommy . . . Make him come to you . . ."

In the third round, Tommy attempts to follow the instructions of his ringside mentors, tucking in his chin, back-peddling, wrapping up his body, the target of Johnson's assault.

Johnson follows taunting:

"Now, don't listen to those folks, Tommy boy. What are you, a back-pedal champion?" In the interim, he slashes and cuts and rains telltale blows to Burn's biceps, already bruised from former punches and being reddened more by fresh ones.

Then Tommy burns in torture, unwraps himself to shoot a straight right to the jaw of Johnson, who retaliates with a vicious left blow to his kidneys, which almost folds him to the floor. The bell rings. This round has been cut into half.

In the fourth round, Johnson comes out with his mocking smile and chatter, rollicking, behind his jibes, with his fists.

"Come on, Tommy boy, and take it," he said lowering his guard. "See, I'm wide open. Come on in and take it, see."

Tommy tears in, Johnson dances away.

"That ain't the way to take it. You got to fight for it, like this."

Johnson rattles a combination of punches off the arms, head and torso of Burns.

"See? That's the way you got to do it, Tommy boy. What's the matter? Yellow? Scared to try it? I thought only niggers were yellow . . . here now, two helpings. Let me show you again."

He moves in and repeats the almost identical combinations as before. Then, moves back, taunting:

"See, it ain't hard, if you ain't yellow. Tommy, you're white. You're as white as the white flag of surrender . . ."

Johnson rattles another series in a flurry across the face and body of the champion, whose eyes are swelling, with blood gushing profusely through his lips as he attempts to answer Johnson, spitting and cursing with his answers.

"Black dog . . . of a black boar . . . of a bastard mother . . ."

Each time, Johnson, still grinning, answers the invectives with a punch.

In the fifth round, Burns rushes out in desperate determination, fighting and flailing wildly, taking the fight to the challenger. Johnson gives, blocking as well as he can, but not before Burns has landed a blow to his face.

He steps back, spitting blood from the split lips.

"See, Tommy—red. Same color as a white man's blood. The same color as a yellow dog's blood. Look at yours . . . compare it."

He throws a right above Burns' eyebrow, then stabs it with his left to open a cut. The blood spurts out.

"See what I mean, Tommy?"

This typical torture goes on into the sixth round. Then the challenger lays on the supreme insult. In the middle of the ring, he drops his arms to his side, Burns lashes at the open stomach. Johnson doesn't budge, but stands there begging:

"Please Tommy, hit me again . . . harder this time, please!"

Then, he takes Burns by the left shoulder, spinning him, and pulls him back into a thunderous right upper-cut, his feet flat, his body bending and releasing as a spring uncoiling behind his right fist. Burns takes the punch, reeling across the ring. Johnson follows patiently and apologizes:

"Sorry, Tommy, old boy."

He delivers a left to Burns' head, whose eye swells to the size of a grapefruit, blue-black and closed entirely.

Burns reels, staggers and holds onto the ropes to keep from falling, as Johnson slugs thunderous punches into the sagging body, the already brush-burned stomach, where the skin is scraped and peeling away.

He holds Burns up, momentarily, and addresses the fans at ringside:

"Didn't y'all say that this boy was good at in-fighting?"

The bell rings and the seconds are forced to come out and literally carry the blinded Burns back to his corner.

Pat O'Keefe, Burns' second, is forced to take a sixpence piece, lance Burns' eye, and then suck the purple blood from the wound, spitting it onto the canvas floor.

Most sports writers agree, "No point would be served in continuing, in describing the fight beyond this point."

Johnson has mastered and even passed beyond, conquering the Heavyweight Champion of the world.

The odds at ringside had changed. No takers! Now it was Johnson to win at two to one. Not even the most loyal Caucasian would bet. Still, the fight went on.

Johnson, venting his fury, taking his toll, exacting his price for the humiliations that he and his people had endured and experienced for years of slavery and slaughter at the hands of the white man. Some of the ringsiders prayed for it to the end.

But, Burns fought back. Grotesquely spitting his anger through shredded lips, sighting dimly through swollen and bloodied eyes, holding up "the honor of his race," retaliating to the taunts of his tormentor and suffering the punishment of doing so.

After the eighth round, Johnson feigned disinterest in his opponent. Toying, taunting, jibing, hitting at will, even joking and playing with the fans at the ringside, which preoccupied him most of the rounds thereafter.

On the far away wall, he had begun to notice a black man sitting on a fence, enjoying the show so much, that he emulated every motion of Johnson, while sitting there. Ducking, feinting, bobbing and weaving, as Johnson did.

Johnson observed him with more interest than he had in Burns. He began to play and entertain the young man. Then, Burns threw a desperate swing, which caused Jack to duck almost to the floor.

When he came up, the black boy was no longer there. Johnson saw that he had fallen from the fence perch. Ducking, like his hero, so that his balance was lost. He had fallen and was getting up from the ground. Johnson broke out in laughter.

Later, he was criticized for his "maniacal laughter at the plight of Burns." He told what really happened. But, in the twelfth round, nobody there was able to account for that cackle of laughter.

The thirteenth round was no variation of the last, except for the slipping and sliding in the blood that spilled from Burns. Then in the fourteenth, Johnson unleashed his right uppercuts at will. Burns fell as a wet flopping, dying fish, floundering as a landed starfish, his body jerking in spastic spasms, in pools of his own soggy blood on the ring floor.

His supporters, no longer concerned with their losses in bets and race pride, called out for compassion for Burns, the tribute which Johnson had intended they should pay for their bloodthirsts, which he had satiated.

He heard their uproar as music, the strained and strange melodies for mercy, for their blood kin. As he stepped up the pace, he heard them cry out:

"No more! No more! Stop it, please. Police. Referee. Stop it. Stop the slaughter!"

The inspector of police was pushed from his seat. He climbed into the ring, gesturing to the promoter-referee, Hugh McIntosh, and motioned his officers into the ring. They responded, swarming under the ropes. The conversation was unheard above the roars, the moans and groans, the screams and the cries. Jack Johnson is now become the king. The Heavyweight Champion of the World.

He had performed as a champion, showing a brutality and fury that the prize ring had never before witnessed, and never to be matched, nor surpassed. He had avenged his people, and ended not only a myth of black inferiority, but that of a black man being yellow, cowardly, unwilling to fight as white men.

He had marked the end of an era. The beginning of a
new one. The Savior, the Prophet, a foreshadowing of
the many who were to follow his patterns. Now, the
black man would cry out, "God save the King. Long
live the King. May his black soul rise and live forever."

CHAPTER NINE

AFTER THE DEMOLITION

Only a few days after the fight, a disastrous earthquake in Sicily killed an estimated 85,000 persons and
devastated the city of Messina—but, to the sports
world, this disaster seemed as nothing compared to Jack
Johnson's demolition of Tommy Burns in Sydney. And,
the worst was yet to come.

To begin with, Jack London, that famed author and
notable white sports writer, left the arena crying in rage.
They say that he hurried off to his typewriter and wrote
his famous report for the *Herald,* which had hired him
to cover the fight:

". . . The Fight! . . . There was no fight! No Arme-
nian Massacre could compare to the hopeless slaughter
that took place in the Sydney Stadium. The fight, if fight
it could be called, was like that between a pygmy and a
colossus. It had all the seeming of a playful Ethiopian at

loggerheads with a small white man . . . of a grown man cuffing a naughty child . . . of a monologue by Johnson, who made noise with his fists, like a lullaby, tucking Burns into a crib of a funeral, with Burns as the 'late deceased,' and Johnson as the undertaker, grave-digger and sexton, all rolled into one . . . So far as the damage was concerned, Burns never landed a blow. He never even fazed the black man . . . He was a glutton for punishment as he bored in all the time. But a dewdrop had more chance in hell than he with the giant Ethiopian. Goliath had defeated David, that much was clear . . ."

Then Jack London went on crying and concluded:

". . . But one thing now remains. *Jim Jeffries must emerge from his alfalfa farm and remove the golden smile from Jack Johnson's face.* JEFF, IT'S UP TO YOU!!"

Now, the matter took on a different complexion, after other white writers had read what Jack London had to say.

They could not help but admit that Johnson had beaten Burns out of his claim to the title. But, according to the way they saw it, Johnson still hadn't earned the championship crown.

They said that by whipping Burns, he hadn't done anything but prove that Jim Jeffries was still The Champ. Since Jeff had retired undefeated. They tried to make out as if the nigger who had won was just a nobody—a non-champion! They argued that Tommy Burns had only been a "keeper-custodian of the heavyweight boxing title," rather than the "real wearer of the crown, he was only a pretender."

Other white writers took the case even further. They started referring to Jim Jeffries as "The undefeated Champion," rather than calling him "Retired Champion," as they had been doing.

By doing this, the white press writers made the matter "a question of race," unwilling "to give a black man his due."

Some went as far as to write, ". . . even if Jack Johnson were white, we wouldn't like him." And these were the *reasonable* writers—those who denied they were prejudiced.

During the meantime, Jack was out having all kinds of lucky streaks. He sat out at the Sydney Race Track and watched Tommy Burns drop every cent of his thirty thousand dollar purse on the horses, while he, himself won fifteen thousand dollars.

Hugh D. McIntosh had been true to his word. He had given Jack three thousand five hundred dollars for the two grand he had bet for Jack on the fight.

Then Jack came home from the track and caught Sam Fitzpatrick in bed with "his wife," Hattie McLay, comforting her. He gave Hattie the eleven hundred dollars that he had borrowed from her father and told her to get to scooting. Naturally, he fired Sam Fitzpatrick.

Sam ran to the newspapers, shouting of Jack's ingratitude. Never mentioning to them what really happened. And Jack with his pride said nothing of the matter of being cuckolded by his manager. One time, years later, he did say that he wondered, "How long the thing between Sam and Hattie had been going on."

But, Jack was champ then. And he performed like a champ, covering his hurt pride, never showing it in the open.

Hattie went home to her folks, unmarried and a drunkard to boot. Her family put her out into the streets in shame. Shortly afterwards, Hattie McLay committed suicide. Of course, the white newspapers blamed Jack for that, never mentioning the part of her family in the matter.

When the papers asked Jack why he got rid of Hattie,

he replied with one of those funny answers he delighted in giving when people asked him personal questions:

"She was a sneak drinker. The bottles she hid underneath the mattress made it all lumpy."

Then Johnson came on back to America. He moved his mother and family up to Chicago and bought a "Nigger mansion" to live in. He picked up again with Belle Schreiber, who had gone on back to work in The Everleigh Club, "the most luxurious whorehouse in the world," of which we'll hear more later.

He also picked himself up *two* new managers, George Little and Sig Hart, who went around trying to find him some fights, while Jack went into vaudeville, appearing on the stage at more than a thousand dollars a week— when he was not out at the race tracks in his spare time. Or chasing white broads.

It was out at the race tracks that he met Etta Duryea, "a high bosomed French-American girl of good family and repute . . . and married." Johnson changed that in 15 minutes. When Etta left her husband to follow him to Pittsburgh, and then married him, the press and clergy threw a fit. Swamped with protests, Congressman James R. Mann of Illinois drew up one of the most durable of all statutes, and then a year later, in 1910, introduced the federal Mann Act into Congress.

When Jack married Etta, "poor li'l Belle Schreiber" was forced to go back to her profession—fuming and planning her vengeance. "Hell hath no fury like a woman scorned." Belle would prove this to The Big Smoke very shortly.

In the meantime Jack was taking on all of "The Great White Hopes" that Sig Hart and George Little could find to oppose him. They came and fell like tenpins in a bowling alley. Everybody who was white and showed he could fight was brought into the act—taking the big chance of cutting the nigger down.

At the same time, Jack repudiated a fight he was scheduled to make with Sam Langford at the National Sporting Club in early 1909. He refused to go through with it on the grounds that the contract had been set up by Sam Fitzpatrick, and since he was no longer his manager, he did not feel he had to honor any commitment made by him. The real reason he refused was that he had defeated Langford before, and now that he was the champion, he could see no reason why he should keep on fighting the same boxers over and over, as he had been forced to do before he won the title.

However, the famed British sense of fairplay was offended at Jack Johnson's "lack of consideration"—though this same famed sense had been nowhere in evidence in the past when the lack of consideration had been aimed at Jack.

Among the various "White Hopes" he fought was Victor McLaglen, who later became a movie actor and won The Academy Award for his role in *The Informer*.

Then came "Philadelphia Jack" O'Brien, whose real name was Joseph Francis Aloysius Hogan, known as a "scientific boxer," fast on his feet, who insisted that the fight be scheduled for "six rounds and no decision." The Champion's managers agreed. They explained that this was in order to get around the Pennsylvania laws "forbidding a fight to a finish."

"Philadelphia Jack" entered the ring with a great deal of fanfare—for he had promised "to put the nigger on the floor." He ended up being beaten unmercifully. Experts called the fight a farce.

After that came another of "The Great White Hopes," a celebrated amateur in the person of Colonel Anthony J. Drexel Biddle, Professor of Mayhem to the United States Marine Corps and author of *The Life of James J. Corbett*.

While Jack was training, Biddle came into the ring

and offered his services as a sparring partner, hoping to pull an upset before the assembled crowd and the others whom he had brought along "to see him put this nigger in his place."

Biddle came into the ring rushing, intent on a quick and fast knockout, surprising Johnson, who held him off.

"Hey, Colonel boy! What's your point. Don't go getting yourself all stirred up."

The Colonel of the Marines stepped back and threw, with all his might, ringing a blow against the ear of Johnson. He attempted to follow through as Johnson stepped back, but was met with the most furious flurry of blows he had ever experienced.

Johnson followed up, until the Colonel was forced into a shell to protect himself from being annihilated, under the vindictiveness he had aroused in the Nigger.

The Colonel was allowed to leave the ring under his own power, but he was visibly shaken after the brief onslaught. A great many observers were dissatisfied with Johnson, feeling that Jack had dishonored the U.S. Marine Corps with his brief display of savagery. Others felt that out of patriotism Johnson should have allowed the Colonel to at least knock him down, for the sake of "Marine Corps prestige and image."

The Caucasian American public was becoming restless and discontented, not only with Johnson's "indifferent savagery and contempt," but with the performances of those who opposed him.

In California it was Al Kaufman, taller, heavier, and with a longer reach than Johnson, who was expected to "put the nigger away." Johnson scorned and taunted him throughout the fight, outmatched him to the point of ridicule, refusing to knock him out, and allowing him to last the full ten rounds by holding him up personally in the last three rounds, refusing to allow Kaufman to

fall down. Then, when the final bell rang, he carried
Kaufman back to his corner and seated him on his
stool, before leaving the ring, grinning toward the fans.

Jack had reached the point where he did nothing
right, as far as the white folks were concerned. If he
carried an opponent, then he was "lazy and insulting."
If he beat him up badly, then he was an "unsporting
savage and brute."

They were racking their brains for a man who could
whip him. The only one they could think of was Jim
Jeffries, who by then weighed more than three hundred
pounds, in retirement.

In desperation, they came up with Stanley Ketchel,
the middle-weight champion, encouraged him to gain
some weight and to challenge Johnson.

Motion pictures of prize fights were getting pretty
popular, so with the hint of vast profits, Ketchel was
encouraged to put on thirty pounds, wear high-heeled
boots and come out "to take on the nigger."

Johnson, while also thinking of "moving picture
profits," assured Ketchel that he would not knock him
out, so that the fight could go the scheduled 20 rounds
for the benefit of the motion pictures.

The fracas took place at Colma, California, October
16, 1909. For eleven rounds Jack carried him, according to the agreement, staying well ahead. But, something happened after the tenth round in the corner.
Johnson's water bottles were switched.

One of Jack's seconds performed the maneuver,
while Jack's nephew Gus Rhodes was looking on.
Johnson weathered the eleventh round with no apparent
effect but of slowing down slightly. The same new water
bottle was fed him in between the eleventh and twelfth
rounds, with more obvious effects, this time.

Ketchel rushed out, swarming all over the Champion,
then with all his force struck Jack below the left ear,

dropping him in his tracks, his legs folding under him like wet pretzels.

Gus was up from his seat, rushing around the ring, screaming from the apron, as the referee tolled the count.

"Dope, Jack, dope . . . your water. Get up . . . you can get up . . ."

Johnson murmured something back, started to rise. The referee while counting also heard Gus Rhodes screaming.

At the count of seven, Johnson rose to his knees. The referee stepped back at eight, a signal for Ketchel to continue. He rushed over to the kneeling but rising black man, only to be met with probably the hardest blow he had ever been struck with in his life.

The blow tore in to shear the front teeth of Ketchel at the gums, knocking him senseless. It was so savage that a priest was called into the ring to give Ketchel the last rites—but it was subsequently found he was not needed.

Johnson revealed later that when he got to his dressing room, one of the teeth was still imbedded in his glove. Such was the price that Ketchel paid for double-crossing Johnson.

Cries went up all around the country, demanding the abolishment of boxing as a sport.

Appeals went to Jeffries as The Ultimate White Hope to come out of retirement, save boxing, and redeem the honor of the white race. Jeffries responded, taking inventory of himself, delving also into the "business aspects" of such a venture. He named himself a manager in the person of a hatter named Sam Berger and dispatched him into conference with Sig Hart and George Little in secret.

Sam Berger stated to Johnson's manager: "This match is such a natural that it's as good as a government license to print our own money."

They made a private agreement to stage the fight at an unspecified, distant date. But, there were considerations. The white man was overweight and worried about ruining his health getting ready for such a fight. First, he consulted with his doctors. Then, he had to be given time to go to the mineral baths at Carlsbad in Austria, now Czechoslavakia, with an entire medical staff accompanying him.

That's where he got the word that he could make it. He even became convinced that he could actually demolish the nigger.

Jack was living all this time with Etta Duryea, introducing her around as "Mrs. Jack Johnson." But he didn't marry her until January 18, 1911.

And even though Belle Schreiber was angry with him, she was at his beck and call, taking time off from the Everleigh Club—the plush mansion, four stories high, over on 2131-33 South Dearborn Avenue, where only the "pure-in-heart white-big-shots" could afford it. It was operated by two sisters who had been school teachers: Minna and Ada Everleigh.

Steak dinners, served in the rooms, cost one hundred dollars a plate. There were more than 44 rooms in reserve, and there were fountains spraying misty-perfume in most of the rooms. Jack himself even said that there was only one other whorehouse in America to compare with it. And that was Mahogany Hall, run by Lulu White, the Negro Madame of New Orleans.

It is said that the piano players in the Everleigh Club played on a gold-plated fifteen thousand dollar piano. The club also contained an art gallery and a turkish ballroom.

Only the white upper-crusts were admitted in the Everleigh Club.

Belle Schreiber was the starlet of the Everleigh Club

staff. But she stayed at Jack Johnson's beck, which didn't make the Everleigh sisters very happy.

Cursing him as she went, loving him as she must have, she went every time that Jack would summon her. And wherever he summoned her from.

But then came December 1, 1909. The big date for getting down to business. The crop of willing promoters had been narrowed to a precious few with the biggest bankrolls standing ready to make their bids in sealed envelopes, in a private dining room at a German Hotel in Hoboken, New Jersey. New York was ruled out for the meeting place, since they had passed a law, because of Johnson, making it illegal to discuss and plan a fight in that territory.

The newspaper reporters had been taken care of with a long table of cold-cuts, hot sandwiches, whiskey, champagne and tubs of potato salad.

There were Tuxedo Ed Graney, Jack Gleason of California, Sunny Jim Coffroth of San Francisco, controller of boxing on the West Coast, who came assuring the principals that there would be no opposition against the fight from Gov. James N. Gillett, nor from San Francisco Mayor Edward H. McCarthy. Then, there was also George Lewis "Tex" Rickard, who came from Alaska to make his bid. He had the backing of Thomas

They argued that Tex was horning in, intruding on the others, but Johnson told them, "Gentlemen, as far Cole, the rich gold-mining Minnesota engineer.

as I'm concerned, money does the talking. Nobody is horning in if he's got the money."

They began to open the sealed bids. Sunny Jim's bid was a purse of fifty-one thousand dollars. Tuxedo Ed bested him with an eighty-one thousand dollar guarantee. Tex Rickard "horned in" with the pledge of one hundred and one thousand and a ten thousand bonus for each of the two fighters signing. This pledge he backed up with draft rights on Thomas Cole's Minneapolis Banks.

That did it. Johnson was so impressed that he insisted that his bonus be paid in one dollar gold pieces. Ten thousand in a bushel-basket.

Jeffries got a little more. He insisted that Rickard pay off a twelve thousand dollar gambling debt that he owed.

The contracts were signed: 60 percent to the winner and 40 percent to the loser. The fight was scheduled to be held on Independence Day, 1910, in San Francisco, California. To be billed "The Biggest Battle of the Century," since the one with Burns had already been billed as *"The* Battle." Anyway, most folks who had been praying and looking for "The Great White Hope," considered that this should be billed as The Greatest. Because "the hope of the white race was now dependent on the sturdy shoulders of Jim Jeffries, the undefeated Champion of all Champions."

Again, it was decided that the man to referee the fight would be the promoter. Others were offered the opportunity. Men with repute for "fair play," among them: Historian and science-fiction writer H. G. Wells, and the creator of Sherlock Holmes, Sir Arthur Conan Doyle. Finally, it was narrowed down to Tex Rickard. The man who was willing to risk his fortune to stage it, could surely risk his life to referee it.

CHAPTER TEN

NOW, AS FATE WOULD HAVE IT

Now, as fate would have it, while everybody else in the world was waiting for the Fourth of July to come, anticipating "The Biggest Battle of the Century," Jack Johnson organized himself a show troupe and set out on a tour of the European Music Halls. Etta Duryea went along as his secretary, "Mrs. Johnson," and also as a participating member of the show, as part of his act.

Jack had found out that Etta could perform on the stage as well as some of the professionals. Jack himself could dance, strut the cake-walk, which Europe was practicing and wishing to learn. They spent Christmas in London.

Together they visited the art galleries and purchased some tapestries and paintings and sculptures. Jack brushed up on his reading, took private lessons on the bass violin, mastered speaking French, Spanish and Italian, and read "most of the classics" in English.

He even made arrangements to play Shakespeare's *Othello* at the Globe Theatre. Only, Jack was re-writing parts of it before playing it.

"Shakespeare wrote it as a tragedy," Jack explained. "I disagree. And after certain modifications, by me, it won't be."

Jack and Etta came back to New York in February, traveling from there to Chicago to visit with his mother, when Jack received the news from a friend that Clara Kerr, his first wife, had been charged with murder.

Seems like dear "Sadie" had met her match. For this was the woman who had nearly ruined Johnson, robbing him, running away with his friend and almost sending him out of his mind, causing him to become a drunken straggler for a time. Clara "Sadie" Kerr had married another man, who turned out to be a chronic alcoholic.

As fate would have it, during one of his "fits," he grabbed Sadie and began to choke her to death, until she broke away, got a gun and blew his brains out. The DA was working to establish premeditation and get himself a first degree murder conviction. And Sadie didn't have a cent to her name to hire a lawyer.

Despite Sadie's treatment of Jack and the fact that she had nearly ruined his life, Jack could not allow her to be convicted unjustly. He took Etta and went down to the prison to visit Sadie, hired her good lawyers, got her free, and then he built her a restaurant and gave her enough money to put her back on her two feet again. This generous and forgiving side of Jack Johnson's nature invariably seems to be omitted from his biographies.

But, he stayed in the headlines. It was while he was in Chicago that the incident of his speeding and the cop stopping him occurred. But, that wasn't the end of that little story. Because that cracker cop waited to see if Jack was coming, speeding back the same damn way like he promised. He did. Faithful to his word.

They took him to jail this time, after his return trip. The crowds had gathered around to see what would happen. Jack told the cracker cop this time:

"Stand back there, white boy, so these people can see me. That's why they're gathered around here."

When the judge heard about the incident, he tripled

the fine. And Jack, with an "I don't give a damn" attitude, paid it without flinching.

In May of 1910, Jack set up camp right outside of San Francisco, taking Etta with him. Belle Schreiber left the Everleigh Club to go, also, taking a couple of the other girls along to keep Jack comfortable while in training.

He even hired himself an "official taster," named Frank Sutton, to test his food and drink before he consumed them. He had begun to take notice of the prophecies and predictions of the fortune teller. Many of her predictions were coming true. He had been Mickey Finned in the Ketchel fight. This time he took no chances. One night, Sutton fell to the floor after testing a drink intended for Jack. He stayed sick for weeks.

Jeffries was making statements from his own training camp. "That nigger's no champ! I own the title. And there ain't no dinge to take it from me. God forbid."

Still, all and the same, there was a merry good time being had by all in the Johnson camp, which wasn't just sports page material. It was front page material.

The California governor, James N. Gillett, was a "Reform Governor," who was attempting to make good his platform promises to clean up California. Especially San Francisco and its "Barbary Coast."

The newspaper reporters were beginning to ask why he was making an exception of Jack Johnson, brawling and balling with all of those white women at his training camp.

The governor decided to attend to this matter himself, personally. He had been fairly successful in sending chills up the spines of the faro dealers, the handbook operators as well as the madams of the whorehouses, along with the pimps, pickpockets, panderers and the street-walkers as well. Why not the nigger?

The governor was a politician. And certainly, "his

personal attention," with the press in evidence, would enhance his voter appeal.

So, one bright morning in May, the governor climbed into his official car, followed by a flock of reporters, and set out for the suburbs of San Francisco and Johnson's training camp.

"Goody-goose" Gillett was also a teetotaler, and election was drawing near. But, he was wise enough to see to it that his caravan of reporters and photographers were supplied with a substantial amount of whiskey and sandwiches for the trip. Soggy sandwiches and the cheapest of whiskey. They arrived at the camp, a resort known as "The Seal Rock House." They followed him on in.

He asked for Johnson and was led into the room where Jack lay on a table, being rubbed down by his handlers, while those pretty white women stood by looking on.

"Goody-goose" gave them the once over and sneered before speaking to Johnson.

"I want to talk to you," the governor said. "But I'll address you only after you've dismissed these. . . ." His words trailed off as he indicated the ladies with a gesture of his hand.

Johnson raised up slightly and narrowed his eyes.

"Now, come on, governor. These ladies are most welcome here. Just as you are, governor."

With that, The Black Fire snaked out his arm and caught the chief executive of California around the neck, pulling him in close and grinned, while hugging him like they were the best of friends.

"Take this picture, boys. Ain't this nice. Me an' th' governor here is lovers like God and Gabriel."

The photographers went to work while the imprisoned Gillett was unable to move. Then, released, he sputtered and moved out amidst the laughter of the bystanders.

The pictures were printed in the papers. "Goody-goose" Gillett—a race mixer!

But his indignation was to be contended with. "Tex" Rickard had just about completed the building of the lumber stadium. He was forced to dismantle it and search for another place to stage the fight, when the chief lawmaker issued an edict. "The fight will not be held in California, under penalty of imprisonment for all concerned." Ed McCarthy, the Mayor of San Francisco, protested, seeking to override the governor, stating:

"The fight will be held. To hell with "Goody" Gillett. I run this town."

But Gillett had a stronger threat. If the fight is held, then San Francisco will lose The Pan-Pacific Exposition, which was scheduled to be held in 1915, five years away. And "Goody" had the backing of William H. Wheeler, president of the San Francisco Board of Trade, who had a telegram from Congressman William "Bill" Bennett of New York, Chairman of the House Committee on Foreign Affairs, which stated that "the prospective fight stands in the way of securing the Exposition."

Jim Jeffries couldn't believe his ears. He was not only a white man but considered himself a personal friend of the governor up until his announcement.

He protested to the Attorney General, who issued a statement:

"Tell Rickard to get himself, that nigger, his fight and even Jim Jeffries out of my state. What he is planning is a prize fight and that's against California law."

On June 15th every newspaper in the country carried the word. "Gillett Vetoes Big Fight."

The "Big Fight" was ready with no place to hold it.

Comments came in from all over the world. Johnson said:

"I don't give a damn where the hell it takes place."

Others said:

". . . just a matter of California politics . . ."

Jeffries said:

"I don't believe it. Gillett just doesn't seem to be that sort of man."

Lord Lonsdale in England stated:

"This is a high-handed action and most unsportsmanlike. . . ."

Congressman Bennet who also happened to be a Lay Candidate to the General Assembly of the Presbyterian Church stated:

"Ministers and laymen of our church . . . voted to commend the action of the Governor . . . further to admonish that all citizens and legislators consider the evil of prize fighting and stamp it out altogether."

The New York Times concluded an editorial with:

"Governor Gillett has assumed national stature. He deserves the heartiest praise of all good citizens."

Still *The New York Times* had been wrong in its estimation of Gillett. He was unable to explain the pictures of him "hobnobbing in the sinful sanctuaries of Johnson's training quarters." He could hardly offer in his defense that he was being held a prisoner in the arms of the smiling black champion. And who, seeing the picture, could believe that he was not a hypocritical race-mixer—"giving his private blessings to the Negro . . . and getting caught?"

Within a few weeks he was defeated at election. Sitting brooding in his quarters, he was asked by a reporter for a statement.

"What shall I tell them, sir?"

"Tell them," he choked and blurted, "that . . . that if that perfidious black ape ever returns to these parts,

I'll have him strung up and castrated . . . with a dull file."

Meanwhile Rickard was conferring with Denver S. Dickerson, Governor of Nevada, total population slightly over 40 thousand citizens, the only state in the Union where prize fighting, along with anything else, was not illegal. Rickard asked to hold the fight in Reno.

The Governor of Nevada gave Rickard his blessings, after Tex had convinced him that the fight was on the up and up. Dickerson even had no objections to Johnson's white women entourage. He visited Johnson's camp at the Willows Roadhouse, four miles outside Reno, displaying his courtly manners as he was introduced to Belle Schreiber, Etta Duryea and the other "Mrs. Johnsons" from time to time.

Governor Dickerson showed an unusually keen interest in and admiration for The Big Smoke and he displayed it in one particular incident while visiting the camp one day.

Among those in his camp, whom Johnson had hired as sparring partners, was Al Kaufmann, whom he had beaten in San Francisco the year before. Then, there was Stanley Ketchel, whose teeth he had sheared off, for attempting that double-cross a month later. One of his sparring partners, named George "Kid" Cotton, got cute and committed the cardinal sin of showing off, moving in to hit Jack in the mouth and "draw a bit of claret." All this while the governor was watching.

Jack moved in so fast that the governor didn't see what happened and Cotton never remembered. When The Big Smoke backed away, they came in and carried the unconscious "Kid" Cotton from the ring. Even when Sig Hart threw a bucket of water over his head, he didn't come around. In fact, he didn't gain consciousness until five hours later.

The governor asked what had happened.

"Johnson put him out," a reporter answered.

"Put him out where?"

"Come on, governor, quit kidding. You know what I mean," said the reporter. "He knocked him out."

"Oh, I see," Dickerson said. Then another reporter asked.

"Governor, didn't you ever see a fight before?"

"Oh, sure, a lot of them. But not like this. The others that I saw were with guns or knives where men were killed. In this little affair, no one seems to suffer much hurt."

No sooner had the governor finished, when the raging Stanley Ketchel came running up, shouting at Johnson.

"He's still out. You big black sonavabitch! If I was a little bigger I'd kill you. I'd beat you to death, nigger."

Jack kept his cool, impassive as Ketchel kept shouting. Then he turned to one of the Nevada state marshals who had come along from Reno.

"I want you to arrest this man," Johnson said to the marshal, who looked to the governor, then questioned Johnson.

"On what charge." he inquired.

"Having sexual intercourse with a prostitute," said Jack, "at high noon, on the main street of Reno, while she was standing on her head. . . ."

Governor Dickerson went into stitches with laughter. Nodding his head, indicating that Ketchel be arrested as Johnson had charged. They carried a raging, kicking Ketchel off to jail.

When his visit was concluded, Dickerson said to the reporters.

"I have never seen a man who can whip Jack Johnson as he stands today, and I am forced now to bet on him. I have also been to see Mr. Jeffries in training a few times."

But the betting odds showed that many, many disagreed with the Governor of Nevada. Still, those odds reflected more the stubborn hope on part of prejudiced white folks, than it did their soundness of judgment. Many of them seemed to think that pouring a flood of money in to back Jeffries was sure to turn the tides in his favor.

All eyes and ears of the world were tuned in on Reno, Nevada. It has been said that more than a million words a day were being written and sent out into the world from that little desert city.

William Muldoon, "The Old Roman," they called him, from New York sent word, "The nigger can't last. I pick Jeffries."

Rex Beach—the literary expert, who didn't even go over to watch Johnson work out, while staying with Jeff at his camp—wrote for his newspaper syndicate:

"I pick Jeffries, because after watching the caveman's work for a month, I can't picture that huge bulk lying on the floor . . . on the other hand I can picture Johnson dazed and bewildered. The difference is both breeding and education. Jeffries realizes his responsibility all the time. . . ."

Equal to Beach, if not surpassing him, was Jack London, who rarely concealed his contempt for Johnson, and who had been first to plead with Jeff to come out, ". . . and wipe that golden smile from that nigger's face. . . ."

John L. Sullivan arrived in Reno. Covering the fight for *The New York Times,* but remembering the destruction that Johnson had performed upon his two protégés, he could only declare:

"This fight looks like a frame-up."

He never did say in whose favor.

Orders for tickets were flooding in from all over the world, from Calcutta to Cuba, from China to Brazil.

From the Arctic to the Antarctic and places located any and everywhere in between.

In the meantime, while everybody else was looking forward to the forthcoming fight, The Big Black Fire was enduring some personal troubles that the golden smile on his black face never revealed.

He was coming to grips with treachery and deceit that would have sapped the strength of Sampson, tried the patience of Job, and which called for the faith of Elijah, the will of David, and the wisdom of Solomon, all in one.

Although he never told the real story till later in life, except to his mother and few close friends, Jack used to get tears in his eyes every time that he told it, recalling the things that had happened to him during this time, which came close to driving him out of his own mind.

The only thing that held him together, he declared later, was his recollection of what the fortune teller had told him, years before.

"She had told me that I was to be champion," he recalled, "and she had warned me of many other things that were then beginning to occur around me. She had said, 'Many women, especially white ones, will pass through your life-span. But three of them will play an important part; two of them will end up killing themselves, while one of them will come close to killing you. If you don't watch yourself, she will succeed. She will be weak enough and at the same time strong enough to sap your strength and your sanity.'"

Jack had told his friends many times, "I've never been a superstitious man. From the time that I was come of age, I never believed in anything, man or God. I believed in nobody but myself.

"But then things begin to come clearer as to the power of God, the one my mother had taught me to pray to, just before my fight with Jeffries. And my biggest fight before that time and even afterwards was coming to grips with me and my beliefs. For around that time, things that the woman fortune teller had testified to happen, came happening, just as she had told me they would.

"I began to take note, and it appeared certain to me that there were other powers working with me as well as against me. Which power was God or the will of God, I couldn't say. But I learned by watching and waiting, listening in silence, with all the noise around me; there was something. And that something was God. . . ."

When Jack learned of Hattie McLay's death by suicide, he remembered more of what the prophetess had predicted. To him, it was more than coincidence when, in San Francisco, Etta Duryea began to show signs of having a nervous breakdown. And if ever a man loved a woman, Jack Johnson loved Etta Duryea. And he knew that she loved him, just as much. In fact, "too much," some folks claimed.

She once shouted at a bunch of newspaper reporters: "I wish that I could meet just one white man on earth as considerate of a woman as Mr. Johnson is of me!"

George Little, one of Johnson's managers, became enamoured with her beauty, which increased his secret envy and hatred for the black man whose earnings paid his salary.

The real situation was not too unlike the main plot of Shakespeare's *Othello*, except that Jack Johnson was no gullible and trusting blackamoor to George Little's *Iago*.

So, George Little had first begun by slyly suggesting to Etta, "Stop kidding yourself. That evil black ape isn't going to marry you. Why do you want to marry him? He's not your class. You come of good stock."

Many of the biased newsmen, when Jack was not within earshot, joined the co-manager in his campaign against Johnson, dropping a phrase here and there, and trying to shake Etta's faith in her man. Then, too, Etta had been sitting, watching George Little, when the water-bottle had been switched during the Johnson-Ketchel fight. It was she who had told her suspicions to Gus Rhodes, Jack's cousin, that night.

The taunts and pressures began to take their toll on Etta Duryea. She developed crying fits, periods of melancholy. Her father had recently died, so that was her explanation, at first.

George Little, beginning to feel ashamed for his cruelties, reversed himself and attempted to be kinder and to comfort her, and he grew to despise Johnson all the more.

He offered to marry Etta as soon as the fight was over. He presented her with a two thousand five hundred dollar ring as a token of his good intentions, which she kept hidden.

Then, too, the California sun had also taken its toll on Etta's sensitive skin. She had blistered and developed a rash from overexposure, which forced her to remain indoors for a period.

Then, George Little pulled his most vicious of all tricks to loosen the hold that the black man held on the delicate strings of Etta Duryea's heart. He explained that her rash was not the result of overexposure to sunrays.

"Everybody in the world knows you can't get too much sun; it's healthy. You've simply picked up a blood disease from that nigger. 'Raging black-pox,' it's called. Few doctors know anything about it. They know its some form of syphilis though."

Jack came into his quarters to find Etta broken down completely, hysterical, threatening suicide. Screaming and irrational.

He lay her down to calm and pacify her, telling her

how much he loved her, promising that they would get married as soon as the fight with Jeffries was over.

It was then that she confided her fears to him. The things that George Little had told her—as well as his confessing his love and intentions, and his desire to marry her. She produced the expensive diamond ring which the white man had given her, and presented it to Jack as proof.

The following day, Jack placed all of his affairs into the hands of Sig Hart, and with no explanation fired Little on the spot, wearing the three-karat diamond ring slipped onto the tip of his index finger where George Little could see it. Etta stood alongside, watching.

When Jack let it be known that Little was no longer associated with him, the Chicago-Inter-Ocean reporter, John I. Day, wrote:

"Few people will be found to exonerate Johnson for the sin of ingratitude."

It was understandable that John I. Day should have written this, for he was one of the newsmen who never lost opportunity to secretly taunt Etta concerning her "disgraceful conduct" in loving "that savage black ape."

It was only Day's position with the powerful newspaper, which kept Johnson from kicking him from the camp, also.

Still, it did not all end with firing of Little, who shouted to the press and John I. Day to be quoted:

"I'm no Fitzpatrick. He can't do this to me and get away with it."

But, for time being, Jack did get away with it. They encamped for Reno and the fight preparations. He assumed that the air would be cleaner there and Etta's fits of depression would clear up. But he was wrong.

The gossip and the rumors flew thick and fast as to,

"How that black nigger is undoing that beautiful young white wife of his."

Jack trained hard during the day. Then at nights he would take Etta for long drives in the desert air before retiring. He arranged for parties, inviting entertaining guests, playing his bass viol, singing, dancing, laughing and joking, hoping to bring Etta out of it and brighten up her spirits. Still, all to no avail.

Rather, the woman drew back further, deeper into her shell from the fear of facing people when she was with Jack. She began to shy away from everybody. Sometimes breaking out into long crying jags, explaining to folks that it was because of the loss of her father, who had recently died.

Much of this began go unnerve Jack. Reports went out that he wasn't paying attention to his training. Which was partially true, for no matter how Jack tried to conceal it, his temper showed up with the sparring partners, because of his lack of success at consoling Etta.

Jack's manager, Sig Hart, his handler, Al Kaufmann, and his cousin, Gus Rhodes, really began to worry when Etta showed no signs of straightening herself out.

Finally, one day she up and told Jack that she was leaving.

"I can't take it anymore. I'm not doing you any good. And worse for myself. I guess it's like George and the others said: 'A normal white woman can't afford to be in love with a black man.' "

In spite of Jack's entreaties, she deserted him and left.

The reporters in camp pledged to keep quiet, but word got to floating around to the effect that "Mrs. Johnson has split the camp and left for San Francisco, under doctor's orders."

Some recalled that Johnson had gone to pot once before because of a woman. The truth was ascertained and for a few days gave comfort to those in Jeffries' camp. But not for long. The Black Fire came roaring back, sending a wire to Belle Schreiber to join him, telling her to bring a couple of other girls along, to brighten things up, to put some cheer back into his training camp.

Belle responded as usual and arrived in a few days. But, when news of Belle's presence in camp reached the ears of Etta Duryea, she called short her rest and hurried back to Reno and Johnson, over the protests and heartbreak of George Little. He was now out his ring and the girl, "both back in the hands of that nigger."

Little complained to the press. He stated that he had loaned the ring to Jack, who now refused to return it to its rightful owner.

Sig Hart and Gus Rhodes got together with the two women, stressing the importance of Johnson's physical and mental condition for the fight, and they exacted promises from them to behave and go easy as he trained. To a great extent, they complied. Confusing visitors in the meantime, for both had been introduced from time to time as "Mrs. Johnson." But mostly they remained as much as possible in the background, behaving with utmost discretion, as The Black Fire, happily trained to his peak, prepared for the fight to come.

CHAPTER ELEVEN

RENO: HUB CITY OF THE UNIVERSE!

That's what they had started calling it by the middle of June. Reno: Hub City of the Universe.

Everybody who could raise the fare was going that way, to be there on July 4th. Signs began appearing on cars, trains and wagons along the road: "MAKE RENO OR BUST."

Then, like The Galveston Flood and the San Francisco Earthquake which had crossed the trail of Jack Johnson, another phenomenon occurred. Halley's Comet appeared over the Nevada desert skies, looming like a signal from God. It shook Jim Jeffries up so that when they woke him up to look at it he shouted:

"Gawd dammit, let me alone. Who cares about comets. I want my sleep. . . ."

The folks around him had begun to notice that Jeff was feeling the pressure and it was beginning to tell. They had placed the entire hope of the white race upon his big, broad shoulders. He had begun to wonder if he had the strength to carry it.

The Chicago Inter-Ocean had written:

"Under his skin of bronze, the muscles rippled like the placid surface of water touched by a gentle breeze."

John L. Sullivan had taken notice, when Gentlemen Jim Corbett had brought him out to visit Jeff's training camp. He asked Sullivan for his advice as to how to fight Johnson. Sullivan answered:

"Jim, all I know is that God Almighty hates a quitter."

Right afterwards, Sullivan began to show his doubts and ventured that "the nigger could, and just might win." He changed his tune and talked of a frame-up, which he had declared a bit earlier. When he visited Johnson's camp, he was told by The Big Black Fire:

"Cap'n John, I'm gonna win. I'm as happy as a kid on Christmas morning."

Sullivan then reported to the readers of *The Times,* the betting should be at least "even money."

The chief book for the fight named Tom Corbett claimed that:

"More than three million dollars will change hands on the outcome of this fight."

Hugh D. McIntosh sailed in from Sydney, Australia, carrying the entire bankroll that he had cleared from the Johnson-Burns fight. Johnson told him:

"Colonel Mac, my advice is to bet the entire thing on me. I can't lose in no way."

Still, Jack went on playing cagey, confirming rumors that he was not even taking the fight seriously. Dancing, playing, singing and entertaining ladies—Eastern ladies who came to visit him, society ladies who came to Reno, if not for the fight, to get divorces from their husbands. Bob Vernon and Harry Lehr, the latter who was social consultant to Mrs. Stuyvesant Fish of The New York 400, would bring them out to his camp in caravans of cars, loaded with Japanese butlers, hampers of champagne and other "goodies."

Man, they say everybody was coming in or had already come into Reno, by the final week before the fight:

Cincinnati Slim, the bank robber; "The Sundance Kid" from Latin America; Won Let, the Chinese hatchet man from the Hip Sing Tong, along with twenty or thirty other hatchet men who had come with him. All of them rubbing shoulders with the likes of Payne Whitney of Wall Street, who had come with four pullman cars to take care of his party. And Tom Shelvin the old Yale halfback. Also H. G. Wells and Sir Arthur Conan Doyle.

Negro "leaders" Booker T. Washington and Rev. C. Reverdy Ransom issued their statements denouncing the fight, an attitude followed by a majority of other minor colored leaders who had found a way to get into print, in white newspapers, by following suit.

Special trains pulled into the sidings from Boston, New York, Philadelphia, Chicago, St. Louis, Kansas City, New Orleans, Omaha, Salt Lake City, Dallas, Houston, Denver, San Francisco, Seattle.

The tops of pool and dice tables were rented as places to sleep, when not in use. But, nobody was sleeping.

Although more than two million postcards had been printed and mailed out, protesting the fight, nearly everybody but the mailers were ignoring them.

Johnson made one final joke, before going to sleep the night before the fight.

"No stolen chicken ever passes the portals of my face . . . chickens and corn fritters are affinities. They are not meant for each other and both are meant for me."

CHAPTER TWELVE

THE DAY OF RECKONING COME

On the Fourth of July, 1910, the Day of Reckoning had come. Jack rose from his sack, ate four lamb cutlets, a half-dozen scrambled eggs, three slices of rare steak and washed it all down with scalding black coffee.

Ol' Jeff ate like a white man, taking a few pieces of fruit, a little toast and tea and made his famous last statement:

"That portion of the white race that has been looking to me to defend its athletic superiority may feel assured that I am fit to do my very best. If Johnson defeats me, I will shake his hand and declare him the greatest fighter the sporting world has ever known."

Then, Jack made his:

"If Mr. Jeffries knocks me out or gains a decision over me, I will go into his corner and congratulate him as soon as I am able. My congratulations will not be fake. I mean it."

Robert S. Abbott, Negro editor-publisher of *The Chicago Defender* wrote:

"If Johnson is forced to fight Jim Crow Delegations, race prejudice and insane public sentiment—and if he wins in the face of all of this—he is truly entitled not only to the Championship title, but should be awarded a Carnegie Hero Medal. . . . When the smoke of battle clears away, and when the din of mingled cheers and groans have died away in the atmosphere, there will be deep mourning throughout the domains of Uncle Sam, over Jeffries' inability to return the pugilistic sceptre to the Caucasian race."

Newspaper headlines cried across the country:

"IF JOHNSON WINS, HE DIES TONIGHT!" The organized Vigilantes and Knights of the Ku Klux Klan, The White Circle Riders in almost every state of the union had promised this.

William Jennings Bryan, later Secretary of State, had wired his good wishes:

"God will forgive anything that Jeffries does to that nigger in this fight . . . Jeff, God is with you."

The odds for Jeff had become 10 to 6 to win and there was some wild talk of one thousand to one.

Johnson reacted in typical fashion of confidence. He had wired money to rent a Chicago theatre where his mother could take the family and friends to listen for the results, also advising his brother Claude and the others: "Bet your last red copper-cent on me!"

There were six hundred newspaper men who came in on free tickets, and a few politicians among the sixteen thousand who sat there. A special box with curtains was arranged for the ladies in attendance.

Tex had hired more than 50 U.S. marshals and Nevada deputy sheriffs, who checked and confiscated all weapons at the gate, to be given back later. Since Tex was to referee the fight, he didn't want anyone witnessing it from behind the barrel of a gun. The pistols, guns, knives, hatchets, etc. were to be given back to their owners after the fighters and the referee were out of range.

They had even taken further precautions, keeping a railroad car with a smoking engine ready to hurry Johnson away after the fight in case of trouble.

In the Chicago Coliseum a crowd of thousands was gathered to watch "electrical figures," illuminated on a nine feet high electrical board, to show every move, blow by blow. The results would be flashed by telegraph after each round, and the reports would be announced to Jack Johnson's mother, his family and waiting friends, from the stage by Bob Motts, manager of the Peking Theatre.

It was as hot as open hell, the sun blazing away, as The Big Black Fire and The Great White Hope came down the aisles, at 11:30 that day. The band struck up a number as Johnson came down to enter the ring:

All Coons Look Alike.

The crowd took up a rejoinder: "Let's hope Jeff kills the coon."

This intensified as Jeffries entered the ring. "Kill th' coon, Jeff. All coons look alike, Jeff. Kill the yellow-bellied black coon."

Jack kept his back turned to Jeffries' corner, still smiling but it was no pleading smile in any manner. Still, if looks could have killed, the look that Jim Jeffries was shooting at Johnson's back could have made him disintegrate into thin air.

"He's scared, Jeff, can't look at you," the crowd at ringside shouted. "Turn around, nigger, and look. Look the white man in the eye. Face him, nigger. Face him. Looking away ain't gonna help you no more, coon!!"

Jeff snatched off his robe with a jerk, not dropping his vicious stare at Johnson. He threw out his chest like Tarzan of the Apes, jabbing his great big arms above his head to show readiness. Only, he didn't beat on his chest or give a Tarzan the Ape Man yell.

Gentlemen Jim Corbett, acting as a second for Jeffries, was watching as the Black Fire took his robe off. Only then he realized that they had been misinformed. That flat-muscled stomach on the black man had not come from leaning over bars and eating watermelons, as he had been hearing. That big ball, which Jack had invented, called "a medicine ball," had now been established as a training instrument for prize-fighters and standard equipment from that time on.

Jack had tricked them again. A few days before the fight he had become a "segregationist," not allowing any white men to come into his camp. They were forced to sleep outside in their flivvers, under cover of the chilly desert night.

Even Jack London had cried out with indignation. "That black bastard won't let us in. He told his boys to sic dogs on us if we tried to get in. And he's got a whole carload of chippy-bitches and boozers in there with him."

"Oh, God," London had screamed, leading the others in a prayer. "Let Jeff come out in the first round and kill that black, lowdown bastard with one punch, please."

And the newspapers had promised: "If the black man wins, it will be the last act of his life."

Now, observing his physical appearance, they were filled with reservations as to whether Jeff could bring it off. And perhaps, they might have to perform the murder of the nigger themselves.

Then Jack crossed the ring, taking Jeffries by the elbows and turning him from the sunny corner to the shady one he had been assigned in the ring.

"Take my seat, Mr. Jeff," Jack said gaily. "You sure can't afford to have no sun in your eyes today."

The ringsiders screamed out, pouring out venom at the cock-sure attitude of this nigger. Then, Jack grinned and went back, stroking the American flag, which he was wearing as a waistband, to hold up his purple, skin-fitting tights, slightly stroking in the direction of his genitals, calling attention to their "legendary size."

The formal introductions of celebrities were made,

and then the handlers were signaled to leave the ring. Corbett took himself a place, leaning on the apron, staring his straight, mean look unwavering at Johnson. He figured:

"The ten thousand that I bet on Jeff will be as safe as a baby's blue socks, after I've broken that nigger's concentration."

The time had come. The first bell was rung. Johnson shuffled out and sent himself a lazy, left lead to Jeffries' face.

Then he slid in and out, moving around and about, feeling and testing the white man, just casual like. Then, like lightning, stepping in, he hooked Jeff to the chin, laughing and calling over to Corbett, leaning on the apron.

"It's the law of jaws, Jim. Sooner or later, they all go down when they hear it."

He pushed Jeff away, still addressing Corbett, paraphrasing Fitzgerald's *Omar Khayyam*:

"The first act of the deed is what the last act of reckoning shall read, Jim."

Then he cuffed Jeff severely, rattling a tattoo of punches which brought the crowd to their feet, drowning out the cursing answer that Corbett was shouting back.

The pattern was set for the next fourteen rounds. Johnson the Executioner, toying, laughing, punishing, delivering with a steady exchange of playful patter, cutting the huge victim down to size as he went. And Jeffries the Defender, while helpless, still an example of Caucasian courage and self-sacrifice, virtually committing suicide that a myth might be maintained.

Round two was but an intensified version of round one. Johnson came forth pumping a barrage of powerful punches, stepping in, so that Jeffries fell forward into him and clinched. The black man laughed:

"Oh, Mr. Jeff, stop loving me so. . . ."

Then, he shot a hard left, followed with a right that sent Jeffries reeling across the ring, while addressing the ringsiders:

"Too much on hand at the moment, eh, boys?"

Jeffries rushed back at him, throwing punches and flailing as Johnson danced and pranced, feinting the white champion off balance, before stabbing him viciously with a rapier-like left.

"Oh, Mr. Jeff, please show me your stuff," he cajoled smiling.

In the third round, Jeffries charged Johnson, who caught him in a clinch, tying him up hopelessly, as he leaned back over the ropes to address the newspapermen and telegraph operators at ringside.

"Y'all catching all this action? I want y'all to get it right, so y'all reports won't disagree with them movin' pictures folks gonna see. . . ."

He then rattled a flurry of punches to Jeffries midsection, pulling him into another hopeless clinch, calling again to the ringside reporters:

"Now if that there was too fast, we're going through it again, the same identical way for y'all benefit. Ready, Mr. Jeff?"

Johnson then pushed him away and repeated the flurry, almost identically.

During the intermission, Jim Corbett could be heard shouting instructions. Admonishing Jeff "to the glory and honor of the white race."

The white man's left eye had closed, his head was already "swollen to the size of a pumpkin." But he went out at the start of the fourth round, pumping to Johnson's body and stomach, where niggers are supposed to be weak. In the breadbasket. Johnson gave him back the same identical treatment, causing him to fall back:

"Aw, come on, Mr. Jeff. Let me see what you got

there. Do something, man. This is a fight for the champeenship. I can go on like this all afternoon, Mr. Jeff," and he proved it.

By the fifth round, it was all too clear that The Big Black Fire was burning off the top and could end the fight as he wished, whenever his "sadistic black sense had been satisfied." So said Jack London, his principal enemy among white writers.

"Those of us who had come betting money on Jeff had started wishing from our hearts that the nigger would go on and end it," said Corbett later.

But "Black-Jack" Johnson did not wish it so. He was in no hurry to end it.

Jeffries waded willingly into and through the torture, throughout the sixth and seventh rounds. And by the eighth round Johnson had found himself a new kind of amusement.

He began to back-chat with the famous ring-siders that he recognized. This infuriated Jeffries so that he mustered the daredevil recklessness of a mad man. Charging in with such force that the crowd rose to their feet with cheers and acclamation, which died down as they watched the consummate ease with which Johnson rode the storm, picking off punches, dancing like a fencing master, blocking, feinting, slithering away as he turned the powerful punches with his gloves, his elbows and his forearms, then clinching, wrapping, tying Jeffries up, calling out to Corbett at the ringside:

"Hello there, Jim. Welcome to the village!"

Then to John L. Sullivan:

"Cap'n? Did you notice that left hand of Jeff's there? Now, watch this one."

Then, he flashed over a left, followed by a right, which sent Jeffries spinning, reeling helplessly across to the far side of the ring.

Jeffries came back. Johnson kept talking to the ring-siders.

"Ah, there, farmer. Ever see a champ who eats leather? You watch now."

He caught Jeff coming up with a right full force in the lips so that he staggered back, his mouth gushing blood in spurts.

"See, he likes it. Loves to swallow blood."

Jeffries came rushing back to receive more. Johnson followed, his fists pumping "One, two, three, four." Jack counted, then commented: "Like it, don't you, champ?"

At the close of this round, Johnson poured it on more. Some of the ringside crowd had become so incensed, the deputies and marshals were forced to restrain them from trying to climb into the ring and to Jeffries' aid. But Johnson grinned and continued, pushing Jeffries back at arm's length, while holding him at bay and calling out:

"How do you like this barndance, Mr. Jeffries?"

Jeffries responded, lashing out a right to Johnson's ribs. He danced back laughing.

"Now, that ain't the one you caved Tom Sharkey's ribs in with, is it?"

The bell rang and Jeffries groped to find his way back to his proper corner. Johnson watched him, still grinning. He had hardly worked himself into a sweat.

The ninth round was different. Johnson showed them his fancy footwork. Driving in digging blows, then ducking, vanishing to come up on the other side of the ring as his stumbling opponent bumbled around the ring to find him.

"Peek-a-boo, Mr. Jeff. Watch yourself. Now, I'm gonna hit you again in the eye. . . ."

Then, he'd do it, sending Jeffries reeling.

"Come on. Protect yourself, Mr. Jeff. You see, I'm giving you fair warning."

Then Johnson smiled and called out to Hugh McIntosh and Tommy Burns, who were sitting together at ringside.

"Here's the one I forgot to show y'all in Sydney," he crowed.

He planted his two feet in a stance, awaiting the onrushing Jeffries. He counted out loud:

"One!" A left hand punch was shorted to Jeffries' midsection. "Two!" A right hand uppercut straightened the body of Jeffries to the point of erectness, before he spun and reeled away to the other side of the ring, catching the ropes to hold himself up. Johnson laughed:

"And they been saying that I couldn't punch, huh?"

Jack went on firing, his head bursting with the sounds and sights of the Galveston Flood, the San Francisco Earthquake; he struck blows as if to make Jeffries explode as Halley's Comet. His body was splattered with the blood of Jeffries, as was the white shirt of the referee, Tex Rickard. He even started toward the corner of Jeffries to get Jim Corbett, who shouted out his curses against the black race. His seconds had to rush out and pull him back to his corner.

Still, Jeffries knew, despite the shouts of Corbett and all the others, the end was very near. He was moving in a nightmare, burned, bruised, confused, he was in a trance as a sleepwalker, unable to tell them that he was no longer confronting just a black man, he was confronting black madness.

He was pushed out to shamble through the unlucky thirteenth. Corbett, John L. Sullivan, Tommy Burns, Sam Fitzpatrick and other veterans of ring slaughter began to turn their heads and close their eyes as The Big Black Fire slithered forward, ramming short blows into the bruised, bloody and swollen face and eyes of Jeffries, without mercy. Taunting, smiling, "cackling with the mirth of a maniac." The women, behind the curtains of their booths, no longer thrilled with typical fascination, bowed their heads and cried. While Jeffries, near his end as the symbol of white supremacy, lumbered forward in a daze. Johnson inquired:

"How you feeling, Jim?"

Jeffries, upon hearing, tried to come back to life. He waded again to the attack, with a flurry that wouldn't have hurt a child.

"I can take you out when I want to, Jim."

No longer was he addressing him as "Mr. Jeffries."

Jack stepped back calmly. Raised his arms skywards, exposing his naked stomach to attack.

"Come on, Jim. Try again. Show me your stuff."

Jeffries lumbered in, a last chance at the exposed stomach of Johnson, his brain forgetting that this was a man who could catch a fly on the wing, with boxing gloves on.

Johnson caught him coming in, sending him back with pile driving force, to sag and sink his weight for support upon the ropes.

Jeffries heard someone say that the fourteenth round was over. The end of the fight had been long delayed, as was the end of a myth, for the white man had never been knocked off his feet but one time, and never for a count.

Johnson tore in, amidst roars of the crowd. "Don't let him be knocked out. Don't let the nigger knock him out. Throw in the sponge. Don't let a nigger knock Jeff out."

They shouted toward the referee and to the corner of Jeffries:

Must not be knocked out by a nigger!

The police heard it: "Police! Stop it! Stop the fight!"

But The Big Black Fire was all over him. Jeffries crumped beneath the onslaught, crumpled to the floor, pulling himself up by the ropes.

He rose to clinch Johnson, who shook him off with contempt, no longer smiling, no longer a look of merriment in his eyes. Rather his was the mask of a hungry puma, intent on destruction of its prey.

He didn't see the tear-filled faces of the spectators, nor the bludgeoned face of Jeffries, turning toward his corner waving his arms, that they throw in the sponge and save him from the disgrace of a knockout. He rose from his knees, waving, but Johnson drove home a full-blooded right, probably the hardest ever thrown in ring history. Jeffries' corner responded, the sponge came flying in, followed by the person of Sam Berger, Jeff's chief second.

But the referee had not seen it, so intent was he on the savage slaughter, as Jeffries lay helpless at this feet. The fight was now officially over. There was no need for a count this time. However, Jeffries rose to his knees as the count of ten was tolled, before crumpling back down to the floor in a sodden, blood-soaked weariness and oblivion.

Johnson had performed the most complete beating the world of prize fighting would come to know.

The Big Black Fire had done it! The Big Smoke was rising, to cover and darken the white skies of every land on earth. Jack Johnson had succeeded in becoming the First Black Heavyweight Champion of the World! Only now was he finally recognized by all.

And he promised, as any supreme king in his splendor:

"I'll make them eat dirt! I'll make them small beer! Until they realize that a black man is now the king!"

CHAPTER THIRTEEN

THE BLACK KING AND
BLOODY CORONATION

Jack Johnson had won the title in December, 1908, with the defeat of Tommy Burns—but it was only now, with the defeat of Jim Jeffries in July, 1910, that he was finally crowned. His brutal coronation was marked with fire, blood and smoke, breaking out all over like bubbles, up from hell.

It started in the streets when folks got the word, "Jeffries, the white man, is down."

"The Black Man wins! By a knockout!

"Jack Johnson now wears the crown. A black man is king, now!"

In Chicago, thousands of his black "subjects" poured into the streets beating buckets and dishpans, whooping and hollering, running and laughing, crying tears of joy, dancing in a long parade up State Street. Firecrackers were popping loud above their heads, moving on in through the white neighborhoods, to make sure that The Crackers got the news right.

Yes, they say that the black folks were cavorting and rolling around in frolic, in practically every city of the country. Even down there, back home, below the Mason-Dixon Line.

Oldtimers declare that they hadn't seen the likes since back when The Emancipation Proclamation was signed.

But, by the time night came to the day of Jack Johnson's Coronation, in some places, the frolics had turned into baby-sized civil wars and riots.

A second cousin of John L. Sullivan who lived down in Muskogee, Oklahoma, got so shook with the news of Jack's win, that he went after two celebrating and cheering "coons" with his bowie knife.

In New Orleans, a Cajun had shot up a nigger for walking into a restaurant and giving what was to become a famous short-order for breakfast:

"Gimme eggs, beat and scrambled, like Jim Jeffries."
"Gimme coffee, black and scalding, strong as Jack Johnson."

That Cajun shot him from behind the lunch counter.

It was the same thing up north, in Brooklyn. It started there when three tough Irish lads heard a black boy talking to a dog he was walking:

"Now, you lay down there, Jeffries," the black was supposed to have said. Then one of the white boys asked:

"You got the nerve to call that dog Jeffries? Why don't you call it Johnson?"

" 'Cause this is a yellow dog. My man, Johnson, is black."

It ended up in a gang war in Brooklyn that night, pitting blacks against whites."

But the worst rioting of the night took place down in Georgia, a town called Uvaldia, which hardly appeared on the maps until, during a gun battle over the fight, three colored folks were killed, a whole bunch of whites injured, and twice as many blacks.

All total, there were eight or more dead reported that night. Whites trying to make black folks pay in blood for what Johnson had done to their boy Jeffries.

But, then, the black men retaliated. A bunch of them

shot up the town of Mounds, Illinois. Even killed a colored policeman while doing it.

Then, over in Washington, Pennsylvania, a bunch of whites shot and killed a nine-year-old colored child when they passed, shooting into a group of colored people.

Down in Little Rock, Arkansas, a Negro shot and wounded a white railroad conductor.

The same thing happened down in Louisiana, when a Negro pulled his gun and shot a fighting mad white railroad conductor.

Reports were coming in from all over: New York, Boston, Houston, San Francisco, Los Angeles; from Mississippi, Alabama, Georgia, Tennessee, the two Carolinas, both Virginias, everywhere.

At the Port of Norfolk, they had to bring in the Marines to restore order.

The niggers even took over the town of Keystone, West Virginia, and held control of it until up till early night of the next day.

The ironical thing was that in Reno, the town where the fight had taken place, only one shot was fired. That was by accident, and there wasn't a report of one single piece of racial violence.

Governor Dickerson had made it clear to all that he wasn't going to stand for anything like that. And then, Tex Rickard had showed his foresight by taking up all weapons before the fight commenced.

While Jack's train was traveling across country to get to his mother and Chicago, rumors were spread all over the nation that they had shot and killed him. And got away with at least a half-million dollars, while the train was crossing the state of Utah, where the Mormon white folks were known as "nigger haters," not even wanting black folks to settle in the state.

But what really had happened was that, as they

picked up coal and water around Ogden, Utah, three crackers did make a try to get at Jack by rushing the rear. All they got for their efforts was a kick in the face, tobacco juice in their eyes, and a few licks about the head with gun-butts, till the police rushed up and saved them, taking them along to jail.

Jack, had just sat there watching, pretending that nothing was happening, not wanting to disturb his "wife." His guards took care of everything, along with a couple of railroad detectives.

On the train, he got the news that "things were not under control in Chicago." Even though they were running more than two hours late, the folks were still waiting for him to come on in.

When the train rolled into the Dearborn Street Station some claim that everybody from "Shady Town" was there, except the disabled and the shut-ins. Every mother's son and father's daughter, along with close kin and far kin cousins. Some claimed they were ten thousand or more strong. Others estimate slightly less. But most of the old folks, the young folks, the strong and the weak claim to have been there to see him come in.

There were bands and groups of local, state and national prominence and fraternal orders: The Odd Fellows, The Bulls, The Zulus, The Elks, The Woodsmen, The Knights of Pythias and Peter Claver, The Mason- and The Shriners; grade schools, high schools, colleges and Sunday Schools were represented.

They all had planned to give Jack a parade, the likes of which New York and those Fifth Avenue white folks had never staged before.

But, the mayor and the chief put a stop to the plans. They were taking no chances on a riot breaking out.

Newspapers around the world were making their string of editorial statements, making his victory a bitter dose for white men to swallow, if there was the slightest speck of prejudice in their hearts:

A calamity to this country worse than the San Francisco Earthquake. THE NEW YORK TIMES

. . . prize fighting has not become a "reductio ad absurdum" when the best fighter comes from the lowest and least developed race. THE NEW YORK HERALD

. . . two brutes, one white, one black . . . pummeled each other publically. . . . Some may not like to see a black American win, but the worst is yet to come. Beware of Japan. . . . NEW YORK TRIBUNE

The days of the ring are over . . . not only because the fight was a disgusting affair, but because it inflamed and further agitated the color problem. THE LONDON *TELEGRAPH*

. . . it is regrettable that the most sacred day of the American civil calendar should be celebrated . . . by the most nakedly commercial prize fight in the history of civilization. THE LONDON DAILY NEWS

If the old-fashioned, straight-forward fighting had prevailed . . . Jeffries would never have been knocked down. THE LONDON TIMES

The reproduction of this barbarous fight in the thousands of picture-show houses around the nation will have it that the minds of boys and girls, future citizens of America will be tainted, corrupted and brutalized by the scenes. THE CHICAGO CHRISTIAN NEWS

. . . intelligent self-supporting Negroes . . . think Johnson's victory a misfortune, encouraging young Negroes to go into prize fighting rather than respectable trades. THE NEW YORK TIMES

Then *The New York Times* changed its tune, seeing that there was no undoing what Johnson had done to Jeffries:

. . . the indirect influence of the black man's victory . . . may be to stimulate respect for quality and fairness

*in more respectable competitions. In that case an oc-
currence so ignoble may prove to have redeeming and
lasting effects.*

"Lord Forgive!" colored folks shouted when they
read that last one. Which simply gave encouragement to
Ol' Cap'n John L. Sullivan of bare-knuckle fame to report hopefully to *The Times*:

*I must say he (Johnson) played fairly at all times
and fought fairly. He gave in, whenever there was con-
tention, and he demanded his rights, only up to their
limit, but never exceeding beyond them.*

Man, after reading that stuff and much more like it,
the reformers and do-gooders got down to business and
went to work. This was prophecy of things to come.
The world would never be the same. And it wasn't.
After the Black Fire had hit the White American fan.

But the coronation of King Johnson still wasn't over.
The Chicago "Nigrew" classy, educated women weren't
accepting Etta Duryea. Some of them, who never would
have considered Jack Johnson as eligible for their "Society," just gave Etta hell. Sneering and sniffling, perk-
ing and spitting everytime they looked toward her face.
Etta was beginning to feel the race pressure and prejudices from both angles of the "Free Americans."

Even during the present time it is claimed that the
free people in the United States of America are the
Caucasian man and the Negro female. 'Cause they're
the only ones free to mix and mingle in daylight or in
darkness without feeling any particular repercussions
from it.

The Negro male and the Caucasian woman are supposed to duck and dart around in the darkness, with the
threat of death and condemnation for being seen together. But Jack "wasn't having none of that, for sure."

And for sure, the reformers weren't going to take it

lying down. Neither was the upper-crust black woman who was being kept by white men.

For two days after getting into Chicago, Etta had to go under the doctor's care for her nerves. After three days, she and Jack left for New York, where she had first met Jack.

And meanwhile, Senator James Robert Mann tried to figure a way to "get Johnson." He got busy and rammed his Mann Act through Congress. This was a federal act making it illegal to transport a woman from one state to another for immoral purposes.

Then Congress went to work ramming through another act making it a federal offense to transport films of prize fights across state lines and show them in public.

᾿ They had a lot of clamor and support, too. Their slogan was:

The Fight Pictures Will Be Worse Than The Fight

Municipal authorities in cities all over the country began passing local ordinances to prevent the fight from being shown. But then Congress settled it once and for all, by making it a federal offense to show them at all.

In the meantime, Jack was with Etta in New York, disregarding what his envious enemies were preparing for him. Rather he spent his time preparing for a fast theatrical tour of Europe concert houses again, writing and arranging the first version of his stage revue titled: "Seconds Out," which featured himself and his talented common-law Caucasian wife. The rest of the time he was spending money, showering gifts upon Etta: diamonds, pearls and other precious stones, silks, satin and furs to wrap around her beautiful body, as they toured New York and the European continent.

But none of the jewels and furs he showered her with was powerful enough to protect her from the abuse of prejudiced people, both white and colored.

The "do-good" Christians were crying out in public:

"She's living in sin. And such living in corruption is the thing that has killed her father."

The jealous white men were crying, "She's ruined. Crippled for life because of the gigantic size of that nigger." Some explained that it was a "scientific fact," white women weren't "emotionally constructed" to consort in sexual intercourse with Negroes.

On the other hand, colored women, in envy, claimed that Etta was contaminating the minds of colored men, who had begun to follow the example of Jack Johnson, seeking out white women for sex partners.

Still, Etta Duryea became a style-setting example for fashions and hair styles.

Madame C.J. Walker became the first Negro millionaire, introducing her famous hair straightener pomade, making it possible to convert the kinky, coarse hair of the black women to the straight silky texture of that hair belonging to white women.

"Palmer's Skin Success" appeared; a skin bleach for dark women's skin, "guaranteed to make you one shade lighter." Dark skinned women used it in secrecy, applying it before sleep, waking in the mornings to wash it away with Palmer's Skin Success Soap, to observe some of the darkness disappearing. Cursing white women the likes of Etta Duryea for bewitching the minds of our best black men, like Jack Johnson.

From their pulpits colored Christian ministers shouted their Sunday condemnations, to the pleasure of the Negro and Caucasian presses, admonishing and predicting the fall of the Black King, whom God had blessed with a Championship and fortune, who like Samson had shaved his head to live in unsanctioned sin, unmarried to a woman of an alien race. "Destruction and Death to his seductress! Damnation to the king who had forsaken his people, to be seduced by her."

The pressures took obvious toll on Etta Duryea. Many newspapers had begun to observe her nervousness. ". . . pale and withdrawn, subject to fits of temper. . . ."

They left for the European concert tour, for Jack figured the change of scenery would be of some good in changing the outlook of the woman he loved so dearly. But it did not. For Etta began undergoing spells of remorse at being pointed out as "Jack Johnson's woman." She stepped up her insistence for a legal marriage.

Jack Johnson's party blazed across the continent of Europe, with his nephew Gus Rhodes as manager of the troupe. Their bookings carried them onto stages of London, Brussels, Lyons, Antwerp, Berlin, Budapest, St. Petersburg and Paris, where Etta was sent into another one of her rages when the famous French actress Gaby Deslys became enamoured with him. Gaby issued statements to the Parisian press: "His great staring eyes . . . simply devour one. His wit? Enchantant. He evokes a desperation in a woman for utter fulfillment."

Christmas found them back in London, where Etta, in her rages, threatened to throw herself beneath the wheels of a speeding train. Jack promised marriage as soon as they returned to the States, at end of the tour.

But Etta's insecurity and jealousies multiplied as a result of Jack's conduct, unbecoming of one who is betrothed. The tour was cut short after Jack had been forced to knock down an official of the U.S. Embassy in London for hurling a racial insult at Etta.

They returned to New York and were married in February, 1911, then left to take up residence in his adopted home of Chicago, where they might be near his mother and family. One member of his family had come to despise him: his brother Charles.

"My mother had got so that she wouldn't even admit that there was a power in the whole universe to compare with him," his brother once stated to the press.

When they asked Jack about his European visit, he declared: "I was a bigger attraction there than the King of England himself."

Johnson had timed his London arrival to correspond with the Coronation of George V. It is begrudgingly admitted that he did take some of the attention from the coronation almost everywhere he went, followed by an entourage numbering between fifteen and twenty.

While the cries and uproars were rising across the U.S. for Jack Johnson's scalp, prayers were being sent out for another White Hope to rise up and remove the heavyweight crown from his head. But there were few, if any, promoters willing to gamble on the white fighters who claimed they could do it.

Jack Johnson then turned his attention to opening his fabulous *Café de Champion*, which was to become the most famous American nightclub-saloon of its time.

It was around that time that Jack began to talk of "settling down in married life, taking care of my business interests, while my wife and I rear ourselves a family."

This idea Etta had somehow never given thought to, even though she had loved Jack enough to want to marry him. But she adamantly refused to hear or discuss the idea of bearing him children.

This was the biggest blow to the Black Fire's pride, to learn that his wife was unwilling to bear children for him. While he was insistent, she was just as unwilling:

"I'll never bring children into this world," she had told him over and over, "knowing what they will have to go through."

"They'll go through no more than I've gone

through!" he had told her. "They'll have a head start. I'm fighting to give that to them."

"You can't even protect me from what I have to go through. How do you think you could protect the children we'd have?"

It was then that Jack became more reckless and restless than ever. His cars blazed up the Chicago streets, causing him arrests and heavy fines in courts.

Then, he started invading the plush and elaborate Everleigh Club, where Belle Schreiber had returned as number-one girl. And Jack proved that he could afford to integrate it. Becoming a "first" of his race to integrate this exclusive white whorehouse.

And he did it in the finest fashion that any whorehouse has seen, much to the distress of Minna and Ada Everleigh. It sent them screaming to the Alderman, Michael "Hinky-Dink" Kenna, protesting:

"He is not only closing the house by hiring the services of all the girls for one evening, propping his big feet upon our Moorish upholstery, but he brings that big bass viol' of his and teaches all of the girls to sing those awful Negro Spirituals until all hours of the morning."

But, Minna and Ada didn't know that Johnson had already started his pay-offs, to open his own club, to Kenna—a fee of about one thousand a month, guaranteed by a prominent Chicago brewery, whose wares he was to feature in his cabaret, exclusively.

Johnson threatened to spread the news, if Hinky-Dink got cute enough to even act as if he intended to bring an end to his "kicks and joys" at the Everleigh Club.

But Hinky-Dink then went and asked Charlie Erbstein, called "The Persuader," who was Al Capone's lawyer, to speak with Jack about his activities at the

Everleigh. Jack's *Café de Champion* was already nearing completion.

When Erbstein asked Johnson:

"Now, how would you like it if the wiring and plumbing of your club is found in violation of the Chicago City Ordinances?"

Jack jumped up, laughing. Then, when he finished laughing, he took "The Persuader" by his collar and tossed him with one hand out into the streets, on his ears. Erbstein went away, forgetting the matter.

Jack Johnson's *Café de Champion* threw open its doors for business October 11, 1911, as one of the most exquisite cabarets in Chicago.

Even the spittoons were solid, polished silver.

When asked to describe it, one politician said:

"Why, on opening night, I saw One-Eyed Connolly sleeping off his drunk under a Van Dyke painting of The Vestal Virgins!"

There were more than two hundred thousand worth of Rembrandts, Rubens, Van Goghs, along with classical tapestries, adorning the walls of the two floors of the club.

Everybody flocked to Jack Johnson's cabaret at number 42 West 31st Street.

11, 42 and 31 became the popular combination of the number players around Chicago. Which was the date of opening, the number and the street of Jack Johnson's cabaret.

Customers stood in line a block and a half long waiting to get in, when the door flew open.

The place was sumptuous; five spacious rooms downstairs, mahogany walls and furniture matched the longest mahogany polished bar that folks had seen up to that time.

Johnson explained that he had planned all of the decorations, "after my extensive travels in Europe. I personally collected these many fine art works, sculpturings and artistic creations. I also, while there, gained a comprehensive idea for the decorative effects, which you see here and about. You must agree that they put to shame many of the similar establishments in Europe and here in America."

Then a reporter asked:

"Mr. Johnson, don't you feel that the 'race-mixing' between black and white in this establishment will have an adverse effect upon the general public feelings and American race relations?"

Jack eyed him levely and answered:

"Emphatically, in the negative! And I might add, a most rude and insidious inquiry."

The Golden Belt which symbolized the championship was on display above the bar. The tapestry told tales of Biblical scenes. There was also a lifesized portrait of "Cleopatra, the Black Egyptian Queen" at the height of her reign. There was a portrait of Jack and Etta, painted by one of the most prominent painters of the time, along with a painting of Johnson's family with his mother and father.

The general public was not allowed to inspect the second floor, which consisted of two private dining rooms, a luxurious apartment for Johnson and his wife, Etta. A lavish parlor across the hall from the apartment with an adjoining, lavishly furnished bedroom, known as *ma joie de fille salon* (Harem room). Jack always spoke of it in French. It had mirrored walls and ceiling decorated in a motif of leopard, zebra, tiger and panther skins.

Etta had come to an arrangement with Jack, allowing for the room to compensate her unwillingness to bear him a child—after Johnson had come close to committing suicide in despondency over her rejection.

In her fear of becoming pregnant, they had come to

sharing separate bed and quarters. Which had led to an increase in his frequenting of the Everleigh Club and other similar places.

By then, both of them had come to live in almost absolute misery over the matter, while loving each other insanely.

As usual, Jack's pride became his undoing. For this was a matter he would never discuss thereafter. But rather he became a legend for his prowess and the many female visitors who climbed the carpeted stairs for an appointment in his *joie de fille salon.*

Etta bore his adventures and exursions with seeming tolerance. Until finally she broke a plan to him. They would adopt a child. Jack rejected the idea. Then, in desperation, Etta came forth with another idea, which was to end almost in a tragedy.

Etta was beginning to show obvious signs of strain, feeling for certain that her husband would leave her for the first of the many beauties that shared his bed who came forth bearing him a child. Nearly all of these were white, like herself.

So, she began to look over the lot of Negro beauties who frequented the cabaret and succeeded in cultivating the friendships of a few of them, generally those light enough to suit her husband's taste.

Finally, she selected one, a married mulatto *passe-a-blanc* or real high-yellow, named Adah Banks, willing to bear a child by Jack and allow the Johnsons to adopt it. The price was right, along with the prestige, so Adah accepted, with her husband's consent. They broached the desperate idea to Jack. Reluctantly, he accepted, hiding his hurt with feigned amusement and concern for Etta's welfare.

After a couple months of this trial and arrangement, Adah proved not only a failure, but began to bore

Johnson, who called for an end of the arrangement, which drove Adah to fury.

She entered the cabaret one night with a gun, facing the champion and his wife, demanding more money or a resumption of the arrangement. Etta explained to her calmly that it was over, since it hadn't already worked. Adah went into hysterics, pulling the revolver to kill the white woman, or her husband, or both. Jack grappled with her for control of the weapon and was shot in the foot as a result.

Although no one knew for certain what the shooting was about, the newspapers went to work on Johnson, emphasizing his "bawdy conduct" and the tolerance of his beautiful white wife, who was showing obvious signs of breaking down.

The injury to Jack's foot wasn't serious, but what the incident did to his life was another thing.

Reformers began to shout for the closing of Johnson's cabaret as a den of iniquity, even though prostitution and larceny were running rampant in Chicago.

Sportsmen in America and England joined in declaring him a "non-champion," a welcher, afraid to fight. Letters came from "Peggy" Bettinson, director of the National Sporting Club, who had forced Jack to stand on the mat outside, reminding him that he was obligated to fight for them.

George Considine, who had also helped finance the trip when Johnson and his former manager Sam Fitzpatrick went sailing to London in chase of Tommy Burns, reminded him:

"You owe an obligation to these men of the National Sporting Club. You shouldn't have thrown over Sam Fitzpatrick. It's cost you every friend that you've had here, in your own country. You've got to honor the plans that Sam made for you."

"Mr. Considine, I don't have to honor a gawd damn

thing. I'm champion of the world and I take orders from no one," Johnson replied.

Then, Jack snatched up the Bettinson letter, walked over and hurled it into the flaming fireplace. "Into the fire it goes. I'm sick of keeping obligations and honoring commitments made for me by slick white men. Now, if you want it honored, then get Sam to honor it. He was the muther who signed it."

A group of die-hard white sportsmen had already begun and concluded an elimination contest among heavyweight fighters, and they crowned Luther McCarty "The White Champion of the World." McCarty was to lose this title to Gunboat Smith, who in turn lost it to light heavyweight, Georges Carpentier, who in 1914 entered the French Forces of WWI.

"The White Championship" was never mentioned thereafter.

Then, under pressure from the American press, Jack Johnson agreed to fight Fireman Jimmy Flynn, a White Hope he had defeated previously, under the direction of Jack Curley, at Las Vegas, New Mexico, on July 4, 1912—exactly two years from the day he had defeated Jim Jeffries at Reno.

It was a miserable affair, despite the ballyhoo of biased pressmen who insisted that Johnson had grown too fat from sipping his Rajah Pegs through his gold straw, while indulging in an overabundance of willing white tramps in bed.

They were sadly mistaken. Only five thousand people came to witness the bout, which found the White Hope, Flynn, up against a superbly conditioned champion, floundering on the ropes in the tenth round, so that the police felt forced to jump into the ring and stop the slaughter.

Etta had accompanied him to the fight. They returned to Chicago, and she planned to visit Las Vegas,

Nevada, along with a sportswriter's wife come September. Some say that Etta was going there to establish residence and obtain a divorce by mutual agreement. But, nobody actually knows for sure.

However, if such rumors were true, Etta changed her mind, or Jack succeeded in prevailing upon her not to leave him, by the time that September 11, the date of her departure, had arrived.

An hour before departure, while her maids, Helen Simmons and Mabel Bolden, made her ready, she claimed to be ill with a severe headache and asked Jack to go down to the station and explain her inability to make the trip to her friend.

Etta Duryea Johnson dressed herself prettily in her night clothes and dismissed her maids, closing her bedroom door, with her last words: "Pray for me."

Then, a few minutes later, they heard the shot ring out, echoing down the halls from the bedroom.

When they rushed into the room, they found her lying there unconscious in a pool of blood. She had shot herself in the head, with a .38 Colt, but she wasn't dead yet.

Helen Simmons ran downstairs to tell Toots Marshall, the manager, screaming for him to call the police and an ambulance.

Meantime, Jack had delivered his message to their friends, bade them farewell and watched the train pull out, walking back in the cool night air—feeling good. He stopped in at one of his favorite tobacco stands, where he had a standing invitation as champion of the world. "Mr. Johnson, you're always welcome to our best cigar, free of charge."

He took his cigar to light up, but looking at the match, the flash of the fortune teller's face appeared before his eyes.

Jack threw down the flaming match and cigar and started to run, not hearing the shopkeeper cry out:

"Mr. Johnson, what's the matter? That's our best ten cent cigar!"

But Jack's premonition had him running, terror and fear gripping his stomach, a foreboding of disaster. As he approached the house, he saw the crowds gathered in front of the cabaret, straining to look inside. Seeing the police, he knew something tragic had happened.

He grabbed one of the policemen by the shoulders, spinning him around:

"For Christ's sakes. What's happening here, man?"

"Don't you already know? Where'd you come from?"

"Is it my wife . . . ?"

The policeman didn't answer as Johnson pushed him aside, shoving and barging past others, pushing his way into the bedroom. He saw the bloodstained pillows and pushed the doctor away, crying his wife's name.

He dropped his head to her chest, heard her faint heartbeat, then lifted her, staggering with her body like a drunkard toward the door. Part of her head had been torn away by the gun shot; Johnson carried her body to the waiting ambulance, which carried them to the hospital. His mother and sisters were already there when he arrived with her. Somebody had called and delivered the news of the tragedy to them by telephone.

Etta Duryea Johnson died a few hours later.

When questioned a few days later, at the inquest, Jack revealed that his wife twice before had attempted to commit suicide, revealing also that twice he himself had attempted it. Each of them had saved the other from self-destruction, on both occasions.

Thus, as it is remembered, this black man and his white woman had lived to be despised by a society they both hated, yet, twice, each of them had saved the other from the deaths they defied as well as welcomed.

Etta was buried and from across her grave he shouted at the reporters and others gathered there:

"She was murdered by those who persecute me . . . by every one of you here. May God have mercy on your souls. *She* paid for me being heavyweight champion of the world."

In his pocket he clenched a small, soiled, crumpled piece of paper, her last words to him. A note, which he later gave to his mother and told her to destroy. It read:

Jack, I love you. But you go on. Forgive me for giving up. Etta.

Later, Jack was to recall, "At the time I lit that cigar, I remembered what the fortune teller had told me: *'two deaths . . . of my wives.'*

"Then I remembered that she also had said, *'But, the worst confrontation with death will have just begun for you. You must remember and keep on going although it will look to yourself as if you can't. You can and you will . . . you must.'* "

Jack refused to reveal Etta's note to the daily newspapers, which had already stepped up their programs against him, attributing the death of his white wife to his black conduct. They openly accused him of "white slavery," inviting Virginia Brooks from Hammond, Indiana, to come to Chicago and lead the fight against the vice, such as Johnson was guilty of. Miss Brooks had come to national attention when she had marked out "Eight Vice-Lords" of her city to be "tarred and feathered and ridden out of town on a rail" by fifty women carrying shotguns and revolvers.

She never brought her plans off in Indiana, but Chicago reformers assured her much support if she came to their city and led such a campaign against "that unscrupulous black nigger."

Upon hearing of this, Tiny, Jack's mother, moved herself in, taking Etta's quarters in the *Cabaret de*

Champion, while his sisters came in alternating spells to see that the business was kept straight.

Jack had intensified his drinking, throwing away the gold straw through which he sipped his Rajah's Peg, and he had begun to guzzle it down from his decanters by the mouthfuls.

"They'll never see the day that I'll stand by and let them break my son down and go to pot, as they think they're gonna do. Not while I live an' breathe," his mother proclaimed.

But Jack ignored business and showed a complete disinterest in fighting altogether.

Promoters would approach him: "Here, Jack. Ten thousand guarantee for fighting Sam Langford."

"Sorry, gentlemen. But I just am not interested. I've beaten him too many times before. Besides, y'all know that Sam's only a middlewcight."

"Okay, same deal for Sam McVey."

"I've beaten him, too. Or don't y'all remember to read the record books to see how many times?"

"Are you afraid of Joe Jeanette? What about Joe?"

"Gentlemen, they are all good. But why don't y'all stop interrupting my drinking and spend your time finding yourselves a fighter who y'all think could beat me, and let me alone in the meantime."

As his drinking intensified, so did his arrests and fines for speeding and disorderly conduct. Business at the *Café de Champion* was slowing down, while no worthy opponent as challenger for his crown was even faintly visible on the boxing horizon.

Then, after a period of some two months, after the death of Etta, The Big Black Fire was swaggering through the spacious rooms of his opulent palace, when he was called over to a table by a white friend named Perry Bauer, who had become somewhat distressed with Johnson's business affairs. There, he was introduced to a smartly dressed, pretty, young, blue-eyed companion, Lucille Cameron, a Chicago University student from Minneapolis, Minnesota.

She listened attentively as the two men discussed the desperate state of the cabaret along with the champion's ever mounting business entanglements.

The white girl sighed gently, after awhile, then opening her saucer-like blue eyes, laid her hand on the champion's forearm, before speaking:

"Mr. Johnson, do you know what you need and want? You need and want a good personal secretary to solve the serious problems of your affairs."

"And I suppose that you think that you are the one," the Black Fire leveled his burning black eyes into the icy-clear blue ones of the lovely white girl. "Tell me, do you know five thousand words, and all of the long ones?" he asked, remembering that Herbert Spencer, the philosopher whom he had met and made friends with had told him, "No secretary is worth a tinkers dam, unless she knows at least five thousand words and all of the long ones."

The young white girl from Minneapolis rose to the occasion, almost "blowing the champion out of his natural mind." She smiled, sighed, taking in a deep breath, then came forth with her answer, with no stop for breath:

"Mr. Johnson, you seem to be a sophisticated rhetorician, inebriated with the exuberance of your own personal verbosity. . . ."

The champion never dropped his gaze, his smile widened slightly.

'Tell me, is that supposed to be good?" he asked.

Her fingers closed around the surface of his forearm, toying with the smooth silk of the suit that he wore.

"But, what do you think, Mr. Johnson?"

"I think that you're hired. Can you write with a typewriter, too?"

"I can write, Mr. Johnson—many kinds of ways. But I'm especially good at typing—even with a machine. I hail from Minneapolis and my age is nineteen. How good are you at judging good type, Mr. Johnson?"

"Good 'nough to know that you can't stay in this place. But I think something might be arranged. My present manager's name is Jack Curley, about the nicest white feller who ever got mixed up in the fight game. He'll be like an uncle to you. And his wife will be just like an aunt. I'll call him and get you and your things moved in with your Uncle Curley."

As Jack later explained it. "I employed her strictly as a business secretary, her association with me was purely of a business nature and devoid of any undue intimacy."

However, as things would have it, this answer was not satisfactory for the newspaper boys, nor for the goody-good reformers. The rumors flew like feathers from a chicken plucked alive.

The gossipmongers got the scent, like hounds chasing a fox on a hot summer day.

When Ed Conkle, the son of a Protestant minister and head of the United Press (UPI), caught wind of it, he shouted to his men keep that vice stuff coming in on Johnson and that white girl; "people like to read 'bout what they're doing."

Virginia Brooks and Alice Aldrich of "The Law and Order League" caught the scent, too. So did the "chicken-eating" black preachers of Chicago and around the country, who saw Johnson and his antics as their only means of being quoted in the white press as "Negro leaders," upon denouncing him. Which they did almost to a man, with few and rare exceptions, in public and in front of white folk.

Those who did not openly condemn him for his actions, which they were never sure of, simply condemned him for his "gross and public indiscretions."

At this same time, the newspapers and the Negro leader-preachers were willing to ignore the fact that Julius Rosenwald, founder of Sears and Roebuck mail order houses, was called before the Illinois Vice Commission, admitting that he paid some 119 "apprentices," fifteen- and sixteen-year-old girls, $5 a week or less for an eight-hour day, along with some four thousand or more women employees less than $8 a week; he was considered not nearly as guilty of the crime of "white slavery" as Jack Johnson was.

According to the Vice Commission, since Johnson was not white, and since they did not consider him a 'philanthropist" like Rosenwald, therefore, only he and a few others like him could be guilty of committing the act of "white slavery."

CHAPTER FOURTEEN

DOWN, WITH THE KING

So, by 1912, the coronation for the Black King was over. The First White Queen had passed on to greater glory, not to be remembered, for a new white queen had replaced her. So they didn't cry, "Long live the king." But rather the cry was:

"Down with the king."

But the Black King wasn't the kind to abdicate. He had won the crown by fighting and he intended to fight to hang on to it.

But the forces against him were preparing themselves, and getting ready for the trial and conviction of the king, heaping tribulation and woe on his reign.

The first trumpet for the big battle was sounded on a windy Chicago morning of November, the year of 1912. That's when a newspaper man from UPI came breezing up to Jack Johnson's apartment on the second floor of the cabaret, demanding to see Miss Lucille Cameron.

The Black King was not only angry at being awakened so early, but much angrier at the white man's demand.

"Where the hell did you come from?" Johnson asked the reporter. "Who in the hell advised you that the lady makes her home here with me?"

Then, after a few well directed words as to where the white man should go, spiced with a few references to his parentage and ancestry, Johnson directed the man to the residence of Jack Curley, where Lucille Cameron was residing.

But the reporter was not satisfied, since he hadn't pulled off an explosive news story for the daily papers. He took it upon himself to send a wire off to Minneapolis, addressing it to Lucille's mother.

Mrs. Cameron-Falconet was off like a shot in search of her brood, leaving on the next train to Chicago, arriving the next evening, umbrella and all. She stormed into the castle of the Black King and, coming face-to-face with The Black Fire, demanded an audience.

to know, what is this I hear."

"I'm Lucille Cameron's mother, Mr. Johnson. I want

Johnson rose to answer her in the style that white folks dislike hearing, coming from the mouth of common-bred, smart alecky niggers:

"Madame, not being cognizant of your audibility, I regret my inability to respond to your query."

"My daughter and you. What are you doing with my daughter, may I ask?"

"You may ask, and my answer is an emphatical negative!"

"What do you mean? I want to know just what you mean," the enraged and indignant mother shrilled, nostrils flaring.

"I mean what I just said, ma'am. Nothing! Nothing is what I mean. Nothing is what I said. Nothing is what I am guilty of doing with your daughter. Does that answer your question?"

"No!" shouted Mrs. Cameron-Falconet. "No, it does not. I want the truth. I came to get to the bottom of this. I'll have you know I've already sent for my daughter, Mr. Johnson. She'll be here shortly. I intend to face her and you with this wickedness, in your presence as well as hers and others."

Johnson burst forth with loud laughter, then subsided.

"Good. Very good, Mrs. Cameron. It will be nice to see her up here. I've always wanted to show her this part of the house."

"Oh, you don't say?" She spat onto the plush carpet.

"Then, we'll certainly see." With that she sat down in a chair as Mrs. Tiny, Johnson's mother, observed her levely, before the bell rang, signaling someone approaching up the staircase.

Lucille entered the parlor, with several reporters following, including the one who had sent the wire to Minneapolis. Mrs. Cameron-Falconet rose immediately.

"Well, I'm here to know what you've been doing. I

want to hear the disgusting things that this nigger has forced you into."

"Why . . . he's forced me into nothing."

"Don't you tell me that. You can't play that game with me. You are underage. And remember, I can force the truth out of you. And by God, I will. Giving yourself to a nigger!" she screamed like a maniac. Lucille matched her scream.

"Giving myself to what . . . ? Who said that? That's a lie. Nobody would say anything like that, but you."

"Everybody's saying it. Everybody in Minneapolis."

"Everybody in Minneapolis! Ha! Everyone in Minneapolis is nobody."

"You wait until you get home and find out what the world thinks of a white girl who would do that with a nigger. Why an animal couldn't be worse."

Tiny, Jack's mother, moved, rushing toward the white woman, only to be restrained in her charge by her son.

"You, get out of my son's house. . . . You white trash bitch, you. . . . Before I forget myself and. . . ."

Johnson moved in front of his mother and towered over the white woman and the reporters.

"You get out of my house. . . . If you were a man, I would break. . . ."

"Don't say what you'd do to me. Think about what you're gonna do!" she screamed. "You're gonna do time, nigger, in prison. That'll be the end of you and your filth!"

She grabbed her daughter by the arm, pulling her towards the hall door, Lucille protesting.

"Try and stop me." She addressed Johnson. "She's nineteen and underage. Lay a finger on me and you've got another five years added to what you're gonna get. . . ."

The Big Black Fire moved past her and pushed open the door.

"I wouldn't lay a finger on you, or your daughter, for all the gold in Ft. Knox. The sooner I see the last of you both, the better. . . ."

The door was slammed into his face. On the stairs they met with federal officers, whom one of the reporters had gone to summon.

It was apparent, after the first meeting with the officers, that the white girl was to be of no assistance as a witness, declaring:

"He never touched me. And I don't care if he is black or white. I love him. . . ."

Her mother shouted to the officers, "I repeat. And I'll repeat again! I'd rather see her dead than sleeping with a black man. . . ."

This much she confirmed as she ordered her young daughter to be jailed, at first as a "material witness," then later to be charged with "aiding and abetting," which the officers knew could not hold, for they had not arrested Johnson, hence the question was: "Aiding and abetting whom, at what?"

So, they released her to the custody of a guardian, but kept her under surveillance in a hotel room, with police on guard.

Charley "The Persuader" Erbstein, working from the federal office, stated to the press, "I think we can get Johnson on the Mann Act," not forgetting the "manly act" of Johnson tossing him out of his ears when he had attempted to threaten him some months before. Erbstein had been engaged by Mrs. Cameron-Falconet to prosecute Johnson and the charges had not been decided upon, yet Lucille had been jailed in an obvious attempt to frighten her.

They explained that her imprisonment, in jail and while under guard in the hotel, was "to keep her out of Johnson's clutches."

Still, her bail, while in the hotel room, under guard,

was set at twenty-five thousand. Johnson withdrew this amount from the First National Bank, while a crowd stood around the bank; they were still milling around three hours after Johnson had made the withdrawal and departed.

Then the court ruled that Jack Johnson was not the proper person to put up bail for Lucille Cameron. The crowd, consisting of mostly "respectable, law-abiding Negroes," hanged a dummy—Johnson in effigy—while some of the group carried signs: *If only we had a real Negro."*

In the meantime, Mrs. Alice Phillips Aldrich of the Law and Order League was allowed visitation with Lucille, to question her and to convince her that Justice would be served if she testified that Jack Johnson had abducted her from Minneapolis, transporting her across state lines "to serve his immoral intents and purposes."

After two hours of this ordeal, Lucille collapsed and this time was taken to jail again. Johnson was not allowed to secure legal representation for her. Judge George A. Carpenter denied him this; then a writ of habeas corpus was denied her by Judge Kennesaw Mountain Landis, who later became commissioner of the national pastime known as baseball.

When Johnson's attorney, Robert E. Cantwell, asked to see Lucille Cameron as a consultant, he was told by Harry A. Parkin, Assistant District Attorney:

"No, you cannot see her. And that is not all. You will not get to see her." Judge Landis confirmed the statement and declaration of the District Attorney.

Mrs. Cameron-Falconet appeared before reporters at the Federal Building with Charley "The Persuader" Erbstein, who was in a jubilant mood.

"Her mother and I feel that Jack Johnson has insulted every white woman in the United States. Despite the consequences that her daughter must suffer, we are going to see that justice is done."

And they had many supporters, influential ones, who cheered him on, such as Mr. J.B. Cummings, president of the Missouri Telephone and Electric Light Company, who wrote the Cook County Civil Service Commissioner, Frederic Greer:

"Dear Fred: If Chicago men let Jack Johnson get away with this insult to our women . . . to all white women, so that he can get away with any one of them that he wants. . . . Then here's hoping that Chicago gets wiped off the map."

Mrs. Aldrich was granted permission to visit Lucille, still in jail without bond or recourse, to continue to point out the error of her ways.

Her stubbornness simply served to increase the public indignation against Johnson.

Mrs. Falconet, her mother, cried: "That nigger has hypnotized my child. He's done it with other white women. Two of them are dead of suicide, because of his mysterious hypnotic powers."

J.W. Bragdon, a prominent Minneapolis civil leader, concurred:

"A slur has been brought upon the fair name of Minneapolis. As president of the Minneapolis Commercial Club, we appeal to your sense of justice to do what is in your power to obliterate the attempts of this notorious obnoxious individual to get into public press. His defiance of the law, disregard of clean morals, and his other numerous crimes should not be tolerated or put forth into print. It is time suppression should be made. There should be a general protest of this character."

The fact that Jack Johnson was guilty of no crime whatever had never occurred to the authorities nor the press and their general public.

Even a member of Johnson's family, his brother Charles, turned against him, reporting that: "Jack should be sent to prison for his actions."

It was further reported that Charles Johnson was giving to the Grand Jury "important evidence" concerning the affairs of his brother.

The pastor and members of the Christian Endeavor League, Bethel African Methodist Episcopal (AME) Church went on record in public support of the condemnation of Jack Johnson as a "bad citizen" and stating further: "We do not condone his breaking the laws of our land."

What laws he had broken was never ascertained, while local and federal prosecutors were wracking their brains to come up with legal charges against him that might hold up in a court room.

Willard Davis, the husband of Adah Banks Davis, appeared to enter a suit of "alienation of affections," on behalf of himself and the wife who had shot Jack Johnson in the foot. Because of Lucille, he claimed. (And Jack had not even met Lucille at the time of the shooting!)

They closed down his business, the *Café de Champion,* by canceling his liquor license.

They dug and searched, in quest for witnesses who might charge and make charges stick.

"Hell hath no fury like a woman scorned." Finally, they got in touch with George Little, who turned them on to Belle Schreiber, still smarting from Jack's refusal to marry her and make of her a "decent woman." Belle was willing to testify not only for the revenge, but because of the fantastic publicity it would bring to her. Along with possible promises of a cash payoff, which was never confirmed.

Sig Hart, Johnson's manger, advised him to flee the country for Europe, upon learning that he had received offers for appearances through George Thomas, a Negro American promoter, who was on a first name basis with the Tsar of Russia.

But the black champion showed his mettle by refusing to leave as long as they kept Lucille Cameron imprisoned.

His decision to delay proved disastrous. The blow fell when a Federal Grand Jury, before Judge Kennesaw "Mountain" Landis, returned with a charge of Violation of the Mann Act, based upon the testimony of a professional prostitute, Belle Schrieber. Making it retroactive. For if Johnson were guilty of the charges, then he had performed such actions *before* the law was passed which made these actions illegal.

These facts were ignored, for they now had the testimony of a "repentant" white prostitute who willingly confessed that:

(1) She had traveled across state lines to fulfill immoral purposes, upon request of Johnson.

(2) Upon his request she had performed acts of sexual intercourse, cohabiting with him upon request.

(3) She had performed, against her will but upon his request, "unnatural sex acts" upon his person.

(4) She had been deprived of work at her profession in cities as Philadelphia, New York, San Francisco, Pittsburgh and the likes when it was learned that she had sexual contact and intercourse with a Negro.

(5) She had allowed Johnson to induce her to prostitution with other men, while visiting his training camps.

(6) Upon his inducement, she had performed crimes against nature, debauchery, etc.

They no longer needed Lucille Cameron, nor her mother. Lucille was released from custody and succeeded in escaping from her mother. She fled to Johnson for help.

Lucille begged Johnson to marry her, but the charges of violating the Mann Act had been lodged against him. He refused. But when she stated that she would never go home to her mother or Minneapolis again, he did arrange for her to go to Toronto, Canada, where she stayed but a few days, then returned, to Jack's mother, Tiny.

"Mrs. Johnson, whether your son marries me or not, it does not matter. But he refused to run away from me. So, I've decided. I will not run away from him until he is cleared or convicted. If they convict him, then I'll stay and wait until he is out, here, at his side with you."

A few days later, Johnson was arrested, then indicted, with an incredible bail of sixty-five thousand! (Later reduced to thirty thousand.) When his attorney, Edwin C. Day, produced memoranda showing ownership of property totaling far beyond this amount, it was refused.

After hours of argument, Judge Landis stated:

"I will not accept a cash bond in this case. There is a human cry in this case that cannot be overlooked in consideration of a bond."

Again, The Black Fire was shackled in handcuffs and led off to jail as the photographers closed in. One got too close and received a kick in the groin, dropping his camera to crumple and crawl away.

He was placed in a cell by himself; calling for candles, cake and wine, he received the candles only.

After four days in jail, Judge Landis relented and allowed Tiny, Jack's mother, to guarantee thirty-two thousand bail with the property she owned.

Ten days later, Mrs. Cameron-Falconet received the news which she had avowed would kill her. Her daughter became the wife of Jack Johnson, heavyweight champion of the world.

She wore the twenty-five hundred dollar ring, which

George Little had reportedly given to Jack's former wife, Etta. Six carets.

There were few friends, among them but four white people, present to witness the ceremony, which was performed by the Rev. Mr. H.A. Roberts.

After the ceremony, Tiny gave the bride a hug and a kiss, stating:

"Sometimes, I say things that Jack doesn't approve of. So this time, I'll keep my thoughts to myself."

"Where's your mother, Mrs. Johnson," one news reporter asked of the bride."

"I don't know. And what's more, I don't care," she answered.

Mrs. Cameron-Falconet closed her eyes and fainted, when she heard in Minneapolis that the couple had been married. But she did not die as she had promised.

Naturally the newspapers and gossipmongers took up the hue and cry. "He just went and married her so that she could not testify against him in court."

"Just like that low-life nigger; slick, cunning, always an angle."

But it never dawned upon even the most enlightened ones among the haters of the black man that Lucille had already refused to testify again him. Also, that Johnson was not being tried upon the testimony of Lucille, nor the charges made by her mother. But rather he was being tried upon the testimony of Belle Schreiber, the professional prostitute, and a couple of other nondescript witnesses whom the prosecutors had dug up.

Still, for more than a week after the marriage, they were shouting condemnations at Jack for marrying the girl. Even on the floors of Congress, one Georgia cracker had got up and shouted:

"In Chicago white girls are made slaves of an African nigger tribe."

The big trial was set for the thirteeneth of May. If

convicted Jack would get at least a year and a day. At least it looked that way. But Jack had a battery of hard working lawyers led by the famous Benjamin Bachrach. He would need them. And could afford them—another thing that this particular black man could be thankful for.

His judge in the case, George Albert Carter, had shown his prejudice and wasn't anything resembling a mental giant when it came to application of the law.

Johnson's lawyers predicted that he had no worry as far as the many counts of the indictment went. It would simply be his word against Belle Schreiber's. But still there was the Mann Act charge. Not only were they going to challenge the constitutionality of the act, but the application of it, in the case of Jack. For the law had not yet been passed when Jack was supposed to have committed the crime of "transporting Belle across state lines." But they warned The Big Smoke that this did not mean that he would walk from the courtroom as a free man. Public sentiment was against him, even for performing such acts with a white professional whore.

They put Jack on the stand to testify in his own defense. He admitted like a man that he had sent the whore money from time to time. The total of what he had sent to her came to something like nine or ten thousand dollars.

The lawyers had advised Jack to talk low, talk nice and humble, to give the impression that he was remorseful and not cocky.

Jack was a very good actor and turned out with an excellent performance. He didn't raise his voice at any time, as his lawyer took him through the motions to prove his points:

"Did you have a telephone conversation with Belle Schreiber on October 10th or whereabouts, 1910?" asked Bachrach.

"Yes, I did," Johnson answered. "She called me up and ask if I would let her have seventy-five dollars."

"Did you?"

"Yes, I did."

"And at this time, did you send her a telegram, telling her to come to Chicago and wait for you here?"

"No, I don't think that I did."

It was here that the judge turned and asked Jack to say yes or no as to whether he had sent the telegram to Belle. Johnson answered:

"I know that I didn't send such a telegram, Your Honor. But it is possible that one of my associates could have sent one without my knowledge."

"When you sent her the seventy-five dollars," his lawyer asked, "did you have any intentions that she should come here for immoral purposes, either collectively or individually?"

"No, I did not."

"When you did come to Chicago, about this time, did you come to see Belle Schreiber?"

"No, I came to make arrangements for a boxing match."

"Did you hunt her up?"

"No. It was she who called me on the telephone. She wanted me to fix up a flat for her and her sister and her mother to live in. I spent about a thousand dollars fixing up her flat. And then gave her five hundred dollars more in cash to keep her going until she could get a job as a stenographer."

Then came the prosecutor with his cross-examination.

"Rather than a gesture of friendship, didn't you fix up that apartment as an investment against Miss Schreiber's future earnings as a prostitute?"

"No, that is not true."

"Didn't you take twenty dollars from her, which she had earned immorally?"

"No. I never took a dollar or a newspaper from her. What would I want with twenty dollars, when I was earning twenty-five hundred dollars a week?"

Then little Belle Schreiber was brought to the stand. They had drilled her well. She went down a list, reciting like from a textbook, of the times and places that Jack had taken her or sent for her to meet him. The bitch remembered every single date, day, time and place to the hour. Almost to the minute that she came and the very minute that she left. She even had the train schedules memorized to the point that would have put a railroad station master to shame.

She even had memorized the cost of the hotel-room-rates and the price of the dinners, breakfast and lunches in the hotel suites, even though she was not the one who paid the bills.

She spoke of it all, like it had been so dreary. As if it were something she did, but was unwilling to do, all that time.

"I was driven out of every house of disrepute in Pittsburgh, Cleveland, Oakland, New York, Philadelphia and other cities, because I had the reputation of being Jack Johnson's sweetheart. The customers did not want me; as bad as the places were, I was too bad to remain in them."

She even let a tear fall as she told that one.

So finally, in concluding his cross-examination of Belle, "Benny" Bachrach asked her in a sympathetic tone,

"Miss Schreiber, did you love Jack Johnson?"

"No," was her reply. "I don't believe that I did. I don't even believe that I -ver knew what love was."

The most hopeful thirg in the trial was when Judge Carpenter addressed the jury with the remarks:

"This court instructs the jury that a colored man has equal rights with a white man under the law. The court protects him, just as it does a white man. A verdict should be rendered as if the defendant were a man of your own color."

Within a couple of hours, the jury returned, and Jack's hopes died, for the jury showed that what the judge had said could be interpreted two ways:

A colored man had just as much right to be convicted as a white man. They proved it by finding Jack Johnson guilty.

The judge then announced that on June 4th of the year 1913, he would pass his sentence on the guilty one, Jack Johnson. Which was just short of one month away, this being May.

The underworld took bets, as the newspapers reported, that under the conditions, Jack Johnson was not going to jail.

But sentence time proved that even the big bettors can be wrong, for Carpenter open the proceedings by denying Johnson's attorneys a motion for a new trial, and delivered the remarks, which chilled the icy winds that swept over the Windy City:

"It is always an unpleasant duty for me to say," he stated, "to say what sentence meted out will compensate our government, for a violation of its laws." He went on:

"The crime of which the defendant, by his own admission, stands convicted, is an aggravating one, has been such as to merit condemnation. We have had a number of defendants found guilty in this court of violations of the Mann Act who have been sentenced from one to two years in the penetentiary. And some have been freed, to go without punishment as circumstances warranted.

"But, in this case, the defendant is one of the best

known men of his race, and his example has been far reaching, and the court is bound to consider the position he occupied among his people. In view of these facts, this case calls for more than just a fine.

"Therefore I pass the sentence of 'one year and a day,' imprisonment in Joliet Penitentiary, plus a fine of one thousand dollars. So be it."

"Benny" Bachrach, the Attorney for The Big Smoke, then begged and was granted a two week's stay of execution to allow himself time to make a formal plea, "a bill of error," in order to carry the case to the United States Supreme Court, by first seeking a reversal of the conviction in the Circuit Court of Appeals. It was granted. Fourteen days of freedom, on a continuing bail of thirty thousand, the bond given at time of his indictment.

CHAPTER FIFTEEN

JUSTICE IS A WHITE WOMAN

I had always believed that "Justice was a White Woman." I am a Nigger. So I was seldom allowed in her company. Being a Nigger, I have always addressed her as "Mis' Justice. . . . Chap. XI, THE NIGGER BIBLE

They claim that "Justice is a White Woman" as far as a Black man is concerned. And this surely was the fact in Jack's case. He loved Justice as well as the next man. And most of the time, Justice loved him.

Still, when Justice betrayed him, that revealed him as a God. For what else is a betrayal but a true revelation of God?

Now, Jack was forced to call the white woman by her proper name: "Mis' Justice."

He now had two weeks to win the beautiful white hand of Justice. Folks told him that he didn't stand a chance of winning the lady.

His mother "Tiny" even warned him:

"Jack, you're black, my son. You're appealing for Justice. But your appeals in the white man's courts won't work. For when your appeal comes on, they are going to uphold your conviction. And that will be the end of you as a man.

"You are out, free on bail. But you still hold the crown. You'll still hold the crown, if you get out of the United States where they can't touch you or take your championship from you."

The old woman nodded towards Lucille, sitting in the chair across from her:

"This girl here is a symbol of the crown and justice. Take her, and y'all get the devil away, from out of this country."

"But, it's you that I'm thinking of," the champion said to his mother. "I don't want to part from you. To me, that's worse than prison or death, mama."

The old woman walked over, reached up and stroked his cheek.

"To me, the worst thing in the world would be for me to know that you were in prison. And if you stay here, that's where you'll end up. In prison! What good are you gonna be to me there?"

"But they still might acquit me," he protested. "The lawyers say. . . ."

"The lawyers say?" she interrupted him. "What do I care what white lawyers have to say. Lawyers are liars, they get paid for that. You'll go to prison, and that will kill me just as sure as putting a bullet in my heart."

The Champion turned to his young wife, Lucille.

"What do you think, honey?"

"Like your mother says, Jack. We've got to get out. I'm going with you, Jack, wherever you go. But like mama says, "We've got to fly.' "

The Black King turned back and looked down upon the head of his mother, whose hair had turned completely grey.

"But when would I see you again?"

The old woman shrugged. "Who knows but my God? Or maybe some of those white politicians you got so much faith in."

The Big Smoke turned to the window, in agony and indecision.

"But it'll look like I'm running away. I don't run away from nothing. Especially when I'm leaving you here to face the music."

"It is running away!" The eyes of the old woman were now flashing fire. "But once you're out of this country, there will be no more music to face."

He then turned from the window. His mind was made up.

"I'll go . . . tonight . . . or tomorrow night, if possible."

Lucille rose and went to stand with him at the window, taking his huge hand.

"The police are still walking up and down out there, watching. The Ku Klux Klan has said that you'd better leave town. Isn't that funny? While the law says that you'd better stay in town and face your sentence."

The old lady walked over to join them.

"You don't have nary a choice, just a slim chance, son. And right now, you've got to take it, while you can."

That night, the three of them laid plans! The black mother, the white wife, and the black man who intended to remain champion of the world.

The next morning, Jack was up with the chickens, leaving the house, whistling, at about sun up, taking his usual walk. He headed on down to the Sporting Hotel Cafe on Washburn Ave, where all of the "Sporting Spades" of note and fame lived and hung out 24 hours of the day.

The Sporting Hotel Cafe was the Chicago headquarters of the American Giants, a professional Negro baseball team, which had defeated the pennant winners of "recognized" baseball, the Philadelphia Athletics, in 1902, led by Andrew Foster, the captain-owner-manager. He was later nicknamed "Rube," because he had defeated the famous white pitcher of that time, George "Rube" Waddell.

According to reports, Andrew "Rube" Foster was a dead ringer for Jack Johnson in physical appearance, and many times he had been mistaken for Jack Johnson in public.

Jack had seen "Rube" Foster perform a few times before. Negro sports had claimed, "Jack, he looks like your double!" Further boasting, "He organized his team up in Canada, before coming down here; all colored men, they can teach those white boys how to play their own game."

It wasn't difficult to be directed to Foster's hotel room and awaken him before breakfast, which Jack ordered to be sent up to the room while they talked and became acquainted. The champion laid out his predicament and his plans, prepared to back up his proposition with money.

"Now, lemme get this straight," "Rube" Foster finally said. "You want to take my place among the boys, after tomorrow's game, while we heading on back up to Canada?"

"That about sums it up, brother," Jack answered. "And it's gotta be then. Already, you must have read of my predicament in the newspapers, for sure."

"But you don't want to play baseball on my team, and you don't want me to go into any boxing ring, as you. Right?"

Johnson laughed. "That's for sure, man. Otherwise, somebody might catch on as to what's happening."

"Rube" Foster laughed and then inquired:

"Now, what am I to do while you're getting yourself across the border, in the meantimes."

"You'll go to my cabaret. It's not open for business, so I'll give you a note to my manager. He'll see that no one comes intruding on your privacy."

"Rube" Foster rose and went to take a long look out of the hotel window.

"I've got a wife and kids, man. A family to support. I don't want to face no prison terms."

"Why should you, man. All niggers look alike to white folks. They can't put you in jail for 'mistaken identity.' "

"But why should I even take the risk, brother?"

Jack pulled out the huge roll of bills from his pockets.

"Oh, I brought along a few reasons with me. A little honorarium, which is what I had in mind, to relieve you of any mental distress you might develop and come up with."

The black baseball player shook his head.

"Keep your dough, man. I've got nothing against money. But, us Negroes don't get much'a chance at helping another brother out of a jam. If things do go wrong, then I'd like to say truthfully that I didn't do this thing that I'm doing simply for my love of the money."

The next two days were filled with haste, preparing for the plan to work smoothly, supervised by Tiny, the black dowager queen, drawing money from the banks, packing trunks of clothes and valuables, shipping, phone calls, telegrams and the like.

Lucille had little trouble going to and fro, departing the country with most of their possessions.

Two days later, The Champion made his slip. Pretending to drive out of town for a week of fishing up at Silver Lake, he switched to become one of the laughing, joking, light-hearted members of the American Giants, as he carried a load of baseball bats and trophies aboard the train, bound for the Canadian border.

The champion had reserved a private car for exclusive use of the team, while his nephew Gus Rhodes had reserved private suites on another car of the train.

He had given "Rube" Foster his suit and coat, along with his large diamond ring, tie stick-pin and jeweled watch before the switch. The federal men followed "Rube" back to Johnson's club, while the fast train sped on into the night toward New York and Canada, by way of Buffalo. The champion went on to join Gus Rhodes in the private drawing-room and went to sleep.

They crossed the Canadian border. And as officials came aboard to inspect the baggage, which was placed outside the drawing-room door, Gus Rhodes stood there with the tickets, informing the inspectors that the occupant of the car was ill and should not be disturbed. They departed the train, accepting this explanation.

At Hamilton, Ontario, they left the train on the "blind side" and picked up an automobile, as pre-arranged, by Tom Flannigan, a friend of Johnson's who had attended every championship fight ever held in his lifetime. Flannigan drove them to Toronto where he owned the hotel at which Johnson was to stay. The date was July 1, 1913.

It was here that Lucille, his wife, joined him. They remained in Toronto until late in the evening, boarding a train bound for Montreal, where a porter got a glimpse of him and his party and went shouting the news of Jack Johnson's presence in the city.

They were shortly besieged by reporters and immigration officials. He gave a signed interview to *The Montreal Star,* explaining the reasons for his trip. Immediately, he was arrested and detained, temporarily, by a justice of the peace, but after a few hours he was freed, when attorneys furnished in advance by Tom Flannigan appeared and obtained his release upon the grounds, "There is no official demand for Mr. Johnson's return to the United States."

Then, officials were shown the tickets, good for passage from Chicago to Paris. Bonds were produced, backed by Tom Flannigan. Under law, the Canadian officials could do nothing to hold him and allowed him to continue on his way.

The champion chuckled later, recalling the incident:

"Those lawyers of Flannigan talked me loose so fast that the J.P. had his head swimming before they finished.

"The Chicago and federal authorities didn't even know that I had left town until they read it in the Canadian newspapers."

Then, Johnson's name once again hit the American fan, causing a world-wide sensation. Accusations flew thick and fast. Prosecutors raved and cursed each other. Federal men blamed the municipal officials. And vice-versa, made all the worse when a rumor leaked out that

Jack had paid a ten thousand dollar bribe to certain politicians. For there was a rule of the underworld at the time, substantiated by Al Capone and the likes:

"For ten thousand, anything can be fixed."

One hundred white passengers were set to sail aboard the *Corinthian* at the Montreal wharf, curious and enthusiastic as to the identity of the passenger-party coming aboard with more than 18 trunks, two lavishly expensive automobiles and other things, until they learned that the party was that of Jack Johnson, his white wife, and his nephew, Gus Rhodes, bound for Le Havre.

"A single white woman and two nigger men, in one party? Unheard of and nothing short of disgraceful!"

The passengers screamed their protests to the captain of the ship. Reverberations of the protests reached back as far as Chicago, to be of some comfort to U.S. District Attorney Elwood Goodman, who summed up the official American attitude as to Johnson's jumping bail to escape:

"This may solve the whole affair. The passengers may mutiny and heave him away on an iceberg."

Immediately after sailing, the white passengers held meetings, protesting and objecting to being seated for their meals with Johnson's party, which was reported to Johnson by the captain with apologies:

"Tell those Paris-bound bastards not to worry. The champion and his party prefer to have their meals served in our staterooms, while en route," Johnson told him.

When the captain had closed the door of the stateroom, Lucille tossed herself upon Johnson's chest, her arms encircling him:

"We are 'The Three Muskeeteers.' "

"Maybe so, honey," her husband answered solemnly. "But what we really are is 'three fugitives from justice,' fleeing from home and fortune. What we find in England and Europe as a way of living is anybody's guess."

"Oh, baby. The champion of the world, is somebody that any and everybody in the world would want to see. And they'll pay money to see him, too, baby."

Gus Rhodes said wisely: "Lu, I hope you're right. You've been right so far. But Jack's got a whole lot of accounts against him in England, too."

"We'll see what we shall see," The Big Black Fire said seriously. "But at least we're putting an ocean between us and the trouble we've been running away from."

CHAPTER SIXTEEN

THE BLACK EMPEROR IN EXILE

It was the 10th of July, 1913, when the *Corinthian* dropped anchor at the port of Le Havre, France, marking the return of the The Black Fire to the Caucasian continent, ending the first leg of his journey into exile, while marking the beginning of many more flights yet to come.

The black champion looked from his port-hole, observing the wharfs, where hundreds of French *gendarmes* were assembled:

"Y'all come look and get ready," he called to his wife and his nephew.

"They sure turn out in numbers a plenty, when they come to get Jack Johnson," he laughed sardonically. "And look at the folks out there who's come to see it."

"Maybe they've all just come to greet you. It's not often people get a chance to greet the heavy-weight champion of the world, you know."

"Let's hope that the lady is right, Jack," Gus Rhodes ventured, as the signal to go ashore was sounded.

She was right. The *gendarmes* had gathered to hold back the crowds assembled there to greet and cheer the arrival of a king, welcoming the return of the pilgrim to the homeland.

French theatrical and fight promotors rushed forward waving contracts and written offers to sponsor the personal appearances of the champion, who had arrived with more than one truck-load of clothing and personal valuables, two new custom made automobiles and approximately seventy thousand dollars.

Thousands were willing to pay to see him.

Johnson immediately went in to rehearsals with a new revised edition of the musical revue written by him, retaining its original title: *Seconds Out,* which would feature Lucille in the role originally played by Etta Duryea Johnson.

While in rehearsals, they became the toast of Paris, touring the cafés and concert halls.

One evening, while attending the *Folies-Bergère* with Lucille, he was spotted in the audience by the star, Mistinguette, "the lady with the most beautiful legs in the world," who called him to the stage to share her curtain calls, announcing that Jack would soon appear in the *Folies* with her in his new forthcoming revue, *Seconds Out.*

Although he did open his revue at the *Folies,* Lucille

was his female lead instead. Mistinguette never came to forgive him for that.

Gaby Desly, the famous French actress, who had once frequented Johnson's quarters and *joie de fille* at his *Café de Champion* in Chicago, during her tour of America, hounded him daily. And much to her chagrin, Jack remained "fairly faithful" to his beautiful young wife, Lucille.

Jack Johnson's revue, *Seconds Out*, did open at the *Folies* very shortly as Mistinguette had predicted, but only for a very brief stay. This was decided on opening night before a sell-out crowd of theatrical celebrities, just prior to the curtain call, during the final act of the revue.

Lucille, Johnson's wife, appeared in a costume of simulated, glittering oyster shells, designed to fall away as she performed a torrid and frenzied dance, eventually revealing her beautiful and well shaped body.

Then, as a climax, amidst fanfare and music, Johnson leaped onto the stage dressed in a leopard-skin jungle costume, taking his beautiful white wife by the waist, and he delivered his lines at the finale:

"Lil Arthur is a loving man!"

The result was bedlam. The theatre audience went into uproar and protest at such conduct and "bad taste," ironically in a theatre traditionally renowned for featuring female nudes and semi-nudes as a specialty in fabulous musicals.

"Mais non! Mais non!" The audience shrilled. "Out! Down! Out of the follies. Out of the theatre! Out! Run them out of town!" they shouted.

And *Seconds Out* was out of the *Folies* and out of Paris within a few nights. Its Parisian performance was sealed a few evenings later, when a few French thugs gathered around the theatre hurling insults at Lucille Johnson objected to the insults. The crowd took sides.

A general melee occured with Jack slinging punches in
self-defense until the *gendarmes* arrived wielding their
lead-weighted billy-clubs and brought the disturbance
under control. Johnson was exonerated and sent on his
way. But he was asked to take his revue along with him
and away from Paris. He shook his head, remarking
and laughing in bewilderment:

"Can you imagine a damn Frenchman being shocked
at anything?"

He also shook his head in wonder at the expert manner in which the Frenchmen could kick each other during the fight. And was intrigued with this particular
method of combat.

So, while taking his "Paris boot-out" good naturedly, he turned his attention across the channel to dear old
England, to open his revue in the London concert halls.

Most London newspapers tried to discourage him, to
no avail, although their sentiments were summed up
conclusively by a prominent Britisher named Winston
Churchill:

"Jack Johnson is not welcome to these, our shores."

But The Big Black Fire ignored Winston Churchill's
statement for the time being, also the objections of the
Variety Artists' Federation, which expressed not only
its astonishment, but resentment when they learned that
the famous promoter Frederic Tozer had signed Johnson and his act to perform in the halls of London and
the surrounding areas on tour, paying him a salary of
one thousand pounds a week. A fee which their own
performers could never demand.

The moral reform and Christian church groups joined
in this protest when Jack and his party arrived in
London. Then The Big Smoke and his promoters called
an English press conference where Johnson issued his
first public statement:

"I am surprised and shocked at the attitude of my

'fellow artists,' with whom I have previously been on excellent terms. Here in England, when you speak of *The White Slave Act*, the people are naturally shocked. But when they speak of *The White Slave Laws*, in the United States, that means something entirely different from what you have here. And I assure you that there is really no need for any good clergyman to squirm and be shaken up about. . . ."

Then Jack sat down and dictated a letter to his wife, addressed to one of England's most prominent clergy who had led the objections to his presence:

Dear Sir:

As a visitor in London, I have read in several newspapers your personal views regarding my character and so forth. I would like very much, sir, for you to come to an audience with me for one half hour, namely, Wednesday afternoon, at 4:00 o'clock p.m. I am also asking the Press to be present.

Yours Truly,

Champion Jack Arthur Johnson

For the record the minister never responded. There was grave concern on the part of the promoter, Tozer, and his partner, Albert Jenkins, who worriedly showed Jack an editorial in the *London Times*, captioned:

Changing Conventions in the Ball-Room.

The writer of the editorial expressed his distaste for "The Turkey Trot," which he heard was performed by little "chillens" in the streets of America. But were forbidden to do so by police, and the respectable element of colored people in Washington D.C. "With the presence of Johnson, England will undoubtly see more of the abominations performed in our ballrooms."

Jack was learning, along with his promoters, Tozer and Jenkins, that racial intolerance worked on hearsay, as much in England and Europe as it did in his native land.

Now, even though they had invested their money and signed contracts to sponsor Johnson with a guarantee, they started to "run scared" as to England's reaction to Jack Johnson.

Then Jack took charge and came up with the decision to visit the *Euston Theatre of Varities* as a guest, to check out the reactions of the people. He was merely going as a member of the audience.

He had box seats reserved for himself, his two promoters, his wife and nephew, Gus Rhodes. When the rowdy musical hall audience spotted him, sitting there "resplendent in white tie and tails," he had his white wife "all decked out in diamonds and jewels that would put a clear, starry night to shame," the audience made such an uproar that the performers were forced to cut their act short.

Jack Johnson was called to the stage, as he had anticipated he would be.

The applause was prolonged, loud, wildly welcoming, drowning the few cries of dissent as he approached center stage.

"My only crime . . . my only real crime, was beating a man called Jim Jeffries . . . Thank you. Thank you."

The cheers were intensified.

"The palms and the feet of all people are white! Unless somebody paints them black with a tar-brush."

Pandemonium broke out in the galleries, as his supporters used fists and violence to silence the objectors.

As The Big Fire stood center stage, smiling, a semi-riot occurred in the galleries, shortly quelled by the swinging clubs of the bobbies. His promoters got the point. He had proved himself fit as an attraction to invade the music halls of London and England. But not without some reservations. For no music hall owner wanted to risk presenting him with the threat and possibility of a riot on their hands. However, some finally chanced it.

Much to the distress of his tormentors and enemies, his stage revue, *Seconds Out,* opened and drew turnaway crowds wherever it appeared. The English fans drooled over his performances as he became one of the most celebrated vaudeville performers of his time—after only a few weeks in London. In the interim he was invited to tea by the Duke of Devonshire.

He toured the countryside, playing to "standing room only " crowds, with consecutive bookings which earned him more than eight thousand pounds a week. He was installed as a Freemason and he played engagements in London, Birmingham, Manchester, Edinburgh, Leeds, and other places.

Still, his promoters Tozer and Jenkins were cautious, and proceeded with extreme caution when booking him in the London metropolitan area.

The English Free Church and The Swansea Watch Committee had demonstrated publicly against his appearances. The underpaid English press reporters took offense at his fine clothes and jewelry and automobiles.

The Big Black Fire created a sensation wherever he went with his excellent shoes, hats, and suits, fashioned by the world's best tailors, hatters and shoemakers. Some newspaper critics called him an "American flash nigger," for his expensive tastes in dress and jewelry defied every rule of "proper British form of dress." For example, he strolled the afternoons down Piccadilly, tapping the pavement with a silver-headed walking-stick, wearing shoes made of soft doeskin and crocodile leather, in a biscuit colored silk suit, a pale soft golden hat, "Trilby style," while a silk bandana trailed in the breeze from his upper jacket pocket, an orchid in his lapel.

Other days he would drive in his snow-white Mercedes-Benz touring car, top folded back to reveal the black and white zebra skin upholstery. While many would stop and cheer, others would gawk and stare, some tossing verbal insults.

"He sullies the fair name of London and its environs." One newspaper editorial remarked, "We do not appreciate his presence here."

This sentiment was echoed in the hallowed halls of the British Parliament by Sir John Simon, Home Secretary, and the Great British statesman, Winston Churchill.

Still, The Big Smoke had supporters in Parliament, for negotiations were underway in 1913 to match him with the Commonwealth champion, "Bombadier Billy" Wells. To make this possible Lord Hugh Cecil Lonsdale, donor of the famous Lonsdale Championship Belt, along with Sir Hiram Maxim, the machine-gun tycoon, performed one of the most heroic diplomatic feats in the history of the Parliament, overriding the objectors to the fight, which was to be sponsored under the auspices of The National Sporting Club.

They even convinced *The London Times* to editorialize:

"England should not be concerned with intimidating this man . . . who has been victimized by the racial injustices perpetrated upon him by our former colonies in America."

New doors swung open when Jack Johnson announced his intentions of fulfilling his former manager's commitment to fight under the promotion of the National Sporting Club.

Within one week he was playing to packed houses and standees at Rocherville Gardens in Gravesend, hobnobbing in between and after shows with the highbrows of London's court.

Lord Lonsdale had told him:

"Everything is going to be all right now. In such cases, we sportsmen must stick together. I want you to tell me all about your encounter with Jim Jeffries."

But Jack Johnson was unfailing in his willingness to antagonize and avenge himself upon those among the British highbrows who had despised him. Also, "the lackeys" of the American Embassy, who dared not refuse to attend any of the functions where he was to be guest of honor.

As Mark Hellinger the famous writer put it:

The Big Boy was still behaving like a '4-11 fire' in a lard factory.

One story is told concerning the first time that Johnson met Sir Claude de Crespigny (Lord Tweedmouth) at tea in London.

The British nobleman, so annoyed with Johnson's arrogance and conceit, and elegant attire—"a black with patrician's bearings" (it is also suspected that Johnson had been sleeping with Lord Tweedmouth's favorite mistress), attempted to find a way of insulting and "putting down" the champion.

He boasted of his possessions, his heritage, among them the many black slaves formerly owned by his family, along with "other cattle," and a shooting preserve which surrounded his baronial castle and estates, for his favorite sport of "killing wild beast and fowl."

"Indeed?" The black champion responded after listening for more than half hour.

"I just cleared six-hundred thousand dollars beating Jim Jeffries," Johnson informed him, then slapping the Britisher on the back in a fashion of familiarity.

"Tell you what I'll do, Tweedmouth. I'll flip, one toss of the coin. Yours against mine. How about it?"

After that little encounter with the British nobleman, his sensational success as a London show piece was not long lived, as his indifference to "the sensitive feelings of English aritsocracy" proved to be a drastic oversight.

But this oversight did not keep Jack Johnson from noticing that immediately after his social encounter with "Tweedmouth," the anti-Johnson demonstrations were intensified, which included a group of London ruffians, who awaited his departure from the theatre and followed him and his wife through the streets hurling angry insults and threats. Two nights later, the confrontation ensued.

On this particular night Lord Lonsdale had been so pleased with his success at making Jack Johnson a socially acceptable "item" of the Commonweath, he played host to an elegant dinner party at his London Carlton House flat.

Johnson arrived late, banging on the door. Then knocking the manservant flat on his back as he burst into the room, shouting:

"Closed for the night!" Before slamming, or trying to slam the door shut and falling into a roomful of distinguished guests, mud spattered and bleeding, with clothing torn.

But he was followed by a group of constables. The officers were torn and bleeding also.

"What is this outrage?" Lord Lonsdale demanded.

"It is about everything, sir," the sergeant of police panted. "This man attacked the patrons outside the theatre, then struck down the manager of the Oxford Music Hall. When we tried coshing him, he snatched away our clubs knocking down two of our men into the orchestra pit, from the stage. One of them has experienced a broken jaw."

"We pursued him," another officer added, "all the way from Shaftesbury avenue to here, worse luck. For another of our squad is stretched, injured, out here in front of your house."

"Then, tell them about the thugs that you didn't stop from attacking me!" Johnson shouted.

The sergeant ignored him, producing a paper from his pocket.

"And what is more, sir. Here is an injuction from the Swansea Watch Society and several groups, prominent among the English Church."

"And the charges?" Lonsdale mustered his courage. "What are the charges?"

"Obscenity! Obscenity is the charge, sir," replied the sergeant. "The obscene dance which this man and his wife performed on stage, this evening . . . she, wearing a 'shell flaking gown,' gyrating her body until all the shells of the costume fell away, leaving her body exposed. Then, sir, he in an animal skin, scantily covering his body, embracing the equally scantily-clad body of his wife, crying out that he was a 'loving' man. . . ."

"Hell, that's the end of our act every night," protested Johnson.

"And that is the end of your stay here in London," Sir Hiram stated to Johnson.

"In fact, you'll never get another fight here, in all England!"

The Big Black Fire smiled, rubbing the bruised knuckles of his hand, then scanned the eyes of the bruised and bleeding English constables.

"You are finished here in England," Sir Hiram shouted through his mutton-chop whiskers. "Finished, you understand that?"

"Well, I don't know, Sir Hiram. If I were you, I wouldn't put it that way exactly, if I were you. . . ."

On the following day, the Secretary of Home Affairs

and Winston Churchill signed papers giving Jack Johnson just 24 hours to leave His Majesty's soil.

Churchill even tried, unsuccessfully, to have the petition read that ". . . under penalty of arrest, Jack Johnson be denied entrance to every part of the British Empire."

As a result of his head-on clash with "The British Lions," there came a wave of public demands for theatrical appearances and boxing exhibition bouts for Johnson from every principal city on the continent of Europe. He filled them obligingly with a tour that covered Paris, Marseilles, Brussels, St. Petersburg, Barcelona, Madrid, Moscow, to name a few.

He arrived in St. Petersburg (which was then called Petrograd) just in time to receive an invitation to the annual Grand Duke Alexis Ball, through the unquestionable influence of George Thomas, a Negro who hailed from the United States and Georgia, who had come to Russia as a valet and climbed to become one of the country's most prominent and wealthiest sports and theatrical promotors and a confidant of Russian nobility and the court, which included Tsar Nicholas himself.

"Jack, son, I want you to meet everybody of importance here," George Thomas declared upon Jack's arrival. "I know them all, including the Tsar himself, who has expressed his wish to meet you. You'll be my prize sensation."

And according to form, Johnson was just that. Especially with the beautiful females of the court, much to the distress of his young wife, Lucille.

"Those Russian women of the Tsar's court just wouldn't let him be," Gus Rhodes commented later. "And from all impressions, Jack didn't want them to let him be. Lucille was getting her first lesson. 'No woman in the world could bring my uncle under complete control.' "

On the night of the Grand Duke's Ball, George Thomas told him in confidential manner:

"Tonight, there is someone special that you might see and meet with. I'll give you one guess. Who do you think?"

"Perhaps the Tsar himself," Johnson suggested.

"No. Not the Tsar tonight. But, somebody equal to, if not more important than, the Tsar. Just stand by and watch. I'll give you the signal, when and if he decides to attend."

The black champion waited with interest, when not ogling the women in attendance, while they ogled back, which took up most of his time. Lucille complained of a headache and Gus Rhodes drove her back to the hotel.

In the meantime, the champion did not know that he was being observed by a giant of a bearded man, who could boast the physical proportions of Jim Jeffries. And whose weird, wild eyes bored into him with seeming hostility.

The Grand March was announced. As formal introductions were called out, George Thomas rushed over to him:

"That's him, man. He's been eyeing you all night. That's Grigori Efimovitch Rasputin. The most powerful man in all of Russia. He hypnotizes. And's got himself in control of Tsarina Alexandra, for healing her son. Now he dominates all of Russia's politics and politicians." Thomas continued as Jack turned to study Rasputin, "The Mad Monk of Russia," of whom he had already read.

"Man, he's known as 'The Holy Devil.' And when it comes to women, he's worse than Satan himself. The talk of his orgies with young peasant virgins and rapings such as Russia's never heard of before. Quiet as it's supposed to be kept."

"Well, hell, Georgie," Johnson laughed. "You know

that I ain't supposed to be any kind of saint myself. Get up and go guide the man over this way. I'll be more than glad to shake hands with him."

"No, Jack. That's not the procedure and protocol. When the Grand March is over, you're supposed to get up and go over to him."

The black champion turned his attention back to the line of notables, the women of the court, now being introduced and parading around the ballroom.

"Oh, I suspect that he'll be coming over this way if he wants to meet me, in particular," he commented.

His calculations were correct, for as the procession rounded the ballroom floor, Rasputin disengaged himself, signaling a body guard-aide, who joined him as he approached the black man, who was eagerly waiting to display his conversational Russian, which he had learned in three weeks so that he no longer required an interpreter.

Rasputin's aide attempted to act as an interpreter and stepped back, amazed that Johnson answered him in Russian, as the "Mad Monk" observed with amused admiration. The introductions were made.

"We two are very much alike," The Holy Devil said to the black one, continuing.

"In my philosophy, one must first sin, in order to repent and gain forgiveness. . . . It is what we term among us here as, *Khlysty!*"

Rasputin raised a glass from the table to toast his remark.

Johnson laughed and reached for his own glass, raising it, then slapped the Russian on the shoulder.

"Khylsty, you call it. That's pretty good," he said in Russian. "I've tossed myself a few parties in my time, too, your highness."

"Only back in my country, it isn't called *Khlysty* or anything like that. It's got another name coined and named by a politican of the same name called James Mann. I am so damned illegal back home in the United States, that they even cut all of my pictures out of the school books, so the kids won't even know what I look like."

The two giants both laughed and toasted themselves again, while members of the court stood gawking.

"Excellent, excellent!" Rasputin exclaimed "Like me, you will be imperishable in history. You must remain and enjoy a bit of revelry here with me."

While The Big Black Fire considered the invitation issued to him by The Mad Monk, that evening he confessed to losing one of the few "man-to-man" encounters with a white man during his lifetime, as he spent the remainder of that fatal night attempting to match Rasputin drink for drink in the many vodka toasts they sat saluting each other with, until long after daybreak.

He went on to admit that he spent the next two days in bed recuperating before he was able to "pursue further social intercourse and philosophical discourses with Rasputin as to the virtues and finer points of *Khylsty*."

Within a week the champion reluctantly departed Petrograd and Rasputin's revelries to complete the remainder of his tour, promising Russia's "Man of Destiny" to return immediately to resume their activities as soon as he had finished his concert bookings and disposed of a couple of challengers in Paris. The tour ended in Vienna, and they soon left for Germany where the Big Smoke went into a bit of training preparing for his forthcoming fight with a young Negro-American by the name of Jim Johnson.

It was here in Germany, while performing his early morning roadwork, that he and his nephew, Gus Rhodes, began to notice the enormous predawn troop movements and maneuvers indicating the forthcoming World War I.

But there were other things to occupy his attention while training in Germany. He developed a taste for Rhine wine and schnapps, extended by a greater appreciation of Nordic female beauty. "Pink toes, blue eyes and flaxen-gold hair."

Within a very short time, he was daily newspaper copy as the foremost German exponent of Rasputin's philosophy, *Khlysty*.

Lucille resigned herself to looking after their business affairs, as she was seldom a part of his social life, for a period of time.

Early one morning, while Jack was doing his roadwork, a Nordic beauty came along, riding her horse. Jack sent Gus Rhodes back home with the car, and, being Jack Johnson, one thing led to another. She introduced herself as Mata Hari, and he accompanied her to her home nearby.

This became a daily habit for a time—this pleasant diversion from his morning roadwork. The affair did not last more than a few weeks—and it was not until much later that Jack came to realize that this had been no chance meeting. He had looked on it as merely an enjoyable interlude but Mata Hari certainly had intentions of a more serious nature—for this was the same Mata Hari who was executed by the Germans near the end of the war. She was executed by a firing squad for espionage, and she has since become something of a legend as being one of the most beautiful—and most successful—spies in the history of the modern world.

After Mata Hari, Jack had taken up with a "voluptuous Gretchen" whose steady lover, before his arrival, was a *kapitan* of the Kaiser's Fourth Dragoons. This blow to German military pride could not be tolerated.

One morning upon leaving Gretchen's flat after having his fill of "her food, fancy wine and her fine fanny," he was confronted on the stairs by her enraged lover, the *kapitan* himself, prepared for combat.

With his cocksure arrogance, the champion eyed him coldly and spoke:

"If I were you, Fritz, I wouldn't bother to go up," he advised the German. "You'd be following too good an act."

Then he lashed out, catching the German officer with a stunning blow that disengaged him from his drawn sword. But the *kapitan* had taken precautionary insurance against this.

Obviously, he had considered his chances before coming face-to-face with the heavyweight champion. For as he was felled by the black man's blow, as if on signal, Dragoons sprang out from the bushes and shrubbery which lined the walk, with swords bristling for destruction.

The Black Fire let out a war-whoop, waking up the ever faithful Gus Rhodes, asleep behind the wheel of Johnson's white Benz, parked but a short distance away.

Gus fired the motor as the champion came ducking, dodging, swinging and running, strewing members of the Fourth Dragoons in his wake.

He sped away seeking other sites to continue his physical training away from Germany for the time being. For he had not simply demolished an ordinary suitor, he had besmirched the battle reputation of "Kaiser Bill's" Dragoons, while striking a military officer.

They raced toward Paris, with Johnson driving, his wife and nephew accompanying him, speeding as the champion loved to do, going more than 80 miles an hour. The car went out of control, sailing over a 50-foot embankment.

The last words that Gus and Lucille remembered

hearing before waking up in the hospital later was the champion's cry:

"Hold your hats! Here we go. . . ."

The car was demolished completely. Gus and Lucille were injured enough to be hospitalized, while The Black Fire walked from the wreckage, unhurt but for "one or two bruises," which he didn't take seriously.

One of the bruises he had not taken seriously enough, was revealed in his fight with Jim Johnson during the third round of their scheduled 10 round title bout, one of the most severe ordeals of his ring career.

He attempted to deliver one of his devastating "Mary Anns," a left hand punch designed by the champion, which consisted of throwing his punch to the extended biceps of an opponent, continuing on with a follow through in one motion to land on the jaw.

As he caught Battling Jim Johnson coming in, he delivered it, successfully crashing it up against the "granite-like skull" of the challenger, breaking the arm, at the small semi-fracture resulting from the automobile wreck, which had not completely healed.

He finished the fight with one arm broken, dangling helplessly at his side. Jim Johnson had sensed his condition and stepped up the pace for the remaining seven rounds. But The Big Smoke was able to withstand and gain a draw in a referee's decision, while fighting his opponent with one hand.

The European reporters called it a dull affair. "Jack Johnson is at the end of his rope. Unconditioned, fat and slow, now ready to be taken by a good 'White Hope.' "

"He is ready to go!" the British editorials cried. Which caused the members of London's National Sporting Club to renew their interest in him. Even Sir Hiram and Winston Churchill relented, as did Parliament.

"Now, the nigger's fit to be tied and taken."

They wired forth offers to sponsor his fight with either Sam Langford, "The Boston Tar Baby," a totally tough Negro-American middleweight whom Johnson had beaten on occasions or "The New White Hope," Dr. Frank Moran, a dentist who displayed great aspirations to become the heavyweight champion of the world.

White people championed Sam Langford, who was considered the ugliest and most ferocious fighter in the world, and the most annihilating puncher of his time. Langford was only five feet, seven and a half inches tall. At his best weight, he was no more than a light-middle-weight. But he was willing to take on anybody. Once, his managers signed and engaged him to fight 18 fights in one week. Later in his life they were to send him into the right totally blind. The sight had gone from both of his eyes when they sent him in to fight a much younger opponent. Langford had fought more than 250 fights in his life-span. He ended up on relief in New York City.

In his later years he admitted that: "Jack Johnson gave me the only beating that I ever had in my life. But y'all got to remember that I was 28 pounds lighter than he was."

His white managers used to put a thousand dollars in his pocket and drive him around, following where Johnson was to appear and have him wave it in the champion's face, daring him to fight him again for the price, anywhere.

The Big Smoke always smiled apologetically and declined the offers, retreating, to the frustration of Langford and his managers, which newspaper reporters would report to their readers as signs that: "Jack Johnson is afraid to face Langford."

To a man, all reporters agreed that Sam Langford was a physical freak, "enough to frighten any mortal."

They cared not to remember that Johnson had floored Sam, while the referee "slowed his count." And Sam had to be placed on a stretcher and taken to the hospital at the end of the fight. Despite the fact, Johnson won by decision as the referee had timed his count so that Sam could be saved from a knockout by the bell.

But the British press joined sentiments with the American Press along with the National Sporting Club members, that Johnson repeat the performance against Langford, or give Dr. Frank Moran a fighting chance.

They felt more certain that the good dentist had better than an even chance, when Johnson agreed to the fight and asked for time to let his broken arm heal.

Now, with a broken arm healing, he was unable to perform stage work, much less fight, allowing any considerable time for recuperation, he would grow considerably short of funds at the rate that he lived.

The London Times summed up his fate: "Johnson can do nothing and has no where to go. His detestable habit of taunting his opponents, within the ring and out, is now able to be curtailed."

The National Sporting Club of London took the hint and offered Johnson a "pittance" guarantee of 3 thousand pounds to fight Langford.

The Times went further to suggest to the champion that despite the threats of the Free Church Council and The Swansea Watch Committee and of those people such as Churchill and Lord Hiram, that unless the champion committed a breach of peace or performed on stage in an indecent manner, there was nothing illegal about his returning to London.

The Times added:

"The tone which Jack Johnson has taken, communicating from Paris, with the National Sporting Club, is

such to preclude the possibility of his making a public reappearance in England."

But *The London Times* had neglected to report the real tone that was taken by the champion, as evidenced in the letter which he addressed to the N.S.C. from his headquarters in Paris:

A.F. Bettinson, Esq.,
National Sporting Club
Covent Garden, London

Dear Sir:

I received your letter this morning and I must say that the offer which you have made to me is ridiculous, absolutely, to my thinking. I have already defeated Langford, and not only that, Langford has been beaten four times in the last two years. He was beaten by Sam McVey in Australia; he was also defeated by Joe Jeanette on two different occasions in New York City, and not so long ago he was defeated by Gunboat Smith, in his own home town, Boston, and the only thing I can get out of the fight is money, because there will be no glory in defeating Langford as I have already done the trick.

And furthermore, the Club has gone so far as to make a match for me. They have also said there must be a 5 hundred pound side bet, and they have also dictated to me how much of the picture privileges I shall receive.

I am very proud that I have made all of my own matches. . . . I myself, being a real champion, do not see where your National Sporting Club has a right to dictate to me how much I shall recieve for my appearance and boxing ability.

If they do not want to give me my price. . . .

*which is 6 thousand pounds, win, lose or draw,
then they do not need to wait until March 1st; they
can immediately call things off upon receipt of this
letter.*

*.You must recall that I received the same identi-
cal conditions from Tommy Burns. . . . win, lose or
draw. I won my title under these conditions, and
any time that I do battle, it shall be under these
very same conditions and none other.*

*I am a boxing man now, and I am getting my
price. I don't care what the public thinks; I am the
one to be satisfied. I have defeated every man before the public with the exception of two, and one
of them is the man who beat Langford, Gunboat
Smith. The other is Frank Moran, who is considered in America the superior of Gunboat Smith,
and after my fight with Moran (which I feel sure
to win) I am going to fight Gunboat Smith, and I
am also going to get my price for that battle*

*Mr. C.B. Cochran, of the Olympia, London, has
5 thousand pounds. Why should I take only 3
thousand pounds from you?*

> *Yours truly,*
> *Jack Johnson,*
> *World's Heavyweight Champion*

But, in the meantime, while the British boxing press
and promoters fumed and fussed with "Jack Johnson's
nigger arrogance," Dan McKettrick, personal manager
for Frank Moran, was in and about Paris, distributing
more than three thousand, six hundred dollars into the
pockets of French newspapermen, trying to stimulate
interests in a Jack Johnson-Frank Moran title fight.

The French were simply responding with the question: *"Qui c'est Frank Moran?"*

McKettrick had observed the "sad performance" of Jack in his defeat of Battling Jim Johnson, a few months before. Then, taking estimate of the time it would take for Jack's broken arm to heal and the kind of wild life he was leading, McKettrick figured that he had the next world's heavyweight champion in his grasp, even though he had no contractual written agreement with Moran.

The Black Emperor was having his usual "press troubles" with Paris newspapers as he intensified his strenuous programs of *joie de vivre,* advancing Rasputin's philosophical theory and practice of *Khlysty* in the capital of France.

Having installed his wife and nephew in a villa at Asnieres, he had begun to reconsider the incomparable charms of the enchanting French beauty, Mistinguette, whom he noticed had sat whimpering as he suffered and inflicted punishment upon the body of Battling Jim Johnson a few months before. So, he had sent his calling card around to her hotel doorman, very shortly after the fight.

Mistinguette had responded admirably. For very shortly she and he were up to their necks in French Cabaret-Salon Society.

She introduced him again from the stage of the *Folies*. Rolling her beautiful eyes for benefit of the audience, she had declared him with the single, but adequate word: *"Formidable."*

He proved her point this time by acceptance to appear with her, booked as a feature of the *Folies Bergère,* "making muscles."

Then he proceeded to "extend the dreams of 'the girl with the world's most exciting legs' " by moving in to live at her *maison*. He even redecorated it, since he felt that he had developed a particular flair for modish design.

While Mistinguette publically taught him to dance the new-fangled tango, Johnson taught her privately and publically "the art of crapshooting," as they gambled nightly for high stakes among the underground habitués of the left bank.

The affair became so torrid that the French press and journals echoed the sentiments of England's Winston Churchill urging that Jack Johnson be expelled from, "not only Paris, but the soil of France."

Johnson retorted in "typical Johnsonian fashion":

"I thought that the French were *blasé*, in matters of this sort."

Still, he adhered to the suggestions and hints of the Paris newspapers, after a few squabbles had developed between himself and Mistinguette, following one in which she had threatened to jump from the roof of the *Folies Bergère*. So, he took her threat of suicide as serious, having experienced it with two other emotionally unstable Caucasian female lovers, by deciding to travel alone, away from Paris, while getting in condition for his anticipated and practically concluded title bout with Frank Moran.

He traveled under the guidance of the famous *Chicorita,* the Spanish matador on vacation, who had assured him that the warm climate of Southern Spain would be ideal for rounding himself into physical and mental shape for his championship match, while enjoying the beauties of Spain in the interim.

He left over the violent and emotional objections of Mistinguette, and leaving Gus and Lucille at the villa. To build up their depleting bankroll, he accepted a match. A wrestling match. He tried to explain it to his wife, Lucille:

"Just a little thing to tide us over, honey, until we finish with this bout with Frank Moran."

The bout was held in Spain, where Johnson had

enthroned himself and Chicorito in the palace of a "temporarily down on his boots Spanish nobleman."

This match became a blemish on the record of Jack Johnson as the bout featured "a multiplicity of fouls on behalf of the champion and Al Spoul the 300 pound wrestler," which ended with Johnson knocking him unconscious with a single punch. The records show Johnson winning by a knockout, even though it was supposed to be a wrestling match.

Even the wrestler forgot. For when he regained consciousness after the knockout punch, he accepted Johnson's apologies.

Jack arrived in Madrid to take up training residence at the villa of the Spanish nobleman. But his stay was short lived.

The Spanish grandee had noticed that each night, as he passed near his exquisite villa, he had heard "strange outcries from within." One night, he decided to enter and investigate matters.

There, he found his internationally famous tenant, along with his famous bullfighter companion, Chicorito, bathing and luxuriating in the main banquet hall, in a half-filled wine vat which they had brought up from the cellar and loaded it with his precious vintage wines, which he had carefully locked up before renting his place. Along with them, slashing about with them in the vat, were a half-dozen completely nude servant girls of his household.

Everything was ruined. The rugs, the crockery and the furniture. As the grandee ran screaming for the police, the black champion ran whooping to his fast car crying:

"*Adios,* muthafucka! *Diabolico. Adios,* Chicorito! 'Till the next time. *Adios!*"

He returned to Lucille and the villa in Asnières disheveled, grimy from dust and driving as a penitent, as she welcomed him with silent displeasure:

"He was like a big panda bear turned loose in a children's nursery. And as childish as a sorrowful big baby who had been caught misbehaving."

The three of them, Lucille, Gus and himself, recognized that the type of training program which he had been pursuing had put him in no condition to fight the title bout, which was only a few weeks away.

Still, while away on his adventures, he had not neglected to visit art galleries, "nosing in and out of picturesque places, chatting with famous artists, writers and theatrical folk, picking up curios and little gifts of art work, which he presented to Lucille for their expanding collections."

In May, he signed the concluding articles for his fight with Frank Moran, which was to take place in Paris on June 20th, the following month, coinciding with the end of the Grand Prix, 1914.

Despite the unpleasantly wet Paris weather, he entered the ring almost totally unconditioned. Yet, European experts and authorities agree, that it was one of the greatest fights ever staged by the black champion. But this was due to a few complicated and unforeseen conditions prior to the fight. And one of the few and first times that Johnson had nothing to do with them.

CHAPTER SEVENTEEN

SPYING ON THE RUN FROM SPYING

It all comes clear, that during this period, Jack Johnson was involved in spying.

His wife knew about it. She wanted what her husband wanted most, for both of them to get back into America together. So, she went along with her man while he made a play for it. By spying on one country for another.

Some speculate that it started in Petrograd while he was partying with Rasputin. Others say it started long before that, when he was invited to Russia by his friend the Negro promoter of prominence from the state of Georgia, USA. Still others say it didn't begin until he came from Russia to Germany. And that his roadwork training in the morning along the roads, was a cover so as to make observations of the movements of the troops.

They even claim that "Gretchen" was a spy, knowing that Johnson had come from Russia, socializing with the Tsar and Rasputin himself, but she wasn't able to make him open his mouth about any of it.

And since he had seen so much troop deployment, while doing his roadwork in the mornings, he wasn't supposed to get out alive. But, he did. And that perhaps explains why Gus Rhodes always slept out in the cold weather, waiting and sleeping in Jack's automobile, while Jack took care of "loving on the warm inside of a broad's apartment."

But one thing is certain. His spying activities were in evidence when Gus Rhodes and Lucille joined him in Paris after their accident and the fight with Jim Johnson.

As has been told, he took up again with Mistinguette of the *Folies Bergère*. He moved in with her, leaving Gus and Lucille at Asnières, only the French beauty had brought a man from the French Foreign Office who questioned him at intense intervals, concerning: His visits with George Thomas, Tsar Nicholas, Rasputin. Then, as to the reasons for his hasty departure and his stay and trouble in Germany, followed by the hasty retreat back to France. What had he observed?

Then Jack fled Mistinguette and Paris. He had planned to return only on the eve of the fight, win, take his gate receipts and move to other parts of the world. For now, the talk of a war was nearing a reality. And as usual, he was playing a part, while involving his wife and relative in it.

Now, 30 days prior to the bout, while back in Paris the interrogations and harrassments were resumed. He had hoped to keep his wife and nephew clear of the matter by the ruse of living alone or remaining in the company of other women.

Then, again, he was called upon by a company of men from across the English Channel. They came with offers, for these men revealed that they knew a war was imminent.

"And America will enter the war on our side," they told him (though this was not at all certain at that time). "Then, it is easily supposed, with your country as our ally, we should be able to resolve the major differences between your country and you. That is, after we have given them our recommendations along with your substantial record for cooperation as a patriot."

The champion fugitive considered and knew that he had no choice. Plus, he was tempted by the prospect of seeing his aged mother again before she died.

"What am I to do?" he asked.

"England will have forgiven you, after your forthcoming victory with Moran, should you bring it off," he was answered. "You will return to London for a brief theatrical engagement. There you will be instructed on what you are to do. We anticipate that you will be ordered to take a tour of Petrograd again. After that, who knows?"

The Big Black Fire got the message. Now he set about making his victory with Moran secure, for he was in the worst physical and mental condition of his fighting career. Which was not aided by the French Foreign Office and the press reporters, who continually made efforts to question him, concerning matters not related to his championship fight with the latest "White Hope."

The champion worried, drank and grew bloated from the drinking, while enduring the frequent talks with members of the French Military Intelligence.

Then he confided his plans to his wife and nephew, instructing them "to pack everything and prepare for a flight to anywhere, just after he had won and collected his receipts from the fight."

But the French Military Intelligence had telescoped his plans. And unfortunately came an uncalculated coincidence of matters, which gave them ample opportunity to thwart the suspected intentions of Johnson.

Seemingly, Moran almost came to blows because Dan McKettrick had sensed that he was about to become manager of the next heavy-weight champion of the world, without a written contract with Frank Moran, who had returned from America, during Johnson's period of recuperation, with a new personal manager, Ike Doran, brother of the sports figure Tad Doran. This had upset Dan McKettrick no end.

"Let's you and me sign a contract, Frank," McKettrick proposed upon the challenger's return to Paris.

"We don't need no contract," Moran replied.

"Well, I need one with you now," came McKettrick's reply.

"I'm sorry, Dan," came the dentist-fighter's rejoinder. "I swore when I got out of the navy. I took an oath, never to sign no papers."

McKettrick then became impossible. Threatening Moran with, "This is something that you'll never get away with."

He made good this threat by going immediately to Paris police authorities and establishing a claim of more than four thousand dollars against the fight receipts, as expenses paid out and issued on behalf of the challenger, instructing his French lawyer to tie up the box office funds from the fight until this matter was settled in the courts. Therefore, no fighter could receive any pay until the matter was settled.

The French Foreign Office chortled with glee. Johnson would not be paid and most likely would be unable to leave Paris for a period.

Still, they had known little or nothing of the visitations by officers of the British Intelligence Office.

And neither did Johnson know of McKettrick's manipulations. As he began manipulations of his own, to insure the defeat of Frank Moran, despite his ineffective training schedule.

Jack got a message through to the challenger. A simply startling message, on eve of the fight:

"Mr. Johnson, heavyweight champion of the world, would love to have the pleasure of a chat with the challenger, Dr. Frank Moran. Before we meet in the ring."

Moran responded. When he arrived and the two were seated together privately, Johnson put forward his proposition.

"Frank, I never thought that there would come a time that I would be compelled to make a deal with a white boy, the way white boys have been compelled to make a deal with me."

"And so? What in the hell does that mean?"

"It means exactly this," the champion smiled. "The arrangement, as it stands, means that the winner will get thirty percent of all the gate. And the loser will get twenty as his share, right?"

"That's right," the challenger nodded.

"Well, I got some bad news for you, friend. There ain't gonna be no fight. And therefore, no 40 percent for you. What do you think of that . . . huh?"

Moran stood. "So you're backing out. Scared to take a beating. . . ."

"Ain't gonna be no beating," Johnson laughed. "Question is, who's afraid . . . afraid of losing his share of the gate?"

Moran's nostrils flared, indicating that he had gotten the black man's point. Johnson chuckled.

"What's the matter with you, Frank. You're a professional 'tooth-pulling dentist.' What's money to you anyway?"

"You can't do this to me, nigger. I'll go to the press. It'll show you up before the eyes of the whole world."

"I'm black, Frank. I know that they even might believe you. But, money. What about the money that you won't get?"

"So, there's something that you want me to do to get it."

Jack smiled, a flashing gold-tooth smile.

"I knew that you'd get the point, Frank. Boy, I just knew that you'd be sensible. Now, here are the facts,

Frankie boy. I just don't feel like fighting now. Let's put it this way, I'm strong and physically fit. But I feel kinda lazy. Us niggers get them lazy kinda feelings, you know. Especially, when there's nothing too much at stake. Mind you, what I'd like is some money, with nothing but a little healthy exercise at stake.

"I want you to give me that little healthy exercise . . . say, for about eight rounds. Then, I want you to lay down and take yourself a little rest."

He shoved a paper forward.

"Now, you just sign this paper, promising that you will . . . that way you earn yourself twenty percent of the gate. . . . Otherwise, you get nothing, Frank."

Moran fulminated, shouted, stormed, shrilled and screamed:

"You can't do this . . . you black bastard, you. Who do you think you are . . . I'd die first . . . I'll kill you first . . . you. . . ."

The Black Emperor sat and widened his smile as the white challenger continued. Then, raised his hand to silence him:

"I've stated the terms, Moran. If you want conversation on philosophical treatises . . . then let's have ourselves a pleasant little chat on the philosophical dissertations of Herbert Spencer. I met and talked with him personally . . . did you?"

The white man stood breathing hard, eyeing Johnson as levely as he could muster to do:

"At least give me time to think it over, huh? You came springing this on me, out of the blue. . . ."

"Take yourself a coupla hours," the champion nodded." Put in a good coupla hours of solid thinking as to whether you want to take home a leather satchel full of dollar bills or not. That's okay with me."

He stood and indicated the door to Frank Moran.

"In two hours time, you come back and meet me

here . . . tell me your answer. I know what its gonna be."

Moran used up most of this time burning gas and rubber, driving straight as he could, to the offices of Theodore Vienne, the French promoter of the fight, who had already sunk thousands of franc notes promoting it. To the promoter, he poured out the story, storming to stress his point, which was to not enter the ring and to broadcast the entire story to the Paris and European newsmen.

But the old Frenchman knew, whatever the solution, the "stink would smell to the high heavens." Then, there was a matter of the audience, already anticipating the fight, the taxis of Paris were prepared to do business. Soldiers coming, attracting carloads of women.

"Women!" The old promoter shouted. "Women, why there has never been an attraction in the history of all entertainment to excite women as the prospects of this bout. If this fight does not come off, then that audience might never be found again. . . .

"No, no, my boy. You must not back out now. You must fight!"

Then the old Frenchman revealed his alternative plan, placing his arms around the shoulders of the challenger.

"We will solve this matter and that nigger quite simply. I'll telephone my lawyer and the divisional police, whose word is strictly law. Now, you will dictate a full and signed statement as to what this black culprit has proposed to you. Then, you will keep a copy of this document in your own possession . . . you will go into the ring . . . and as the first bell rings . . . inform that fat, overly indulgent nigger that this fight is on the level. . . ."

The old Parisian danced about in a series of pirouettes about the office, bristling and exploding with argument and thrilling with the excitement of his plans. Which was contagious as the challenger caught the fervor and agreed to them.

The old man wept for joy, realizing that the twenty thousand pounds collected as advance gate receipts would not have to be returned to the customers, after all.

The people came and formed into one of the greatest sporting fan crowds in the boxing history of France, up until then, paying the top price of 15 pounds for a single ringside seat.

And well over three thousand women had come out to be there, dressed up like they were going to the theatre or the *Folies*.

Celebrities galore, as never gathered before were there. Including those who came to curse and see Johnson lose, like: the actress Gaby Delsys, who Johnson had put down. And even that slick and long legged Mistinguette was there with Maurice Chevalier, who hated Johnson and made the point clear, along with the Dolly Sisters, Eleanor Gwyn, the novelist and the Princess de Polignac who had joined the Johnson haters.

Even the deposed King of Portugal, Manuel II, was there. He later had a party and conversation with Jack after the fight.

When the newspaper reporters asked Johnson about the conversation later, he replied:

"Gentlemen, I endeavored to put him at his ease. And I do believe that I succeeded. I've always tried not to be hard on a chap simply because he has fallen."

The fuming and vindictive Dan McKettrick observed his mistaken over-estimations of Frank Moran's chances of wresting the crown from the slippery black bald pate of the champion beginning the first round of the bout which took place at the Velodrome d'Hiver, 20th of June, 1914.

Johnson drew all eyes as he climbed between the ropes, smiling his sweet golden-tooth smile, gazing hungrily at the cheerfully exposed cleavage and white bosoms of the fabulous women sitting at the ringside, paying little or no attention to his opponent, in the opposite corner.

Georges Carpentier, "The White World's Champion". served as referee while on furlough from his military service duties. He received the loudest of the cheers.

Carpentier called the principals to the center of the ring for instructions. Then, at the handshake, Moran followed the instructions of Theodore Vienne the fight promoter:

"Go for yourself, nigger. The deal is off. This fight is on the level. . . ."

He declared it loud enough for the ringsiders to hear.

The champion took the challenger at his word and warning, beginning slow, pacing as a master, who recognized he was on the first leg, with 19 rounds possibly to go.

The cheers were sporadic and intermittent as nothing exciting occurred as Johnson waited for the challenger to take the lead, while laying back toying in the center of the ring.

The bell rang announcing the end of an uneventful first round.

The second round began as a monotonous repetition of the first. The crowds jeered recognizing that Johnson as champion was attempting to force the challenger to bring the fight to him, which he had to do, if he intended to win.

He lunged forth to try, the crowd came to its feet as Moran finally landed a punch, which the big black was unable to parry or side-step. They cheered, as if a victory punch had been landed.

In utter mockery Johnson stepped back, and joined the applause by clapping his gloves together:

"My sincere congratulations, Frank," he called out. "Now allow me to return my respects."

He then stepped in and sent Moran reeling across the ring with an onslaught of punches.

"On the level, Frank," he grinned. "Remember, after the eighth, you'll still have twelve more to go...."

The fans screamed out with indignation, as the bell rang.

They danced through a nerve wracking third round. And even the champion's tantalizing and taunting could not inveigle the challenger to come in and carry the fight.

"That's not the way to win it, Frank. You've got to come in and fight, if you wanna take it."

In the fourth Johnson continued his jibes and taunts, contenting himself to pad around the ring, still dominating the scene with slapping the challenger about the ring with ineffectual, but point making blows.

In the fifth round Moran exploded, leading with a powerhouse left to the champion's head, who retaliated, moving in with old form swiftness, jolting a right and then a short left into the rib cage of the challenger, wrapping him into a clinch, as Moran held on, Johnson attempted to wrestle free of Moran's.

The referee called for them to break. Moran attempted to step back as commanded, but Johnson caught him by the shoulder, pulled him back by his neck with his left hand, then stepped in to deliver his thunderous right uppercut, on target, the punch cracked Moran's nose as a large beetle being crushed by a hammer.

He reeled back out of range, blood gushing into his mouth almost choking him as he coughed helplessly.

"Foul! Foul!" was the cry heard rising to the rafters of the building, amidst indignant curses.

Moran was the smaller, the white underdog, the favorite. He fell back protecting his shattered nose, spitting the blood spurts which threaded into his gasping mouth, his only means of taking breath.

"Get down, Frank. Give it up, man. Things will be getting worse as this goes along."

At the bell, the fat and unconditioned champion pranced back into his corner, thumbing his nose at the tormented fans, then grabbing his crotch in a defiant invitation, which aroused them all the more. He was still grinning.

The Notice Board announced: *"Johnson has received a warning. Another breach of the rules and he will be disqualified."*

But, The Big Black Fire did not need any longer to risk any questionable moves. For from there on breathing becomes so difficult for Moran, it was miraculous that he was able to withstand the remaining 15 rounds without gagging to death from his own blood.

Moran pegged on through the sixth round, attempting to pace himself and adjust his breathing. Backing away, covering to protect the broken nose which Johnson peppered away at, followed with "gibbering insults.'"

The crowd cheered wildly at Moran's seventh round courage and aggressiveness. He switched his stance and landed a solid punch, which rocked the Black Smoke back onto his heels. He tried to follow through as Johnson showed his mastery of ring dancing, while his head cleared. Then he reached out and gave Moran a condescending pat on the shoulder:

"That's the way, Frankie boy. You work on that

punch. Get it down real good. And one day, you'll be a champeen, man."

Even the fans who sat hating him, were forced to join him with laughter.

At the eighth round bell the champion charged out swiftly. Crowding his man into a corner, pleading seriously.

"This is the eighth, Frankie, honey. Come on, give it up and let's go home, baby."

Moran stepped back and charged in, more determined. The black panther slithered out of reach, still pleading.

"Come on, Frank, now!"

But Moran continued to shake his bloody face retorting:

"You come on, Jack. Come on and fight!"

He saw that Moran had reneged on the deal for certain; then he obliged the challenger, stepping up the pace and punishment. His weariness seemingly disappeared, as he got down to serious work of demolishing the white man who faced him, working as a skilled swordsman, pricking a pig to the point of ridicule.

This was the story throughout the 10th, 11th, 12th and 13th rounds, extending on up through the 17th. Although Johnson's form improved as he went, he treaded through these rounds while visible signs of his weariness and lack of condition became more and more obvious. Cautious, lest the lumbering, bleeding challenger connect with one of his wildly swinging right hooks.

He ceased to dance away from these lumbering assaults, but rather grappled the lighter challenger to toss him across the ring with sheer brute force. But Frank Moran kept coming back, rushing, swinging, determined.

Although the champion's traditional "split, semi-second timing" was off, Moran was still no match to connect successfully with the champion's chin.

In the eighteenth round the tired black man pulled Moran into a clinch.

"It's been a nice fight, boy. But, let's take it easy, from hereon til the bell, huh?"

The incensed Moran simply doubled, redoubled, then tripled his efforts to land a punch as Johnson ducked, dodged and shuffled away.

Finally, the 20th round gong was heard. The tired black champion sprang from his stool, leaped forward to stab a vicious straight left to Moran's face, which almost took his head from his body. Moran retaliated, with a left of his own. Johnson snarled as he brought the "Mary Ann" into play, bouncing it off the biceps of Moran, continuing on like lightning to his face. But the challenger had dropped his head and the blow landed too high to be fatal. But it stunned him so that he staggered backwards, his hands almost touching the floor as he went.

Johnson followed him grunting vengeance and rage with every punch, each delivered with deliberate and expressed design for destruction. Moran whimpered, as the blows landed home, as did the weeping women at the ringside.

The champion summoned his final strength, in a last twenty-second effort. Chuckling from his throat like a madman intoxicated with power and speed, inflicting his final moments of torture with a sadistic pleasure.

The bell rang. Johnson stood center ring laughing as the dazed and beaten Moran staggered back to find rest in his corner.

The black man's face was a picture of drained energy as he made his way down the aisle to his dressing room, receiving not one cheer from the crowd.

As he moved into his dressing room, Lucille greeted

and kissed him, wiping the tear from his eyes, smiling. He smiled back as he heard the thunderous cheers and applause, signifying that the beaten challenger was leaving the ring.

It was about this time, after he had showered, that his nephew Gus Rhodes entered the dressing room to inform them. Just as Jack had suspected, the French police officials had confiscated the gate receipts pending investigations of Dan McKettrick's complaint.

The Big Smoke listened as his bitter smile turned into a laugh of jocularity. As he shook his head:

"Goodbye money, you're gonna be long gone, for some time."

The threesome drove on back to their villa at Asnières for a private victory banquet of quail, lobster, whiskey and champagne, all purchased from an inn on credit.

His premonitions concerning the money had been correct. For he would never see any part of the fourteen thousand four hundred dollars, his part of the purse for fighting Moran, even years after the war, which was immediately imminent.

The very next week signaled the beginning of the war. It was on the morning of June 27, 1914, that they received the news, as flashed around the world:

In the Bosnian town of Sarajevo, a political assassin had shot and killed Francis Ferdinand, Archduke of Austria.

The following day at their villa, no sooner had the Johnson family received the news of the assassination than they also received important callers from the French Foreign Service offices.

They had enjoyed his fight, while regretting his unfortunate circumstances with the gate receipts.

"Mais, c'est la vie. C'est la guerre. . . ."

But since this was now a reality, what were Mr. Johnson's plans, they inquired.

Perhaps, remain in France, accepting some minor position with the French Office, while awaiting the "gate receipts affair" to become straightened out?

Then Mr. Johnson and his party might have an opportunity to refresh their memories as to what they had actually heard and observed while on their travels in Russia and Germany?

They were further reminded of anticipated travel restrictions, since Mr. Johnson was now "a man without money or a country during war time. . . ."

They departed, leaving Mr. Johnson and his little party with some time to consider their proposals. Then, it might be possible, when the war is ended, serious consideration would be given to his becoming a naturalized citizen of France. Which would be based on his patriotic services performed on behalf of the French nation.

"Eh, bien. C'est la guerre. . . ."

The problem of coming to a decision concerning the proposals of the Frenchmen was solved a few hours later, with the visit of their next callers, a company in guise of British promoters from across the Channel, whom he had met previously, but prior to the Moran fight.

They were aware, they so informed the champion, of the French visitors who had preceded them. And of the conditions of their offer. They spoke this time with more diplomatic precision and directness than before, displaying letters of invitation from London sports promoters who were eager to sponsor a match between Johnson and Sam Langford, while Johnson would be able to reopen his revue *Seconds Out* at the Hippodrome. Since they were sympathetic and aware of his present financial crisis.

The Three Musketeers departed bag and baggage for London immediately for a short stay and fulfillment of a few theatrical personal appearances, which had been arranged for the champion there.

Now, as to what Johnson's instructions were, as a British Intelligence Agent, have never been told. But it is for certain that during this theatrical season in London, he was given instructions.

And he was given protection from the London "bad press" and his objectors and enemies in Parliament.

There is no doubt that some mighty and powerful strings were being pulled for him. Even Winston Churchill and Sir Hiram made no public comments concerning his return this time.

Although the Big Smoke still took his regular strolls up and down Piccadilly, wearing his orchids, displaying his flashy clothes and jewelry, seemingly he had become a model of behavior as a husband and a proper family man. For generally he took his wife, Lucille, along to be seen with him.

It seemed as though he was undergoing a period of rehabilitation, for the public's benefit.

He dropped in frequently at Covent Gardens, for long sessions with promoters of the N.S.C. concerning his proposed fight with Sam Langford, which was never to come off.

Again, he resumed visits and teas with The War Lords and Diplomatic Lions of England, experiencing an unprecedented cordiality among them.

Then, as predicted, offers came through from his friend George Thomas in Russia. With negotiations completed, Johnson and his party headed across the continent to Petrograd, where he was to appear at Thomas' huge amusement park called *The Aquarium*, which consisted of restaurants, residences, hotels, cafés, exhibition centers and other facilities.

The Aquarium was known as "a city within a city." From all reports George Thomas owned it all. Lock, stock and barrel.

The party was allowed to cross the continent without interference, obtaining first class accommodations, despite the vast shipments of arms and supplies and movements of troops.

In his party was a Frenchman, part of the troupe. Also with them was an English secretary-aide.

Arriving in Petrograd they found the city in terror and confusion, with the mobilization of troops, with diplomats and the military running over each other, going to and fro.

His friend George Thomas was in the thick of it, revealing much to Johnson, Gus and Lucille. Things were happening.

Another assassination attempt had failed to take the life of Rasputin.

There were few if any foreigners who knew as much, nor more, about the inner workings of the military and political circles of Russia, beyond a shadow of a doubt, than George Thomas.

As a confidential agent to Tsar Nicholas II, this Negro was frequently allowed to sit in and take part in military councils of top priority. He confided more than this much to his friend, the champion.

Some say that it had been arranged beforehand, that George Thomas would make reports to Johnson, who was to pass them on to his contacts.

Which would account for Jack having those sealed secret envelopes which Thomas had given him, and which the British stole off of Johnson.

Others say that it was a matter of friendship . . . "two black brothers, stickin' together in foreign lands."

They say that happened after Jack confided his plight to George Thomas—the pressure that the French, along with the British Secret Service Agents, were putting him under, to force him to spy for them.

But, whichever way the truth is to be told, we know that Jack Johnson ended up taking that sealed packet of secrets out of Russia and back to London.

His stay in Russia was cut shorter than expected, for Johnson came under suspicion. This was obvious as he immediately resumed his relationships with Rasputin, who was finally assassinated by a "friend" some two years after the champion's departure.

He had remarked this much to Lucille, Gus and Thomas after he had returned from a visit with The Monk.

"Somebody's going to kill that man here, for sure."

Thomas assented, with some reservations, recalling the fate of those who had attempted and failed to bring it off, just a short time ago.

But it was Johnson whom they first tried to kill.

About a week later Jack rose to depart from the tables about daybreak, after "a drink for drink" bout of vodka with Rasputin. Staggering back to his hotel a gunshot split the silence of the morning and smacked into the brick wall of the building, inches from his head. Running and ducking for cover, he was headed off by several men with cruel looking knives in readiness. These were confident professionals, experience had taught him to recognize.

As they charged in silence, the champion brought his feet into play, kicking high as he had learned from the French rowdies along the Left Banks of Paris.

He screamed and shouted as he fought like a wild man for his life, hoping to attract attention, which his assassins obviously didn't want.

People joined the shoutings from their windows. The police came on the run as his attackers, nursing their wounded, hastily vanished into the shadows and corners of the dark buildings as they had come.

He tried to explain the occurrence to the police, who listened as he was escorted to his hotel.

As Gus and Lucille helped him bathe his lumps and bruises, his recounting was interrupted by a return of the police. He was instructed to leave Russia immediately.

"They invoked their 'five and ten law,' the champion recalled later of the affair.

"Which means, five minutes to pack, and ten minutes to get out of town."

Through the powerful influence of George Thomas, Johnson was able to get all 18 of their trunks packed and made ready for the next train, leaving Petrograd.

It was then that Thomas called his friend aside.

"It was because of that cat Rasputin, wasn't it?" The Big Black Fire asked.

"No matter now. Too many things could account for it," Thomas commented, continuing on. "The thing is, what are you gonna do. Where do you plan to head?"

"Back to Paris or even London," I suspect.

"It'll just start all over again. They've got you by the balls, man. America's coming in, too. Nobody knows whose side they're coming in on, right now," Thomas pointed out.

"You don't want to give yourself up before they come in, do you?" George asked.

The black champion shook his head. "It would kill my mother, man."

"Well, if America comes in as allies with Britain, or France, or both. And you didn't cooperate with them, they might just throw you over to them."

"Maybe I'll try Spain. . . ."

George Thomas shook his head. "Come with me. I'm moving to Constantinople as soon as I've liq-

uidated as much as I can here. Go there, I've got contacts there expecting me. I'll turn you on to them and
join you later there."

Jack shook his head: "No, then I'd really be out in
the cold, at least until you got there or if you didn't make
it. At least in Paris or even London, I might be able to
strike a bargain of some kind with them."

George Thomas slipped a packet of papers from his
pocket.

"Then, you're gonna need some kind of bargaining
point, my friend. Just in case, you might be able to use
these. Keep in touch and I'll be able to give you a few
instructions on how to use them."

The black giant took the sealed packet and pocketed
it.

"But what are they?" Johnson asked.

"I'll tell you. But whatever you do, don't open and
break that official seal to find out. Trust me. They are
letters, personal exchanges between the Tsar of Russia
and the Kaiser of Germany. Notes and data concerning
Russia's decisions to enter the war. Plans of attack, de-
fenses and other agreements, indicating that together
Russia and Germany could rule the world. . . ."

"But, what should I do with them?"

"Just keep them for now. I'll tell you when, where
and how. But whatever you do, don't let them get out of
your hands. Holding on to them can be your life insurance. Now, we better be getting you aboard that train.
Or perhaps you nor that packet will get away from
here."

They caught the last train at the border leaving Russia, changing trains at Warsaw and were forced to leave
their truckload of baggage behind on the loading plat-
forms of the railroad station there.

Forty-eight hours later they arrived to change trains
in Berlin, where the champion elected to stroll around

outside the station, while Gus Rhodes ran about distributing bribes to porters, conductors and station masters to get the party and their remaining baggage aboard the crowded train.

Outside the station Johnson immediately got himself into a near-riot fight, by going to the aid of a Frenchman who was being beaten almost to death by a group of angry Germans. But the incident rather aided their eagerly awaited departure from Berlin.

The German police had quelled the near-riot and officials decreed that his party should leave Germany at once. Which was exactly what they were attempting to do. But police and a wedge of porters were more than helpful at forcing them into an overcrowded train car bound for the Belgian frontier.

A short distance from the Belgian border, the train stopped and all passengers were ordered to get out and walk.

Soldiers and sentries stood in rank along the tracks. One of them recognized Johnson and warned him.

"Run fast, Jack Johnson. The President of France has been assassinated!" He announced into the ears of the black man. "We expect to be in Paris in two weeks."

Taking hold of their suitcases, the champion's party took a fast three mile walk across the border into Belgium. They arrived in Paris the following day, finding everything in an uproar with war preparations. Jack and Lucille elected not to remain.

The Three Musketeers crossed the channel into the United Kingdom, after Johnson had gotten his automobile and their other belongings out of storage in Asnières.

As he drove, the port roads were choked with traffic of troop movements, ammunition, weapons and war supplies, horses and cavalry mules.

When he got to England, Johnson immediately went to visit his promoters, Tozar and Jenkins, proposing the feasibility of booking him for public appearances as an entertainer, along with his show, "as a morale booster, taking the people's worries and fears away from the war."

The possibilities were challengingly profitable, but there were reservations as to whether the champion was one of the people to do it.

They elected to test the public reactions of London, as they had once done before, by attending a large London music hall with him as a guest, to be called to the stage.

As before, Johnson was correct concerning the magnetism he held with British vaudeville-musicale audiences.

"The British could be as forgetful as forgiving at times," the champ laughed and commented as he was called to the stage, during the closing song, "It's a Long Way to Tipperary."

Then The Black Fire seized the occasion and went "patriotic," which blew the audience's mind. He jumped to the stage to lead them in song, waving his arms and calling out:

"Now, come on now . . . everybody sing it."

They joined him in chorus.

One newspaper noted favorably the following day:

"For once Jack Johnson has done the right thing before an English audience."

Seconds Out reopened with a banging success. Johnson resumed his daily walks along Piccadilly Square, waving, tossing his friendly greetings and receiving them from passers-by, stopping long enough outside Gatti's to purchase flowers for Lucille and an orchid for his buttonhole from "Fat Bessie," the flower seller.

After a few weeks of this, playing to capacity houses in the evenings, he arrived home to receive a letter from his friend, George Thomas.

"Things blew up here, for the worse. I was nearly killed going about my business to liquidate my affairs. . . ."

It was true. George Thomas was nearly lynched by a Russian mob, jealous and enraged at his properous living, and his race was held against him. He had fled from Russia, taking as much as he could with him, and settled, as he had promised, in Constantinople.

"Take the packet that I gave you and go to the top persons! Don't break the seal, but tell them of the contents, as I told you.

"It is time for all good men to come to the aid of their country . . . remember? A British-American wrote that line. Remember that and God bless you, Jack. Your friend 'G.T.' Good Times."

As Jack put the letter away he was reminded of the packet of sealed envelopes, stacked away in the bottom of one of the wardrobe trunks. He made a mental note to find it upon his return from the theatre. Then, he and Lucille could decide what to do with it, after she had had a chance to read the letter from George Thomas.

The champion arrived at the theatre and was engaged in some byplay and banter with a couple of policemen:

"I saw that dance of your wife's the other night, Mr. Johnson. She's great, sir."

"Mr. Johnson took proper precautions with her costume this time, I bet. Didn't you, sir?"

"Oh, my wife's a pretty clever girl. But, I don't think that *Seconds Out* is a bad show, do y'all?"

Just then a third policeman joined the group. "Mr. Johnson, sir," he was holding his smile, but dropping his voice. "I just thought that I would warn you, sir. You're being followed."

The Big Smoke held his pose, showing no reaction. He then smiled good naturedly, shaking the policeman's hand.

"Thank you, son, thank you. But there's not the slightest reason in this whole round world why anybody would be wanting to tail me."

He strolled toward the rear of the theatre calling back.

"But thanks for telling me, anyway.

As Jack moved on to approach the stage door, he was confronted by the theatre manager and a United States Senator, from the South, serving on a top priority War Aid Committee, presently visiting London. He remembered that the Senator had attended his fight with Jim Jeffries in Reno. He hadn't seen the Senator since that time. But he spoke to him politely and attempted to pass.

"Good evening to you, Senator."

"Don't you come speaking to me, you gawd damned nigger."

Jack smiled, then turned to the manager:

"Do you allow your stars to be talked to this way," he inquired.

"I don't care how he talks to you," the manager stood and faced Johnson squarely. "The way we hear it, there are a lot of people 'talking rough' to you now."

Johnson turned and entered the door. They followed him.

"And talk isn't where it's going to end, neighbor. Nigger," the Senator threatened. Johnson spun around livid, lips quivering. He clenched his two fists as he spoke in a hiss, "You . . . get out of here. . . ."

The cracker Senator laughed. "It's not me that's getting out of here, boy." He turned to the manager. "Show this nigger that new contract that you've got for him, mister. . . ."

The manager stepped over to his office door and swung it open. A huge detective stepped out.

"Are you Jack Johnson, mister?"

"Who do I look like, Snow White?"

"That's him all right. Jack Johnson, supposed to be the world's champion fighter . . . who'd just better not show his face in any state in the Union."

He spat in his direction, barely missing the toe of Johnson's expensive shoes.

"Then, I take it, you are Jack Johnson, sir?"

"Then go and take it, man. It's all yours," Jack was eyeing the Senator.

"Then, it is my duty to inform you. . . ." He produced a paper, handing it to Johnson. His face was completely dead-pan, as he continued to drone his message home.

"I am to serve on you this order to leave our country within twenty-four hours."

Johnson moved to stop him at the door.

"What the hell is this, man?"

"I have nothing more to say, sir. Those were my orders. I have carried them out." He moved out the door into the passageway, Johnson following him.

"But, my God, man! What's this all about? What've I done to be ordered out of England? And twenty-four hours? Tell me!"

The detective paused in hesitation, then faced him.

"Listen, sir. I can't tell you what it's all about. But, I can say one thing, sir. You've got enemies, here in this country."

"What do you recommend that I do," the big black man asked the white one, who continued speaking.

"But you've also got friends, from what I hear . . . big friends. Well, sir, when you've got big men as friends, then this would be the very time to call on them. Good day, sir."

The man walked away and a worried Johnson turned back into the theatre to take people's mind off their worries for a few hours of the evening.

Out front, the impatient audience was calling out for him; the curtain flew, the music was playing as he stepped out onto the stage calling cheerfully to them:

"Good old England!"

"Good old Jack!," the crowd chorused back.

They were unaware that this would be his last performance before them, as he led them into the closing song, standing there smiling his gold smile, contrasted only by the sparkle of the tears which flowed down his black cheeks, encouraging them to sing with him:

It's a long way to Tipperary
It's a long way from home....

At the conclusion of the show that night, the two, Jack and Lucille, talked their situation over, while en route home. They summed up and took fast account of the conditions and resulting consequences, which were somehow coincidental with their present predicament, placing the occurrences and incidents in chronological sequence:

(1) The proposals from both British and French Secret Services, encouraging them to participate in espionage.

(2) The favorable reception they had received, following the Frank Moran fight and their return to London.

(3) The finalized offers, as British agents had predicted, which assured their return to Russia and Petrograd.

(4) The assassination of the Archduke Ferdinand, immediately after the Moran fight.

(5) The first, but unsuccessful attempt to assassinate Grigori Efimovitch Rasputin, after their first departure from Petrograd. The second, but successful at-

tempt to bring it off, after their dismissal from Russia and the attempt upon his own life, just minutes prior to his "five and ten" eviction from the country.

(6) The sealed envelope packet which George Thomas had entrusted him with, at his moment of departure, along with the instructions given.

(7) The zeppelin which had trailed their car along the port roads, as they left Asmières for Bologne to cross the channel for London.

(8) The talk of a promised bout with Sam Langford. The questioning by the British agents, upon their return, along with the favorable press upon their return.

(9) The presence of the southern cracker Senate Committee member, that afternoon, and the subsequent papers, ordering him out of the country in 24 hours.

(10) The letter and instructions from George Thomas, which were so similar to the suggestions made by the detective who served him with the orders. George had said: "Take them to the top persons." The detective had suggested: "You also have friends . . . big men . . . this would be the very time to call upon them."

By the time that they had arrived home they had decided.

The champion's wife reminded him:

"We haven't done anything . . . and no Ku Klux Klanner's got any pull over here. So, tomorrow we'll go see the biggest shots that we know and get all of this straightened out."

They entered the house as her husband kissed her. "That we'll do. And for being such a daring and brave woman and wife, I'm gonna play your chef-servant and cook you the finest 'Chicken Maryland' that you've ever tasted."

She playfully pulled away and entered their bedroom quarters, only to call out in panic:

"Jack, come here. For God's sake look. . . ."

He went past her into the bedroom. The trunks all piled high had been opened. The pages from his four volumes of Herbert Spencer had been ripped from their covers and scattered about the room.

The two of them, suspecting robbery, raced frantically about through, drawers, trunks and closet to ascertain what had been taken. He counted the spilled contents from his jewelry boxes, as she checked hers.

"But, nothing seems to be gone, honey. All of my valuables seem to be here."

"And all of mine . . . no one came here for nothing?"

"Oh, Jack, of course not. No one would come and do this just for nothing and leave with nothing . . ."

The trunk with the papers. This flashed across his mind as he tore past his ties, silk vests, silk shirts, which seemed to be in good order. Finally, he turned to her and spoke:

"They came looking for something all right. And they must've got it. That packet of papers that George gave me to keep, and wrote about in his letter today, is gone."

"They came for those secret documents between the Kaiser and the Tsar. . . ," she said.

"His letter said to take it to the folks in high places. Looks as though somebody in those places couldn't wait . . . . George had said that they might mean my only bargaining point. And I never broke the seals to see what was in them. . . ."

"What are we going to do now, Jack?" Her question was delivered in the tone of a helpless child.

"We're gonna eat. I'm still gonna cook you that Chicken Maryland. I don't want to talk with Hiram Maxim on an empty stomach in a crisis. And I plan to go and see him, in the bright and early."

But he wasn't up to see Sir Maxim bright and early enough. Sir Maxim couldn't help. Even though he had such great admiration for the champion. For he, before he had invented the machine gun, had been a pretty good boxer himself. He informed Johnson that the British government would not listen closely to what he had to say in the matter.

He had heard rumors concerning this matter. Grave rumors to the effect that perhaps Johnson had not cooperated as fully as he might have on behalf of British security, while experiencing and enjoying their asylum and charity, although he was a fugitive. But still the nobleman could do nothing in this case.

"Why don't you go over and speak with Lonsdale about it," Sir Hiram suggested. "I'll call and make the appointment with him this afternoon for you." Which was the best that the machine-gun tycoon could suggest for the moment.

Lord Lonsdale was just as cordial and obliging as Sir Hiram Maxim had been as to the sport of boxing, while explaining that he was equally as unable to help him.

They stood in the drawing room of Carlton House Terrace as the old man reminisced over his admiration for Peter Jackson, the former Negro ring master, whom Lonsdale believed to have been the finest exponent of the art who ever lived. He had known Jackson personally, just as he did Johnson.

"For his sake alone, I'd do anything that I could to help you." He took a relaxing draw from his cigar, a special brand he was famous for smoking. "And of course I will. But, this is war, Johnson. And countries get hysterical in the times of war."

"But Lord Lonsdale," the champion asked. "What in the devil do I have to do with the war?"

"Aha. That, Johnson my man, is the main question. What?" He blew his smoke out and continued.

"There are some speculations as to the answer. You have been in Germany. You've just recently returned from Russia. A mystery man you've become in some circles."

The Britsher toyed with the head of the huge Borzoi at his side. The wolfhound responded warmly.

"Lovely creatures, aren't they?" His change of subject indicated that the meeting had come to an end as he continued to fondle the head of the animal concluding:

"But, not nearly so lovely as that Peter Jackson, stripped down for action as he had been on the day I saw him beat Slavin, I say, eh?"

The liveried footman, upon signal, arrived with Johnson's exquisitely tailored, Russian fur coat, lined with silver and violet silk. The nobleman took it from the hands of the lackey.

"Allow me to help you with this, Mr. Johnson."

Now, as he slid into the coat, he pondered the wisdom of having chosen to wear it on this particular occasion.

"And what would you advise me to do, your Lordship?"

"Go see your solicitor. Tell him the truth. Everything you know. And whomsoever else you tell ... well, tell them ... anything else. But see him this afternoon, no later than tonight, without fail, eh?"

"Thank you, My Lord."

The senior partner of the Solicitor's office had listened without a single question of interruption, studying his fingertips and nails as he did. The black man could see that he was more acquainted with the details than he could afford to have Johnson believe.

"I can advise you, that if you should fight this order to leave the country, you may succeed. And I do mean *may* succeed. That is, if you have told me everything ... and if everything that you have told me is the truth. ..."

"I swear to you, sir. I never knew what was in that

packet of envelopes, I never broke the seals to even find out."

"That much has been substantiated. And so far, that much is presently in your favor. But, the Home Office does know of the contents. Perhaps, because some enemy who stole them from you has told them, and that is why they no longer consider you a welcome visitor here in England, for the moment. . . ."

"But don't you believe me, sir," the black man asked.

"What I believe is of no consequence with the powers that be. Then, I never disbelieve a client, until I am forced to.

"But my sources have informed me that somebody in the Home Office does not care to believe you. Somebody in high authority, so I am informed. . . ."

"But, sir. They know that I'm no spy, or traitor to Great Britain. For all that I may be, there's been nothing in my life to even suggest that. . . ."

"Suggest, maybe not!" the senior partner interrupted. "But to suspect is precautionary. Especially during war. Let me advise you of this much. It is already precluded that America will join the war as our ally."

"So, somebody from back home, like a southern Senator has convinced them that I'm a spy. . . ."

"Somebody in the Home Office has seen those documents . . . somebody who knows what information you brought back from Russia."

"But, I didn't know. . . ."

"You'll have to convince the Home Office of that fact, which might be difficult, as your friend George Thomas seems to have vanished from sight, after contacting you by mail. . . ."

Now, it dawned on the champion that they had intercepted his letter, mailed to him by Thomas. The senior partner continued.

"And I don't feel that you'll get much help from the

Russian Embassy here. For at least the time being, they are our allies and friends. All they report is that you went to an army barracks, where you got your orders to leave Russia at once because of your friendship with certain suspect persons in Petrograd. And also that there was an attempt to eliminate you shortly before the orders were issued."

"But I was instructed by British agents not to neglect those friendships, on behalf of Britain, in case I might learn something of importance, sir."

"So you've told me already." But I repeat, Mr. Johnson, the Russians are our allies. And with your traveling around with documents like that in your possession, you surely couldn't expect them to welcome you under such conditions."

"Then, I've got no choice but to leave England."

"Or to cooperate with England . . . to prove yourself innocent. That would be your decision."

The black man got the message. The old "squeeze play." Fight a "no decision" fight or lose.

"And if I don't decide by tomorrow, then I've got to leave?"

"As you like, Mr. Johnson."

"And then, how much do I owe you, sir?"

The man brushed the offer aside as the champion pulled the bankroll from his pocket.

"My clerk will send you a bill."

"I like to pay as I go along, sir. If you don't mind." He peeled a hundred pound note from the roll and placed it on the desk. "Will that cover it?"

The old barrister held the note up to the light and studied it. Then he unlocked his desk drawer and counted out nine ten-pound notes. And from his vest pocket he pulled a purse and from it counted out six golden sovereigns. Finally, from another pocket of his trousers he counted out six half-crowns, one shilling and two sixpences. He pushed them toward the champion. "Your change, Mr. Johnson."

The two of them exchanged smiles, Johnson's broke out into a laughter. He had been outwitted and got the message again.

"And now, since I've accepted and paid for your advice, sir, is there anything else to give, by way of suggestion?"

"Nothing beyond the sound advice to leave England, Mr. Johnson. You've become, shall I say, an enigma, world-over. Whereas your enemies failed in their attempt to take your life in Russia, they have friends here, who might not fail. . . ."

"Unless I am able to convince the Home Office here of my worthiness to be here?"

"Exactly! Then, it could prove a source of embarrassment to the Crown to have you meet your death on our soil, at present. . . ."

"Then, you can tell the Home Office that I'm leaving, sir. I don't want to be in any country that doesn't trust me or my wife. But I'm going at my own time. Be so kind as to tell that to the *gentlemen* who run the law here, the next time you meet with them. . . ."

The Black Fire departed, bristling upon that note.

For the next few days he bristled the same way as he strutted carelessly to the Strand Theatre for his performances as if nothing had happened. He had sensed the change of attitude in the glances and greetings from the policemen and some passersby, which made him feel like anything but the heavyweight fighting champion of the world.

But he was comforted by the fact that neither the Home Office nor anyone else made any official move against him. He even felt that he might have called off their threats and bluff.

Then it happened. In the wee dawn hours of a London morning, while he made his way home down Shaftsbury Avenue, following a drinking and gambling party, of which he came away winner, feeling good.

The ambush came from the darkness, as in Petrograd, but this group was more determined and better organized, as a half-dozen of them appeared like ghosts, waiting and blocking the way he was to pass.

He turned to see one emerge from the shadows of a book shop doorway, charging with a wild swing, which whistled over his head, but knocking off his hat as the champion ducked and crashed home a punch to the solar plexus, which felled the man. Then, the second appeared in an attempt to back-heel him into the gutter. Jack caught him with a right cross, bouncing him onto the pavement.

The men were quiet and deadly as they moved in. Two more came. The champion shouted and waded in to meet them. He felt himself fall back as one lashed him to the cheek with a blow that sent him reeling, tasting blood as he noticed the thug moving in to slash him again with the heavy buckle of the belt. He took another blow on the arm and chopped the man down. Still screaming as once he had done when performing the Battle Royals . . . somewhere back in the recesses of his memories. Then he heard the whistles as he moved in still swinging. The other thugs melted into the darkness and street shadows as police came rushing, feet pounding, blowing their whistles. He was allowed to stagger home, holding his silk bandana to the ugly gash on his bleeding cheek.

As Lucille Johnson watched her blood-spattered husband enter their apartment and hobble almost helplessly to a chair, explaining that he had gotten into a little friendly fracas with a few fellows, she made her silent decision that either she, or the both of them, would leave England as instructed.

She helped him to the bed, washed and bandaged his wound without question. In a short while after feeding him two large portions of strong brandy he slept, snoring loudly as she stood at the window, looking out, burning cigarettes until sun up.

CHAPTER EIGHTEEN

THE SQUEEZE PLAY

When Jack went to sleep that morning, he realized that he was caught in the middle of something bigger than he had ever faced in his life. But what he didn't learn until a long while later was that he was in the middle of the biggest squeeze play ever.

For Jack Johnson had gotten himself so caught up in "the thick of things" that it had then come to the point that where, when, and how he lived, or even died, would have serious social and psychological as well as political effect, if not directly upon the outcome of the big war, then certainly on the condition of things which were to come after the war.

The first proof of this came about sun-up, after his fight with the London gang that night.

Lucille was still at the window, looking out and worriedly smoking cigarettes, when a carriage rolled up; a man got out and knocked on their door.

Lucille went to answer it, for she had recognized the man, the English secretary-aide who had gone with them on their last trip to Petrograd.

He came into the room, inquiring about Jack, seemingly he had heard about the fracas already. He didn't take the time to tell her how he had heard, neither did he bother to explain as to why he had come in person, instead of using the telephone.

She refused, at first, to wake up her husband, until the aide informed her that he had located their baggage and it could be obtained with proper identification at Moscow. Someone had to journey to bring the baggage back, because of variable border troubles and restrictions, due to the war.

Lucille Johnson, at the English aide's request, went to wake up her husband to hear the rest of it.

The champion's face was so swollen from the gash received in his fight, that she insisted she call the theatre and announce a cancellation of his appearances, at least for one evening. She left the room to do so, while the former secretary repeated his story of the recently located, lost baggage. Then he got down to the real business at hand, by the time Lucille had come back into the room.

Now that the cancellations for his evening's performance had been confirmed, she joined her husband, sharing his joy at their baggage being located, along with the opportunity to regain at least a small personal and family fortune in clothing, jewelry and furs.

"But the main point of my concern," the Englishman explained. "Although I had succeeded in relocating your baggage some weeks ago—there was a trunk of mine along with it—there was a question of my ability to accompany you on the journey to claim our things. Because of my present employment.

"However, upon hearing of your orders to leave the country I was so taken up with the prospects of leaving with you, I took the liberty of checking out potential engagements for you in Spain, Portugal and even Germany. The latter was immediately responsive. It came from that Hamburg brewer, who admired you so much while you were there. He is eager to have you return for a series of 'wrestling exhibitions'. Germany is eager to have you return."

He produced written responses to his proposals for the theatrical reappearances of the champion in Germany.

"Then, in the interim, we, or one of us, might go on to Russia—by way of Sweden—and retrieve our baggage."

The champion and his wife exchanged glances. It was all too pat to be on the level. He once remarked, recalling the incident sometime later:

"It was too pat for believing—even if offered to a white man. But definitely these proposals were of too pat a nature when offered to a man of my color."

When Lucille went to the kitchen to prepare tea, brandy and coffee for the three, the English aide confided to the champion that a former German paramour of his, Mata Hari, whom the aide had continually kept in touch with, had expressed her hopes and anticipation of Jack's return to Germany.

After finishing their tea, coffee and brandy, the aide rose to go, with a final remark:

"The prospects of recuperating our lost baggage, and the return to Eastern Europe just enthralls me, Mr. Johnson. I do hope you will allow me the privilege of going with you."

He was no sooner out of the door, than Johnson

called for his cousin Gus Rhodes, to whom he gave all
the papers, proposals and claims, which the Englishman
had left with him, along with instructions:

"You will leave for Russia this evening," the champ
told his nephew. "See if you can bring the baggage
back. In the meantime on your way back, you will stop
off in Germany and check out the feasibility of our
going there."

With little discussion Gus Rhodes hurried back to his
quarters, preparing to leave for Sweden that afternoon.
But right before Jack and Lucille had settled down to a
rehashing of their situation, a messenger appeared at
the door with a written invitation: "From Jack Curley!"

Jack Curley, who had once promoted Jack Johnson's
prizefights, was in London, and was inviting the Johnsons to have dinner with him that very night at one of
the city's most fabulous restaurants, private dining
room and all. "Business to discuss with good news!"
How long he had been in London, from America, the
note did not say. What Curley had in mind they were to
learn that evening.

The way the evening dinner had begun proved the
earlier suspicions of Jack and his wife, that the white
American promoter had more than a dinner celebration
for them on his mind.

There was a spray of orchids by Lucille's place at the
table. Vintage champagne and brandy was placed
alongside Jack's, for the mixing of his favorite Rajah's
Peg, which Jack Curley had remembered that Jack
loved so well.

It was obvious that Curley not only knew something
of their predicament, but had some form of a proposition to make. Even in his casual and cheerful banter,
while their main courses and desserts were being served,
not once had Curley inquired about the condition of
Johnson's battered and severely swollen face.

The after-dinner brandy was served; Curley passed one of his two huge Havana cigars to Johnson and they lit up, while he produced smaller ones called "Henry Clay's" and encouraged Lucille to try one. She refused, selecting one of her own brand cigarettes, with impatience.

"Listen, Jack Curley. What's on your mind? Now all of this has been nice. Jack belongs in bed," she reminded him. "So let's get it on out in the open, okay?"

Curley rose and walked over to the window, as they watched him.

"Okay," he agreed. Then turned from the dining room window to face them.

"Jack, do you know what they're calling you back home in America?"

"Oh, I can imagine a lot of names. Bail jumper, fugitive from justice, a black no-nation sonovabitch. But most of all, they'd come to one true name: 'Jack Arthur Johnson, the unbeaten heavyweight King of the World, and exile from the very same world that he is ruler of.' "

"This is serious Jack," the white man became more intense. "I mean upstairs, in Washington, the big boys in the White House and our State Department. They're calling it treason . . . your pro-German sentiments .. . ."

"Hell, I like the Germans. They like me. And they were a damn sight more cordial to my wife and me than people were back where we both were born."

"You know that we'll eventually fight Germany, don't you, Jack?"

"Man, I've seen war, and heard rumors of war. But, when you get back there, you tell them what I said," the black man rose from the table. "That I'm no traitor. I call it as I see it. But you also tell 'em that if they do go to war, I'll be on my country's side."

"Would you like to see your mother again, Jack?"

Lucille was up alongside her husband shouting so

angrily that the waiter ducked discreetly from the dining room.

"Oh come on, Jack. What are you trying to do? You know that Jack wants to see his mother more than anything else in this world. Why, what's with you?"

"Don't press your luck, Curley," Johnson warned.

"If I don't press it, Jack, then somebody else'll press it for me." The white man continued. "I heard, while back in America, that your mother's in a pretty bad way. And not expected to live very long. I also heard that over in Europe, like here in London, that quite a few parties were pressing their luck with Jack Johnson. And pressing them pretty damn close."

"Make your point, man. Before you 'crap out.'"

"Awright. Awright. How's this for openers. Now, it's the talk of the town that you've been asked to leave England again. They don't want your spilled blood on their hands. I hear that they feel the same way in France as well as Russia. And as words have it, they say a few German promoters are 'making sweet eyes' at you."

"So, I ask again, Curley," the champ said. "What's wrong with Germany?"

"For anybody else right now, I'd say, nothing's wrong. But Jack Johnson's not just anybody else. You're not only an American, but you hold the heavyweight title of the world. When America comes in, your being in Germany wouldn't set too well in some circles."

"And just who says that we'll be in Germany when that happens, Curley? If it happens," Lucille said sweetly.

"It'll happen and you will be in Germany when it does, if you go. The Germans will make sure to keep you there . . . for propaga 'a reasons. If Jack says the right things, during the war, they'll let him walk around on the streets. If he gets out of hand, or you try to leave, they're gonna hold him there as a suspect . . . No three ways about it. . . ."

"So, you're saying I should go back and sit it out in prison, kill my mother and be a patriot, huh?"

"I'm here to tell you there's another way," he walked over to his briefcase and placed it on the table, taking out papers, as he talked.

"It's a way that you can fight for it, Jack. You can fight yourself free. I've got you a heavyweight title match already prearranged. We'll call it, *'The Fight for a Pardon,'* only it won't be advertised that way, I wish it could. Jack, how would you like a full pardon, going back to America and no prison term? I've been in Washington working on it. Here read these papers. . . ."

He extended a packet of letters to Jack; Lucille took them and began to open and read them with her husband.

Now, although the letters have never been made public, it is certain that that the contents were correspondence exchanged between the very high people in U.S. Government, which included the Secretary of State, the southern senator from Georgia who had insulted Jack in front of the theatre and others among his critics and enemies, who could pull strings "and get things done."

The letters contained no promises nor commitments, but they indicated that if Johnson showed some public indication of "respect for the laws of his country by returning and 'facing the music' . . . trusting the integrity of the American Courts, there is no reason why an appeal for pardon could not be given serious considerations . . . a re-evaluation of his case . . .

". . . as to how this might be effected would be entirely up to Mr. Johnson and his advisors. Perhaps it could be settled, dependent upon the outcome of a title

bout, whereby the Champion removes all reasonable
doubts as to his future public conduct within the ring
and out of it. . . ."

After finishing the letters, the champion looked at the
promoter and chortled:

"What they want me to do? Take a Bible into the
ring, say a loud prayer and say I'm sorry. Then, beat up
Langford, McVey and Jeanette all on the same card?"

"I've signed a fighter for you Jack. I own him. I want
him to succeed you as world's champion. . . ."

"Good for you, Curley," Lucille chided. "And what's
his name. Or is everybody keeping it a secret?"

"He's a young cowboy from Kansas; the biggest thing
you'll ever see. Six-foot-six, 250 pounds stripped
naked, with an arm reach of 83 inches, named Jess
Willard."

"And they'll give me a pardon for beating him?"
Jack jeered.

"Who says that you'll beat him, Jack?" Curley smiled.

"But suppose an accident happens, like Jack knocking him out, or he falls on his face, Curley. What then?"
Lucille laughed. "What about the pardon then?"

"Jack gets the pardon for seeing that such accidents
won't happen to Willard . . . a pardon plus fifty thousand on the side, guaranteed by a few of those gentlemen whose names you read on those letters. . . ."

"So that happens and I'm pardoned by the government. I make pretty nice speeches for them and all that,
too. But I'm still a fighting champion by profession.
Will those nice gentlemen even guarantee me a return
fight with your cowboy from Kansas and his 83-inch
reach?"

Curley produced a contract. "Check the papers.
Since I'm becoming the manager of both, champion and
challenger, what can I lose? I'm all for it."

Johnson laughed. "Curley, I heard a man say something to another one, which I never forgot. I'm gonna say that li'l sayin' to you. 'Man, if I wasn't myself, I should prefer to be you.'"

"For this one, Jack, you'll sign a contract with me, for conditions identical with those you had Dr. Frank Moran sign in Paris, okay? That's the only proof that I can take home to the big boys. In writing is the only way I can bring them to understand that you're serious."

Jack looked to his wife. Lucille showed her eagerness to go home. But obviously pained at the price which her husband was being forced to pay. The black champion smiled reassurance, then turned back to Curley.

"You'll get it all down in writing okay. But there's something in writing that I want, on the side from you. . . ."

"Like ten percent of whatever your cowboy earns from fighting, while he's playing champion, until he meets me again. I want that from your share, on the side from you-to-me, in writing, too, Curley."

Jack Curley held his poker face. He knew that the wrong reaction on his part would blow it.

"We'll draw it up together," he extended his hand. Jack took it, and holding Curley still, with an equally straight poker-face asked:

"How long do I carry your boy, before making him look like a champion?"

Curley pulled away, as if thinking it over. "I'd say that fifteen rounds oughta do it. That's long enough to get the betting down right, huh?"

"Uh, huh. And just long enough to make the motion pictures good and exciting," Jack mused, with a wink to Lucille, to perk her up. "I want a copy of the fight picture negatives to deal with, too, Jack."

Curley winced and let out a loud breath of wind before whining his complaint,

"Oh, come on, Jack man. Be reasonable . . . I'm. . . ."

"Be reasonable," Lucille shouted angrily. "Be reasonable? Why you stand there asking him to throw away his crown . . . and be reasonable. Where'd you come from, Curley?"

"Okay, Lucille. Okay, Jack. You get the negatives. I don't know how I'm gonna come out on this deal, for all my efforts and performances."

"You get a world's champion, man. And a world's champion means money in the bank. I'm giving it to you. Where do we fight, back home in Georgia?"

Curley was back in good spirits again. He had chosen Mexico City, which he had big plans for putting on the map as a sports capital.

He had arranged for Jack and his party to take up residence in Buenos Aires, while he negotiated a "tune-up" bout there, to take care of expenses.

Jack Curley and his backers had figured almost everything out in detail as to when, where and how, before they had even consulted Johnson. They had been that sure of themselves; Curley made that much clear as he explained the plans to Jack and his wife, while adding:

"Oh, we had alternative plans, Jack. But it won't be necessary for me to tell you what they were, now."

After they had laid out the general plans for the bout, signed the initial papers and agreements, they prepared to part for the night. Curley making arrangements for his immediate trip back to America, while Jack and Lucille went to prepare for their trip to Buenos Aires. As the champion and his wife left the Savoy, Curley called out his parting remark:

"Say, Jack, I wanted to tell you. I bet when your nephew, Gus, returns from your errand in Petrograd, he'll come back with every one of your trunks, with not the slightest piece missing."

His predictions were correct. Gus had little or no

trouble going to, or returning from, Russia with all 18
trunks intact, after seven months, except that a pair of
boots were missing. They hurried back home, cleaned
out their apartment and set sail for South America,
sharing the fears of submarine attacks as they crossed
the war-torn seas.

They were received in the South American city with
such acclamation that Jack was immediately booked for
innumerable personal appearances in Rio de Janeiro as
well as Buenos Aires. He quickly organized an act and
began to fill theatre engagements. "Making money,
hand over fists."

He performed strong man stunts, which he called "a
part of my physical training for the fight." He lifted
weights, broke chains with his muscles, carried four
men around the stage and as a further exhibition of his
strength, his act consisted of pulling a team of horses,
then allowing one horse to stand on his chest.

He also took time out to fight the "warm-up" bout
which Jack Curley had arranged for him, by knocking
out Jack Murray in three rounds, at Buenos Aires on
December 21, 1914. By then the fight site of Mexico
City had been changed, due to a revolution.

Jack Curley had a "near miss" when he got the President of Mexico, Venustiano Carranza to agree upon
their staging the fight and making Mexico City "one of
the greatest sports capitals of the Western Hemisphere,
or the world. . . ."

The President was forced to flee Mexico City and
take up residence at Tampico, as the Revolutionary
forces of Pancho Villa, "The Mexican Bandit-Gen-
eral," had swept in to take hold of the capital.

Carranza, seeking intervention and aid, did an about
face and announced:

"If Jack Johnson appears in Mexico, I will have him

arrested and returned to his country, from which he is a
fugitive. . . ."

Of course, Carranza issued his declaration in panic,
when he learned that Pancho Villa had invited the parties promoting the fight to still hold it:

"I assure you that Mexico City will be peaceful for
the fight. As long as I get my cut," Villa is supposed to
have assured them.

Then Jack Curley pulled a bluff, with a press campaign to rival Hugh McIntosh or "Tex" Rickard. He almost succeeded in pulling off the trick of getting the
public to agree to allowing the fight to be held at El
Paso, Texas. *Every red blooded American demanded
it. To see the fight 'The Republic of Mexico did not have
the courage to stage!"*

Curley's campaign for support of his proposal was so
effective that when objectors cried out into the ears of
William Jennings Bryan, Secretary of Sate and Johnson's avowed enemy in high places, he responded to
their appeals that he denounce the fight being held anywhere in the USA with the statement:

"I know this Jack Curley, who's promoting the fight.
He's all right. Besides, I saw a prize fight once and it
was very interesting."

He neglected to mention that the fight he saw was the
films of Johnson's brutal defeat of Jim Jeffries, to whom
Bryan had sent his famous telegram: *"God will forgive
anything that Jeffries does to that nigger in this
fight. . . ."*

Nor did the newspapers mention that Jack Curley
had once been manager and promoter of a lecture tour
for Bryan, which accounted for Curley's ability to produce a letter considering a Johnson pardon, in order to
sew-up the agreements for the fight.

But Curley still would not risk El Paso, when he
could get no political assurances that Johnson would

not be arrested when he came into El Paso for the bout. Instead, Curley chose Havana, Cuba, where he was allowed a lease on the Oriental Race Track to stage the battle. The papers were signed, the match was scheduled for April 5, 1915, then but two months away.

Jack spent most of this time, as newspapers reported it, "training on the sea shores of South America, soaking up sun and senoritas, when not touring in and out of theatres and night clubs of Buenos Aires and Rio de Janeiro."

Such reports upset Jack Curley to no end, as his ballyhoo for the fight pictured the champion as an "aged champion 37 years old . . . strenuously working himself to prepare for what could be the fight for his life . . . against a young white giant, who towered above him by almost six inches, outweighed him by 50 pounds, outextended him in arms' reach by at least ten inches."

Curly had pressed his newpaper campaign in America, emphasizing *"tired old black jack, filled up with the folly of European living, longing for his mother, watermelons, down-home cookin' and fried pork chops . . . penitent, seeking forgiveness for his sins, but like a brave old champion, facing possible imprisonment and even extinction, was dutifully training to give his supporters perhaps the last good fight of his life . . . win, lose and no draws. . . ."*

Meanwhile, down the South American way, newspaper pictures and stories were showing and saying otherwise. Curley sailed in scolding:

"Look man, we're doing this for your good. To make your pardon more palatable to the general public. You've got to cooperate!"

"I am cooperating, Curley, my boy. I'm giving you and your boys a 'temporary championship,' while laying a program to at least let your backers be able to explain my defeat. 'Cause anybody in their right minds knows

that Jack Johnson got penitent and went into strenuous
training for possibly the last fight of his life . . . like
you're telling those papers. Then, there are many folks
who know that your cowboy from Kansas wouldn't get
past the first round."

"But what about your pardon?" Jack Curley protested. "Think of your pardon."

"I am thinking about it, that and nothing else. I'm
giving up my title for that pardon and fifty thousand,
which is supposed to be delivered in a package of five
hundred bills before I go out. So you go think about
getting that together, okay. And let me do the thinking
about my behavior and training like I've always done.
We're not going to be able to get the fight and a pardon
arranged to suit everyone. You just remember that," the
champion concluded. In despair, Curley went back to
Havana to finalize his fight preparations, as the Champ
instructed.

CHAPTER NINETEEN

THE FIGHT FOR A PRISON PARDON

On Monday, April 15, 1915, at Havana, Cuba, they hauled out and dusted off the same old title for the third time of Jack Johnson's career: "The Battle of the Century."

The Havana sun was blazing away at 1:45 p.m., driving thermometers up over the one hundred mark, while fifteen thousand spectators sat there waiting and sweating in shirt sleeves and sun hats. The women present showed their reactions and discomfort with the heat, by fanning themselves with the hems of their garments affording the lookers a shameless but slight display of shapely white legs.

It was notable to observe that most of the times The Black Fire had fought with his championship at stake, as with Tommy Burns in Australia, Jim Jeffries at Reno, as now here in Havana, the sun had always been a scorcher, roasting away at everything.

The day was what the Cubans called "a good day for nothing but drying out tobacco."

Only this was the big day for the third battle of the century, between The Big Black Fire and the last of the White Hopes. Jack Johnson, champion, and Jess Willard, the Kansas cowboy, challenger.

The rumors were floating around like sweaty steam from the red hot sun.

"Johnson's old, over the hill, this sun will kill the old man. . . ."

"He's dried up . . . too much good living . . . ain't in a proper condition to hold up under Willard, for long. . . ."

By fight time the betting, based on hearsay of a fix, was even money on Willard to take the crown by the fifteenth round.

Johnson entered the ring without his prearranged guarantee, but with a solemn promise from Curley that it would be put in the hands of Lucille by the end of the fifth round. Lucille would be sitting at ringside within Jack's view. When she rose to leave that would signal that the pay-off had been received.

Each man was cheered as he climbed through the ropes. Cuban soldiers stood at each ring corner, relieving the Havana police of the responsibility of keeping order. After preliminary introductions, the referee called them to center-ring for instructions.

"This is a contest for 45 rounds and the Heavyweight Championship of the World. Shake hands and come out fighting."

"The nigger goes in fifteen," cried a ringside gambler holding a fistful of bills over his head, waving it to any takers.

"You got a bet, fellow . . . over here," a spectator shouted above the cheers of the crowd. Then the bell rang and there was a deadly silence as they moved out to face each other, Johnson still grinning at the gambler's shouting. "The nigger goes in fifteen. . . ."

Since the pay-off was not in, nor was the assurance of his pardon, the champion moved out determined to use the first five, and perhaps the next ten rounds, proving to his negotiators that they had received a bargain.

He knew that the pay-off had been delayed in the vain hope that a slight thing like a knockdown on behalf of Willard, or even a promising showing during these earlier rounds, would mean that the pay-off need never be made.

After more than a minute of feinting, dancing, feeling out, aiming tentative blows and withdrawing them, still grinning and making leers at the cowboy giant, in the middle of the first round he let go a convincer, whistling over a vicious left, which cracked like a whip against the challenger's upper jaw, and sent him reeling, staggering back into the ropes. There were no cheers as he followed up, sinking a series of solid blows into the body of the big man, grunting savagely as he dug them in, before the bell sounded. Grumbles were heard, but still no shouting or the throwing up of hands.

The second round was almost a repeat of the first. Except that Willard displayed an admirable restraint of his nervousness, by backing away, respectfully unwilling to step in and test again the bombs, which the champion had lowered upon him in the first round. Then, midway of round two, Johnson drew the challenger's guard, flashing in to unleash a right uppercut, this time the cowboy reeled forward catching the champion into a clinch, who pushed him away and commented:

"I devoutly hope that I didn't happen to hurt you, Jess."

The ringside rose to a man. "The nigger had started his taunting again." Jack laughed, stepped in and peppered the body of Willard until the bell rang.

The same gambler who had cried out for even money on fifteen, then stood, still waving his bills.

"Come on. I'm still betting. Whose giving what, sayin' the nigger will make it to twenty-rounds?"

Jack came out at the third round bell, laughing at the sudden change of the man's odds, allowing Willard five more rounds of grace.

He moved in to Willard, pumping his body with blows. Then stepped back, grinning:

"Now, that's the way to do it, Jess. Lemme show you again."

He stepped in, to the howls of the crowd, repeating the flurry, before stepping back and almost bowing.

See, it ain't hard. . . ."

Willard stumbled around the ring, swept away by the flurry.

Johnson continued to follow, taunting until the bell rang. The crowd didn't like it. But the black champion looked toward his wife and winked, hopefully.

The fifth round came. No pay-off was in, but the crowd saw now that the nigger was winning, well ahead on points. They cheered Willard for the slightest tap he made. They yowled and booed as Johnson worked him over in retaliation.

The "tired old washed up nigger" wasn't looking so tired and old as he bundled Willard into the ropes and battered him at will, keeping a running stream of chatter, antagonizing his opponent and his audience as well.

"This boy is a cowboy, who forgot to bring 'long his two guns."

At the round's end, Jess Willard walked back to his corner on wobbly legs, bent at the knees. Jack moved back to his own corner, looking in expectancy at his wife, who shook her head sadly indicating, no. No pay-off had come.

The sixth, seventh and eighth rounds wore on in the same repeated fashion. Johnson staying on top by points; even if there were some ruse employed to stop the fight, he was ahead without question. Willard reeled and rocked about the ring, taking punishment, bleeding from the mouth since the fourth round. Now everybody sensed: "He is too slow. Johnson's cutting him to pieces."

He had hit the champion, of course. But just by

slapping out. No punches, causing Johnson to stand back and laugh:

"Patty-cake, patty-cake, baker's man . . . Harder, harder, now! Hard as you can. . . ."

The Cuban soldiers were forced to make ringsiders sit down, preventing them from climbing into the ring.

Johnson was now beginning to sweat, during the ninth round, which Willard's supporters took for weariness and cheered the challenger on.

His manager, directing from his corner, signaled for Jess to go for the champion's heart, by pumping his fist against his chest. Willard followed these directions, coming awake, he closed in pounding heavy artillery to Johnson's rib cage. The crowd again rose to a man, shouting:

"Kill that black bastard. Kill that big bear," forgetting that Willard was by far the larger of the two in all measurements: height, reach and weight. The champion laughed again, slid away like a jackal, then flashed forward, thudding one, two, three right jabs in succession, each punch blotching a red, painful bruise against the pale skin of the challenger, who winced as each punch landed home. He grimaced in pain, some of the fans wincing with him in sympathy. The bell rang, ending the ninth. Thirty-six more rounds to go. Jess Willard hadn't won a single round.

Some critics report that at the end of the tenth round:

"There haven't been any redder ribs than Willard's, during a championship bout, since those of Jim Jeffries in his tenth round with Johnson."

Still Willard stumbled on, backing, charging, then reeling back, bending under the onslaught of The Big Black Fire, who punched and slapped him at will, sending him rolling across the ring from savage flurries, with Johnson smiling and taunting:

"You should have studied up on footwork, Jess. To keep yourself out of range. . . ."

He moved back to his corner, looking toward his wife. Who now shook her head again, closing her eyes, that he would not see the tears fall.

In the sixteenth, Johnson tore out as stark terror, resembling the tidal wave of Galveston, the San Francisco earthquake, the speed of Halley's Comet. Until then, there had been some hope for Willard, perhaps Johnson might have slipped, or broken an arm, or something. But, now there was wonder if the white giant could survive. But he did, standing, rocking from blows that came like rain, shaking his big body from stem to stern, like a ship in a raging storm. He stood helpless, receiving a barrage that made many customers close their eyes. Willard couldn't last.

The fifteen round bettors had lost their fortunes. Those remaining, who had bet Willard to win by knockout, felt hopeless. There wasn't a taker for any bets against Johnson's winning, as he moved back to his corner after the sixteenth.

The black champion moved back to his corner, smiling in determination, looking toward his wife, this time not asking. He knew, the double-cross was in. He raised his fist, causing Lucille to smile through her tears of concern and worry. He was going for the win. A knockout.

As he sat down, one of Jack Curley's aides came rushing to the corner, mounting the apron and spoke hastily into the ears of the heavily breathing champion, who nodded as he listened, then commented:

"You tell 'em then, they got but nine minutes more, three rounds at the most," he gasped through his heaving for air. "This thing's long past due . . . tell them count it out fast. And Lucille had better be moving by the twentieth round at the most."

Johnson was ahead by a mile, on points. He slowed the pace, on assurance from Curley's aide. The money was there, they were counting it out, getting it packaged and ready as stipulated.

He realized the gamble that he was taking. This wasn't Paris, where the referee could render a decision. This was no twenty-round fight. There would be no referee's decision . . . or any decision, despite the points, could go against him. Yet, he was allowing three rounds, that the white man could regain his strength, while immediately on verge of going down. Now!

The fight slowed down to a jog and a foxtrot. Johnson was even struck in the mouth by Willard, now both were bleeding from blows struck.

Before the twentieth round, the aide came rushing up again, whispering into the champion's ear, who nodded and smiled. As the bell rang, he looked over toward Lucille, his wife, as she rose smiling and started up the aisle, not looking back.

The bell sounded for the 21st round, also sounding "the turn of the tides" as white writers saw it. Forgetting what they had already seen for twenty rounds past, they elected to tell it, not as it happened, but as they had been promised and they had come to see it happen that way.

Johnson, the champion, acknowledged as potentially one of the finest stage performers of his time, became:

". . . A tired old Negro . . . slowed down by time and fast living, weary of the onslaught, began to sag. . . ."

Jess Willard, the challenger, "finding renewed strength and courage moving in . . . daring, stronger, bouncing his punches off the chin of the black man, driving him backward until the worried look replaced the cocky smile from his visage."

They described the twenty-second round as, "instead of a black panther, licking its horrible maw for the kill, there was a weary old Negro, circling the ring with a hope of leering and grinning his way to victory.

"All through the twenty-second round Willard's counterattack poured in. The weary white forearm, like Arm and Hammer Baking Soda, found renewed strength to level punches as the Negro's sagging bronze (not black any longer) jaw."

It was Willard all the way through the 23rd round, as well as the 24th, swinging the battle against the champion of the world, in his own favor, as the Negro went stiff-legged, backing around the ring from his full gale assault.

The man who led now, driving his victim around the ring, was a white man. The former insults, which had withered Tommy Burns and devitalized Jim Jeffries, had dried up on black and bloody lips now.

The Negro hadn't the strength to mutter anything . . . no more bitter jest to spit out. "Uncle Jack was standing at the feet of his master . . . obliged to take a well deserved whipping."

As the rounds rolled on thereafter, they were all Willard's.

In round 26, the bell had tolled for Johnson, coming out of his corner, shuffling as "the tired old man," that he was, long arms drooping, shoulders sagging. This was the black man who years before had clubbed Tommy Burns to his knees, reduced Jim Jeffries to a gibbering idiot, calling and pleading for his corner to throw in a sponge and save him, while the Nigger laughed as they carried a white man from his corner to his dressing room, semi-conscious and helpless.

Now it was his turn! As he lunged forward to meet his doom. . . .

Willard led with his left, backed away to take measure of his man, then, with a punch that Johnson himself had become renowned for, delivered a "right upper-cut," bending Johnson to his knees. Stepping back, he allowed the black man to slide to the floor, roll over on his back, with his head almost through the ropes on the apron.

Gus Rhodes rushed around to the ringside, looking at the champion, as the referee tolled off his count. Johnson winked at his nephew, raised his gloved hand and forearm—which many claim to have been near enough to see—with the comment:

"Lawdy, I sure wish that somebody would shade this sun out'a my eyes."

When the count tolled ten, the white race was avenged. A Nigger was no longer a champion of the world. The white folks had learned their lesson well. For it would be a long time to come, more than 20 years, before they'd give another Nigger the chance of becoming a champion again.

He left the ring amid boos, as Cuban soldiers cleared a path to his dressing room, while he endured their jeers of spite and hateful taunts.

Thereafter, smilingly, he admitted that he had been beaten by a younger and better man, with the belief that this gesture would cinch his plea for a pardon.

But there was no pardon, nor freedom to return to his mother and his country. His defeat, as well as his victory, only meant continued exile.

Newspapers refused to accept his story of the "fix and the doublecross," even when Johnson produced affidavits. They refused to break the story, some years later, when he returned to enter a penitentiary and to serve his time.

He remained in Cuba a short time as a guest, under the sponsorhip of General Mario Menocal, President of Cuba, becoming a personal friend of the family, the wife and the children, while dispatching Lucille to London to complete negotiations with an English syndicate for distribution of the fight films, which Jack Curley had promised to deliver to him in Cuba, when ready.

Then the Cuban President revealed that his intelligence service had learned: "There is to be no pardon. And Jack Curley and his backer plan to renege on their promises to grant Johnson Eastern Hemisphere rights to the fight films, which was to have included England and Europe." This was further substantiated when he received, "a reel of blank films of the fight." Menocal also revealed that his intelligence agents had learned that Curley and his backers were already en route to England to negotiate with London promoters, for release and distribution of the films.

Jack set sail for London immediately.

England received him, once again with no comment as to his ouster. He was no longer champion of the world, just another "has been" nigger, whom they might tolerate as a source of amusement.

He reopened his stage attraction: *Seconds Out,* while waiting, keeping an eye on the agents of Jack Curley. The films arrived and Johnson presented himself, snatching the films from Curley's man, Mr. A. Weil, under threat of violence.

He was then able to place the films, by contracting the London syndicate for distribution. But not before "almost bending Mr. A. Weil out of shape."

There were no assault charges launched against him this time, but a few days later *The London Times* announced:

"Jack Johnson is leaving the country in compliance with a ruling of The Home Office, under the Aliens Restriction Act."

They headed for Spain, as had been the advice of the Cuban President, Menocal. "In Spain, they will love you, for I have many friends and associates there, whom I will write to aid you to live well there."

They arrived in Santiago, Spain. And true to his words, President Menocal had sent correspondence to precede them. Johnson began immediately to set up an advertising agency, while beginning a career as a motion picture actor, appearing in his initial film, a drama *False Nobility*.

Very shortly, he took up residence in Madrid, then traveled on to Barcelona, where he was featured as a wrestler, while opening a School of Boxing. Two of his students were the famed Spanish matadors, the thin and small-framed Belmonte, and the six-foot-one Joselito, both of whom had been introduced to him by the aging bull-fighting star Chicorito.

It was these two who encouraged and challenged him into his (brief) career as a bull-fighter in Barcelona.

"It is an excellent idea, to make yourself a fortune," Joselito danced about enthusiastically, after making the proposal to the reluctant Johnson.

"You are a natural! Almost the same size as Joselito, here. You couldn't be any more clumsy, for the both of us are willing to teach you!"

"Your footwork is fair," agreed Joselito. "Under our coaching and sponsorship, you could not help but become a sensation at bullfighting."

"That is, unless you are afraid," Belmonte commented sadly. "Men who are afraid have no business in the bull ring."

"I'm afraid of nothing, man. Especially a bull who can think of nothing but a red flag that you wave in front of him."

"Yes, but the bull will kill, not box for a decision, like fighters. You have to kill him, or be killed, when the time comes. There is the rub, the difference, unlike with prize fighters."

"It is a fight unto death, my friend," Joselito added. "Each time that you face a bull, it is a dance unto

death. For you or for the bull. And you know that the
bull, with his hard head, has decided already. It is you
who face the decision of the bull. For he knows, and he
has already decided."

Johnson retorted to Joselito, "Well, I sure don't see
how decided he is when he fights with you. For you stay
too wide open to hold off a man in the boxing ring.
That's a fault that the bulls you kill must not notice.
Man, some of the men that I've fought would actually
kill you."

But that is his skill!" Belmonte shouted in Joselito's
defense. "He dares the bull to take advantage of this
weakness. For he is more intent on the kill. The crowds
love him for it."

"But one of those bulls is going to kill him, mark my
words. If I were fighting bulls, I'd do just as I do with
the fighters that I've fought. Stay close, make it look
good to please them, thinking that I'm within the inches
of death, keeping a margin for safety."

Although Johnson's prediction came true, a short
time later, when Joselito was gored to death by a bull,
he threw back his head and laughed.

"You are right, Jack Johnson. I do stay open, stand
open all of the time. With your style, they would boo
you out of a bull ring. I must tell Juan and Ramon to
follow your suggestions more. For that is what they do,
cover up, cover up, like they are fighting the 'Dixie Kid.'
But I stand out, alone, in the open, like you say. Forcing the bull to come out and challenge the mistake,
which is his mistake."

"Joselito is right, with all of his clumsiness," Belmonte replied in support of his friend. The crowd
comes to see you carry the fight to the bull. You must
make them see that you are a split second ahead of the
bull with your skill, like partners in a dance to death,
showing that you are the master, at all times, that you

can bring the dance to an end when you wish to. The
sword must flash too quickly for the eye, as a woman,
helplessly sinking back to be seduced by her lover, in
the last moment. . . ."

"The killing of a bull is a poem that we write to all
the women we love," Joselito added. "The poem must
have all the bells of heaven and hell chiming in unision,
eh, Belmonte?"

"He's right, Jack. You've got to be able to feel it,"
Belmonte agreed. "It is not just a sport, Jack Johnson,
it is art, poetry, music and painting all rolled into one,
climaxing with the sweetest love affair that a man can
possibly dream of."

Jack smiled, but was fascinated at the description
and ecstasy displayed by the two Spaniards. Belmonte
continued:

"It is love, incomparable! Ask any hot blooded
woman, would she rather have a great bull dedicated to
her, or to sleep in the bed with a prince. You may judge
the woman by her answer."

"Your first fight would be like being a virgin, Jack,"
Joselito added in dreamy recollection. "Like possessing
a woman for the first time in your life. . . ."

"You must take our offer, Jack, to train you," Belmonte continued. "Or, at the age of thirty-two, you
must confess that you'll spend the remainder of your
days wondering what true love, death and living can
really be like."

"But, look here," Johnson protested. "If I don't
know the rules of the game, I'd offend all of the gods of
the game."

"We told you already, we would not allow for you to
do that, Jack. You'd be our protégé. They would spit
upon us, if we sponsored you and failed, the very next
time that we appeared in the bull ring."

"Of course, if you are afraid, Jack. . . ." Joselito let

his voice trail off to blend with the strumming music of
Spanish guitars. "That would be the end of it, of course.
Bullfighting is no sport for a man with the slightest fear
in his heart."

"Are you afraid, Jack?" Belmonte asked, looking at
the black man, feigning sadness and sympathy. "It's
all right, you can tell us. Then, we can drink and forget
about the whole thing."

"I'm not afraid of anything existing between God and
the devil, friend. What a couple of Spanish *hidalgos* can
manage, any Negro like me, from Texas, can master.
When do I meet your bulls?"

Belmonte jumped up pumping Johnson's hand. "As
soon as we have signed contracts and given you a
course of proper instructions."

He then turned to Joselito and laughed, while pumping Jack's hand.

"See, I told you," he laughed at Joselito. "I told you
the sucker would take it. Now you owe me one hundred
pesetas."

Within the period of one week, The Black Fire was
well into intensive training, from sun-up to sun-down,
under the severe and double scrutiny of two of Spain's
most celebrated matadors, his sponsors, in typical
Johnson fashion—much to the concern of those who
loved him, as well as to the chagrin of those who hated
him.

Among the latter was one Juan, Matador of Seville,
who openly resented Jack's entrance into the bull ring
as an intrusion. He had shouted at Belmonte and Joselito:

"He has no right! I spent a lifetime of apprentice-
ship. He did not. I do not invade the prize fight ring. He
should not invade the bull ring!"

His protests were drowned under echoes of drunken
laughter. After a short course of intensive training by

two of Spain's foremost stars of the bull ring, Johnson was scheduled to enter and make his premiere in the bull ring in July of 1916.

His two mentors, during his training period, had persuaded him to become a Catholic convert, which entitled him to receive the sacrament and the "last rites" which were rendered by their favorite priest.

Belmonte had loaned him his sword. He wore the golden-striped satin trousers of Joselito. He was given a cloak which had been worn by a Spanish matador of the past, who had flourished it during his life as a victory flag, before he had been gored to death by a bull.

As he was dressed in preparation, Belmonte took him by the arm, leading him to the chapel.

"Now, I will teach you the prayers of all matadors since the history of bull fighting began."

"I want to talk with my wife," Johnson said airily. "You go, and you pray for that bull."

Belmonte's eyes narrowed at the foolish bravery and daring of his black pupil, replying, "Later for your wife, my friend. You will come and pray with me, all the same. When down on your knees in prayer, you will find that faith dies hard . . . harder than the bulls die."

Johnson went with him to the chapel. Upon returning he confronted his wife, Lucille.

"If he kills me, hon," the black man said to his wife. "Then I will you my solid gold teeth. That'll be enough to finance your passage back home, won't it?"

She tried to share his laughter, before turning away and rushing off, before he could see her tears.

Joselito and Belmonte stood there observing, exchanging glances, before Belmonte stepped forward to touch Johnson.

"Perhaps, my friend, it is not at all even worth it. Your life, your wife's sorrow. Why shouldn't we just call it a private little joke between the three of us?"

"Because nobody would believe you," Johnson answered solemnly. "Everybody in this wide world knows that I'd never offer my life as a private joke and amusement for anyone."

Joselito stepped forward and touched his arm.

"Perhaps it is just as well, my friend. For the President of the Council has just gone to your dressing room. Paying you the great honor of calling upon you before you go into the ring. Shall we go?"

As they entered the dressing room, the *presidente* (prime minister) turned from his party and faced him, as Johnson bowed, the grandee also bowed in return, a gesture that was offered few foreigners.

"You are a brave men, Mr. Johnson. You are not content to be champion of the world, for after your career is almost over, you risk everything for the first and possibly the last time. I salute you."

"When I saw Belmonte and Joselito in the bull ring, for my first time, I knew that I'd given my life to the wrong trade, sir. I should have begun with the most beautiful and exacting sport in the world, then."

"Then you must allow me to give you one piece of advice," the *presidente* said. "Remember this infallible rule. You mustn't ever take your eyes off of the bull. Not for one split second! If you want to survive, Mr. Johnson, remember. There is no rest between rounds in bull fighting. Not even one second."

Johnson bowed stiffly in appreciation as the grandee passed from the top room.

"Your turn next, Jack," Joselito announced, turning to Belmonte. "How the devil did he get in on the draw?"

A fast exchange of glances between the two Spaniards indicating mutual understanding of the fact that in last minute concern for the black man's life, Belmonte had gone to arrange for Johnson to draw the smallest bull of the lot.

"By sorcery, perhaps by luck," Belmonte answered. "But what does it matter, for he has managed to draw the smallest bull in all the history of Barcelona. A bull about the size of a cat!"

Joselito almost laughed with relief, pretendng sadness. But thankful that his partner had taken the final course of precaution against Johnson's first encounter in the bull ring would not end with his death.

"What does he mean?" the black man asked Joselito.

Belmonte eagerly interrupted. "Oh, don't you worry about it, Jack, it is just that—bull fighting, the bigger the bull, the louder they cheer. But, that's of no matter, for you are simply a curiosity to them. They will almost for certain grant you the tail of the bull, out of good manners to a stranger."

"That is providing that this 'small bull' which you have drawn does not get your tail first," Joselito joked.

The three friends looked at each other. The time had come. Both matadors embraced Johnson almost in tears, wishing him luck, before leaving him alone, as they went out into the stands to watch.

But they had not reckoned with the bitterness and anger of Juan, Matador of Seville, who had followed Belmonte, then bribed the attendants to switch bulls. He had killed the smallest one, assigned to Johns͟ leaving the outsized bull that he was to have fa͟ the Negro, in his debut as a bull fighter.

Belmonte and Joselito noticed the s͟ alarm; they encouraged the *banderi͟* to work more on the bull. But ͟ served to increase the bull's madne͟

The Black Fire walked down th͟ arena, moved from the darkness into͟ um filled with colors, shouting and cheering people, beautiful senoritas, alive in the splendor which he loved so. Then the idea dawned upon him that very shortly he might not ever see life again.

He recalled part of the prophecy which the Los Angeles fortune teller had told him years ago. He had laughed at it, so incredible it had seemed, as she stated:

"You are destined to meet with large animals in combat for life and death . . . huge beasts of battle and burden. You will see death, touch death, but death cannot harm you. It is only your living that will bring you harm."

Amid the roars of the crowd, he heard these words thunder back into his ears. Then more thunder was added . . . the thunder of pounding hoofs as the bull, as big as a steam engine, charged.

A lifetime passed as he braced himself. He flourished the *muleta,* brought his body into play and sidestepped as the bull charged by, snorting as he tossed his head up into the air, hooking the empty place where the tall champion had stood one split second ago.

Now The Black Flame knew terror, as he had never known before. He wished that he could run, but the tight trousers seemed to constrict his legs and prevent movement. The crowds roared. The first charge of a fight to the finish was over.

He spun on his heel, as his tutors had shown him, facing the big bull again, in readiness, noting that the bull was slow. He smiled. He could make it, for the bull was much slower than the men he had faced in the prize fight ring.

The bull charged again. This time with confidence ~k feinted away with seconds to spare. But the third ~ge was shorter and faster. The bull had cut down istance as well as his movements, allowing little and a shorter time for his tormentor to deceive him. His horns dipped then came up slashing at Johnson's vital area. The black man's ability to jump back ten feet, from a standing position, came into play. Awkward, but effective, and not before he felt the pangs of pain as the dagger-sharp horn-tips of the animal had gashed across his thigh. A fraction of a second less, Johnson wold have been dead or severely injured.

He could wait no longer. The bull had sensed the kill. Each movement now was a final movement of survival. The longer the wait, the better the chances for death.

Now, the bull whipped back in angry charge again. The black man turned, holding his *muleta* too high, but it rippled around his legs as the bull passed once again. He tried to remember to execute all of the movements which his mentors had taught him. But he had no time to think. Sweat blinded his eyes, blurring his vision. He heard the warnings of *El Presidente*: "Your eyes . . . not for one second . . . not for one split second. . . ."

The bull passed again, his whistling noises blending into the blood-thirsty screams of the crowd.

He taunted the bull for their entertainment, grinning, waving, playing to infuriate him more, for the pleasure of the crowd, while preparing himself for the kill, recalling the instructions of Joselito and Belmonte. "The death stroke. . . ."

"Up with the body . . . eyes fixed upon the spot of the beast's neck . . . poised on your toes . . . deliver swift like an arrow in flight . . . wrists steady . . . poised ~ steel spring, ready to uncoil. . . ."

As instructed, he tried. His sword flashe~ hind the shadows of his *muleta*, he whi~ the spot. Perfection! He thought body of the great brute spun his cuperating just in time to avoid ~ swirling horns, remembering Belmon~ "Remember, no reflection, my fr~

reaction! To reflect at the point of death means, 'tardiness,' too late! Tardiness with death is fatal."

Johnson heard the crowd groan. Then the charge again! Poise! Ready! Slip! Failure! Again the bull turned, pawing, aiming with madness and bloodshot eyes! The last time!

This time, up! One toe! The *muleta* whirls, the bull head follows its movement, tossing to expose the spot which the champion saw. His sword slivered as a flash of lightening, his body followed lunging its weight, following in force and grace, as the slim steel shaft followed its point to the hilt. Home!

The massive hulk of muscled steel halted. Paralyzed, then shuddered in its tracks, hot steam exploded from its nostrils in a burst. Eyes still glazing, reflecting at death, then turning, heaving at his foe, in recognition. He was dead!

Johnson watched his eyes register this, before the brute closed his eyelids softly as he slumped, his front legs folding as if in a gesture of prayer, it sank forward, then slowly rolled over onto its gored and bleeding side, its head shaking in convulsions, nodding, as the bull had finally, consciously, conceded to accept the state of death.

The rumbling noises from throats of the fans rose into a fanfare of wild cheers, swelling as high as the clouds as a single thunderous applause.

He saw the barefoot Spanish boys, leaping, swinging and clambering from the stands, dropping over into the ust and bloody area, running toward him.

He dropped his head to hide his tears as he mumbled er of thankfulness as they flooded toward him. It that he raised his hand in salute to the presireceiving the bow of acknowledgement be- engulfed him, lifting him to carry him, e around the arena, exposing him to cheers and hugs and kisses, planted and tossed, before rushing him off to his dressing room, where his two mentors, Joselito and Belmonte, waited in tears of joy, relief and pride.

Belmonte flung his arms around the neck of the huge black hero, laughing and crying into his ears:

"Oh, Jack, my friend. The time he slashed your thigh, I thought it was over. I prayed for you, Jack. I prayed! If that bull had known as much about bull fighting as I do, then you would have been one dead matador, my friend."

Lucille stood aside with Gus Rhodes, smiling, her eyes brimming with watery pride, as her black, sweating husband made his way toward her. She turned her head from his kiss causing him to laugh as he playfully pulled her mouth to his lips.

Jack was to kill more bulls that day. And during the final encounter, his confidence having grown so, from two earlier kills, he executed one of the trickiest and most unusual maneuvers ever seen or witnessed in Spanish bull rings.

During what did not have to be the final charge of the bull, The Black Fire employed a foot step which he had learned in the ring. Standing head on into the charge, he struck the bull in the nose, before moving aside for his pass, causing the animal to bellow out, turn, stunned, whipping his head about, exposing the spot, into which the black matador slid the sword with grace and ease, for the kill.

Now some say that the bull was knocked out by the punch.

Others say, in disagreement, that the punch simply confused the bull.

So, what does a bull know about the rules of bull-fighting? The bull did not know that he had been fouled.

But the fans who witnessed it loved it, and were overjoyed, predicting, as Joselito and Belmonte had done, that Jack Johnson had a successful future as a bull fighter, if he should choose to follow it.

CHAPTER TWENTY

THE FLAME GONE A WANDERING

Jack didn't follow bull fighting as a course, after a few more appearances in the bull rings of Barcelona, Madrid, and Santiago, although he had become a Spanish sensation.

He received the news that Tiny, his mother, had been felled by a stroke and confined to her bed indefinitely. He longed for a means to get home.

Prize fighting was his natural game. His bull ring experiences had so increased his popularity that Spanish promoters were willing and ready to sponsor him at anything he chose. He returned to the theatrical circles, touring while seeking the promised return bout with Jess Willard, to be staged in Spain or elsewhere on the Continent, all to no avail. It had become clear that despite written agreements with Jack Curley, he would not meet Willard, nor would he ever collect the ten percent of the cowboy, which he owned with Curley. And without an entrée into the United States, he was unable to enforce any kind of American agreements or signed conditions.

He was eager to fight and issued challenges to all "American imports," just as the Spanish promoters stood eager to sponsor such engagements. That year there were only two. Frank Crozier, he knocked out in Madrid in 4 rounds on March 20, 1916.

Shortly after this fight, he received the news that Tiny Johnson, his mother, had passed in Chicago, causing him to lose interest in almost everything.

Cheered on by Lucille and Gus, Jack prepared to meet and knock out the famous poet-prize fighter, Arthur Craven, in one round, on July 16 of that year.

But his yearning for home was only increased, despite the fact he had become one of the most adored Spanish attractions of that time.

Now that his mother had passed on, his return and imprisonment would no longer harmfully effect her. The Three Musketeers began to consider plans to go home.

They began to exchange correspondence with people in high places, politicians who were known to pull strings as "to a deal, or series of deals" that would enable him to return home. But, after a few months of this, their hopes were cut short.

America entered the war on April 6, 1917. It had finally come, just as Curley had predicted it would, even though the sinking of the *S.S. Lusitania,* which allegedly provoked her entry, had happened some years prior, on May 7, 1915.

It had taken that long, but now America was in, as anticipated, which called for an immediate reevaluation of their position, as he recalled his conversations with Jack Curley almost three years ago back in London.

Spain remained out, as a neutral nation, which was an open invitation, as agents of espionage, "spies and counterspies" from all nations, flocked into her major cities.

The German agents were not long in making overtures to Johnson. Although he was no longer the champion, he was no less a world renowned figure, also a fugitive from the justice of an enemy country. He could be employed in many ways.

The American agents in Spain also recognized this factor, upon learning that the Germans were after the celebrated American Negro.

Johnson seizing his opportunity, while recognizing the necessity of remaining a popular figure, turned to wrestling. After a series of matches, even though wrestling was only secondary to bull fighting as a sport in Spain, he was again in the headlines after defeating the wrestling champion of the Latin nation, Juan Ochoa.

By then American agents had secured the official permission from Washington to approach Johnson with propositions and offers to serve his country as a spy. The Black Flame accepted.

Without any previous training, he pursued his assignments, working under a Major Lang, U.S. military attaché in Madrid.

Immediately, he was instructed to join in with the small American colony there, which must have suited the black man's early American training around the ports of Galveston. For within a short period of time, he had earned profits, as well as a reputation as one of the most prominent smugglers of the port of Cadiz dealing with Germans, Spaniards, Americans, British or any other nationality "ready to pay the price."

"You are on your own at all times," Major Lang had warned him with regularity as he would return from the coastal inlets traveling the musky waters with smugglers, to return with information concerning German submarine bases around San Sebastian and Santander, and traveling as far as Sweden, Denmark and Norway in the guise of a wrestling exhibitonist, sailor, smuggler, exile and even at times an American traitor on the run. Reporting the locations and movement of various ships, which served as refueling posts for the deadly U-boats.

"Your country can never claim that you are working for them, until perhaps years later, after the war," the Major had frequently added. "And, perhaps, not even then. We work for the love of what we are doing, many times without credit or approval."

"Major Lang, sir!" Johnson would often laugh and remind him. "That's the story of my life up to now. Working without credit or approval, but for the love and hell of what I'm doing."

Lang was later to comment, "That sneaky, sly black bastard had the makings of an excellent agent. No matter where he was sent or assigned, he not only tried to make a point of coming away from it alive, but he made another point of coming out of it making a profit for himself on the side. He didn't need to concentrate. He was concentration itself, without even giving a damn about concentration.

"Although it is sad that much of what he did in service and risk for America cannot be told, I am certain that the personal satisfaction gained from the deeds that he performed was sufficient unto itself," Major Lang observed.

"When making his reports, the relish and exuberance with which he embellished the reports, as he spoke of the narrow escapes and results, was enough to put the finest of our writers to shame. He would force you to listen or he would deliberately leave out an important factor. Then, when I would inquire about a detail, he would begin the story all over from the beginning ,until you had heard well what he wanted you to learn of his fantastic adventures."

For example, Johnson came across the captain of a Danish spy steamer in a saloon. And during a drunken spree, he learned that the captain was fueling U-boats that very night, which were scheduled to contact and destroy an American-British convoy at sea. The Dane had particular navigational information concerning the convoy, which he was to deliver to the fleet at the time of refueling.

Johnson gathered together a small group from the American contingent at Madrid, followed him and engaged his crew in combat. It is alleged that the captain was killed or nearly killed, during the action. Johnson did succeed in relieving him of the documented materials as full proof.

The Danish captain was not heard of again. Johnson got credit for the kill, or the near kill.

Then, more concerning his activities became apparent, when he sought financial aid based upon the strength of his clandestine operations on behalf of his country, evidenced when the American Consul at Malaga wrote the American Ambassador, Joseph E. Willard, on April 3, 1918, as follows:

I have the honor to report that Jack Johnson, ex-champion pugilistic (sic) of the United States, called this consulate today and requested me to notify the Hotel Regina, where he was staying, that he would meet his bill for bedding and boarding.

In this connection, he informed me confidentially that he was employed by Major Lang and that he was expecting money from him. Jack Johnson was informed that this consulate was unwilling to make guarantees for anyone. . . . The above is brought to the attention of the Embassy for its information.

I have the honor to be, sir, your obedient servant, Louis G. Dreyfus, Jr., American Consul.

Then beyond this was another U.S. State Department

correspondence which was uncovered later, written from London to a Washington department representative by an official named L. Lanier Winslow, addressed to Edward Bell, which read:

I want to give you a little information about your colored friend, Mr. John Arthur Johnson, otherwise known as Jack Johnson, the former heavyweight champion. ..

From an instruction No. 165 of June 4, 1915, from the Department, in which Jack is described as a colored person of wide reputation in the pugilistic world, I gather that he is a fugitive from justice of the United States, and is not likely to set foot in his native land in the immediate future. It may interest you to know that in the course of the past year, while in Spain, he offered his services to the German organization in that country for the purposes of espionage against the Allies, including his native country. The German Organization in Spain referred his application to Berlin, where it was turned down.

So far as I know, Jack never engaged in espionage against us. It was not his fault, however, and I think it just as well that this should be borne in mind. . . ."

It also should be borne in mind, as we read the files today, that Johnson may have been acting on instructions in treating with the Germans, attempting the hazardous role of double-agent. It is significant that no action was ever taken against Johnson for approaching the enemy.

This letter above was not revealed until after World War I was over.

Still, with the documented proof above, nobody in our government came out officially after the war to say anything good on this black man's behalf. Others wouldn't believe and give credit when Jack Johnson himself attempted to make public the services he had performed.

When the war seemed like it was coming to a close, and the allies felt reasonably sure of winning, they no longer needed the spying services of The Black Flame. Once again, he turned loose to fare for himself.

The Big Smoke then began to look toward the shores nearer home. Late in the year of 1918, he was encouraged by promoters in Mexico City, who suggested that he come to promote boxing and wrestling for their syndicate. There were also included Mexican offers to sponsor him in a bull fighting tour. The Mexican Revolution seemed to have come to an end. Thus Mexico City had become an international headquarters for criminals, gamblers, spys and counter-spies, propagandists, world renowned pimps, prostitutes and peddlers of everything from pepper to stolen jewelry, politics, sports and fabulous masterpiece-paintings. "Counterfeits, duplicates or originals."

He sailed for Mexico City on the 28th of March, 1919, he and Lucille, while he dispatched his nephew, Gus Rhodes, to New York, to round up and make arrangements for sending prize fighters down to box in Mexico City against Jack Johnson.

Then, Monte Cutler, George deBray and Jack Heinman were contracted by Gus to proceed on to Mexico to fight, in matches where Johnson would be the principal attraction against them.

He arrived to fall in with the riotous and bawdy crowd of military men and millionaires who sponsored him; among them was Paulino Fontes, the railroad tycoon in Mexico, who took him to a celebration at Chapultepec, the palace of restored Presidente Carranza. And he became an immediate favorite of the man who had banned his fight with Jess Willard.

"I regretted preventing that bout in Mexico City,"

the *presidente* explained. "But things are different now. I support your fighting anyone that you wish in Mexico City now. Perhaps we might induce Mr. Willard to come down."

Johnson accepted Carranza's presidential invitation to remain a few days as his guest, "for amusement and conversation."

The Black Flame accepted and remained, establishing one of the most cherished friendships with the Mexican President that he had ever known.

"You are a man of experience, Mr. Johnson," Carranza told him. "And you have met all kinds of people, world over. I would rather talk and listen to you than to hear a skillful oration from a polished politician. I can learn more from you."

He opened himself an advertising and theatrical agency, a boxing school, a dancing school, while appearing in boxing exhibition tours against the five fighters he had imported for the syndicate's benefit and his own. He also included bull fighting for the benefit of the tourists and Mexican fans. Mexican newspapers made complimentary appraisals of his skill at their native sport.

His political and civic activities and interests were not neglected, either. A State Department communiqué sent from Washington to the American Embassy in Mexico City, will attest to this:

It has been reported that Jack Johnson, of pugilistic fame, has been spreading social equality propaganda among the Negroes in Mexico and has been endeavoring to incite the colored element in this country. Please report any activity of this character on the part of Johnson as well as the manner in which the propaganda is distributed.

Now although there are no official records concerning the effectiveness of Johnson with a "social equality" program and propaganda among the Mexican people, there is some evidence in that it was to save him and a whole train load of passengers just a short time later.

A new Civil War broke out in Mexico which brought an end to the tenure of Venustiano Carranza as that nation's president. And as usual, right on schedule, Jack Johnson was right there in the thick of it. Since he was a personal friend of the man who was making hasty preparations to depart the scene as the reports were made public that the military strong arm, General Alvaro Obregon, was approaching Mexico City with his armies to take possession and shoot Carranza on sight, when they found him.

But Carrenza took time out to send Johnson a message advising him to follow suit and quit the city:

I feel certain that Obregon will seek to destroy any and all people who might have shared a personal friendship with me. If I do not return as President, then perhaps we will see each other again, elsewhere in the world. Paris, Madrid, Switzerland? Who knows? But it is something to look forward to, as you know I share with you the fate of fleeing as a fugitive from your own native land.

Johnson, Lucille and Gus Rhodes fled the city as Carranza had advised, headed north for Tijuana, the Mexican City just across the border from the United States and San Diego, California. It was during their flight they learned that they would never see Carranza again. The forces of Obregon had caught up with him before he reached the coast. They shot him.

Johnson's group was to travel overland by train to Mazatlan, and there take a boat up north via the Gulf of California, then, overland to Tijuana. Their train was running irregularly, as all of them were, risking holdups and robbery by Mexican bandits and savage Indian tribes, who made a practice of slaying the passengers as well as robbing them.

The threesome arrived in Mazatlan without incident, and then they attempted to find a boat which would sail the route they wished to take. There was little choice, but they managed to come across the captain of a gasoline launch who was willing to take them. The captain was easy to deal with, and the party learned why when they set out to sea, headed up the Gulf of California. The boat was smuggling fifty Chinese passengers who had recently arrived from the Orient. They were seeking to be smuggled across the border from Mexico into the United States.

They were no sooner out to sea than the skies opened up with a violent storm. The captain, who had sailed these waters for a quarter of a century, fought to make it to land, but was tossed many miles off course, out toward the open seas. The black man later claimed that never before had he seen waves rise so high—and he had lived through the Galveston Tidal Wave.

Finally the launch was swept toward land and the captain made for a tiny cove where they could wait until the raging sea had died down. Starting forth again, the captain was wary of the coast guard and government boats, out searching the sea for survivors of the storm. He confided his fears to the members of his crew while Lucille was within earshot. The fifty Chinese passengers were to be dumped overboard into the sea should a government vessel elect to challenge them.

Johnson tested his weapon, as did Gus Rhodes. Then, keeping their guns in readiness but out of sight, they approached the captain and attempted to persuade him not to do what he had planned. Johnson offered to stand there with him and attempt to talk to the patrol boats, should they appear.

The captain seemed grudgingly agreeable, although

he gave no assurance, for, already in the distance, a patrol boat was approaching. The captain gave no order to
execute the orientals. Johnson waved to the patrol boat,
and their crew waved back; the launch was not challenged.

"I sighed with relief," the Big Smoke recalled later.
"I didn't want to kill the man, but had he given that
order, I'd have shot him dead."

The rest of the voyage was without incident. They
made their way up the Colorado River for a day or
more, until they arrived at an isolated spot where the
smuggled orientals were put ashore, to hike for many
miles toward the border of Arizona and California.
Hopefully they would be successful in entering the
United States. But if they managed to avoid death from
hunger or the elements, there were still the American
Border Guards to contend with. For the favorite sport of
some of the Border Guards was to use the orientals as
"two footed runners at a rabbit shoot-out," spotting and
shooting them as they came across the border.

The threesome, Jack, Lucille, and Gus, caught a
train for Mexicali, but it was near Sonora that they were
stopped by a horde of Yaqui Indians who claimed to be
supporters of the revolutionary forces, using this as an
excuse to stop and pillage the trains and passengers.

The passengers were driven from their coaches—
sometimes thrown, when the bandits were finished with
searching them. Johnson and his party alighted from the
train as ordered; he began to talk with them, for he had
mastered enough of the language to make them understand. He told them who he was. His name was passed
down the line, with enough interest that the Indians
stopped their looting temporarily, out of curiosity of
seeing *el hombre* who calls himself Jack Johnson. He
was surprised that many of them recognized him.

The leaders of the band came forward with enthusiasm.

"You are a champion of the poor people. You have spoken out on our behalf, we hear."

They then offered profuse apologies for stopping and robbing the train that Jack Johnson was riding. They had not known. They even asked him to remain and enjoy a bit of celebration with them, as they set about restoring what loot they had already taken from the passengers. He declined the invitation to remain, explaining the importance of his leaving. Although he did promise to return someday, as he moved freely among them, laughing, talking and drinking of their brewed mixtures, until the passengers had retrieved their valuables as well as they could and the train was readied to move away. And under armed guard, all the way to the outskirts of Mexicali, as assurance and insurance that "The Jack Johnson train would not be molested until it had reached its destination." His preachments for Social Equality had paid off among the peon Yaqui Indians. And for which a trainload of passengers felt at least temporarily indebted. For, but for the Black Fire, they might not have lived to relate their experiences.

Jack, however, had kept his gun in readiness—just in case—and it had accidentally gone off, wounding his nephew, Gus Rhodes. He was seriously injured and bleeding profusely, and they were still 150 miles from their destination: Tijuana.

Jack immediately sent for an automobile from Tijuana, while they nursed Gus in an old abandoned cabin. The auto arrived and they rushed him to a hospital in Mexicali, where he remained for several weeks, Jack and Lucille continued on to Tijuana to take up residence. And to prepare for his nephew, who had suffered the ordeal of braving the drive across the desert, wounded and almost to the point of death from the lack of blood.

The promoters were waiting to greet him. Since he was overdue, they had already arranged several bouts for him. His mettle and superb physical condition was evident. This much he proved. For after the grueling travel at sea, the harrowing experiences of travel with Gus Rhodes across the Mexican desert, The Black Fire took on his first opponent in two days, knocking him out at Mexicali. This was Bob Wilson from San Francisco.

He toured the nearby provinces in boxing matches, accepting any and all who dared to cross the border to meet with him in Mexico, a challenge which was also hurled across the border to fall upon the deaf ears of Jess Willard, the champion, and Jack Curley, the manager-promoter. Even the sounds of Mexican money supporting his challenges failed to remove the wax from the ears of the champion.

Very shortly after arriving, The Big Smoke and his wife opened their exquisite Gambling-Cabaret which was immediately successful and popular, well patronized by visitors from the United States and all over the world, who were flocking into Tijuana, because of the "lack of restrictions" placed on fun lovers and fun seekers there.

Jack, knowing well how to "take advantage of the lack of restrictions," set a Tijuana pattern to be followed by others, by offering anything and everything to suit even the most peculiar tastes of his clients. "From bribing, betting on the race horse, the drop of the card, the roll of the dice. From the finest in drink and food, to freakish, sex-filled sideshows. All under one roof."

The Cabaret jumped, twenty-four hours around the clock, filled with diplomats, dignitaries, politicians and prostitutes, "the do-gooders and the do-badders" from all over the world. Yellow men and women, brown men and women, black, beige and red among all the human species would cross over into Tijuana to see Jack Johnson again.

But, all of this by no means could satisfy his yearning. Many a morning the tall black giant could be seen standing, watching the sun rise and looking across the invisible barrier which separated him from the land he had been forced to flee from.

Sometimes folks would notice two figures standing there in the twilight, holding onto one another as they looked out across the hills. What they said to each other, nobody got close enough to hear, because after about two months of this Jack Johnson developed the habit of cornering prominent officials and politicians who visited the Cabaret, talking earnestly as to the possibilities of returning to his country.

Now that seven years had gone by Johnson sent lawyers back into the USA, pleading for a more lenient judicial review and re-evaluation of his case. The black man insisted that he should not be made a moral scapegoat, for he was nothing like his prominent moralistic-at-home clients, who visited the brothels regularly in secret, while holding him in condemnation for their own guilts.

Many Americans joined in supporting him on this point, but he was convinced by Tom Carey, a Chicago politician and one time candidate for Mayor of that city.

Carey was vacationing in Tijuana at the time, some six months after Jack had opened the Cabaret. They began a close friendship the day that Jack had furnished him with six winners out of the seven races that the politician had placed large purses on.

In consideration, Carey offered his services as

bondsman and mediator in Jack's behalf, to make it easy for Jack to return to America.

'But the wisest course, Jack, is to turn yourself in first, at the border. This move would make it dramatic enough for a public support build up," Cary advised his black friend.

"The publicity will be worth something then, when I start to pulling for you. Think it over, you and your wife. Let me know. I'll be pitching for you either way. You're quite a man, Jack," the politician continued to persuade him.

"The law must take its course, Jack. Surrender your passport and yourself at the border. Take a chance on clemency. You're not champion of the world any longer. That's why they were mad at you. But, now? Why should they come down heavy on you now? They got their crown back. That was the main issue. And everybody knows it."

That night Jack Johnson and his young wife were seen again, looking across the border together, marking the last time they would be observed in this manner. As he gazed he simply said to his wife,

"We're going home, honey. I'm gonna try it."

They hurried back to the Cabaret, sweeping through to go to their quarters as Jack called out to Gus:

"Call up Billy Silver, Gus. Tell him I'm coming across sometime in the morning."

The black fighter had gone down many times to stand and joke across the border with Deputy Sheriff Billy Silver and his men. He had promised that Silver would be the first one notified, if he ever decided to step back, over across the line into his country.

The few "stringer," hang on reporters who heard the statement broke out to find telephones.

"Jack Johnson Gives Up!"

They drove up to the border; the Sheriff had gone away.

"He'll be right back," an officer informed. "Went to see a coupla his chickens some devil of a Mex' slipped over here and stole."

"Well, run and tell him that Jack Johnson is here."

"Say, that's right, you are him. . . . Mr. Johnson, this here is sure an honor. I'll fetch him. But just wait until my son in Santa Barb' hears about this."

The Deputy Sheriff Billy Silver climbed out of his jalopy as Johnson did likewise. He noted that the Sheriff was accompanied by his crew of two photographers.

They approached each other, extending hands as Jack stated ceremoniously, for the benefit of the reporters and photographers:

"My passport, sir," the champion flashed his big smile. "My name is Jack Johnson. I am wanted in Chicago, Sheriff, for breaking bail seven years ago."

Headlines blazed across front pages of newspapers all across the country, with photographic evidence of his surrender, which indicated that Deputy Sheriff Billy Silver had done a profitable business, selling pictures of the surrender.

"JACK JOHNSON IS BACK," Chicago, Illinois, newspapers shouted.

"JACK JOHNSON SURRENDERS," "FUGITIVE RETURNS,"

"JACK JOHNSON CAPTURED," "JOHNSON DELIVERED AT BORDER,"

"NEGRO GIVES UP," "FUGITIVE SURRENDERS," cried the front pages of newspapers throughout the southern cities and states.

Billy Silver turned Johnson over to Federal authorities while Lucille caught her train, traveling alone to Chicago.

The Black Fire's trip back to Chicago to stand retrial took somewhat longer as he was celebrated all the way. Crowds turned out to greet his train, even larger than those which had turned out to greet him after he had won the title from Jim Jeffries. His escorts participated and enjoyed it, as toasts were made from the rear of his train car. Food and drink were brought and presented as offerings and sacrifices to The King Returned. Jack began to agree that Tom Carey had been right in his predictions.

"You're still a hell of a hero to them, Jack! Why you'll get an ovation in Chicago as never heard of. You might even do a little time. But that blue-nosed Wilson is dead and Harding's president. And Harding's got a mistress himself; folks know it. Then, too, there's rumors out and almost substantiated that Harding's either a Negro, or has got a good deal of Negro blood in him."

The politician "Cagey Tom" Carey was correct in two of his predictions: The reception in Chicago and Jack's doing a little time.

More than ten thousand Negroes had crowded around the station to await his arrival and to receive him. But they were disappointed by cautious authorities who took him from the train and carried him by fast automobile to a cell in Joliet Prison.

While awaiting trial there, Jack Johnson was allowed out of Joliet three nights a week, ruling the roost, until newspapers began to complain and editorialize that the prison authorities were indulging him.

He was then transferred to another prison, just on the outskirts of Chicago, at Geneva. There, the authorities elected, for some reason, to indulge him more. For thereafter up until his trial, he was allowed to go home and spend the nights with his wife, every single evening of the week.

Judge George A. Carpenter had obviously heard

about such things and disapproved, for he denied The Black Man's plea for clemency, or mercy:

"I can see no reason for making a change in the sentence," the judge said. "If the conduct of the defendant had been such to indicate that he regretted his criminal act, I might feel differently concerning a reduction of his sentence. But on the contrary, Johnson has behaved in a manner to indicate a complete disregard for the laws and institutions of this country."

So, upon finishing his little, but decisive speech, he gave the order that Jack be sent to "the walls"—the Federal Penitentary at Leavenworth, Kansas—where Jack was to serve the time exacted for his crime. "A full year and a day at the walls."

But even "the walls" weren't big enough to hold Jack back. As fate would have it, Jack Johnson was introduced to a long, lost friend. For the Leavenworth Prison Superintendent was none other than Denver S. Dickerson, the ex-governor of Nevada, who had supervised his championship fight with Jim Jeffries at Reno in 1910.

The Big Fire was back to burning again, as his old friend, the ex-governor addressed him in a fatherly manner:

'You just play it on the square with me while you're here, Jack. And you won't find things too bad here at all. Now, what job do you want to do, while you're here with us."

Now, it is not true as his enemies tell, that Jack Johnson was allowed to run Leavenworth while he was there. He was simply made physical director, organizing and directing drills in calesthenics. But for this he was granted certain rights befitting his station.

Like any other king in repose: He was allowed to employ his own personal cook from among the prisoners; allowed to keep his own private supply of liquors

and cigars. He had a personal butcher to cut up and re-
frigerate the wild game which his "hunters" could kill
as: rabbits, wild birds, but especially possum meat,
which was one of his favorites.

When, occasionally, he was forced to mete out his own
form of justice, without fear of repercussions. Which he
only had to do once. This was after he had put in his
order for a possum to be prepared for a special supper
to be given for three guests he had invited. But the
clever trusty instead caught a cat and butchered it and
delivered it to the chef, who naively cooked it. But it
did not fool Johnson, who was an expert at the appearances of a naked possum.

The Black Fire was furious. His special supper party
had been ruined. The king refused to deal personally
and soil his hands on the sneaky trusty. But he delivered his verdict.

A few days later he was to smile upon hearing the
trusty "possum hunter, a killer" had regained his consciousness, resting well, in the stirrups and trappings for
broken bones in a prison hospital bed.

The Superintendent had come around one morning
to watch Jack shadow box and spar, giving boxing lessons to other inmates. When it was over, Dickerson
asked him:

"Jack, why don't you think of making a comeback?"

'My last fight, Mr. Dickerson, was in Tijuana," the
champion shook his head. "Then, I'll be a mite on the
old side by the time I get out of this calaboose to pick it
up again."

"Why should you wait to get outside to pick it up?
Why don't you start right now, in here, picking it up,
Jack?"

"Super' Dickerson," Johnson laughed. "Now what
would people say, when those newspapers start reporting. 'Dickerson allows Johnson to do roadwork, jogging

around outside the Leavenworth Prison Walls, getting ready for his outside comeback.' "

"I mean, begin that comeback in here, Jack. You can find suitable opposition in here. We'll promote it, you and me, inviting the principal sports figures to look you over. Meantime, I'll work on an early release for you, based on good behavior. Let's say we'll set it for Thanksgiving Day. That's an order, Jack," the superintendent walked away.

Jack Johnson took him seriously, and went in strenuous fight preparations for Thanksgiving Day. The day of his comeback, behind "the walls." The year was 1920.

The prison was decked in a flowery motif, with bunting and flags hung out all over the place. The Prison Band stood playing all of Jack's favorite tunes, as Gus Rhodes, who had been acting as his secretary outside, in business affairs, came along bringing Lucille, joined by sports writers, officials of big and small stature, other well wishers who were able to and willing to pay costly bribes to get in, all joined and milled around the prisoners, awaiting the comeback of the king, Jack Johnson, who was scheduled to face two men that day: George Owens, a 267-pound fighter of popularity and note, who had been brought in "from the outside" and Chicago. Along with "Topeka Jack" Johnson, a former sparring partner of Jack Johnson, who was doing a stretch along with The Big Smoke.

Three more bands arrived, along with hundreds of people, cars parked all over the place. By noontime, an hour before the bout, the seating capacity was exhausted, make-shift seats and lean-to sun shelters of canvas were improvised for the convenience of the visiting customers.

Johnson slipped through the ropes, beneath a roar of applause, some there to cheer him on to victory, others there out of curiosity to see if Jack Johnson still had it, at the age of 42. "A man couldn't punch his weight at the age of 42," they said.

According to later newspaper reports:

His skill and form was of that equal to any former occasions. When he attempted to entertain his fighting audience.

His first bout was a fighter who resembled an Angus bull, George Owens . . . the crowds had never seen such an outsized customer like a seventeen-stone, since P.T. Barnum had left town with his sideshows . . . this trial horse was worthy of his showing . . . for several rounds Jack let his man lead, counter-punching like the Johnson of old. Then, in the fifth round, he proved it, not with one, but two, three, then four! Four grand right hands in succession! Which shook the giant from his foundation. "A man could punch his weight at 42, especially if the man was Jack Johnson."

In the sixth round, he took Owens out for the count. Johnson had fought with his fists, not with his mouth . . . not once did he lash out with his taunting tongue. A gentlemanly fighter now, was Jack Johnson! Not even grinning as they carried Owens from the ring.

He sat modestly to await his next opponent, displaying no conduct which would make Super Dickerson embarrassed or hesitant about suggesting his early release from Leavenworth for good behavior.

Although "Topeka Jack" Johnson, as a former sparmate, knew most of the champion's moves, he was helpless to match Johnson's incredible speed, as he picked up the pace proving that his swiftness could match that of his punching power. Resulting in two victories in one day.

The crowd stood and cheered, which through the enclosed walls of the prison, sounded louder than those cheers which he heard bouncing back, after resounding against the hills of Sydney, Australia, in his fight against Tommy Burns, The *First* Battle of the Century, or those sounds that rolled across the plains at Reno, in The Battle Number Two of the Century. They were even louder than those he had heard for Jess Willard at Havana, in The Third Battle of the Century.

This one, inside the walls of a prison, he hoped would make certain number four, forthcoming, when he got out.

Super Dickerson was pumping his hand:

"Well done, Jack. Well done, my man! Indeed, this does make you Heavyweight Champion of Leavenworth Prison."

"Governor, that's the finest compliment that I have received in many a year, thank you."

He started back down the corridors to his cell, the cheers and applause still resounding. He had proved himself a champion capable of coming back. He thought of the other deposed rulers he had known who now could never do so: Tsar Nicholas of Russia, Grigori Efimovitch Rasputin, "The Mad Monk," Kaiser Wilhelm of Germany, Poincaré, President of France, his close friend Venustiano Carranza of Mexico. Georgie Dixon, the Negro fighter who was sent up against 22 oponents in one week's time, only to wind up insane. Tom Molineux, The Fighting Slave from Virginia, who died fighting in the ring that his master might earn a fortune. Sam McVey who died after 17 years in the ring, starving to death in rags.

He thought of Manuel II, deposed King of Portugal, who had also become his friend and admirer, of Joselito, king of Spanish bull fighters, all now who had passed on, beyond the point of come-back or return.

He went to his liquor cabinet, poured himself a brandy and prayed for God to hasten the few months to pass, when he would be free, to prove that a king can make a comeback. A fire which once burned might falter and flicker, but it was still alive, when the coals burned red and hot enough to be fanned into flame again, burning brighter than ever before.

And true to his words, ex-governor, Prison Superintendent Denver S. Dickerson had arranged for Johnson's release, three months ahead of his full-sentence time, based upon his good behavior. It was more clear to him now than ever before, as many other champions of his race would learn: "The rewards for being a Black Champion depended much less upon the Champion's ability to fight in the ring, than it did on, 'Behaving yourself, like a good, docile and modest boy.' "

CHAPTER TWENTY-ONE

BACK OUT, INTO THE CHANGING WORLD

Willard hadn't worn the crown for too long, before he fought "The next greatest fighter to Jack Johnson." Another Jack, whose last name was Dempsey, who had snatched away his crown, while giving him a beating almost rivaling the one that Johnson had inflicted, while he himself had cinched the title, on Jim Jeffries.

So, after doing a stretch of eight months and a few

days, out of an eleven-month sentence, Jack Johnson ended his prison confinement.

"My vacation at expense of the United States Government," he used to call it.

They turned The Black Fire loose, once again. "But back out into a changing world."

Denver Dickerson had succeeded, like he had promised, in getting Jack off, this time for "good behavior," by making a special plea to the authorities:

"A prison term has done this man good. It has made him ready for rehabilitation into the freedom and order of the American society he once offended. And we must remember that it was Johnson himself who elected to return and accept his punishment that he might be restored into this order. He voluntarily returned to square his debt. He now offers this society the great opportunity to vindicate itself, for no good purpose could be served in denying him freedom and access of this society for the brief, no more than 90-day, remainder of his sentence. Surely, he has proven himself worthy of being freed now. He is a changed man."

The plea of Dickerson was accepted. But Johnson still further confirmed Denver Dickerson's "changed man theory," as he was asked to deliver a farewell address to more than a thousand of Leavenworth Prison inmates.

His speech indicated for certain to his black listeners, "Jack Johnson was takin' the preacher route." He addressed them on "the virtue of redemption through suffering" as the Golden Rule was about the most sure-fire con and convincer for any Nigger in knee-deep trouble with any white man, North or South.

Some shook their heads knowingly as the tears fell. For experience had taught them that for years to come thereafter Johnson had condemned himself to follow the low the legendary pattern set for "Black Princes on

Christian Soil," helpless and speechless to object any longer against the forces which had reduced him to the role of a commoner.

The black prisoners knew, as Johnson winked to them many times during his speech, that he still saw himself as a master of Christian Caucasian cunning.

He had committed himself to the traditional "Role of the Uncle Tom Preacher," sinner converted, convincingly rectified, in order to gain a 90 day lease, hurrying anxiously to get free, get back out into the world which he himself was helping to change.

As he smiled at them, winking, while making his speech, the other black prisoners became hopeful that he might pull it off. They cheered, while keeping their own reservations to themselves.

For the next 25 years, slightly more, they would follow his progress: from the role of a black prince, who became the black king, exiled to return later as a convict, converted to a preacher to be released and to returned, back out to challenge a changing world, which his own black reign had done so much to change. At the age of 42, he would try it again. Coming back, this time, another damned way. Coming back in the role of the convert, after his conviction.

But, for the next 25 years or a little more, they noted that Jack Johnson was never a serious threat to the law, as an offender, in anything more reckless than a fast drive arrest, his only obvious means of Black Fire letting off steam.

Now, even though he tried to take it slow, from the time that they gave him "his leave from Leavenworth." They had prepared to restrict his law-breaking, to an outburst of speeding by auto, as an outlet for his pent-up energies, outbreaks of fire which burned away at his inside and entrails.

He arrived at home, Chicago, five days after his release, along with his pretty white wife, Lucille, on July 14, to be greeted by an entourage of Negroes not nearly nor so large in number as the crowds which had formerly greeted him. And the reception committee explained: "The brass band which was engaged to serenade your arrival has not arrived as yet."

But the Black Fire responded in a style befitting him:

"Chicago, and my friends, look mighty good to me. With or without the music."

They cheered and applauded his further statements at the train station. Especially when he stated that he was ready to "take on Jack Dempsey."

The black king, had issued his challenge to Dempsey, whom he chastened as a pretender to the throne.

Chicago blacks then cried out the challenge to the whites of New York, the place where Jack Dempsey was supposed to be staying.

The bait didn't work, for Jack Dempsey ignored his challenge, while making it clear that he was one white man who was not afraid of drawing the color line.

Dempsey later proved this by paying a fortune, in forfeit, for not meeting with Harry Wills, the leading contender, who was colored; a man who was listed among those that Jack Johnson had defeated.

So, Jack Johnson was forced back into his preacher-type-Nigger-role, in an effort to seek big money again. And big money Niggers, as well as big money whites, were unwilling and too suspicious to back him. So, then, he could not compete with "Tex" Rickard, Jack Curley, or Jimmy Johnston (The Boy Bandit), as a top promoter of prize fights, as Sullivan, Corbett or Jeffries had done as ex-champions of the ring.

Now The big Black Fire was forced to acknowledge a fact which very few of his race would be willing to recognize: The big money is unwilling to fan the ashes of a black coal's ambitions, back unto even a flicker-flame of life that it once knew. No matter how promising the rewards or returns, especially after they had once witnessed the brilliance of its fire.

Still, while the former black champion was no longer rich, neither were all of his fortunes depleted. For he was one of the few black niggers, since that time, up till now, who had no fear of being buried in a pauper's grave.

But he was forced to contain his play at fury and fearlessness for the remainder of his life; pretending, in role of "The Preacher type," the quiet and reformed, conservative and religious Nigger man, when seeking money-making arrangements in his dealings with white men. He was even forced to perform more convincingly among those Christian Caucasians who had once fought each other for the privilege of kissing Jack Johnson's black ass.

When he did give way, on infrequent occasions, to express his resentment against the gross humiliations which he was subjected to, he would step into the "ready-made trap."

"Jack Johnson has not changed! He has not learned his lesson! Therefore, he is still undeserving of help, recognition or cooperation. He is not as reformed as we believed him to be."

So, for his first two years out of prison he remained on trial, held under suspicion while he attempted to emerge as a fighter or promoter, among the same white men who had at one time or another attempted, succeeded or failed, to criminally exploit and cheat him.

And in the years that followed, Jack was forced to revise, and many times refine his "reformed, religious Nigger role." And compelled to play it to such a perfection that even cautious observers were forced to comment:

"He continued to develop a gift for extemporaneous

chatter, in a mystical elusive style, not unlike that of an evangelist, or that of a fanatic Negro religious cult leader."

For quite a few years his lectures and talks had taken a moralizing turn, as he sought the use of various Negro-church pulpits in order to exhort his condemnations of Judeo-Christian hypocrisy and pseudomorality. With no particular set patterns and text, he would "wind his way gloriously through moralistic discourses entered around such Biblical characters as: *Job, David, Solomon, Esau, Jacob, Daniel, Joseph,* the *Book of Revelations* and the writings of the *Apostle Paul.*

But as the years wore on, none of these implicit signs of a Nigger's Reformation made it possible for Johnson's reacceptance back into our social order, to experience any prominence in the businesses at which he had been a champion.

As a sideline he continued to appear in the prize rings, whenever offered such infrequent opportunities.

Although skillful as ever, winning as he did, in all bouts with knockouts, sound decisions, and even in exhibitions, he displayed "too much of his old stuff," causing champions and their challengers to take special precautions at avoiding to meet him. He traveled to and fro—north, south, east and west—begging for a bout of any promise, until reaching the age of 46.

He proved himself continually, all to no avail, until 1924, "he hung up his gloves as a challenger," after beating a young fighter, 20 or more years his junior, Homer Smith, by a decision at Montreal, Canada.

Some say it was caused actually by Lucille Cameron, his wife of a dozen years, who finally took the advice of her mother, Mrs. Cameron-Falconet, who was still alive and kicking back in Minneapolis, and ended her marriage. She was granted her suit, an uncontested divorce, on the grounds of adultery and infidelity, which is still the most popular means of legal separation in the State of New York.

However, Lucille disappointed the newspaper people, who interviewed her, wishing to buy, or to "ghost-write" her life's story: *"Twelve Years of Marriage to Jack Johnson,"* or: *"A Dozen Years of Marriage to a Black Man."* Rather, Lucille retired, fairly well fixed, from all appearances, to fade into obscurity with deliberate resolution.

But the Black Fire went raging, burning up the highways and roads again, racing up and down like mad in his search for another constant love life. His terrifying road pace, became a matter of public headlines, emphasized with numerable traffic tickets for speeding, culminating with an auto wreck, along the highways of Connecicut, which almost took his life, while marring his hard-earned reputation as a reformed, slowed-down Negro.

But it was only after his second wreck, of the same nature, which happened later at Benton Harbor, Michigan, that the Big Smoke finally admitted to newsmen:

"I must confess that I now have, as I have always had, a terrible weakness for driving fast."

But his respectable weakness for fast driving could not be applied to his earning power, which had then been reduced to the point and past the point of something cruel. So he publically announced his decision to professionally enter the field of speed car, automobile racing.

Despite his reputation as "A Wizard on Wheels," no offers came forth to encourage him. This could be attributed to his speed and pace at love and marriage, for within the period of less than one year, in 1925, Jack Johnson had selected another white beauty for a bride, thus pulling off the cover of his "reformed Nigger" role, forever.

Her name was Irene. She was a blue-green-eyed, golden-haired "pink-toed" divorcee, who had recently been legally released from a marriage entanglement with a white husband, Harry Pineau, an advertising tycoon, who had made the mistake of taking his wife to spend a day at the race track as a means of reconciliation, averting a pending divorce. He made the further mistake, while attempting to entertain her, of introducing her to "the famous and charming Negro, Jack Johnson, who had once been Heavyweight Champion of the World."

"Interesting fellow," Mr. Pineau had told his estranged and beautiful white wife. "But much too fast and too far ahead of his time. And he doesn't know it yet."

But Mr. Pineau had underrated the prowess and speed of the Black Fire, for within a short time, his reconciliation period to his beautiful wife was pronounced a failure, cut short by many months as newspapers across the nation declared, with blaring headlines, in bold print:

Jack Johnson Does It Again! Johnson Takes Another White Wife. Third White Woman Taken by Negro. Black Man Marries Another White Woman!

Comment and tragi-comic cartoons flooded the editorial pages of daily newspapers, in epic proportions, emphasizing Christian Caucasian protest and condemnations:

"Any negro who has experienced so many love affairs with women of the white race, no matter how common-place she be, can never be of any benefit to the production of our civilization."

"Already, two fair white women have come to their tragic ends, by means of suicide, while struggling to make a meaningful marriage with this black monster."

"How long must self-respecting white men stand by

*and accept the affront of this black mad-man upon our
white womanhood."*

*"Johnson has abused the privileges of our system,
forgetting his place . . . flaunting the rules in our faces."*

In order to step up the program, where "Niggers
would come to know their places," comic strip characters and caricatures began to appear in the featured
funny-papers of our daily and Sunday morning supple-
ments, extolling the virtues of "fighting white champions of the prize ring," with a faithful punch-drunk
black lackey as his handler, working as a spar-mate,
carrying bucket and towels, cheering his "boss" against
other prize-fighters, who were all white, similar in appearances to the men that Jack Johnson had defeated.
They appeared under such titles as:

Dynamite Dunn, Champion of the World, adhering
to the advice and relying upon the faithfulness of his
loyal man, "Smokey."

Then there was Moon Mullins, with an aide some-
what similar who looked after his "boss," named
"Mushmouth." This strip later included Lord Tweed-
mouth (Plushbottom) the mustachioed caricature of the
British nobleman, who had joined in promoting Jack
Johnson's London prize-fights.

Tarzan of the Apes, the Edgar Rice Burroughs' hero,
reached a zenith in popularity; Tarzan found apes for
his allies, those who were loyal to him, while depicting
the prowess of Jack Johnson. For a while he even had
an African native tribal assistant, who later died at the
hands of an ape, which Tarzan was later to defeat in
vengeance.

Mandrake the Magician developed himself a physically strong sidekick, faithful Lothar, who resembled
Johnson in all appearances.

Other such comic strips appeared and vanished, with
Great White Invincible Fighters, aided by a black as-

sistant, Friday the Faithful, who, with enormous strength, knew his place among white me nand white women. Speaking only when spoken to, fighting only when told to, while *never* offending a white man, except to take his complaint to his "boss" who was certain to defend him and such nobility. A reward for docility.

The playright Eugene O'Neill came forth with his classic drama, "The Emperor Jones," whose tragic hero was Brutus, the black American commoner who became a king, but displayed the vital flaw by revealing his emotional instability. In his many drunken moments O'Neill would admit that Jack Johnson had been his model and prototype for the hero of his play.

It was the life of Jack Johnson, America's first and only true black fighting hero, by any Caucasian standard and classical sense, who was responsible for establishing the long lasting and unwritten code in American literature, be it fact or fiction, in the novel, biography, or otherwise: *No Negro hero, unless he ends tragically, especially if he has been intimate with a white woman. Or unless he has been converted and redeemed for the sin of opposing the pride or wishes of a white man.*

This became the established pattern in American literature which was to last for the next half-century or more, thus fulfilling the prophesy of Rasputin, Mad Monk of Russia:

"Like me, you will be imperishable in history."

It had become the popular fad among white folks and colored folks alike to slay and slander the character of Jack Johnson, by comic insinuation, criticism and comment. So much so that people actually forgot that Irene Pineau Johnson lived with him as a happily married woman longer than any of his former wives had by refusing to become a public figure at his expense.

And for the sake of preserving the only fully successful marriage relationship of his lifetime, Johnson set about trying harder, but, not for the lack of effort, unsuccessfully, at any kind of endeavor to amass another fotune, which she might share and enjoy with him as his former Caucasian wives had done in the past.

He tried promoting fights and other sporting and theatrical events, selling stocks as a broker on Wall Street, working as a pioneer as a Public Representative for a Brewery and Liquor firm. (A position that many middle-class, college-trained Negroes and celebrities would later accept and welcome, as one of the finest assignments that a Negro male could obtain, as proof of "progress, integration and affluency.")

The Big Smoke even attempted to produce and present himself in the role of Shakespeare's Othello, while legitimate theatre producers conducted a "talent search," for another, and other Negroes, who met the physical requirements of Jack Johnson, to essay the role of the noble Moor. This campaign effected the discovery of Jules Bledsoe and an intellectual, physically complete and scholarly genius, a Rutgers College Phi Beta Kappa All American football player, named Paul Robeson.

The Big Smoke was rather relegated to the roles as a film extra on the motion picture lots of Warner Brothers, in Hollywood, while filling in as a Master of Ceremonies in night clubs along Los Angeles' (then fabulous) Central Avenue.

It was on the Warner Brothers' lots that Wilson Mizner, prominent Broadway writer and Hollywood dialogue director, upon hearing that Johnson was working as an extra, rushed out from the "big throne," where he habitually slept all day long behind a huge desk to greet and embrace Jack Johnson, admonishing studio officials:

"This is no ordinary man that you have hired here.

But a figure of great importance. And you should be grateful to treat him so."

But still, whereas the studio officials treated him thereafter with pleasant politeness, he remained a less black light in Hollywood and was forced to give way to greater and more preferable black lights such as Stepin Fetchit, Mantan Mooreland, Pigmeat Markham, Clarence Muse and Willie Best, and Bill "Bojangles" Robinson, all Negro "film heroes" of that period.

There were too few among the white men to come out and speak openly, or to suggest capitalizing upon the greatness of Jack Johnson, "The most colorful and publicized heavyweight champion of all times." Rather their excuses could be summed up in a sentence or two for not doing so:

"Can't take the chance," they would say, shaking their heads. Or:

"Ain't sure that his white-fever has been chilled enough."

Biased newspaper writers intensified their efforts, keeping a constant pressure to make certain that the Jack Johnson of old would never emerge again, even though he had reached the mellowed age of 47.

So vicious were their campaigns that an obviously heartbroken wife, Irene Pineau Johnson, who had remained a demure, quiet and soft-spoken woman, who avoided publicity like the plague, for the sake of her husband was forced to speak out in letters, addressing herself to a few of the most prominent newspaper columnists of that time, first to one who had attempted to do a story on the life of Jack Johnson. She wrote two particular missives for which she is remembered:

"Sir, it seems fitting that I, Jack Johnson's wife, should insert a few words in this matter of his life."

She then followed in length and detail, seeking to

clarify the means by which she had come to meet, fall in
love with and marry the black man.

*I was introduced to him at the race track in Aurora,
in the fall of 1924 . . . by a mutual friend William
Bernbach, while in the company of my dear friend
Helen Matthews. In February the next year, 1925, we
met again . . . by this time I had started divorce proceedings against my former husband, Harry Pineau.
Our friendship progressed so rapidly, until it came to an
issue, as to which one of us, between the two, Helen and
myself, that he liked best.*

*"I was the favored one, which made me not a little
happy, since my feelings for him had graduated and developed from those feelings of friendship into those of
love. After each succeeding time spent in his company
my affections for him grew, until the day came when I
knew that I would have defied the world and anybody in
it, to separate us.*

*"During all of this time, my divorce was going for-
ward, and regardless of the many promises I had made
to myself to avoid and stay away from a second marriage, I knew that nothing could have kept me from
marrying Jack Johnson at the earliest possible moment,
since he had asked me to become his wife."*

Irene Johnson went on to describe in her letter of
Jack's being felled with a severe case of appendicitis,
which effected an operation and a short period of con-
valescence, two weeks or a little longer, while she remained at his bedside, never leaving, which did little to
help in the matters of public opinion.

Shortly thereafter her divorce was granted. She described to the writer her feelings when they married in
August, 1925.

*"What a wonderful day it was for both of us! How
different is the real soul-stirring love from that which we
often mistake for real love, but that which is no more*

than a passing infatuation. What great things are not possible, when one loves and is also loved, truly and deeply?

Since our marriage, we have not changed one iota, except to have our love for each other grow stronger as time goes on.

"As a husband, Mr. Johnson is everything he could possibly be, loving, considerate to the smallest details, generous to the nth degree, loyal and kind. To many people who might be a bit sceptical about marrying a man of a different race, let me say that there could not be a man from any race in the world more worthy of being loved and honored than is my husband.

"It took him to show me what a real love and a happy home is, and in comparing mine, with the lives of all my friends and acquaintances, I can say without fear of contradiction that none can boast of a more harmonious and happy home than we.

"A predjudiced writer once said of my husband 'that Jack Johnson has a sinister influence over women, white women.'

"And I answer, 'If to be a man, in every sense of the word . . . and to treat a woman with utmost respect, kindness and loyalty, is "sinister," then a lot of men would make this world a better place, to emulate my husband and become "sinister," too.

"My husband has been accused of 'having the affections of a "levee Negro,"' of being 'primitive' . . . 'just a "happy-go-lucky-Negro," who wasn't much outside of the ring.'

"There deliberate statements of falsehoods, with no foundation of personal knowledge on which to base them, have so greatly aroused my anger, that I could not read such malignments of my husband's person and allow them to go unchallenged. They must know from me, how wrong they are."

Now, although this first letter from Irene was never challenged when made public, the reactions to Jack Johnson's love life and his women became more mixed-up and muddled than ever. For writers had made a point to busy themselves classifying his female companions and wives as: *"Low-grade forms of white-trash." "Prostitutes and flappers!" "Soft-brained white women, hypnotized, while seeking strange excitement and erotica."* Or, *"Pathetic creatures with masochistic and suicidal tendencies." "Frenchy-freaks" or "European bitches." "Thrill seeking nymphos."*

While in some private and selective circles her letter had not set too well, she did gain a few sympathetic supporters among white women who expressed admiration at her daring to speak out in defense of black men as lovers, making quite a few private female sentiments public.

But her letter was simply passed off among numerous Negro women, those who dared to voice an opinion of her letter:

"Just trying to cover up for that no-good black nigger. Nobody could be happy with a nigger like that."

"She wrote that letter to get herself in the headlines. Now, that he's gone down, she's using him to get her white picture into print. Bet she got paid some money for writing it."

"She's a public disgrace to the white race anyway. Who is she? Nobody knows her. There's a lot of colored women of better class than her. She's trying to pretend that he's still something at his age."

"That white bitch is just cashing in before he dies. Any colored woman knows of Johnson's reputation."

"Talking 'bout his being a lover. Why doesn't she have some kids for him. None of them other white bitches that he was married to did either."

And so ran the female comments across the back

farmyard fences of the Negro South, and among the indignant outraged elements of Northern Negro womanhood, many who slept with and afforded the sleeping privileges of their daughters to satisfy the lusts and desires of white men by daylight as well as nighttime.

The reactions of the Negro-American male contingent was without public definition, especially among those of the educated, well behaved and schooled "muddled-class." Some were forced to bless Johnson as "one lucky black dog," for having latched on to a white woman who married him and loved him enough to speak out in his behalf as a man. But few or none would express this when queried in conversation by white men.

Among the cautious and reserved, "Jack Johnson was all wrong for allowing his wife to write such a letter without his permission." The woman had set a bad pattern by "pulling Charlie's coat-tail, "hepping him to the fact," that some white women of culture and refinement could fall in love with a Negro.

"Too many Negroes will die, by means of the rope and faggot, thinking they can make it with a white woman the likes of Irene Johnson," said some.

And they backed their statements up with factual evidence called the "Famous Tuskeegee Report," which was to account for the numbers of lynchings, dating back from the Civil War, up until that time. For a period of some fifteen years, 19 of such lynchings were unofficially attributed directly to the performances of Jack "Li'l Arthur" Johnson, for his actions in the ring and outside of it, in the role of a "white woman's lover man."

The Tuskeegee Report was probably the first, among the many to follow, "Federally Financed Studies," designed to influence future conduct and public behavior of Negro males in America. It was conducted and supported by the adherents of Booker T. Washington, who had performed his job effectively as principal instructor and spokesman of Negro public opinion.

Even W.E.B. du Bois was baited to offer an opinion as to the moral influence of Jack Johnson and his effect upon the American racial problem, concerning his marriages to white women. DuBois wrote:

"... *the masses of Negroes see all too closely the anomalies of their position and the moral crookedness of yours. You may marshall strong indictments against them, but the counter-cries, like with Jack Johnson, lacking though they may seem in formal logic, to you ... have burning truths within them, which you cannot wholly ignore.*

"*Oh, Southern gentlemen! If you deplore our presence here, then we ask, who brought us here?*

"*When you cry: 'Deliver us from the visions of intermarriage,' then we answer: 'that legal intermarriage is much better than systematic concubinage and prostitution.'*

"*And if, in just fury you should accuse our vagabonds of violating your women, then they in a fury, quite as just, must reply:*

"*'The rapes, which you gentlemen have performed upon helpless black women, in defiance of your own laws, is written in blood upon the foreheads of two million mulattoes.'*

"*And finally, when you fasten the crime upon this race, or a personage of our race, as some peculiar trait, they must answer you back with an answer:*

"*'That slavery itself was the arch-crime, while lynching and lawlessness are its twin abortions; Race and Color are not crimes! And it is we Blacks who in this land receive the most unceasing condemnations for it.'*"

Of course it is notable to say that following that answer, du Bois was demoted from the top echelon of the

NAACP, which he had helped found. Instead of remaining executive editor of *Crisis,* the official journal of the organization, his position as a spokesman was reduced so that he was no longer the final editorial authority and policy setter for the *Crisis,* or even a spokesman for the NAACP.

The word came down, right down from the top, from the prominent white president and treasurer. For his statement concerning Jack Johnson and his white women old W.E.B was censured and silenced. Still, to prove that it was not a matter of his public opinion on intermarriage that brought it about, the NAACP went so far as to bring in Walter White, an almost white Nigger, who could "pass," and frequently did, with his light skin, soft hair and blue-eyes to serve as Field Secretary of the organization. One who could mix well and marry white women without serious question, which he did; while Jack Johnson was just too damn black to be afforded the honor.

Thus, our leading organization was to stand idly by while the program to bring Johnson to his knees was continued. It was intensified by the second letter from Irene, written to the famous Jim Tully of *Vanity Fair,* who had published an article in that magazine titled: *"Colored Fighers"* which pictured Johnson as a "subhuman black, with supernatural, hypnotic powers over white women," provoking the indignation of Irene once again:

"I have just finished reading your article, and feel sufficiently wrathful to write you a few lines. I am referring to your statements concerning my husband Jack Johnson, of whose personal side you know nothing.

"Must a man, because of his color, be disparaged and ridiculed by every white man who takes a pen in hand to scribble a story, for the already over-prejudiced people? Cannot someone be human and decent enough to

*give a man his just due? You writers from whom words
and stories flow so glibly, most of the time will not look
beneath the surface to even see the facts in a case.*

*"This letter is written by one who knows Jack John-
son intimately, and who resents seeing him being slan-
dered.*

*"Is not accepting misery stoically a form of bravery?
We call people weak who go about crying their troubles to an unsympathetic world, do we not?*

*"There was never a man who was more sympathetic
and loyal to his friends, generous to a fault in every
cause of charity, in helping those who were in need of
help. Let me add, that many a white man has been
aided by his black hands. He is quiet, gentle and soft-
spoken, contrary to your statement and declarations of
him being a 'primitive.' And within his head is more
knowledge than most men alive can boast of. I am not
alone in this opinion of him. Anyone who knows him
will bear out this statement.*

*"He has a wife who is intensely in love with him, and
whom he loves equally as much; and she is proud to be
married to a man who is honestly and truly the gentle-
man that Jack Johnson is.*

*"I go about life with no expression of shame on my
face. Instead, you will find a look of happy confidence
and love in my eyes. All of these things that I write are
true. Why not give credit where credit is due? And
leave out all of the sneering and riducule, too often present in articles, such as yours, to be read by a gullible
public?*

*"How many men would be willing to survive the
uphill climb and struggle, enduring the bitterness and
heartaches, as Jack Johnson has done, and who could
still remain the steady, temperate man he is today?
Very few!*

"These virtues have not the ear-marks of a 'levee

*Negro.' You are entirely mistaken with your impression
of him.*

> *Written and signed by his wife,*
>> *Mrs. Irene Johnson*

Now, the writing of the second letter made some
folks sit up and take notice, to take a better look at
Irene Johnson and the husband she had written in defense of. But, seems like it was much too late in the
game to do or say anything about it. Then, in the top
circles, her letters had made it more certain that Jack
Johnson would slip lower, down another notch or two,
on the white man's totem pole for Niggers. For "good
words and good letters" written by a white woman on
behalf of a black man can guarantee a conviction, sentence and imprisonment socially, even worse than anything behind the walls of Leavenworth Penitentiary. Despite her sincere and desperate pleas, Irene Johnson,
the white wife and woman, had sealed the fate and future of her black man and husband, as he would live to
inspire the observation, to be recorded eventually in
The Nigger Bible:

"WHEN YOU TAKE A WHITE WOMAN to a love-
couch, my Son, consider the common status you share.
You are both refugees from different cells of the same
prison. You have filched the keys from the sleeping
Warden and met in the darkened corridors, along the
cell blocks of time. Remember if you would be free, you
must flee together. The consequences are terrible upon
recaptured escapees."

And the consequences were terrible, and this observation, inspired by the fate of Jack Johnson, stands ap-
plicable as a prediction. For Irene and Jack Johnson
lived as a fulfillment of those words.

His life became filled, following a multiple of careers,

which ranged from boxing exhibitions, religious evangelism, vaudeville stage work, as the Ethiopian General, a walk-on in the opera *Aida*. As a salesman, pitchman or performer, The Big Black Fire brought excitement and dignity and spectacular sensation to practically everything he attempted to earn a living at. One critic observed:

"He even brought excitement as a lecturer in a Flea Circus, and excelled as a traveling sideshow freak, placing his foot on a handkerchief in a circus tent boxing ring, taking on all comers, offering a cash prize to those who could hit him solidly enough to make him move."

And it is a matter of record that he decisively defeated a prominent heavyweight title contender named "Dynamite Jackson," in a three round exhibition, when he had reached the age of 53 years.

He had by that time established a legend of fear and suspicion of black prize-fighters, which was to last for more than 25 years, whereby they were forced to prove themselves as "well meaning boys," who had taken up boxing just for the fun of it.

His conduct had forced the great Joe Louis, his next black successor, to become the classical example of a "well behaved, quiet, humble and well meaning heavyweight champion of the world."

"A poor and humble, Bible-reading, 'Mama, I glad I won,' boy, unable to do nothing except annihilate opponents in the prize ring. Patriotic and unwilling to do anything that would offend the white public."

This point was further emphasized when Jack Johnson was kicked out of Joe Louis' training camp, his 25 cents returned, after he had paid to come in and to watch the Negro challenger in training. Louis was said to have later remarked:

"We're still paying for him. When I was coming up,

back in 1934 and '35, they didn't forget about old Jack. I had to live like a saint to get a break. I even had to take what they give me for fighting. Like in my fight with Roy Lozer, out of a forty thousand gate, they only paid me four thousand, four hundred for knocking him out. Even before my big fight with Primo Canera, there were people trying to stop it, because of race troubles they were scared of."

However, hard it was for Joe Louis to make hey-day, it must be pointed out that he was rewarded accordingly, for being "a good boy" in public. For when time came for him to go to jail for infringing the Federal Laws on income tax, an unprecedented provision was made, that he remain out of prison "because of his good behavior." Whereas in Jack Johnson's case, the law was provided *and made retroactive,* in order to make sure that he went to prison.

Most black heavyweight champions would be forced to make a note of this in the future. And took heed, while a few others were compelled to follow the path of The Big Black Fire, in defiance.

Now, after a period of almost another quarter of century, The Big Black Fire, although still burning, was reduced to something like a "flicker-flame." For another World War had started, white men against white men (and yellow men) and black kings had become nothing more than figure-heads. Joe Louis, the heavyweight champion, was inducted into the army as a sergeant, while former white champions were made into commodores, captains and commanders. Haile Selasse, Emperor of Ethiopia, was given the "charity of exile" in London. Other past champions and kings of color were forgotten temporarily if not permanently, watching as white men went about burning up the world. Unlike in the former War of the World, even the espionage talents of Jack Johnson could not be utilized.

He was no longer considered "a threat to world order," for the world order was a semblance of chaos. So he settled for steady employment as a lecturer in Hubert's Museum, along with its noted collection of "educated fleas" as a feature.

It was after Joe Louis, the black, had defeated Max Schmelling, Hitler's example of the Aryan superman, that writers in our nation became somewhat benevolent in recalling the greatness of the first black champion of the world:

"Jack Johnson is the greatest heavyweight of all times," said *Ring Magazine*.

After years of "devoted study" of heavyweight fighters, said the editor, Nat Fliescher, "I have no hesitation in naming Jack Johnson as the greatest of them all."

But what more are tardy acclamations than combustible fresh coals heaped onto a human flame which flickers in eager hopes to become fired again?

As Jack Johnson approached his "twilight years," he was still the healthy affirmation of excellent living, robust, clear-eyed, slightly scarred about the face, but none resulting from his fights in the ring, his face unlined with wrinkles which generally mark a man of 68.

His bearings were still that of a king, or that of "the other wise man" whose name had not been listed among the three who had visited the manger, by following the star which had led them to become among the first to gaze upon the Christ child at birth.

Some of his critics remarked in print:

"He began to look something like an old-fashioned English butler, except that he wore smart, double-breasted suits, well tailored, set off by a beret, spats and his traditional showman's walking cane."

Among the millions who had worshipped him for more than a half-century, during their fondest recollections of his greatness and brilliance, he was still the star, the king, the lord, the black prince (or the Black Christ), who had endured, who had carried his cross without flinching, endured his own crucifixion while crying silently within his heart:

"Father forgive them, for they know not what they do."

The emerging "Negro spokesmen" had learned that one sure way to protect their selfish interests and to assure their personal gain and favor among the cautious and ever watchful white folks, was to discredit, or to pretend not to remember, anyone resembling Jack Johnson.

So the Messengers of Heaven must have decided that it was time for the king to come home and take his place among the arch-angels.

They say that he was traveling by car, headed back to New York from an engagement down South, June 10, 1946, with a single witness and companion, Fred L. Scott, whom Johnson had brought along, "to spell him at driving" when the Big Fire grew tired.

Now, as the same age-old story is related, the two black men cruised in for coffee, along U.S. Highway No. 101, somewhere between Franklinton, North Carolina, and Raleigh, stopping just long enough to order sandwiches to go, while seeking relief and use of the cafe's rest-room facilities.

With no sign of recognition and complete disregard, the café owner, upon noting the color of the black men, refused them service, denied them use of the washrooms, while ordering them out of the establishment. He was supported by his hostile white cracker clientele in doing so.

This was the incident! The primer that lit the fuse, precluding the final blast of the Black Fire on earth, as he smoldered, climbing back behind the wheel of his powerful Lincoln Zephyr into the angry dark of the night.

He stepped on the gas pedal, pressing it to the floor, as release to his pent up fury. Approaching a gentle curve in the road, he ignored it and swung left past the traffic, and faced the oncoming glare of headlights. A large truck loomed into view. Unable to swing back into the traffic line on his right Johnson swung the car to his left, twisting it across the "wrong side" dividing line, jumping the road-shoulder, leaving the highway at incredible speed, to crash headlong into the base of a tree-trunk on the driver's side. As they hit, the door on his right was sprung open and his companion Fred Scott was thrown free and clear of the car.

The gasoline hissed, as did the stream, while Jack Johnson crawled out from behind the wheel, moving but a few feet from the car before the explosion occurred.

A brilliant burst of flame, puffed a large cloud of smoke skyward. The black champion slumped into a state of unconsciousness, for the first time since Joe Choynski, the Professor, had delivered the chopping right hand punch to his temple at Galveston, Texas, in what had been billed as "A Fight To The Finish," some forty-five years before.

They took his broken body to the Catholic St. Agnes Hospital at Raleigh. He was pronounced dead thirty minutes after he was brought in. Ironically, his death was attributed to "Internal Injuries." So, no other external forces could be blamed.

Now, the story of his life, as well as that of his death, can be traced to internal injuries. His beginnings, like his end could be consummately described: "Crossing the white-line, with dare and deliberation, traveling with too great a fury, rage and speed."

THE END

INDEX

314

315